ROCKET
Hell's Handlers Book 5

Lilly Atlas

ISBN: 1-946068-30-6
ISBN-13: 978-1-946068-30-9

Other books by Lilly Atlas

No Prisoners MC
Hook: A No Prisoners Novella
Striker
Jester
Acer
Lucky
Snake

Trident Ink
Escapades

Hell's Handlers MC
Zach
Maverick
Jigsaw
Copper
Rocket

Join Lilly's mailing list for a **FREE** No Prisoners short story.
www.lillyatlas.com

Logan "Rocket" Carrera has a history he prefers to leave buried under prickly layers of standoffish personality. He's seen and done things that would make most people lie awake at night. A master of compartmentalization, he's never had trouble moving on until the night he rescues the redheaded Chloe from a sadistic gang.

Kidnapped, beaten, and abused by criminals, Chloe has a difficult time assimilating back into the world after the most traumatic experience of her life. With each passing day, her anxiety builds until she's forced to find an outlet. Finally, Chloe discovers her own way to make sense of the world and steal a few moments of peace. There's just one problem: she can't tell a soul what she's doing. Who could ever understand the risk she's taking?

Unable to stay away from the fascinating woman who's screwing with his head just by breathing, Rocket tails Chloe as often as he can. His curiosity over her actions borders on obsession. Before long, and despite the MC president's orders to keep his distance, Rocket succumbs to the urge to approach her.

Logan, the handsome man Chloe meets in a bar, gives her exactly what she needs. He's accepting of her unusual requests in a way she hadn't thought possible. The fantasy unravels, however, when she discovers who he really is, the outlaw biker who saw her at her very lowest moment. Will Chloe be able to accept Logan as the biker, Rocket, and allow him into her life enough to help her heal? The answer won't matter if his violent past sucks him away before she has a chance to try.

Table of Contents

ROCKET

Lilly Atlas

PROLOGUE

Was it finally over?

Could she dare to take a breath? To release some of the tension in her coiled, ready-for-battle yet exhausted muscles?

Not that any of her vigorous struggling, foul-mouthed screams, or hostile threats had made any impact. From the second the two flea-ridden thugs nabbed her in the parking lot of a Subway restaurant of all places, Chloe had been as helpless as a baby lamb. One needle full of God knew what and some duct tape ensured she hadn't been able to do more than wiggle in vain.

The moment she'd woken, bound and stuck in the trunk of a car, she'd known she was in deep trouble. Before she even had time to assess just how screwed she was, an itch had sprouted up on the tip of her nose. With her arms secured behind her back, and unable to alleviate the problem, the annoyance had turned into a full-fledged drive-me-crazy itching. What she'd have given to have had that insignificant irritant be her biggest problem. She'd trade full-body intense itching over what she currently felt any day of the week.

A strangled laugh left her, causing her chest to lurch up and down in a painful spasm. "Uggh," she groaned as the movement brought her back to the present and reminded her of the agony she'd endured in the hours since they dragged her from that car.

Fifteen minutes ago, the four men who'd made her last two days a living hell had exited the dingy motel room they'd delivered her to, and all had been quiet ever since. Well, if she discounted the incessant noise in her own head. One of the men, a vile piece of shit in a filthy wife beater with a red bandana tied around his head, seemed to be the ring leader. Wasn't too hard of a deduction to make. Each time the action-movie wannabe opened his mouth, the other three, his minions, jumped to do his bidding.

They'd called him Lefty. The way they used his name freely should have been a clue that she was in seriously hot water. The first time she'd watched them scramble to complete his orders, she'd snickered. Bunch of no-balled weaklings unable to do anything more than follow a Rambo-look-a-like's demands. Then the sadistic bastard gave her some insight into why they all rushed to do his bidding. That snicker had won her a first taste of true, all-consuming fear.

Sure, she'd been afraid when they stuffed her in the back of her trunk—damn her for being too lazy to cook dinner that night. But after she let that tiny laugh escape, the very second it had tumbled from her lips, she'd received her first nightmare come to life.

Lefty's grimy hand had closed around her throat in a move so quick her brain didn't catch up until her air supply disappeared. With her arms flailing about, her eyes bugged, and her mouth uselessly flapped open and closed. In what felt like only a second, blackness had encroached in her peripheral vision. The darkness had closed in until Lefty's face was a pinpoint, and the room loop-de-looped. Just as her body began to fall limp, he'd slackened his hold. She'd sucked in air like it was water for a parched man in the desert.

For about forty-five seconds there, she'd been certain death was coming for her. But the torment hadn't stopped there. The next forty-eight give-or-take hours had been full of enough trauma and terror to alter the entire course of her life.

Rocket

They'd planned to sell her. *Her!* A twenty-seven-year-old redhead who was too tall, and too vanilla to be desirable by any man who'd be in the market for a plaything. None of that seemed to matter to Lefty or his crew. She knew because she'd tried every tactic she could drum up to get them to release her.

She'd told them she'd only slept with two men in her entire life.

She'd told them she was boring.

She'd told them she had six burly brothers, all SWAT cops who'd be hunting them within hours. A stretch, but what could it hurt to try? Besides her body, that is. Each time she'd tried to manipulate them, she'd been hit with fists, a belt, or sometimes a boot.

Despite her efforts, nothing had worked. Hell, she'd been so desperate, she'd told them she was HIV positive. All that tall tale got her was the men's laughter and a particularly brutal kick to her ribs. Once, when one of the men had leaned in to whisper how they'd break her, how when this was all said and done, she'd be so used up she'd be good for nothing but sucking and fucking, she'd bit him.

His earlobe to be precise. It was the only thing she could reach being tied to a chair and all.

He hadn't liked that one bit.

At one point, on the second day of being a prisoner, all but one of the men had disappeared. The lucky guy left behind had leered at her for about an hour before growing bored and disappearing from the room she was held in. For two blessed hours, she'd had peace. Until bad turned to worse.

Lefty had returned with his thugs, ranting, raving, and smashing things around the...house? Shack? Apartment? She still never found out where they'd taken her. She hadn't been alert enough to take note of her surroundings after the ride in the trunk. Plus, it'd been dark as hell. Most of what Lefty had uttered during his tantrum had been muffled by the closed door, but she'd caught phrases like, "Who the fuck are they to give me orders?" and "Fucking Handlers."

The Hell's Handlers? It was the only thing she could associate with Handlers. The Hell's Handlers were a motorcycle gang from Townsend, Tennessee, a town adjacent to the one she lived in. The most she knew about the Handlers was that they were criminals and not the type of men she'd ever associated with.

The final thing Chloe had caught before the shit really hit the fan was a bellow of rage from Lefty followed by, "I'll deliver her, but she's gonna be a fucking mess when they get her."

A shiver charged up her spine. Not thirty seconds later, the door burst open revealing the furious Lefty. After screaming slurs she could never have dreamed up, he proceeded to beat her until she'd lost consciousness. Something had changed because he had no qualms about taking his rage out on her face this time around. The blackness had been a far better alternative to the crushing pain of his heavy blows.

When she'd woken, the real horror began in the form of three men who deserved castration and worse. Naked, spread eagle, and tied to a bed in what now appeared to be a cheap as hell motel room, Chloe had been completely helpless to prevent what was coming. Despite her vulnerable position, she'd fought for all she was worth. Spitting, screaming, biting, bucking hips. She even managed to get a few deep scratches in.

None of that prevented the vicious assault. To her everlasting shame, she resorted to begging and bargaining, offering them money, and anything else she could think of to just make them stop. In the end, she drifted somewhere in her mind. Somewhere quiet. Somewhere safe. Somewhere she could pretend she was someone—anyone else.

Which brought her to now. Battered, bruised, naked, and so freaking cold her entire body shook in an attempt to warm itself. While she was hurting, terrified, and shamed beyond belief, at least she was finally alone, and the attack seemed to have ended.

Rocket

Someone would find her at some point, right? Friends and family would wonder why she wasn't taking their calls. Hot tears rolled down her cheeks. How would she ever face them again knowing what had been done to her? What would they think of her? Would she be subject to nothing but pity for the rest of her life?

A sob broke through, but it was so painful, she forced the rest of them down.

The motel's housekeeping staff would be in to clean the room in the morning. It was night. At least that's what the darkness peeking through the slit in the curtains suggested. Time had ceased to make sense hours ago. She felt bad for the unsuspecting woman who'd open that door and discover the mess of her body tied to the bed. Chloe barked out a laugh.

Shit. She was losing her mind. Shock, maybe? Pain induced delirium?

Did it matter?

The question now was why was she there? Didn't seem to fit with their plan. Would a guy who wanted to purchase a live sex toy want one with a swollen, bleeding face who'd just been raped? Unless that's what he got off on...

God, she couldn't even go there. No, this had to be something else. But what?

Right before he'd...finished, Lefty had whispered in her ear. "You can thank the Handlers for this." There it was again. Reference to the Handlers.

Chloe carefully drew in a long, slow breath. As she started to exhale, the air caught on a sob.

No! This wasn't the time to think about what they'd just done to her. This wasn't the moment to let the reality of what she'd endured sink in. That could come later. In order to survive, she'd have to remain detached. Think of it as though she were watching an episode of Law and Order SVU. She could recognize the horror of it, but it wouldn't actually touch her. Later...later she could shatter.

She craned her neck, trying to get a peek at the binds securing her hand to the bed, wincing as the action stretched the abused skin of her face. A quick tug of her arm made her gasp then hiss. Her shoulder ached from being trapped overhead for hours. Oh, and the arm wasn't going anywhere. There had to be an entire roll of duct tape wrapped around her wrist, which was then secured to the leg of the bed with another million yards of tape. Where were the scissors when a girl needed them?

She couldn't even think about how badly she had to pee.

With an uncomfortable groan, she gently returned her head to a neutral position. Relief was instantaneous. At least for her face and neck, the rest of her still throbbed in an angry rhythm.

The door knob rattled seconds before a loud thud had a man appearing in the doorway to the room. Instinct made Chloe freeze as though being immobile would somehow shield her from discovery. The guy was big. Big and dressed in black from head to toe. Black boots, black jeans, a black leather jacket, a black helmet with the face shield down. If it weren't for the dim light shining outside her motel room, he'd have probably blended in with the dead of night.

Boots, leather, and a helmet.

A biker.

Her breathing sped until she was practically hyperventilating.

You have the Handlers to thank for this.

Was he a Handler? Had he come to finish the job? There she was completely vulnerable once again to whatever this newcomer wanted.

"Goddamned, motherfucking, pieces of shit," the man behind the helmet said.

Chloe trembled, unable to utter a sound beyond a squeak of fear at the vehemence in the man's tone.

Had she just hopped out of a scorching hot frying pan directly into the fire?

* * *

Rocket

LEFTY WAS GOING to die. Slowly. Painfully. In the most agonizing way Rocket could dream up, and he had quite an arsenal of horrific torture scenes to choose from.

Unharmed.

That was Copper's decree. Lefty was to deliver the woman he'd kidnapped to this motel room *unharmed*, or else he'd have the Handlers after his ass. Looked like the guy was in the mood for a good ass fucking.

Shit. Even through the dark face shield of his helmet, he could tell the once gorgeous woman had been brutalized. Bruises, cuts, and blood caked her naked body. Shivers wracked her, whether from fear or the cold, he had no idea. Probably a combination.

This wasn't the scenario he'd expected, and fuck did it complicate shit. Plan was to rescue the woman, maybe act a little gruff and spook her into keeping her mouth shut. Keep her away from the cops.

Further frightening a woman who'd been kidnapped and assaulted wasn't exactly Rocket's idea of a stellar plan, but it was the best they had. If they wanted to deal with Lefty in their own way, and they fucking did—now more than ever—then she had to stay away from the police. Usually a few well-placed threats the MC never intended to carry out had people jumping on board with their plan, no questions asked.

Now? Well, now the hospital was their destination which meant the cops would be involved no matter how much he wished it wasn't so. A woman didn't pop up at the ER looking like this one and not have the damn pigs called. But it was unavoidable. She needed medical attention beyond what the club could provide. They really needed to get a doctor in house.

Eyes that held a familiar terror stared back at him. Years of highly classified, black-ops missions had found Rocket in some of the worst hellholes on earth, witnessing atrocities far worse than he'd seen since he joined the Handlers—and he'd seen plenty there, too.

Yeah, scared gazes were all too recognizable to him.

He lifted both hands in as non-threatening a gesture as he could pull off considering he had one thing on his mind.

Murdering Lefty.

"Won't hurt you," he said, the words somewhat muddled by the face shield. He fell silent. Often, keeping his mouth shut proved to be the best way to get what he needed. He'd give her a minute to process, let her decide if she wanted to trust him. Not that she had much choice. He was her one ticket out of there.

"Y-you, you're a b-biker," she said through chattering teeth.

Even Rocket noticed the chill in the room. The bastards must have cranked the AC just to fuck with her. Both her nipples stood fully erect and Rocket would bet his nuts she was the furthest thing from turned on a woman could be. "I am."

"Hell's Handlers?"

His eyebrows drew down, not that she could see, but he remained silent. She'd continue talking. People always did. Silence needed to be filled.

"Don't t-touch m-me."

"Fuck." Keeping his hands at shoulder height, he advanced five steps into the room. Even though the woman couldn't go anywhere, she seemed to shrink away from him.

"P-please d-don't come c-closer."

He nodded again. "I'm here to get you out of this place."

The woman huffed some kind of laugh and groan combination that would have broken his heart if the damn thing hadn't hardened to steel years ago. "Sure you *can*, but will I be alive?"

Her breath hitched as though she was going to sob, and who could blame her? But then, before his eyes she transformed, steeling herself and shoving back the hysteria.

"Yes, you fucking will. I'm not here to hurt you, sweetheart. Just here to get you and all that gorgeous red hair out of here." He pointed toward the empty second bed. "Can I cover you with the blanket? I won't touch you."

She stared for a few beats, then her chin dipped. The movement must have hurt. She winced and held still. "Y-yes, please."

Rocket pulled the frayed comforter off the additional double bed and laid it gently over her. Despite the feather light landing of the material, she flinched and hissed out a breath.

"Are—are you really going to get me out of here?"

"That's the plan. Though I don't know how you'll ride on my bike in that state. I'll have to call one of my brothers to bring a cage."

Her eyes flew to his face mask. If she thought it odd he didn't remove it, she didn't say. No way was the fucker coming off. Whatever she thought she knew about his club, she didn't exactly trust him and he wasn't going to risk her being able to identify him down the road.

"Sorry, I mean a car. We call it a cage."

"Oh. I-I'll be fine on the m-motorcycle."

"I don't think that's a good idea. I know I'm guessing here, but you're naked and you've been beaten. I'm guessing they did more than just hit you. You don't want to sit on a bike for thirty minutes, sweetheart."

"Chloe," she said with a snap that had his lips twitching. Good for her. The fact that she was so damaged yet could still toss attitude his way gave him confidence she'd recover. At least as well as any woman could recover from this kind of horror.

"My name is Chloe. Not sweetheart. And we aren't discussing what happened to me. I want out of this hellhole more than I want a comfortable ride. If you're really here to get me out, then the bike is fine."

He stared at her for a few long seconds before nodding. And damn if she didn't earn his respect right there. "I need to get you free of the bed. I'll try not to touch you, but I may have to touch your wrists or ankles. I'll warn you before I do."

With another nod, she said. "At this point, I'm not sure I'd care if you cut my hands and feet off. I just want out."

Rocket grunted as he got to work on freeing her. There was a ridiculous amount of duct tape around each wrist and ankle. Whoever had bound her made a rope out of the tape then secured it to the legs of the bed. Easy to saw through with a knife, but impossible for Chloe to break free from. Working the tape off her skin was pointless. He'd leave that unpleasant task to the medical professionals. Pain medicine would come in handy.

Chloe. It was a good name. Pretty, like she'd been on that grainy security video he'd watched over and over. From the intel his brothers had gathered, she was a well-liked woman. Sweet, kind, a bit of a homebody, but willing to help anyone and everyone. It remained to be seen, how much of that woman still existed inside Chloe now.

After about five minutes of slicing through the four man-made ropes, he had her completely freed. Each time he released a limb, she flexed and rotated the joint, biting her lip as she groaned through pain. A pile of clothes rested in the corner of the room. Leaving her to soothe her muscles, Rocket inspected the pile, and discovered the outfit she'd been kidnapped in.

Without speaking he handed her the garments and turned his back. She snorted out a laugh. He got it. Her dignity had already been stolen and he'd had more than a glimpse of her naked body. Even if she didn't think the gesture of privacy mattered anymore, it did to him. He wouldn't compound the worst night of her existence by gawking at her while she dressed.

Chloe was tough, never asking for help as she struggled to a stand. The urge to swing her into his arms and carry her outside was strong, but Rocket resisted. For one thing, she'd probably freak if he touched her and for another, he had to know if she still had some fight left. Recovery would be a long road. Most of it alone, since the club was about to ask her to keep all details of the attack to herself. If she couldn't dig deep and survive, they'd all be in trouble.

"I'm ready," she said, voice weak but determined.

Rocket

"Follow me," he said.

When they got to his bike he turned to face her. "I'm taking you to the hospital. They will call the police. I need you to make up a bullshit story that will never lead them back to my club or Lefty." Best to dump all the cards straight on the table.

She gasped, the move nearly toppling her over. Just as Rocket was about to break his rule and scoop her up, she grabbed the seat of his bike for support. "What?" she whispered. "No. I want him found. I want him in jail for what he did to me. He-he's a monster."

The urge to stare her straight in the eye was almost too much to ignore, but he managed to keep the face shield in place. "He'll pay, Chloe. I personally promise you; the man will pay in ways you can't even imagine. Might take us some time, but we'll get him, and we'll destroy him. Can't do that if the cops are sniffing around my club. You can't talk to a therapist either. No one can know what happened. Lives depend on it. Are you going to be able to keep this to yourself?"

Sugar coating, being warm and fuzzy, all that shit wasn't his style. Straight and to the point. No bullshit. That was him.

Chloe stared at his face mask and even though she couldn't find his eyes, he swore she gazed straight through them and into his soul. So many emotions flittered across her face before she finally gave him a single nod. "I can do that. Y-you'll get him?"

Rocket threw his leg over his bike. "I'll get him."

"Okay." Chloe stepped close and lifted her leg with a flinch Rocket tried and failed to ignore. A soft whimper left her as she settled on the bike.

Maybe he'd deliver Lefty's dick to her, let her toss it in her fireplace. Seemed fitting payback for what he'd done to Chloe.

"You good?" he asked when he felt her arm close around his waist.

There was that disbelieving laugh again. "Fuck no, I'm not good. But I'm on the bike, so get me the hell out of here."

CHAPTER ONE

What the hell was the infuriating woman doing?

Two months of this bullshit, and Rocket still didn't understand what the fuck her deal was. He wasn't a man that appreciated unanswered questions. He tended to dig and dig until he uncovered what he wanted to know. That tenacity was a part of his personality and it had served him well in the past, but sent puzzles like Chloe to obsession level.

"What'll it be, man?" the bartender asked. Rocket spared him a quick glance. This lounge had one man and one woman working the highly-trafficked bar. Smart business move. A broad to subtly flaunt her tits and draw in the men, and a dude with the sleeves of his collared shirt rolled high enough to show his tatted and bulging forearms for the ladies. Rocket's friend's ol' lady, Toni, had described the look as badass gentleman or some shit. Guys who dressed all proper and suave, but under the pricy threads were bad to the bone. Apparently, the look worked to get women's motors revving. At least the women he knew.

According to Toni, when Rocket dressed up—which was usually rarer than a hot pink helmet on one of his bothers, he had much of the same look. Might explain the table of women currently eye-fucking him. With no choice but to blend in with the professional crowd, he'd slipped into some slacks, a tailored shirt, and a tie.

A fucking tie. Noose, more like it.

Rocket

Enter the table of late-twenties women sending him come-fuck-me vibes. Whatever. While the release would be nice, they weren't a part of his plans for the evening.

"Jack Daniels." He held up two fingers, and the bartender nodded before turning to the bottle-loaded shelves.

Rocket's attention strayed back to the woman who'd set up camp in his mind almost five months ago and had yet to leave.

Chloe Lane.

Five-foot-nine-inches of sex appeal wrapped in a curve-hugging purple dress. And damn, did that woman have curves. Instead of sleeves, the dress had thick straps and a low square neckline showing off her tits in the most appealing way. Every man in the bar got an eyeful of creamy white cleavage, but not too much of it. Classy, while still being erotic as fuck. But it was the color of the dress that had half the men in the room slobbering into their martinis. The deep purple made those green cat-eyes ten times more intoxicating than the overpriced liquor.

Like some kind of witch, she cast a spell over every man within a ten-foot radius, Rocket included. When the hell had he even noticed the color of a woman's outfit, let alone what it did to her eyes?

The fact that she was currently conversing with a man didn't seem to matter in the least to the other dogs in the room. Nor did the fact that many of them had dates or at least hook-ups of their own. No, all over the damn lounge, eyes strayed in her direction, fixating on those small but high and perky tits. Or maybe it was the short skirt riding up a pair of toned thighs that did it for them.

The woman was fine as fuck.

And she was out of her goddamned mind.

"Here you go, man," the bartender said as he placed Rocket's double of Jack in front of him. "You starting a tab?"

"Nah, just the one, thanks." He dropped a twenty on the bar top, and waved the bartender away when he lifted a brow in an unspoken, *need change?*

One drink was all he'd have time for, if that. Chloe wouldn't stick around long. God knew, after practically stalking her for months, Rocket had her routine down pat. And it was a disturbing fucking ritual.

For the first three months following the assault, Chloe rarely left the house. While concerning, her self-imposed house arrest wasn't exactly surprising considering what had been done to her. Then, one night, out of the blue, she emerged looking like sex on a stick. She drove to this very bar, had one drink, picked up a polished and manicured gentleman, and drove to a fairly nice motel. The pair had disappeared into a room, and Chloe emerged an hour later almost to the second.

And so began a habit she engaged in every Friday and Saturday night.

Every week.

For the past two months.

The bars changed, the dresses changed, but the pattern never did.

One drink.

One guy.

One room.

One hour.

And Rocket, being the stupid fuck he was, followed her every single time.

He told himself it was to protect her. To make sure Lefty never came sniffing around again. In reality, it was the unsolved mystery of what the hell she was doing that drew him in like a fish on a hook. And the boner he got pretty much any time he laid eyes on her? Yeah, that had *nothing* to do with his stalker act.

Any one of the men she invited to the hotel room could hurt her in ways he'd describe as unimaginable, but unfortunately Chloe didn't have to imagine. She knew exactly what the fuck could happen to an unprotected woman.

Which made this entire thing, including Rocket, crazy.

What the hell was she doing in there?

Drugs? Crying on their shoulders? Raging?

Surely, she wasn't fucking them? Not after what she'd been through.

Drugs seemed the most logical answer. Self-medicating to chase away the demons she hadn't been allowed to purge through therapy. But why snag a random guy? And she always left the hotel room looking as put together as when she went in. Not a hair out of place. Not a wobble in her step. She even drove home without swerving.

Drugs were seeming less and less likely.

Most nights, Rocket lurked in the shadows to avoid being spotted, but tonight, the overcrowded bar had him sitting much closer. In fact, he was on the barstool next to her, however her attention was fully trained on the man sitting to her opposite side. The suit had come on to her before Rocket made it through the door, and she'd never so much as glanced his way. Some snooze fest in a fucking Armani suit. Actually, most of the men in the bar, including Rocket, were dressed in professional attire. The place was hands down a martini and banker bar.

As were all the establishments Chloe visited. Swanky, post nine-to-five meet-up locations Rocket wouldn't be caught dead in, if it weren't for his newfound obsession. A whiskey swilling, music blaring, dive bar was much more his speed. But concessions had to be made if he wanted to continue stalking Miss Chloe. He'd have stuck out like a sore thumb in jeans and a leather cut. Not that he gave a shit. Fitting in with this crowd was dead last on Rocket's priority list, but remaining incognito was at the top. She'd never seen his face, but a Handlers' cut carried the risk of freaking her the fuck out.

"Excuse me if I'm overstepping, but that dress makes your eyes look like two sparkling emeralds," the bro on Chloe's left crooned.

Rocket couldn't keep his eyes from rolling skyward. Was that the shit women in these snazzy joints wanted to hear? Sure, the guy's description might be dead on, but, shit, who spoke like that? In his experience, women preferred a dirty mouth working hard between their legs to a sweet one whispering in their ear. Talk was cheap, but oral? Yeah, that was the shit.

"Thank you," Chloe responded, her soft voice stroking over Rocket's dick.

No doubt about it, he was a sick fuck. No matter how many times he jerked off before tailing Chloe, or how many lectures he gave his damn cock, the prick wouldn't lie limp in her presence. No, it filled to capacity just from the sight of her. Now that he was close enough to smell and hear her? He was in some serious damn discomfort.

A hard cock was probably the last thing Chloe wanted anywhere near her. A mere five months ago she'd been raped. By three vicious men. Rocket gripped the glass in his hand to a near shattering point. His hands ached to squeeze the life out of Lefty. The MC was working hard on finding him, but it'd proven more difficult than they'd anticipated.

"Do you live nearby?" the dude asked in his cultured voice. Cultured, hell, that was just a fancy word for snobby and obnoxious.

Come on, there was no way she'd choose this guy for whatever would go down in that hotel room.

"No," she said. "Just in town for business. I head back home tomorrow morning." Her voice dropped, taking on a husky quality that left no question as to her desire.

The woman wanted to be fucked and she wanted to be fucked now.

Didn't. Make. Sense.

The sultry way Chloe spoke did nothing to stem the flow of blood to his cock. Through the mirror along the wall behind the bar, he had a clear view of her body language. Yep, the woman was open and ready for business, at least that's what her heavy-eyed, pouty-lipped look portrayed. She leaned in, giving the guy an even better show of her stellar cleavage, and her crossed legs brushed against his thigh. On any other woman, this would scream *do me big guy*. But surely not on Chloe. He just couldn't let himself believe it. What the fuck was her game?

"That's too bad," douche bag replied. "I was hoping to take you out, show you a good time."

Chloe tilted her head, giving the man an assessing gaze. Then, she tossed back the last of her Cosmopolitan. Shit, even the way her throat worked swallowing down the liquid, had Rocket ready to bust a nut.

"You can take me back to my room and fuck me. That'd be a good time."

Rocket choked on his whiskey.

Guess that answered that.

No longer caring if he blew his cover, he spun and stared at the back of Chloe's head. The man she'd propositioned had a deep tan, platinum blond hair that must have come from a bottle, and ten perfectly shaped fingernails. They probably topped off ten very soft fingers. Rocket glanced down at his own chipped nails and calloused skin.

A man's hands.

He sure as fuck could do a lot more with them than this motherfucker.

With a bug-eyed stare, the guy gaped at Chloe. He looked as shocked as Rocket felt. For the life of him, he hadn't really thought she was fucking the men. Why would she do that? Her bruised and broken body knew firsthand the damage the wrong kind of man could inflict.

"Uh, yeah, uh, fuck yeah. We can go to your hotel room."

Rocket almost laughed. What happened to the Casanova with the smooth lines?

"Great." Chloe reached out and put a hand on Mr. Smooth's chest. "One thing before we go."

"Sure, anything."

Yeah, Rocket just bet that guy would agree to anything. He was about to get between those very sexy thighs.

"My room, my show," she said. Gone was the come-hither tone, replaced by an undercurrent of steel. "Before we go you need to agree to fuck my way. It's non-negotiable. If you can do that, we'll head out now. If not, I'll keep looking for the man I need."

"No, yeah, that's good. I'm down for anything."

"Okay then." Chloe's voice brightened. "Let's go."

Rocket's gaze fell to that absolutely bitable ass as Chloe led him to the exit. He rolled his shoulders as he processed the new information.

Chloe *was* fucking the men. And she was fucking them *her* way. What did that mean? He turned his gaze away from her, telling himself the unease in his gut was concern for her safety, not envy of the man who was about to spend one hour between the sheets with the only woman Rocket had gotten hard for in months.

If his brothers could see him now.

They'd be in hog heaven watching him act like such a fool. Meanwhile their ol' ladies would probably castrate him for slobbering after a traumatized woman.

Or was she traumatized? Maybe she'd moved past the assault. Maybe this was how she'd lived her life before Rocket met her. Maybe her coping skills were stellar and the trauma she'd endured was all behind her.

He rejected the idea as quick as it came. Just didn't sit right.

As soon as they were out the door, he would follow. While he waited for them to navigate their way through the throngs of thirsty patrons, Rocket switched his phone back on. Earlier that morning, he'd received a text that had him powering down and getting his hackles up. Three words, that's all it had taken to have him looking over his shoulder for the past that might coming back to haunt him.

I need you.

Fuck no, he wasn't needed.

Rocket

He was out. Done with his former life as a glorified mercenary and had the walking papers to prove it. Didn't stop his old employer from seeking him out every so often. Not once had he been remotely tempted to return to that way of life. With each rejection, the requests grew a little more hostile. One of these days, his reprieve would run out and they'd send someone to bring him in. For now, he'd continue to avoid them with radio silence. Hence the turned off phone.

"Fuck," he ground out as the screen came to life. Fifteen missed calls and twice as many texts screaming at him to check in. All from Zach, the club's enforcer.

Some shit was going down. He'd flaked on church last week while tailing Chloe to the grocery store. Copper would roast his ass on a spit if it became a pattern. But calling in meant leaving Chloe.

Torn between loyalty to his club and the hot gut-punch he experienced knowing Chloe was minutes away from fucking some businessman, Rocket paused. What the fuck was wrong with him? It was getting harder to call the souring in his stomach anything other than jealousy.

He had to put an end to this shit. Chloe was a big girl. She, more than anyone, knew what could happen at the hands of a madman. For his own sanity, he had to step back. He couldn't continue to watch over her so much. Not when his club needed him.

Without bothering to listen to the voicemails or read the texts, Rocket left the bar, heading straight for his bike. If he pushed it, he'd be back in Townsend and at the clubhouse in thirty minutes. The guys could catch him up in person.

With any luck, they'd finally gotten a bead on Lefty.

That thought had a sinister smile curling his lips.

Just as he was pulling out, he caught sight of Chloe turning onto the road with Mr. Smooth's car hot on her tail.

Now that his head was screwed on straight, Rocket hit the throttle and shot off toward the clubhouse.

There were just some questions he might never get the answers to and he'd have to learn to live with that.

CHAPTER TWO

She used to be normal.

For ninety-seven percent of her life, Chloe had been perfectly and predictably normal. Born the daughter of a middle school principal and a home economics teacher, she grew up with three older brothers and an overweight pug in the suburbs of Knoxville, Tennessee. Throughout her school years, she earned A's and B's, played some mediocre soccer, and had a summer job at the local ice cream parlor from the time she was fifteen until she graduated high school. Afterward, she went to the University of Tennessee, graduating with a degree in accounting. After passing the CPA exam, she moved to Pigeon Forge where she'd started her own small accounting business and had been living and working ever since.

She'd had exactly one serious boyfriend, two bed partners, and a beloved group of close-knit friends. Once a week, she'd spoken to her parents and kept in close contact with her brothers through texts and her favorite new app, Marco Polo.

Normal.

Normal.

Normal.

Not overly exciting, not boring, just a regular life.

And then in one forty-eight-hour period, everything was shot to hell. Now, there wasn't a damn normal thing about her.

No, now she was just a screwed-up rape and assault survivor who hated leaving her house unless it was to pick up the random men she fucked on Friday and Saturday nights.

Who did that?

What kind of woman who'd been through what she'd endured went out and slept with multiple arbitrary men each week? Especially knowing exactly what could happen if she chose the wrong one.

Fucked-up women, that's who.

"Shit, babe, you're an animal in bed." The man beneath her said, giving her a satisfied, post-orgasm grin.

"Mmm," she said with a roll of her shoulders. Shoulders that were just as tense as when they'd walked in the room. "Don't call me babe. I'm sure as hell not your babe." Swinging her leg around, Chloe climbed off his adequate body before searching for her dress. Without so much as a glance at the man on the bed —Jon, Joe, James, something like that—she walked straight into the bathroom.

Here was the part she hated. The post-sex re-dressing while she tried to avoid catching a glimpse of herself in the mirror. For a few short hours, from the moment she walked out of her house until she scurried into this bathroom, she felt good. More than good. She felt powerful, sexy, in control, excited. And then, without fail, she'd see her reflection, and it would all evaporate.

As the high of her conquest began to wear off, Chloe stepped into her dress. After shimmying it over her hips and working her arms thorough the straps, she stood in front of the mirror with her eyes closed.

"Just do it," she whispered. Hiding from the mirror was a pointless exercise. She'd have to face herself at some point.

With her palms planted on the surface of the vanity, Chloe opened her eyes. She took a hard look at the woman in the mirror. As the seconds ticked by, her heart sank. Physically, she looked good. None of the damage to her face had left any scarring. Her body bore a few small reminders of the beating she'd suffered, but nothing unsightly, and nothing that truly bothered her. All the problems were squarely between her ears.

The woman staring back at her might look the same on the outside, but her soul had been permanently altered.

Sometimes, a sick part of her wished the men who'd hurt her had left some kind of hideous scar for all the world to see. Maybe a big gash across her cheek. At least then, people she encountered could tell from first glance that she was messed up. Hiding the internal struggle was an exhausting practice that took a huge toll on her every single day. No one expected her to hate being touched or panic if men she didn't know spoke to her. But maybe they would if they could see her scars.

"Uh, babe? You planning to release me anytime soon? I'm game for another round, but I could use a few minutes to stretch my arms first."

With a resigned sigh, Chloe bowed her head. This had to stop. One of these days, she'd end up hurt or worse from the reckless behavior. She'd been through hell and honestly wouldn't survive another attack. Neither would her family.

So why the hell did she continue to pick up random men at bars and fuck them? Why, and how did she manage to do this again and again when she'd flip out if a man so much as offered to shake her hand otherwise?

Because she was so very fucked up.

And because it was the only time she felt anything besides fear, depression, and disgust.

She flipped off the mirror. "What did I say about calling me babe?" she asked as she exited the bathroom.

"Sorry," the guy shrugged. "You never told me your name." He gave her a grin that was probably supposed to be boyish and playful, but now that she was done with him, it just made her skin crawl.

"And I never will," she said scanning the floor for her clutch.

"Oh, that's fine. My name is—"

"Nu-uh." She held up a hand, using the other to rummage around for the handcuff key. "Don't care. Didn't care the first time you told me. I'll uncuff you, then I'm taking off. Room is paid up through eleven am if you want to stay."

His forehead wrinkled. While not her type with his fancy suit and over processed hair that probably cost more than her own highlights did, he was an attractive man.

She'd chosen this hotel for its beds. They had headboards with wooden slats, perfect for handcuffing her conquests. Spread out and at her mercy, what's-his-name had the type of body her friends went nuts for. Gym honed muscles, sprinkling of dirty blond chest hair, smooth, ink-free skin. Way too clean cut and polished to get her motor revving, but then again none of this was really about sexual attraction.

At least not for her.

"You sure? I'm pretty much ready to go again now. We could switch positions and I'll tie you up." He shot her a wink.

Chloe's heart nearly stopped dead in her chest as an icy wave of fear washed over her. Not for all the money in the world would a man ever restrain her in any way shape or form. Hopefully, would never do anything to get herself arrested, because she'd have the mother of all freak outs the moment the cops broke out the cuffs. With a shake of her head, she pushed past it. "Not how this works."

She moved to the head of the bed and rested her knee on the mattress as she unlocked his right wrist.

Immediately, his freed hand landed on her thigh, giving it an affectionate squeeze. Chloe reacted without thought as though someone had pushed a button springing her into action. Her hand shot out, slamming into the man's throat.

A strangled half choke, half wheeze came from him as his body jerked.

Shit. Looked like those instructional self-defense YouTube videos were actually working.

"Jesus Christ. What the fuck is wrong with you, lady?"

Well that was a loaded question if she'd ever heard one. His words came out slightly garbled, like someone had throat punched the guy.

Oops.

"I'm sorry. You startled me." Even to her own ears she didn't sound very apologetic.

"That's it? You try to kill me because I fucking startled you? You're a crazy bitch."

He had no idea.

Chloe slipped her feet into her heels. She'd be making a speedy getaway this time around. Quick as she could, she scurried to the other side of the bed. After unlocking the remaining cuff, she grabbed her clutch and darted toward the door. "Sorry again. Just be out by eleven."

And now came the part of the evening that almost gave her cardiac arrest each time. Mace in one hand, keys threaded through the fingers of the other, she ran to her car like the devil himself was hot on her heels. After being kidnapped from a dark parking lot, she made sure to park directly under a lamp and always had her weapons at the ready.

Once securely in her car with the doors locked, Chloe allowed herself a moment to relax. Eyes closed, head resting back, she breathed in the fresh mountain air. With her tension finally at a manageable level, she started up her Volvo and navigated her way out of the parking lot. Sticking around to see just how angry what's-his-name was wouldn't be the smartest of ideas.

Halfway home, her car connected Bluetooth rang, jarring her so bad her heart nearly flew out of her mouth.

"Shit," she muttered as she used the steering wheel buttons to lower the ringer's volume then accept the call. "Hello?"

"Seriously, sis? It's ten on a Saturday night. Why the hell are you answering your phone?"

"Scotty!" Man, it was good to hear her brother's voice. "Are you in the country? Please tell me you're home?" Nine years older than she was, Scotty had enlisted in the army the moment he turned eighteen. Now, with nearly two decades years under his belt, he was a Ranger and deployed more often than not.

His laugh, healthy and strong filtered through the car's speakers. "Yeah, sis, I'm home. Arrived in country yesterday."

She couldn't hide the sigh of relief. Another deployment survived.

"How long you here for this time? Any idea?" As she spoke, she steered the car onto the highway that would take her back to Pigeon Forge. Or at least in that direction; she lived right outside the vacation town that was the home of the flashy Dollywood tourist attraction.

"Actually—"

Static had her smacking the dashboard as though the jolt would somehow end the crackling. Always happened on this stretch of the highway.

"Sorry, Scotty, dead spot. What did you say?"

"I said I'm taking some time off and coming to visit you."

Her heart simultaneously seized and soared. Visiting meant he'd be staying with her, and an end to her nocturnal activities. Scotty would flip his shit if he found out what she'd been up to these past few months.

Nerves skittered down her spine. Since she'd made the decision two months ago, she hadn't missed a Friday or Saturday. Would she be able to hold it together without those nights?

"Nothing? Thought you'd be at least a little excited."

Chloe blinked and laughed. "Oh, God, sorry. My mind ran away for a second. Yes! Come here, please. I'm super excited. What's it been, almost a year and a half since I've seen you?"

"Something like that."

She flicked her turn signal on and coasted over to the exit ramp. This time of night on a Saturday she was pretty much the only one on the pitch-black road. A shiver overtook her. Three more minutes and she'd be safely in her home.

"So, when are you coming? Gotta make sure I have enough food to feed your huge ass." And huge he was. Most of her family was tall, but at six-six, Scott was the largest by far.

"Got some shit I gotta take care of here before I can bug out. I'm thinking three weeks from tomorrow. That work for you?"

"Yes, of course. Anything works for me." She smiled into the night as she pulled into her driveway. "God, I can't wait to see you."

He didn't respond for a moment which had her frowning as she put the car in park. "Scott? Did I lose you?"

"Nah I'm here." His voice had grown serious. "How you doing, honey? I'm sorry I've been off the grid so much over the past few months. Nearly killed me to be out of the country when you were hurt."

A now familiar sorrow swamped over her. It wasn't a surprise. The attack was always there, looming on the sidelines, just waiting to jump in and ruin a good moment. A healthy dose of guilt joined that sorrow. Her family didn't know the full story of what she'd suffered. They knew the same version she'd told the cops. A partial truth.

"Ahh, so that's why you're visiting. Not because you can't stay away from your favorite sister and my brownie recipe, but because you're checking up on me. Mom making you do this?"

She'd kicked her mom out after five days, unable to take the incessant mothering—smothering—any longer.

"Clo…" He sounded pained. As though thinking about what happened to her physically hurt him.

She almost snorted, but thankfully found enough control to keep the rude sound at bay. Didn't anyone get it? Didn't they realize she couldn't handle their hurt on top of her own? It was just too much. Too heart wrenching. She hadn't asked for what happened to her, and the fact that it caused almost as much agony for her family as it did for her was more than she could take.

"I'm okay, Scott. Dealing with it." *In a way that could get me killed.* "Getting better every day." Because she'd found tying men to a bed and fucking the shit out of them was the only thing that gave her a sense of command over her life. It was the only time she felt powerful, strong, in control. The moments she was dominating some random man were the only ones that banished the fear she'd lived with every second since she was stuffed in a trunk and kidnapped.

So yeah, she was dealing with it, and she'd continue to do so until it blew up in her face. As dangerous and unhealthy as her unconventional therapy might be, it was far better than cowering in the corner of her house as she'd done for the first three months following her rescue.

It'd been a while since she thought about the rescue. About the mysterious biker who'd saved her life and delivered her to the hospital. He was the man who'd seen her at her very worst and somehow, he'd known what she needed. He'd known not to touch her both because she'd freak at the touch of a man and because she'd needed to climb off that bed and walk outside on her own two feet.

Needed to salvage some shred of dignity.

And he let her.

Even though he was her savior, and she owed him her life and then some, he represented the worst possible moments in her existence. Not to mention he was a member of the Hell's Handlers. Lefty's message placing blame on the bikers ran through her head whenever she thought of her rescuer. Like a true coward, she avoided the entire city limits of Townsend, his motorcycle club's territory.

She sure as hell hoped to never run across the biker again.

CHAPTER THREE

Shit had blown with the club.

From the moment Rocket left the bar three weeks ago, it'd been one explosion after another.

Copper, the club's president, had been kidnapped.

Boom.

They'd rescued him only to find the giant red-bearded man stabbed and beaten to a pulp.

Boom.

Rusty, Copper's psychopathic brother was murdered.

Boom.

Lefty, the man whose blood Rocket wanted more than anything, slipped through their grasp yet again. Gone to ground without a trace.

Fucking boom.

Thanks to Copper's strong leadership when he returned to the chair less than a week after being injured, the clubhouse had only descended into mild chaos. A full-on manhunt was in effect for Lefty, the one-time leader of the Gray Dragons gang. Almost two years ago, Lefty had been the number three dog in the Gray Dragons' food chain. Shark, a sadistic motherfucker, ran the gang at the time. Shark had a nasty history with Toni, the ol' lady of the Handlers' enforcer. The sea predator had been killed in a showdown between his minions and the Handlers, but not before causing a shit ton of grief for the MC.

Once Shark was out of the way, Lefty murdered the number two and took over the gang. His primary source of income had been twofold, drugs and trafficking women—unwilling women. It wasn't long before the Handlers shut that shit down, sending Lefty underground. Unfortunately, not fast enough to save Chloe from her fate.

Recently, Lefty had poked his head out of whatever hole he'd been hiding in long enough to commit a few murders before disappearing once again.

Rocket had hit his limit with this fucking guy. Hell, Copper was at his limit, and that's what mattered, because he ran the show. So now, the Handlers were searching under every rock and in every dark corner for Lefty.

It was time for him to die.

And though either Copper or Zach would be the ones to do the honors, Rocket wanted to end Lefty's life himself so bad he could see the moment the man's heart stopped as though it was right in front of him. Never in his years with the Handlers had he so much as thought of going against his president's wishes. Now, he wasn't sure he'd be able to keep himself from slaying Lefty long enough to deliver him to Copper, were he the one to find the gang banger.

And Rocket was determined to find him.

For Chloe.

Shit. Rocket poured himself a drink, then returned the bottle to the shelf behind the bar. It'd been exactly fourteen days since he'd laid eyes on the woman. Each of those twenty-four-hour periods, he'd woken with a hard-on courtesy of raunchy dreams starring Chloe, wild and uninhibited. He'd stroked off in the shower every morning, her name falling from his lips as he shot his release down the drain. Then, after an exhausting fifteen-hour day dealing with tension-filled club business and cranky as fuck men, he'd find his fingers wrapped around his dick once again.

Rocket

He'd come more times in the past two weeks than the previous six months combined. And all by his own hand.

After downing the Jack, he glanced across the room to where Screw was shooting pool with two of the Honeys. If Rocket were smart, he'd grab one of the girls and unload into her instead of his fist. The Honeys weren't typically his first—or even second—choice of lay, but desperate times and all. The one he had his eye on let out a high-pitched giggle as she blew her shot. It earned her a slap on the ass and quick tit-grope from Screw. Someone she'd also be blowing before the night was up, unless Rocket stepped in and claimed the prize.

"Wanna join us, brother?" Screw called across the mostly empty clubhouse. At three on a Saturday afternoon, most of the guys were home, gearing up for another night of debauchery. Screw liked to prepare for a night of fucking and drinking by fucking and drinking. Even though his name came from Screwball, he tended to live up to the more obvious meaning as well. Hell, that pool table was his favorite substitute for a bed. Not a weekend went by without him bending some broad over the felt. Screw squeezed the ass of the redhead. "Got more than enough to go around."

What the hell? Something had to snap him out of his Chloe-induced funk.

"Yeah, I'm in." He poured himself a second drink, then meandered on toward the pool table at the back of the room.

Screw lifted his chin toward the redheaded Honey. Tina, if Rocket remembered correctly. She caught his meaning and grabbed a pool cue. With her head cocked to the side and her crimson-painted lips pursed, she winked at Rocket. Step by step, she walked toward him, bony hips swaying, hand stroking the cue like it was a skinny dick.

Rocket shook his head once. Not Tina. No redheads. Not when there was already one fucking with his mind. He wasn't known for being chatty, probably considered an asshole among the Honeys, but Tina caught his drift. After sending a pout his way, she shrugged and turned her attention back to Screw.

"I'll take the blonde," Rocket said.

"She's all yours," Screw replied, giving blondie a hard slap on the ass that propelled her in Rocket's direction.

"Oooh," she said with a giggle. "Lucky me." When she reached him, she plastered herself against his side. The scent of three-dollar perfume singed his nose. "My name's Lacy," she said, stretching onto her tiptoes to reach his ear. Her breath reeked of alcohol and menthol cigarettes.

Even in her five-inch stilettos, she barely reached his chin. At six foot two, Rocket preferred his women taller and with some curves. Women with a little height and cushion fit him much better. Just an issue of alignment. Plus, he didn't have to worry about snapping them in half if he got a little over exuberant, which happened from time to time.

"Rocket," he answered, taking the pool cue from her hands.

"I know that." She giggled again as he lined up his shot. The sound resembled loose change in a tin can, grating and unpleasant. Shit. What was with him? Didn't matter what the fuck she laughed like. If she could kneel and suck, she'd provide the tension relief he needed and be happy to do it.

"Four. Side pocket," Rocket said.

Screw snorted. "No fucking way." The kid had been spending a ton of time with Zach, both assisting in enforcing for the club, and managing the gym. From the way he stood with his hands wrapped high around the cue, Rocket could see the extra hours at the gym were paying off. Thick biceps ringed with new ink stretched the sleeves of his T-shirt almost to the point of no return.

The difficult shot sailed into the pocket.

He raised an eyebrow at Screw.

"Sorry, oh master of pool," Screw said lifting his arms in defeat. "I'll keep my comments to myself from now on."

Rocket straightened. "You do that. Starting to look like a meathead there, Screw."

Another laugh, this one followed by a kiss to each flexed bicep. "I'll take that as a compliment, brother."

Rocket's lips twitched as Tina oohed and aahed over Screw's bulky muscles. "Baby," she whined. "When are you gonna take me upstairs and put all that strength to good use?"

Screw might love the company of the Honeys, but he did not like the girls making demands on him. His face tightened. "When I'm good and fucking ready." He stepped away from Tina and bent over the table. Along with hardening muscles, his personality had firmed up as well, taking him from the near goofy screwball to a serious, sometimes harsh member of the club.

"Nice shot." The words were cooed in Rocket's ear as a set of silicone tits engulfed his arm. "How about you line up a shot toward my center pocket."

Rocket groaned at the same time Screw burst out laughing.

Christ, he was either getting too old or too smart for this shit. There was a time he'd have shrugged off the comment, grabbed Lacy's hand, and found a dark corner of the room. Now, he needed a little something besides swirling air between their ears.

"Yeah, Rock, when you gonna shoot—"

Rocket sent Screw the glare that had scarier men than him backing down. Of course, the scowl only made Screw laugh harder. With a roll of his tense shoulders, Rocket glanced at Lacy. Her brown eyes were wide and expectant as she waited for him to give her the fuck she wanted.

Wasn't gonna happen right then. Hell, who was he kidding, it never was going to happen. His dick had pretty much given up the ghost unless Chloe was around. She was better than an entire bottle of Viagra for waking his cock up.

Just as he opened his mouth to blow Lacy off, his phone rang. Saved by the bell. "Gotta take this," he muttered as he glanced at the screen.

Fuck.

Esposito wasn't backing off this time. Rocket hovered his finger over the decline button as he stared down at his old boss's name flashing across the screen. The impulse to send it straight to voicemail was only eclipsed by the need to know what they wanted from him. His neck had been itching for days and that usually meant a shitstorm was rolling in.

"Everything okay, brother?"

"What?" He glanced up at Screw as he realized his face must have shown his displeasure. "Yeah, s'all good."

"You coming back or you want me to entertain Lacy for you?" Screw leaned his hip against the pool table, arm slung across Tina's shoulder. The Honey was lazily tracing the Hell's Handlers logo printed on his T-shirt.

"Have at 'er. Sorry," he said with a forced smile for Lacy.

"No worries," she chirped, making her way back to Screw. The three of them would be up in Screw's room going at it before Rocket finished his call. He'd bet his Harley on it.

"What," he barked into the phone as he stepped outside. A quick glance around revealed he was alone. Good. This call required privacy. Copper knew the details of Rocket's life prior to prospecting for the club, but he was the only one.

And Rocket planned to keep it that way.

"No hello? Didn't your mother teach you any manners?" the familiar yet unwelcome voice said.

"My mother didn't teach me shit. She was a strung-out crack whore who died in a raid on her coke den. Surely you remember."

A grunt was the only response.

"Need you, Logan."

Rocket pinched the bridge of his nose. "You must, if you're busting out the Logans already." Same manipulative shit as always. "Wasting your time, old man."

"Don't even want to hear the job?"

Rocket laughed. "Fuck no."

Rocket

Silence fell over the line. Rocket had met Lt. Colonel Nicholas Esposito at Parris Island back when he was an eighteen-year-old grunt in boot camp. The guy had followed Rocket's career, even afteer he became General Esposito, and eventually retired from the Marines. Two years after that, he'd sought Rocket out for his private security—aka government sanctioned black ops—organization. All gung-ho and oorah after multiple tours with the Marines, Rocket had separated from the military and signed a very exclusive contract with Esposito's company, DarkOps. He'd convinced himself he'd be saving the world and making bank doing it.

What wasn't to love about that?

"This is important, Logan. And dangerous. A real adrenalin rush of a job, just how you like it."

"How I liked it, old man. Past tense."

"I need your skill set for this. You're the fucking best and you know it."

So, the job required explosives. Or maybe a sniper. Rocket had excelled in both arenas, but explosives were where his true talent lay. Hence the handle Rocket. Esposito employed plenty of other snipers, but no one as good or as fast at assembling bombs which were virtually impossible to defuse.

"Been out of the game for five fucking years, old man," Rocket said using the nickname he knew drove Esposito nuts. The man wanted nothing more than to be smack in the middle of the action himself, but at sixty, he was long past his operational prime. "My skills are rusty at best. I'm liable to kill myself along with your mark."

That was bullshit and Esposito knew it. Rocket hit the range at least once a week. His skills with a rifle, and a hand gun for that matter, were as tight as ever. Not to mention his little explosives lab in the basement of his house. He may not use the shit often anymore, but he'd be a damn fool to let the skills slip.

And he was no fuckin' fool.

Except when it came to one curvy redhead.

Thoughts of Chloe invaded his mind and filled his dick. Fuck, now he was trying to get rid of Esposito while he had a damn boner.

Wonderful.

"Look, old man, I'm gonna make this simple for you. The answer is no. It's always going to be no. Every one of these phone calls is a waste of your time." He'd said those same words more than once since he walked away from DarkOps. Each time Esposito had eventually backed off.

"Can't accept that this time, Logan. You owe me and I'm finally calling it in."

Fuck.

It was the truth. With the shit Rocket knew, he never should have been allowed to walk away from DarkOps. Esposito had paved the way to his freedom without any backlash. Sort of...

There'd been those three little words that followed Rocket out the door the day he left it all behind. *You owe me.* He'd had known all along Esposito would come to collect one day. And he had, a few times, though each and every one Rocket managed to wriggle out of it.

"Won't do it," Rocket said.

"You don't have a choice," Esposito shot back, the unspoken threat clear in his tone. *Do this or I'll make sure what should have happened to you five years ago happens now.*

The line went dead.

Fuck.

"Fuck!" Rocket yelled. He was going to have to involve the club in this. DarkOps would send someone for him. Hell, they'd probably go after one of his brothers or sabotage the club's business dealings to get him to fall in line. The club knew little of the past that might be coming to bite them all. He couldn't and wouldn't leave them vulnerable like that.

But goddamn, this was the worst possible time to bring mayhem to the club's doorstep. Copper was hobbling around with a broken leg and healing stab wounds while all the club's energy was focused on tracking Lefty. They didn't need his shit mucking things up even more.

He glanced at his phone. Seven p.m. In about an hour or so, Chloe would be heading out to find her boy toy for the night. Or for an hour. Despite his mood, Rocket almost laughed. An hour. Who were these jokers she was fucking? He had no doubt he could drag the encounter out longer than a measly sixty minutes.

A smile curled his lips. He loved a good challenge.

With the threat from Esposito, Rocket was well and truly fucked.

Might as well go get fucked in a more pleasurable way.

CHAPTER FOUR

Heels click-clacking across the polished hardwood floor, Chloe weaved her way to the mahogany bar. Her head was high, shoulders back, and her body was hugged tight in a hunter green dress she'd splurged half her paycheck on. But, damn if it didn't portray her as a confident woman on the prowl. A woman who knew what she wanted and went after it. A woman who didn't suffer from crippling self-doubt and anxiety.

Appearances sure could be deceiving.

The dress was an off-the-shoulder bandage-style bodycon number. The thing fit her like it'd been designed with her body in mind. Not something that happened every day. Or ever.

Tonight had to count, had to hold her over, and keep the stress at bay for a few weeks. Tomorrow, Scott arrived. He'd knock her out and stuff her in a closet before he'd let her cruise the bars for random men to fuck.

"Day-um, woman," the bartender said. "You are looking extra fine tonight. You know," he said with a wink as he leaned on his elbows, a damp drying rag in his hand. "I can serve you way more than just a drink."

Chloe tossed back her head and let out a laugh. Her long hair tickled the backs of her bare arms, making goosebumps sprout across her skin. Rich was nice to look at, had her favorite drink memorized, and flirted like no other, but that's where the appreciation ended. At least on her end. There was no way in hell she'd risk taking him back to her hotel room. Sleeping with him would mean the end of her visits to that particular lounge, and she wasn't willing to sacrifice her favorite meet-up spot for a quick romp with him. Besides, picking up a complete stranger was the only way this exercise worked. And the casual banter she always shared with Rich made him a friend of sorts, or at least put him on a level above stranger.

"Hmm," she said, making sure it came out as more of a purr. Might as well have a little fun with him. "I'm sure you can. But I'll stick with a vodka and club for now."

He winked again. "Sure thing, gorgeous. You change your mind, you know where to find me. I'm off at two." He rapped his knuckles on the bar.

She almost laughed. Long before two, she'd be tucked into bed, snoozing away. "I'll remember that," she said blowing him a kiss.

He caught it and pretended to stuff it in his pocket—their silly routine whenever she visited his lounge.

Chloe sat on the barstool and used the mirrored backsplash to scan the room. More than a few sets of male eyes were fixated on her back. A smile formed as the familiar rush of excitement flowed through her veins.

In here, she was the star. The men came to her and came on to her, but it was ultimately her decision who would be gifted her time and body. If a man annoyed her? She sent him away. If he laughed in a way that grated on her nerves? A drink slurper? Bye-bye buddy. They all wanted her, or wanted the assertive woman she pretended to be. These men fought for her attention with their winks, lusty grins, and offers of alcohol. But in the end? Each and every one of them was helpless to do anything but wait for her decision. Wait to find out who she'd choose, if anyone.

The ultimate power trip.

Though, she always chose one. The second phase of the night was where she really got her fix. Where the high was so good, it eclipsed the fear living under her skin the other twenty-three hours of the day.

"Here you go, gorgeous," Rich said, setting the drink in front of her.

"Thanks," she handed over a twenty, then took a small sip. Legs crossed, she used the bar for leverage and spun on the stool. Time to identify her next conquest.

As she perused the dimly lit lounge, her gaze landed on a table of giggling women, and for one second, her heart ceased to beat.

It's not her.

Chloe lifted her glass and gulped down a mouthful of mostly vodka. If she didn't know better, she'd think Rich was trying to get her hammered. Damn, that was a close call. For a hot second, she'd thought she'd recognized one of the giddy women laughing with her girlfriends. Upon closer inspection, it wasn't her old high school peer, but damn, what a wakeup. A little reminder to be careful and not get arrogant.

She'd die if she ran into anyone who knew her. The woman sitting on the barstool in the tight as hell dress wearing Chloe's skin was not the Chloe anyone knew. Hell, she didn't even know herself anymore. Never before had she dressed up to attract men. She'd dated some, but was never focused on hooking up or sex. Before her world had imploded, she wouldn't have accepted a million dollars to seek out a different man or men every week.

But now? Now it had become an obsession. If anyone who knew her witnessed her in action, they'd think aliens invaded had her body.

She'd found that trying to psychoanalyze herself only led to increased anxiety, guilt, and shame, so she'd given up and did what she had to do to keep from losing her sanity completely.

After another healthy sip, Chloe continued her inspection of the room. A few potential candidates caught her eye and sparked a bit of interest. Just as she was about to take a second gander at a sandy-haired business man chatting with two similarly dressed guys, she locked gazes with a set of piercing blue eyes.

Her heart skipped a beat, and she had to glance away. *Wow.* The intensity of that gaze nearly burned her. She peeked again, this time out of the corner of her eye while directing her head away from him.

He hadn't so much as twitched. Those two blue orbs zeroed straight in on her. She swore lasers shot from them, warming her skin to the point of flushed. Swallowing another sizable mouthful, she faced the bar once again. The view wasn't as good, but at least she could stealthily spy on him through the mirror without him being aware.

The man was downright delicious. Not only did he have eyes that made her swoon, but he filled out that dress shirt with some serious muscle. He'd skipped a tie, or had already taken it off, and the top button of his crisply pressed gray shirt was open as though he'd shed his professional persona and was ready to kick back for the night. He wasn't a regular, she was there often enough to know the usual crowd. Something about the man was familiar, but she was near ninety-five percent certain she'd never seen him before, which was a requirement for her one-offs, but without knowing a damn thing about the man, she could sense the raw visceral power radiating from him.

Which made him an automatic no. Too risky. That kind of animal would never allow her the control she required. And she couldn't even fathom being alone in a room with a man who wouldn't give her control, let alone naked with one who possessed five times the strength she did.

Unable to redirect herself, she continued to trail her gaze upward over his thick neck. Then came the five o-clock shadow that looked just scratchy enough to elicit a round of shivers as it brushed against naked skin. That dark stubble covered a strong jaw and framed firm, smooth lips. And finally, back to those blue eyes that were…staring straight into hers in the mirror.

Shit!

He'd known she was eye-fucking him all along. His face seemed too severe for a true smile, but one corner of his mouth twitched, letting her know he was at least somewhat amused by the situation.

Stuck like a deer caught in high beams, she was unable to tear her focus away. Even when he rose, keeping eye contact through the mirror, and ambled his way toward the bar.

Shit. Double shit.

The hairs on the back of her neck rose to attention and the temperature in the bar shot up by at least ten degrees. Chloe tugged at the suddenly constricting neckline of her dress. Didn't the place have some kind of air circulation? And what was with her deodorant? Clearly it wasn't made for this woman.

Blue-eyes stalked straight toward her, oblivious to the appreciative glances women threw his way. Of course, they looked and admired. The man had that potent mix of power and beauty with an air danger. He was magnetic.

Without asking if the seat was taken or issuing some kind of cheesy pickup line, he parked himself on the empty stool next to her. Chloe swallowed around her dry throat then lifted her drink to her lips only to discover an empty glass.

"Another?" Blue-eyes said.

Before she thought the better of it, she nodded.

Shit.

One drink was all she ever allowed herself. She nursed it for hours if necessary, until she was ready to leave. Sliding into tipsy territory was far too hazardous. Being tipsy meant feeling comfortable, friendly, hell, even amorous. It led to letting down her guard and that could be a fatal mistake.

No, she needed to remain in control each and every minute of the night.

The man lifted his hand toward Rich, then motioned to her drink. Two minutes later, eyebrow arched in question, the bartender slash friend of sorts slid a second drink her way.

Rocket

She gave Rich as reassuring a smile as she could. His eyes flicked toward the entrance where a muscle-bound bouncer sat checking identification. Chloe gave a subtle shake of her head.

Wasn't necessary. Blue-eyes hadn't done a single thing wrong or creepy. Hell, he hadn't done anything. Just ordered her a second drink, something men did for women every night in bars all across the world. Having him tossed out on his ass would be quite the overreaction.

Rich just shrugged, sent the man a chilly look, then moved on to the next patron.

Chloe blew out a breath. Just because he'd bought her a drink didn't mean she had to drink it or choose him as her companion for the evening.

Steeling her spine, she faced him only to find a slight smirk on his full lips. Damn, why couldn't he be a hideous ogre? She cleared her throat and lifted the glass. "Thank you, uh…"

"Logan," he said, the deep timbre of his voice washing over her like a warm wave.

"Thank you, Logan." Shit. Why the hell had she acted as though she wanted his name? Learning his name wasn't necessary. In fact, it was a hinderance to the evening's goal.

He lifted his own drink, scotch if she had to guess, and tapped it against her glass. "And thank you for not having the bouncer haul me out to the parking lot." His expression remained serious, but there was a teasing quality to his statement.

A shaky laugh escaped her. So, he was observant as well as sexy. "You from around here?" she asked, then immediately wished she could take the words back. They were part of her well-practiced spiel. The script she used when choosing a partner for the night. Since she'd already ruled him out, she needed to take a different path.

"No. Just in town for the weekend." He didn't offer anything beyond that. Usually the men she spoke with enjoyed talking about themselves and why they were visiting the area.

A quick peek at his left hand reveled a naked ring finger devoid of tan lines. A good indication he wasn't married.

You're not picking him.

"You?"

"Huh?" Why did he have to smell so good? Not cologne as most of the men she met wore. Hell, she could pretty much tell them all with a single sniff by now. No, this guy smelled, clean, fresh, with an undertone of...sawdust? Interesting, unexpected, and masculine as hell.

"You live here?"

Yes, yes. Say yes. If she did it would seal his fate. She'd never leave with him if he knew she lived nearby. "No. I had some business in the area. I'll be heading out of town tomorrow morning."

Shit. She sucked back half her drink in one gulp. So much for not drinking it. So much for not picking up this guy.

Double shit.

"You here alone?" He asked, his already sexy voice leaving no doubt as to his intent. They weren't touching. Not even their knees had brushed though they faced each other. Yet somehow the heat of his body was already flowing its way into hers. Watching him trail a long finger around the rim of his glass, she shivered. Those hands would probably feel amazing...

What the fuck was wrong with her?

Even if she'd been planning to leave with him, he wouldn't be touching her. The game didn't work that way.

"Um, yeah. Just me." God, she was losing her mind. She sucked down another gulp.

He looked her straight in the eye. "You got a room nearby?"

As though a puppeteer was controlling the movement of her head, her chin lifted then fell in a single nod.

"Wanna get out of here?" he asked.

Completely mesmerized by the play of his lips as he spoke, Chloe had the distinct impression he was a spider drawing her into his web, a complete reversal of her usual role.

Again, she nodded without even giving her head permission to move.

He stood and held a hand out to her. "Uber?"

Probably a smart idea. She'd had just enough to make her unsafe on the road. "Sure," she croaked. As she stared at his outstretched hand, the magnitude of what she was agreeing to finally kicked in. She'd chosen this man for the night. Or maybe he'd chosen her. As that second option wasn't acceptable, she went with the first.

She'd chosen him. That knowledge was an icy bucket of water, dousing some of the lusty spell he'd cast. Now she had to make sure he knew the rules of the game. "Wait," she said, some of her usual confidence and authority making its way back. "I have some conditions."

He tilted his head. Clearly, Logan was a man of few words.

"I, uh…" Shit, where was her usual bravado and control? This was such a stupid idea. The man muddled her head too much to be safe. Why the hell couldn't she kick him to the curb? As those captivating eyes stared at her, she straightened her shoulders. Fuck it. She needed an epic night and dominating this powerful man would be just that.

"We do this my way," she said, stepping toward him. She didn't have to try to inject a husky quality to her voice, it came naturally just being near him.

"Your way?"

"Yes," she said, finally getting into the usual role. "My room, my show." The familiar words settled her. "Before we leave you need to agree to fuck my way. That's non-negotiable. If you can do that, we'll go now. If not, I'll keep searching for a man who'll give me what I need."

He stepped right into her personal space, his lips mere inches from her ear. Though she was tall, especially in her heels, he still had an inch or two on her. Immediately a barrage of lust and panic warred for dominance. Chloe clenched her fists and bit her lower lip to keep from whimpering, whether with need or fear she had no idea.

"Fuck your search. I'm exactly the man you need, baby." His warm breath had shivers racing up and down her spine. "But sure, your room, your show."

Holy shit. The man might not be overly verbal, but the words he did use got the job done. When he drew back, he was smiling the first real smile she'd seen from him and her knees weakened. With a wink, he turned and started for the exit.

Chloe stared at him for two seconds before tossing back what was left of her drink. Liquid courage.

As she followed him, her eyes fell to his perfectly rounded ass draped in a pair of fitted black slacks. Her nipples puckered.

Shit. This was bad.

CHAPTER FIVE

Rocket had thrown her off her game. That much was obvious by the slight tremor in her hand as she inserted the keycard into the hotel room door. Flustering her hadn't been the plan. He wanted the authentic experience. Wanted to uncover exactly what she did with the other men who crossed this very threshold, but he just couldn't help the primal pull to her that had him coming on strong.

Chloe was hands down the most gorgeous woman he'd seen in years, maybe even ever, all wrapped up in that tight as fuck dress. The damn thing wasn't even overtly sexy. Nothing was on display, not her back, not her tits, hell, not even too much leg. But it molded to her length as though it'd been painted on, accentuating each and every curve and dip of her womanly body, and making a man's mind think of nothing but what might be hiding underneath the slinky fabric. And the way that green looked against the waterfall of auburn hair cascading down her back?

Fuck, she had him practically thinking in poem.

Once she had the door open, she preceded him into the room. Without so much as a glance in his direction, she marched her pert behind straight to the dresser. "Clothes off. Lie on the bed. On your back." The no nonsense tone was in complete contrast to the heat in her eyes and the subtle quiver he'd felt when he whispered in her ear just fifteen minutes earlier.

Now, it seemed as though she didn't give a rat's ass who owned the cock she was about to take. She was all business. The last thing Rocket would ever be described as was submissive. Yes, he'd spent much of his adult life obeying orders, but that was the nature of the military. And his job. Once he entered the private sector, he'd been given more freedom. Now, he only answered to one man and that was Copper, his MC's president. He certainly never gave up control when fucking. But, curious to see where this was going, he complied.

After stripping out of the uncomfortably proper attire, he reclined against a stack of pillows and folded his arms behind his head. Chloe still hadn't given him so much as a flicker of her attention. Back to him, she shimmied the tight dress up and over her ass, revealing two smooth globes separated by a ribbon of dark purple fabric. Next came a smooth, creamy back. That was all it took; his shaft rose thick and proud between his outstretched legs. For a split-second, he recalled what she'd been through and almost covered himself with a pillow, but clearly, she wanted to fuck. That was the entire reason they'd come to this middle of the road establishment.

Right?

Hips shifting back and forth, she drew the dress over her head and dropped it on the thin carpet next to her feet.

Her manicured fingers came around her back, unclasped the purple bra, and let it fall as well. Rocket's mouth went dry while his cock twitched in anticipation of seeing her tits.

There was no seduction attempt, no carefully planned sexy reveal. Chloe spent a moment rummaging in the top dresser drawer, then spun without ceremony. On the smaller side, her breasts high and damn tasty looking. Something dangled from her hand, but he couldn't tear his gaze away from her body to check what it was. "Fuck, you're beautiful," he said as she started toward him.

Her steps faltered a second before her surprised gaze met his. "T-thank you." It was as though she was realizing for the first time that the man in the room with her was an actual person who could think, feel, act, and speak. "Thank you," she said. Still, she didn't preen, sex up her walk, or stick those tits out farther. If it weren't for her nudity he'd think she was getting ready to walk into a grocery store.

Rocket let his gaze wander her body for another moment. As he once again reached her tits, his mouth turned down. Her nipples, while gorgeous, were completely soft. Sure, the room was warm, but they were both buck ass naked and about to fuck. Shouldn't she be a bit aroused even pre-foreplay? In the lounge, those green eyes had smoldered, small flecks of gold seeming to shimmer with lust. Now? She might as well have been sitting down to a business meeting.

The woman wasn't remotely turned on.

Rocket wasn't an idiot. He realized she might not get as wet as he was hard just by looking at his erect dick, but with the way she'd reacted to his clothed body in the bar, he'd expected something. Not this almost cold reception.

She walked toward him, hips and tits jiggling in time with her steps. Behind his head, he squeezed his fists to keep from pouncing on her. The need to know what she was playing at outweighed his physical ache.

Just barely.

When she reached him, she stopped next to the bed. "My room, my rules. Still good with that?"

He nodded.

"Okay, you don't do anything unless I tell you. That includes touching. Understand?"

"Got it." Damn that went against every instinct he possessed. Hell, he'd had the same conversation with women in the past only in reverse positions. He was a dominant guy, just his nature. Lying back and taking it wasn't exactly his M.O. Still, the combination of curiosity and a raging hard-on had him agreeing.

Chloe bent forward slightly, and his brain completely fuzzed. Her nipple hung just two inches from his mouth. The woman was crazy if she thought he could resist a taste. Sneaking his tongue out, he circled the bud then sucked it into his mouth.

Hard.

She cried out and jerked back, stumbling away from the bed. "What the fuck?" she yelled.

Rocket leaned forward only to realize his wrist was circled by a metal cuff attached to the bed. He hadn't even realized she'd touched his arm. One taste of her and his awareness went to shit. "What the fuck, indeed," he said, unable to keep the amusement out of his voice as he jangled the cuff.

"I just explained the fucking rules to you," Chloe said, running a trembling hand through her hair. "And you agreed to them. This was a bad idea," she muttered more to herself than him. She might be flustered and nervous, but at least she wasn't unaffected by him. Both nipples had tightened to stiff peaks and a red flush brightened her cheeks.

Whatever she was up to, she wasn't accustomed to pleasure.

"I'll behave," he said.

She eyed him with a look of disbelief.

"Here." He held out his left wrist. "I assume you want to shackle this one too."

Her lower lip disappeared between her teeth. "If this were any other weekend," she grumbled as she stomped around the bed. Pointing a finger in his face, she said, "Next time you break the rules, I'm walking."

"Understood." He felt like a kid chastised by the principal.

Not sexy at all, yet with Chloe in the room, he had a feeling she could be covered from head to toe in sludge and he'd be hard as stone.

The click of the locking mechanism had him testing the strength of the handcuffs and bed rails. Not flimsy, but if he really wanted free, he could splinter the fucking wood slats in no time. "Now what?" he asked, raising an eyebrow.

"Now we fuck," she said. It might as well have been, "now we vacuum" for all the heat behind it.

Rocket

Chloe crossed the room, grabbed a few things from the dresser, then returned to the bed. Two seconds later, she straddled him. His cock wept at the mere feel of her silken thighs brushing his. Didn't bode well for his staying power once he got in what he knew would be some prime pussy.

There wasn't much he could do besides lie there and take what she dished out, so that's exactly what he did. She sure as fuck was hot, sitting astride him with her shiny red hair flowing past her tits.

A tearing sound had him pulling his gaze from her hair to inspect her hands. Chloe was back to efficient, almost clinical actions as she removed a condom from its foil packet. Without so much as a caress, she rolled the latex down the length of his straining cock with as much enthusiasm as a kid in health class, learning on a banana. Hell, those horny teens were probably ten times as excited as Chloe right then.

Rocket was so busy clenching his jaw and trying not to blow at just the feel of her fingertips smoothing the condom in place, he almost missed the soft click and squirt that came next. Chloe squeezed a large glob of what he assumed was lube onto her hand then immediately slathered it on his suited-up cock. The moment her hands and the cool liquid hit his shaft—chilly even through the condom—he cursed.

"Sorry," she said. "Too cold?" As though she was a physician placing a frigid stethoscope on his chest instead of fisting his cock in her delicate hands.

"No," he ground out. "Feels fucking good. Like your hands on me."

"Ah."

So she wasn't one for dirty talk. "You know, you wouldn't need that shit if you let me—oh fuck."

Without ceremony or so much as a millisecond of foreplay, Chloe positioned herself over his cock and started to work him into her body. He saw stars as the heat of her began to engulf him. She was tighter than tight and hot as the fucking sun. But she wasn't ready to fuck. Not by a long shot.

"Babe," he said through clenched teeth. Fuck it was near impossible to think with the strangling squeeze of her pussy neutralizing his brain cells one by one.

"Shut up," she practically barked at him. "No talking. No moving. Keep your legs out straight." Her eyes were closed, face screwed in concentration as she slowly worked herself down his length. Once he was fully seated inside her, she paused, probably to adjust to his size.

The reprieve gave him a second to get his rational head in the game and keep from blowing his load already. In an unanticipated moment of clarity, Rocket wondered why the hell she was doing this. Nothing about it seemed to be working for her sexually.

The thought was fleeting because the next thing that happened nearly rendered him stupid. Chloe rode him. Like a fucking jockey gunning for the win. She started with a steady pace, but quickly ramped up to fast, almost frantic movements like she couldn't get *him* off fast enough. But what about her pleasure?

Something was way the fuck off here.

If Rocket was any other man, or Chloe was any other woman, he could probably close his eyes and ignore the signs, but as it was, he'd spent months stalking the sexy woman and could easily tell this wasn't doing shit for her. There was absolutely no connection in their fucking. Not that he was unused to fucking without emotion, in fact he only fucked without emotion, but he never fucked without both parties being hot and desperate for each other. Even if it only lasted a short time, they wanted each other, at least physically.

And while Rocket wanted the fuck outta Chloe, he was pretty sure she saw him as nothing more than a two-hundred-pound vibrator.

Don't get him wrong, he was gonna come, and come hard. Encase a man's dick in a pussy as hot and tight as Chloe's, and that was pretty much a guarantee. But he wanted Chloe as hungry for it as he was. When she came, he wanted her to go off like…well, a rocket.

Chloe picked up speed. Her small tits bounced and swayed as she fucked him, drawing his attention. Before long, the feel of her eclipsed all his other thoughts. He groaned and strained against the cuffs as she clenched her sex around him. Damn, the woman had some skill. She swiveled her hips, letting her head fall back on her shoulders. Her hair was so long, the ends brushed Rocket's thighs. That added sensation, the slight tickle combined with her vigorous fucking had his balls drawing tight and his gut coiling with impending release.

"You almost there?" Chloe asked, eyes still shut tight.

"Fuck, yeah, I'm close, baby. You?"

"Yep."

Yep? She gave him a yep? Chloe leaned forward, slapping her palms on his chest, she braced, threw her head back and moaned long and loud. As she did so, her pussy rhythmically squeezed around his cock, nearly blowing his head straight off his body. Her moans grew in volume before she let out one last high-pitched whimper, shook a little, then let her chin drop to her chest while she panted.

An Oscar-worthy orgasm performance.

And Rocket wasn't buying a single shudder of it.

What. The. Fuck.

He tugged hard on the cuffs while thinking about his next construction project. Hopefully the combination of work and bite of pain would keep him from unloading inside her for the next few minutes.

Chloe lifted her head, eyes wide and mouth in a perfect O-shape. "What…uh…you're still very hard. You didn't…?" She waved her hand around.

Rocket smirked. "Nope, I sure didn't. And neither did you." As he spoke, he slid his heels toward his ass. The movement shifted Chloe's position. She fell back a bit, cradled by his thighs, still full of his cock.

"What are you doing?" she shrieked, gaze darting around the room. He'd laid there like a goddammed corpse long enough. Now it was his turn to move. "You're wrong. I already—oh!" There was a note of hysteria in her voice until that last gasped "oh."

That's right, baby. Not leaving this fucking room until you come for real.

Using his shoulders for leverage, Rocket powered his hips upward for the first time, grinding his pelvis against hers as he held her in place with his thighs. He might be the one in cuffs, but Chloe's reign of control was fucking over.

"You have to sto—oh, my God," she said as her eyes fluttered closed. Yeah, a little clit action will do that to a woman. Rocket smiled as he started to fuck her with intent.

Chloe remained uncertain for all of two point five seconds before she lost herself in the sensations and started to fuck him back. Tiny whimpers flew from her mouth each time their hips collided. She slammed herself down in time with his upward thrusts taking an extra second to grind her clit against him.

This time, when her head dropped back and her moans grew to near screams, it was real fucking pleasure he heard in her voice.

"Oh, my God," she said again as Rocket drove down through his heels and rammed her with his cock. He felt it then, a small ripple in her pussy as she spiraled toward orgasm.

"Work your tits," he growled. Someone needed to give those beauties some attention and if he wasn't allowed, she'd have to do it herself.

Curling her fists at her sides, she shook her head.

"Fucking do it. Pinch 'em. Tug 'em. I want to see it."

Chloe groaned then did as he asked. As her fingers closed around the stiff buds, she gasped, and her eyes flew open. "Logan," she cried.

"That's right, baby. Make 'em feel good while I made this pussy feel good."

She gripped her nipples, hard, tugging them away from her body. "Shit, I'm gonna—fuck!" she shouted as her entire body became racked with spasms. Gaze locked with his, she cried out again and her pussy squeezed him so hard, he was completely defenseless against the powerful orgasm that stole through him.

"Shit, yeah," he shouted as he burst into the condom. Keeping his eyes open was a struggle but he wasn't about to miss a second of Chloe's pleasure.

"Goddamn," he said as his body began to relax and his eyes dropped closed. "Now that's a fucking orgasm. Don't know what that fake bullshit was, but the real thing was fucking beautiful."

She didn't respond.

"Babe?" He opened his eyes to find her still as a statue, a look of horror on her flushed face. "Hey, you okay? Shit, did I hurt you?" What the fuck was wrong with him? He'd been rough, as rough as he could be while restrained to a bed, and she'd been attacked just months ago. Fuck, if she didn't make him forget all about that while she was riding him. If he'd set her back, he'd never forgive himself.

But it made no sense. He wasn't the first guy she'd fucked. She'd been at this for months.

"Hey!" he said with bite this time.

The sharp tone seemed to snap her out of whatever trance she'd fallen into. "Shit," she said as she scrambled off him.

Her hands went to her mussed hair. She gripped the strands as though she was about to yank it out of her head. "What the fuck was that?" she yelled.

Rocket blinked. Anger? He'd just fucked her to a screaming orgasm, and she was pissed? "Um, fucking?" he said.

"You didn't follow the rules!" She gathered her dress and shoes. "My room, my show, remember? You didn't follow the fucking rules." Her voice cracked. After she'd collected her belongings, she disappeared into the bathroom.

Well, fuck. What the hell just happened? He listened, for the most part. Didn't touch her. Didn't try to taste her again. Hell, he remained cuffed to the fucking bed when he could have broken the damn thing.

Five minutes later, hair in a pony tail and eyes red rimmed, Chloe burst from the bathroom and marched toward the hotel room door.

"You gonna leave me like this?" he asked, jangling the cuffs.

Hand on the doorknob, she turned to him. Regret was plain in her eyes. "Yes. I am. I'm sorry, but I don't trust you anymore. You didn't follow the rules. You took control. The key is in the dresser and the maid can use it to let you out in the morning."

Then she was gone.

And Rocket was left bound to the bed feeling like the lowest shit on the planet.

You took control.

Her actions made sense now. The cuffs, the strangers, the no touching rule. Even the sex in general. Chloe wasn't fucking these men. She was waging war against the horrors in her mind. Horrors she'd unfortunately experienced firsthand.

Chloe was assassinating an evil adversary, one cock at a time.

And if there was anything Rocket understood, it was how to eliminate an enemy.

CHAPTER SIX

"One more time. Just tell it one more time. Promise I won't ask again," Maverick said, one laugh away from having Rocket's fist rearrange his smug face.

"You know you're an asshole, right?" Rocket asked.

Mav shrugged as though totally at peace with the title. "Come on, brother, be a pal. I had a shitty day and could use another laugh. Just one more time." As he spoke, he dug through a small leather case. "Here we go." He held up a handcuff key.

"Gotta say, I'd be up for hearing it again too," Zach chimed in from across the room, holding his beer bottle in front of his mouth as though it would somehow disguise his snicker.

"What the fuck do you ladies see in these dipshits anyway?" Rocket asked bouncing his gaze between Stephanie and Toni.

"Well," Izzy chimed in, not for one second pretending to hide her smirk, "I for one—"

Rocket lifted a hand. "Wasn't talking to you. You're the worst ball buster of the bunch." And it was true. Fierce as ever, Izzy had her ass-length black hair swept back in a tight braid that combined with her sharp mouth and take-no-prisoners attitude made most men's balls shrivel. Not Jig's though. He ate that shit up.

"Hey! I resent that. Being pregnant has really mellowed me out."

The room grew dead silent as everyone avoided eye contact with Izzy.

"What? It has! Tell them, Jig." She elbowed her fiancé in the gut. Hard. "Tell them how soft and maternal I'm becoming."

"Oh yeah, sure, babe." Jig rubbed his ribs with a wince. "You're a fucking marshmallow."

Izzy scowled at her ol' man, lifting her elbow once again.

Jig flinched before grabbing her arm and yanking her close for a deep kiss.

The group chuckled at their typical exchange, except for Mav who made gagging noises. Regardless, the distraction allowed Rocket a moment out of the spotlight. He should have known better than to show up at Maverick's door with the perfect ammunition, but Mav was the only brother he'd known for certain would be able to get the damn cuffs off. Figures, he'd forgotten Mav was having some kind of couples' night or some bullshit.

Bunch of pussy-whipped fools his brothers were turning into.

After Chloe's dramatic exit, he'd broken the slats on the bed with ease, dressed, then Ubered back to the bar, grabbed his truck, and returned to the hotel where he fixed the broken headboard. No point in leaving it in pieces when he could repair it in under fifteen minutes. At least Chloe wouldn't be charged for damages.

Though with the way she left him shackled with his sticky dick flapping in the breeze, she might have deserved it. A smile curled his lips. He could think of a few more...interesting ways to punish the little runaway.

Once the room was in tip-top shape, he'd knocked on Mav's door, cuffs dangling from each wrist, only to be greeted by three of his brothers and their tipsy women. The jokes began before his boots had even crossed the threshold.

Fuck my life.

"Just get these damn things off me, Mav."

"Sure, brother. Happy to." Maverick's eyes twinkled.

Oh fuck, here it comes.

"I'll get 'em off you. Soon as you tell us the story again."

Rocket narrowed his eyes and glared at Maverick who just laughed. Waste of a good glower. "Fine," he grumbled. "Met a chick at a bar. Took her to her hotel. Fucked her. She left. I came here. Happy?"

"Uh, no," Stephanie said with a giggle, half hidden by Mav's shoulder. "You kinda left out the best part. How'd you end up cuffed to the bed?"

"You too?"

With a sheepish grin, she shrugged.

"Maverick is a bad fucking influence. You used to be much nicer."

Stephanie's cheeks pinked.

He needed to get the damn things off, so... "She cuffed me, obviously. Then she left. I broke the fucking bed then drove here to get them off which was clearly a mistake." He turned to Maverick. "You gonna help me or what?" Rocket held his right hand up, cuff swinging in Maverick's face.

"You know," Mav said as he grabbed Rocket's wrist, spinning the cuff to find the keyhole. "Didn't figure you for the submissive type. Tell me, brother, did she wear leather? Oooh maybe latex?" Mav bobbed his eyebrows. "She whip ya? Maybe drizzle you with candle wax? Damn, baby," he said over his shoulder. "We may have to kick everyone out sooner than I planned."

Stephanie's face flamed even darker, but the heat in her eyes was unmistakable.

One cuff off. Rocket destroyed the enamel on his molars as he held up the other wrist.

"Let's see," Zach said, passing his beer to his ol' lady, Toni. He darted across the room, and before Rocket had a chance to figure out what Zach's intentions were, his shirt was being lifted and Zach was inspecting his skin, no doubt for red splotches.

"Huh," Zach said, dodging Rocket's swat. "Looks like bondage is his only kink." He rose to his full height which was about a half inch taller than Rocket. "Unless the marks are somewhere we can't see."

"You touch my pants, and you'll be looking for a surrogate to fuck your woman."

"Hmm," Toni said from across the room with a sly smile. Rocket had always admired her. The slender five-foot-five woman could handle their MC's tough as nails enforcer with one arm tied behind her back. "Would I get to pick who he was?" One light brown eyebrow rose, but she kept her face neutral otherwise.

"Hey!" Zach turned to her. "You're supposed to be on my side."

"I am totally on your side, babe," Toni said with exaggerated sweetness. "It's just, if he does unman you, I'd like some say in who will take your place in our bed." She gave him an owl-eyed innocent smile.

"Fuck that," Zach growled. "He rips off my dick, I'll bronze it and still fuck you with it."

Toni's expression morphed into one of disgust. "Sorry, Rocket, you're on your own. Having your back isn't worth the risk."

"So, you *were* trying to help him?" Zach stalked over to her. "Toss me those cuffs when you're done, Mav. Someone needs to be taught a lesson."

The sound of the second handcuff being released was eclipsed by Toni's husky laughter.

Jesus, it was like he'd stepped into a fucking soft-core porno flick. "Knock yourself out," he said, tossing the cuffs to Zach who caught both one handed while trying to sneak his other hand under Toni's blouse.

"Hey, Rocket, all kidding aside, are you okay?" Stephanie asked, teasing gone. The room grew quiet.

Fuck, he wasn't about to talk about any of the shit going on in his head. He knew he had to answer for some of his erratic behavior lately, but he'd be doing that with Copper, and Copper alone. "I'm good, babe. No need to worry about me. You got more than enough to worry about right there." He pointed to Maverick who slid his arm around his woman's waist and tugged her close.

They were tight. All his brothers had close relationships with their ol' ladies. Beyond close. When they patched in, every man pledged to put the club above all else, relationships included, but Rocket had no doubt their priorities shifted when they claimed their women. He'd never experienced a relationship like that. Where there was one person who meant the entire world to him. One person he valued above all. In the military, he'd learned to trust and work with his brothers in arms, to function as a team before an individual. Then again in the MC, the brotherhood was strong and bonded by fire and blood. He'd lay down his life for any of his brothers, or even their women, as he'd have done for his fellow Marines.

But the connections his brothers had with their women were different. He couldn't fully explain it because he'd never experienced it, but it was even more than being willing to die for someone. It was being willing to live for them.

He ran a hand down his face. Jesus, he needed some fucking sleep.

"Wanna hang for a while?" Mav asked.

With all the monogamy? Fuck no. "Nah, I'm out, brother."

"Hey," Zach said as Rocket started for the door.

He stopped and faced his brother.

"Prez wants to talk to you Monday afternoon. You free?"

Ahh, his day of reckoning had finally come. "I can move some stuff around." With so much going on lately, including being gravely injured, Copper hadn't set the time aside to talk to, or chew the ass off Rocket.

Looked like tomorrow was the day.

CHAPTER SEVEN

He'd made her come.

He'd made her *come.*

It was the first orgasm she'd experienced since the kidnapping. And it was a gooood one. One of those toe-curling, mind-numbing, soul-shaking orgasms that left her feeling both exhausted and energized at the same time.

Actually, she'd only had one or two of its kind in the past. There was just one problem with that kind of orgasm, for her anyway. It made her all gooey inside.

Emotionally speaking.

The other times her world had been rocked in such a way were with the first man she'd slept with. Her college boyfriend whom she fancied herself marrying for a time. Of course, as with many young relationships, it ended and she moved on, but at the time she was head over heels. After that she'd only slept with one additional man who hadn't exactly been a Casanova in the sack.

Now, in the light of day, she was a mess of jumbled emotions. Confusion and anxiety were the primary reactions keeping her unproductive. With a heavy sigh, she folded the corner of a top sheet and tucked it between the mattress and box spring of her guest bed. It'd been taking her about six times as long as it should to make up a bed for Scott, and she wasn't even to the comforter yet.

Rocket

How on earth did Logan worm his way past her very well constructed defenses? How and why did she allow him to? Really, he didn't worm his way anywhere, he'd demolished her walls with a freaking wrecking ball. None of the other men she'd been with since the kidnapping had come close to knocking her out of her head and getting her to go off script. She cuffed them to her bed, lubed them up, and rode them until they came. And in that time, the power she experienced having a man at her mercy alleviated the fear and anxiety she had been struggling with for months. When it was over, she uncuffed and left.

That was that.

But she'd not only let Logan break the rules, she'd allowed it to continue until she shattered with pleasure. What she needed to do was forget the entire incident, finish making the bed, and get ready for her brother's visit.

But that was much easier said than done. Mainly because of how damn good Logan made her feel. So good, she wanted a repeat. Wanted to come again. So much so, she'd whipped out her trusty vibrator only to chuck it across the room in frustration twenty minutes later when she wasn't even close to climax.

So, there she was, confused, anxious, slightly horny, and feeling some unnamed affection for the random man who'd rocked her world. That last part, the affection, she refused to give credence to. Way too complicated.

With a huff, Chloe grabbed the sky-blue comforter from the floor and dragged it up the bed, smoothing and tugging it straight.

Then there was the guilt. Probably the most powerful of the morning-after emotions. For fuck's sake, she'd left the poor guy naked and defenseless guy handcuffed to the freakin' bed.

She'd officially become a monster.

The guilt was so strong, earlier that morning she'd staked out the parking lot of the motel, hoping to see the maid venture into the rom. She had to make sure Logan had been freed but was far too chicken shit to check on the room herself. When the maid knocked on the door, entered and exited a moment later with the dirty linens, her heartrate had skyrocketed. But nothing happened. No pissed off man exited the room. No cops were called. No angry demands to speak to management.

Somehow, he'd gotten out of the room. What the hell had he done? Broken the bed apart? Would she receive a bill from the motel in a few days? With her brother due to arrive, she hadn't had time to linger, so she hightailed it back home to obsess in the comfort of her own house.

A knock at her door had her tossing the last pillow on the bed before jogging down the stairs.

"Coming," she yelled then rolled her eyes.

Yeah, she freakin' wished.

A quick peek through the peephole revealed her handsome big brother standing with his hands propped on his hips. He may have been the closest of her siblings, but they looked the most different. His hair was blonde to her auburn, and his freckle-free skin tanned like he wasn't of the same Irish descent as she was. They did, however, share the same green eyes.

It took a minute, as it always did these days, to unlock the four deadbolts, but once she had the door opened, she flung herself into her brother's arms. "Scotty," she said as his thick arms closed around her.

"Hey, sis." He engulfed her like he always did, in a bear hug that stole her breath.

All she experienced was a quick flash of alarm before she remembered it was in fact Scott. Her favorite sibling, who'd die before hurting her. He'd also kill before allowing her to be hurt, hence the elaborate lie she'd cooked up regarding her attack.

"I'm so glad you're here," she said, the words muffled by his broad chest. A good thing because the sudden rush of emotion at having family close had her throat closing and her eyes filling.

"Me too, sissy. Me too. You gonna invite me in or are we gonna stand here hugging all day like a bunch of chumps?"

It was the exact perfect thing to say. Knocked her out of her emotional moment. "Yes, of course." She drew back, and thankfully he ignored her sniff and nose-swipe. "Just drop your bag by the door and we'll take you to your room later."

He let the long green military-issued sea bag drop to the wood floor as he took a look around. "Nice place, sis. You've done well. Proud of you."

Her heart swelled under the praise just before it deflated again. Proud of her. Ha. He wouldn't be so proud if he knew she was getting over being attacked by fucking hordes of random men.

Jesus, just the thought of him, or anyone she knew finding out had her gut churning.

"Hey." He cuffed her shoulder. "It was a compliment, weirdo. You're supposed to say thank you."

God, she loved their sibling banter. With a mock punch to his gut, she said, "Come on, you giant. I made a fresh pot of coffee."

Scott followed her past the den with its oversized plush couch and leather recliner. The chair was a little more masculine than the rest of her furniture, but she'd always loved the feel of soft leather against her skin. They entered her kitchen, which was hands down her favorite room in the place.

"Wow, Clo, this is sweet."

"Thanks. I love it too. It was owned by an elderly gentleman who remodeled the kitchen after his wife died. He'd planned to sell after updating the place but passed from a heart attack before he ever had the chance to enjoy it. His kids just wanted out from under the responsibility of it all, so they sold it for a song."

"Shit, unlucky for the old guy but lucky for you."

Chloe laughed. "You're as sensitive as ever, I see."

He just grunted. Typical Scott.

"Seriously though, sis, stainless appliances, granite counter tops, is that a Viking range? Shit, you must love cooking in here."

Chloe motioned to a chair at her round oak table. A thrift store miracle find. "Have a seat. I'll grab you some coffee. And I do love to cook, but since it's just me, I don't actually do it much. So it'll be great to have you around to spoil with some home cooking for a few weeks." She grabbed two large mugs from the cabinet directly above her coffee pot.

"Oh man." Scott stretched back in his chair, rubbing his flat stomach as though he'd already devoured a huge meal. "I can already feel the pounds I'm going to pack on being here. Bring it, girl."

Chloe smiled. She'd hadn't been as excited for Scott's visit as she should have been, more concerned with her own anxieties and issues, but now that he was here and the enjoyment of being with him sank in, she was beyond thrilled. Having someone around, Scott especially, would be good for her. She'd been alone far too much lately. Having another person to cook for was just what the doctor ordered. She loved to cook and really hadn't done her near-professional grade kitchen justice. Well, she'd be sure to give it a workout over the next two weeks.

"Black?"

"Yep."

She drank it the same way. One of the many things she had in common with her oldest sibling. After placing his steaming mug on the table, she took the empty chair directly across from him. With a deep inhale, she savored the comforting and invigorating smell of the premium java. As she lifted the cup for a sip, her gaze collided with Scott's very serious, and pretty grim expression. "What? Is it gross?"

He huffed. "No, the coffee's great. It's you I'd like to talk about."

Well damn. She flicked a glance at the analog clock on the wall. He'd given her a total of seven minutes before diving right in. Guess she should have been glad, he could have started in on her before he stepped in the house. Or before she got her coffee —even worse.

Rocket

"I'm good, Scott. Better every day." The words sounded so rehearsed she wouldn't even be cast in a Soap Opera. She smiled but even that felt contrived. Hopefully he'd buy it anyway.

Scott burst out laughing. "Nice try, Clo, but I've known you for twenty-seven years. You think I can't tell when you're full of shit?"

No, he could tell. So could the rest of her family. Which was why, after their initial flocking to see her, she'd distanced herself over the past few months.

"Tell me, what the cops have done? Where are they with your case? Are they staying on top of it because I can speak with them if you'd like." As he spoke, he straightened his spine as though preparing to posture for the police.

"Whoa there, speedy." Chloe held up the hand not wrapped around her coffee. "Take a breath. I do not need you to speak with the cops."

Mostly because there was nothing to speak with them about. She'd given them a cock and bull story that led their investigation to a brick wall within minutes. As for her family, they'd gotten a completely different tale.

"You sure, sis? You don't have to do this all alone." His half glare half scowl was full of disappointment. "You don't have to push your family away." As he spoke, a yellow lock of hair fell in front of his eyes.

There was the heart of the issue. "I'm not, Scott. But I'm an adult. And I can handle it on my own." Even if handle it meant becoming some kind of man-dominating junkie. "Besides, he's been arrested. Trial is in a few months." By then Scott would be off in some other country saving the world and unable to butt in. She sipped from her mug; the coffee not nearly as bitter as her lies.

"And it was someone you'd dated?" He shoved his hair back in place in a move that appeared frustrated. With the errant hair or with her?

"Mm-hmm." Sounds were easier to lie with than words, but Scott was a trained interrogator. Wouldn't take much for him to grow suspicious. Chloe forced herself to look him in the eye. "We went out a few times. I didn't know him too well though."

"Fuck." He scratched his bearded chin. Normally, the military didn't allow facial hair, but with special ops, they were often required to blend in with the culture, so those guys frequently sported facial hair. Or so Scott informed her. "Half the world is fucking psycho, Clo. Please tell me you're being extra cautious with the guys you meet now."

His expression was pained. For her. He'd suffered because she did. And because he was too far away to come comfort her and kick someone's ass. That's just who Scott was. He took care of everyone he knew and had a protective streak ten miles long. "Um, yeah, sure. I'm very careful."

Lying to him made her stomach hurt, but no one could know her secret. She couldn't imagine a single scenario where someone would understand what she was doing and why. Even others who'd been in a similar horrifying position didn't react as she did. She'd rather lie than see shock and disgust reflected back at her.

He stared at her, clearly not believing her. "Don't lie to me, Clo."

Shit. Why the hell did he have to be so observant? "I, uh—"

His brow furrowed. "You're not going out at all, are you? Not dating? Not even hanging out with your friends?"

Well...he wasn't wrong, per se. She wasn't actually dating and had pushed most of her friends away by constantly declining invitations. But how the hell was she supposed to explain to Scott the only time she could handle being around men was on her *special nights*, so to speak? Leaving the house wasn't the issue; she could drive around in her car all day. It was being close to people. Other men mostly. In a space where they might brush against her or try to touch her. Men who might appear normal on the outside, but how was she supposed to know what lurked beneath the surface? One of the men who'd kidnapped her had looked totally normal. Sure, one looked like a stereotypical thug, but the other could have been her bank teller for all she knew.

She almost laughed out loud. She couldn't bump into a man in the grocery store without losing her shit, but she had no problem taking strangers back to a hotel room for sex.

Jesus, she needed therapy.

Big time.

But that wasn't an option. The man who'd rescued her asked her to refrain from telling her story to anyone. He'd promised his motorcycle gang or whatever it was would take care of the situation for her. So, she'd lied to the cops, lied to her family, and avoided therapy so there wasn't anyone who could report the truth to the cops. Lying to a therapist was an option but seemed like nothing more than a waste of time and money. Though, if she were honest, she didn't think she'd have gone anyway. She was too embarrassed to divulge her deep dark secret. Even to a paid professional who'd probably heard it all.

Bet they haven't heard this one.

"Clo, you with me?"

She blinked. Shit, what had he asked? "Sorry, what did you say?"

"You all right? You kinda checked out on me for a minute there." He reached across the table and took her hand in his.

Shaking her head, Chloe said, "Yeah, big brother, I'm good. Just got lost in my mind for a second. Uh, you asked if I was going out. No, I'm not. I'm just not ready for that yet, Scott. And I'd appreciate it if you'd just let it lie. I need to work through it at my own pace."

Staring at her as though she was a code he was trying to decrypt, he sipped his coffee, swallowed, then sipped again. She squirmed under the weight of his assessment. He wouldn't even have to interrogate the bad guys, just bore into their heads with his x-ray eyes and they'd spill their guts.

"Jesus, Scott, stop trying to Ranger me and just be a normal big brother." She lifted the mug to her lips; anything to distract from the way he tried to tunnel inside her brain. Damnit, when had she finished the coffee?

Scott rose and grabbed her cup as he made his way to the half-full coffee pot. He stared out the window as he poured. "You know," he said. "I was hoping to get out a bit. Explore the area a little while I'm here. Maybe do some hiking, take in a movie, eat at a few restaurants. Normal things I haven't been able to do in more than eight months."

"For sure. You should definitely do all those things. And more. Enjoy your time off. You're welcome here as long as you want."

He turned, holding the mug out to her, and for the first time since he walked in her house, she got a glimpse of the boy she'd idolized growing up. Scott had nine years on her and to say she'd followed him around like a loyal puppy would be an understatement. "I don't want to do all this shit alone, Clo. I want to do it with you. I want *you* to show me around and hang with me."

With his intense military career, he didn't get much down time. Much time to just be a regular guy enjoying life. If all he wanted was to spend time with her, she could force herself out of her comfort zone and rejoin the real world.

Maybe. At the very least she could try.

With an internal sigh, she accepted the fresh coffee. "Of course, Scott. Just because I haven't been ready to dive back into the single scene doesn't mean I'm locking myself away in my house." Hopefully that came off believable. "I'd be happy to take you to all the local sights. Hell," she gave him a saucy grin. "We can even go to Dollywood. I have to work some, but should be able to spare plenty of time."

He threw back his head and laughed. "Looking forward to it, sis."

Rocket

Chloe swallowed the anxiety already creeping up her throat. Maybe having big, strong, and sometimes scary Scott with her would keep the demons at bay.

Or maybe by next weekend she'd be so stressed, she'd need the one thing keeping her sane.

The one thing she could never pull off while Scott was around.

CHAPTER EIGHT

Rocket knocked on the heavy wooden door his president was working behind. To say he wasn't looking forward to this meeting was quite an understatement. Disappointing Copper sucked worse than letting a parent down, mostly because he respected the hell out of Copper, whereas his parents were useless.

"Come in." Copper's accented voice came through the door.

Prepared for his fate, Rocket entered the sizable office. The prez wasn't much of one for decorating, but his ol' lady, Shell, had added a few touches to the place years ago. A plush leather chair, some badass skull and motorcycle knickknacks on the desk, black and white photos of bikes mounted to the walls. In the space behind Copper's oak desk was a large twenty-four-by-thirty-six-inch framed picture of himself, Copper, Mav, Zach, and Jig. The good old days. They were all a good five years younger and twice as many years softer.

Well, maybe not Rocket. He'd hardened up ages ago. Both his heart and his mind.

"Hey, prez," he said as he took the empty chair across from Copper.

The stare he received had him thinking he wasn't leaving with just a verbal slap. Fuck, Copper might just swing one of those giant fists his way.

Rocket

Dropping his pen to the desk, Copper leaned back in his leather chair. Both thick arms folded across his chest, all the while he seared Rocket with that pissed off glare. Even injured, with his left leg in a cast and his body beat to shit, Copper was a formidable foe. "Ain't gonna bother with bullshit, Rocket. Just come straight out and tell me what the fuck is going on. You in trouble?"

And that, right there, was the reason Copper had the respect of every man in the club. Rocket had fucked up. He'd missed church a few weeks ago which was a sin worse than murder, and he'd been unreachable when his president was abducted. While Copper was being tortured by a psychopath, Rocket had his phone shut down and was off the grid. Yet as pissed off as he was, Copper's first thought was to go to battle for his men.

There wasn't a man in the club who would balk at an order issued by their prez. Cop already knew all about Rocket's past, though he was the only one. The club had an unofficial full disclosure policy. Copper's policy, really. If a guy patched in, the club would have his back in any situation, no matter what. Something from a man's past came creeping back around? The MC would be all over it, no questions asked. But that meant full honesty about the skeletons in the closet.

Copper wasn't afraid of a fight, but he fucking hated surprises. As long as he knew what a man brought to his club from the get go, he'd take it on. So would any of the brothers.

Keeping shit from the prez was the ultimate no-no. "Esposito," he said.

Copper's shoulders heaved "Well, fuck," he said.

"Been hounding me. I turned off my phone, and that's why Z couldn't reach me when the club was looking for you."

Nodding, Copper rubbed his red-bearded chin. His signature *I'm thinking* move. "Much as I was hoping that fucker got killed in the field, I figured it was something like that. Ain't like you to flake on the club."

His laser gaze came back to Rocket's. Copper didn't say shit, just to say it. He knew something else was going on. Fuck.

"That's not why I missed church though." Rocket cleared his throat.

"It's the woman, ain't it?"

He couldn't help it. Rocket laughed though nothing about this situation was funny. Leave it to Copper to figure out exactly what was going on with his men even when they were trying to be stealthy. And Rocket could do stealth. Copper was just that in tune to the pulse of his club.

"It is."

"Hmm." There went the chin stroking again. Lasted about thirty seconds before Copper rested his beefy forearms on the desk and leaned forward. "Ain't gonna happen again, right?"

Missing church? Fuck no it wouldn't happen again. He felt shitty enough about it. "No, Cop."

"And I trust you aren't doing shit that would endanger the club?"

Rocket swallowed. Did fucking her count? She didn't have a clue who he really was. "No, prez. I'd never risk the club." And that was the truth. Chloe would never learn who he was.

"Okay. I'm trusting you on this. I know finding that woman in the violated state she was in fucked with your head. You're a stand-up guy, Rocket, figures you'd want to make sure she was handling shit."

Rocket snorted. He was about as far from a stand-up guy as one could get. A stand-up guy wouldn't lie to a woman to get her to fuck him. No, he was an obsessed guy, not a good one.

"You don't agree?" Copper raised an eyebrow, a small grin visible through his beard.

A shrug was all Rocket could come up with as an answer to that question.

"You're a protector. Have been from the moment I met you. Why do you think I made you Sergeant at Arms?"

What the fuck? "A protector?" Rocket nearly choked on the word. "I'm a killer."

Now Copper was chuckling. Laughing at him. "Yeah, you've killed, to protect. Fuck, Rocket, how do you not see this about yourself? When we freed Mav, you were in on it. When we rescued the girls Lefty was selling, who drove them to the shelter? I swear I'd have had a fight on my hands if I told someone else to get the woman from the hotel room."

Rocket shifted in his chair. This meeting wasn't exactly going as expected. Receiving the praise and lesson in insight was almost worse than having his ass handed to him.

"You know what it stems from, right?"

Oh, no. Copper wasn't going to bring up...yeah, he was. Couldn't the ground just open up and swallow him whole?

"Yeah," Copper said. "You know. Goes back to Elena."

"Cop..."

The president shook his head. "Can't believe I'm telling *you* this, but shut up. When that buddy of yours from the Marines died in your arms, you took it upon yourself to look after his wife, right?"

That was a time in his life Rocket never revisited, even on his worst days. Damn Copper for exposing that festering wound. His friend's name had been Evan and they'd been closer than brothers. Even with his death being nearly a decade ago, thinking about him brought a fresh wave of agony.

"Right?" The prez waited with an atypical look of patience on his scruffy face.

"Right," Rocket growled.

"They'd only been married a few months. She couldn't live with his death, and killed herself only months after hearing the news, am I right?"

Jesus Christ. Rocket scrubbed a hand down his face as memories of the second worst moment of his life bombarded his brain. The sick feeling he'd lived with for nearly two years following that tragedy returned as well. "You're right."

"And you were the unlucky fuck who found her passed out on her bedroom floor, an empty bottle of pills next to her. Ever since then, you've made it your personal mission to protect those around you. Never could figure out whether it's penance for what you think you didn't catch in time, or just your way of making sure no one you care about gets hurt again. If it's the first reason, you're wrong, because that shit wasn't your fault." Copper shrugged. He knew he'd never break through Rocket's guilt over Elena's death, so he didn't bother to try too hard. "Makes for a damn good SAA. Also makes you willing to go above and beyond for someone you care about. But if it fucks with club business again, I'm stepping in, hear me?"

Rocket nodded. As he'd been doing for years, he shoved aside the past and forced himself to focus on the here and now. "Heard and understood, prez." He started to rise. Time to get the fuck out of here before Copper started telling him how handsome he was or some other equally ridiculous bullshit.

"Now, what's Esposito want?"

Fuck. His ass hit the seat again.

Just hearing the name fall from Copper's lips had Rocket's hands itching to wring someone's neck. "Wants me for a job."

"You tell him to fuck off?"

"Yeah."

"And I'm guessing he's not accepting that answer."

"Nope."

"Jesus, Rocket, talking to you is worse than talking to a fucking teenager. Give me something here."

Seconds ticked by. As much as he trusted and respected his president, he loathed the idea of bringing his personal shit to the club's doorstep. Taking care of it himself came naturally to him even after years of helping handle the rest of the brothers' issues. Why endanger his brothers if he could shield them? Huh, maybe he could be a bit of a protector. "Whoever the target is, Esposito wants me for it. Only me. He won't even consider anyone else. I've been putting him off for weeks. Guessing at some point he's going to turn up the heat. He's an underhanded fucker who'll do just about anything to get what he wants. I don't have any blood family I give a shit about so I'd normally say he'd come after my club family, but he's not stupid. He'd know that was a fucking mistake. Still, if he's desperate enough…" Rocket shrugged.

"If he's desperate enough he might fuck with the club."

Rocket nodded.

Copper rolled his lips inward. "Okay. What are you thinking? What's his style?"

"Well, his usual style is to threaten a wife, or kids. Show his face, let you know he can get you whenever. I've known him to fuck with people's finances and shit too. Best guess? He'll send the local PD sniffing around. Maybe make a few false reports. That kinda shit. Worse case, he goes after an ol' lady, but I have trouble seeing him take that route. He doesn't want a pissed MC on his ass." Truth of it was, if any of the ol' ladies were threatened, Rocket would go apeshit. He may not be overly chummy with them, but he considered each and every one of his brother's women family. He'd maim, kill, or take a bullet to protect any of them.

Protective. Copper's voice sounded in his head.

Two more strokes of his chin and Copper said, "I'm not ready to bring the entire club in on this yet, but you need to wrap your head around the idea that you might have to share your past with them if shit gets hairy."

"Hairy shit. Fucking awesome." Hence the rat that'd been gnawing at his gut the past few days. His club brothers wouldn't judge, they weren't that type, but it was shit he didn't like thinking about, let alone blabbing to everyone he knew. "I get it."

Copper chuckled. "Okay, keep me posted and let me know if he's escalating to the point he wants to take some action. We'll batten down if we need to."

"Thanks, prez."

Copper held out a fist which Rocket bumped his against. "Keep your head in the game, brother." His tone was grave. "We'll get Lefty and find a way to let the girl know he'll never hurt another woman again. I get that you feel territorial and need to keep an eye on her, but don't cross any lines, get me?"

Too late.

"Yeah, Cop, I get you." Oh, the lines he'd already crossed. "Any news on Lefty?"

With a shake of his head, Copper said, "No. The fucker can hide, I'll give him that much."

The day Lefty died would be the best fucking day Rocket had in years. The club had a contact that owed them. They'd done a favor and were supposed to receive Lefty as payment. Only the damn gangbanger was way too good at living underground. "You know, Cop—"

"Don't even think about it."

Rocked grunted. "I didn't even fucking say anything."

"Yeah, but I know you. Known you for years. You were about to offer to reach out to some old contacts. Ain't letting you do that."

"Cop, I know guys with connections we only wish we had. Guys who could flush Lefty out with less effort than chewing fucking gum." And he did. His contacts worked, even lived in the shadows. It's where they thrived. Lefty wouldn't stand a chance.

"Yeah, and before you could grab your dick, word would get back to Esposito, and he'd have exactly the ammunition he needed to get you to do his dirty work. Ain't happening. We'll get Lefty. And we'll fucking end him. But it won't happen at your expense."

"Thanks, Copper."

"Ain't a thing, brother."

Rocket extended his hand across the desk as did Copper. Just as they were about to clasp, Copper pulled back. "Oh wait," he said. "One more thing."

Rocket

Rocket froze, hand in midair. Oh fuck.

The hair around Copper's mouth parted, revealing an evil grin that had Rocket's balls shriveling. The next words out of Copper's mouth were not going to bode well for him.

"Gonna patch-in LJ next Friday. Shoulda happened already, but with all the shit that's been going on, I put it off. The guys need a party and they need a big one. I'd like you to plan it."

What. The. Fuck.

"Uh, don't the ol' ladies usually take care of that kind of thing?"

His president's smirk grew. "They sure do. And they'll be around to help. But you'll be running the show."

Narrowing his eyes, he pulled his hand away as he rested back in the chair. Fuck if he was gonna shake the president's hand now. A punishment. That's what this was. A damn joke of a punishment. The moment his brothers found out he was acting as party planner the torture would commence. "Shoulda known you wouldn't let me off the hook."

Copper laughed. "Sorry, brother. That's the way it is."

"Goddammit. All right. You want a piñata? Maybe some pin the tail on the fucking donkey?" He'd take a fist to the face over this damn punishment any day. Copper knew that shit. It's why he chose the punishment.

Still laughing, Copper said, "You can have your first planning meeting tonight after church. Shell's rounding up the ladies for you. Have fun, brother."

"Fuck," he muttered under his breath as he rose.

"Damn, brother, the look on your face is priceless. I'm gonna enjoy the fuck outta this." Copper rubbed his hands together like some kind of evil genius enjoying his master plan for world domination.

With a roll of his eyes, Rocket yanked the door open only to find Shell standing there with her fist raised, poised to knock.

"Oh, Rocket, hi!" she said, face splitting into a huge welcoming smile. She stepped in the room. "Hey, hon," she said to Copper. "How you feeling?"

Copper rolled his eyes and huffed like her attention was a nuisance, but his eyes were soft as they landed on his woman. "I'm good, babe, same as I was an hour ago."

"Don't you get sassy with me, mister. I've already dealt with one whiny child this morning; I'll take away your dessert too." She winked at him.

Copper held up his hands. "I'll be a good boy. I promise."

Rocket snorted. Somehow, he didn't think Copper's dessert had anything to do with sugar and flour.

"Don't be too good," Shell said, her cheeks turning pink.

"All right, I'm out before I vomit."

Shell grabbed his arm. "Wait. The girls and I can all meet tonight after you guys get out of church. Everyone is so jazzed to plan this party for LJ. Thanks so much for offering to help. We want it to be epic, since he's been so patient waiting for his patch. Poor guy has been prospecting for almost fifteen months."

Rocket's eyes narrowed as he forced himself to nod in agreement.

Copper burst out laughing all over again. Goddammit, this was going to be his life for the next ten days.

"That's fine, Shell," he said sounding gruffer than he'd intended. Without so much as a goodbye, he stormed out the office, middle finger held high over his head.

Instead of pissing anyone off, all it did was kick Copper's laughter even higher.

"What'd I say?" Shell asked, her voice laced with confusion.

"Nothing, baby. Close and lock that door. I got twenty minutes before I gotta get. Plenty of time to get a taste of your sweet—"

The door closed.

For a moment, Rocket looked over his shoulder at the blocked off room. The sound of Shell's happy giggle followed by a squeal hit his ears. Cop sure seemed to be enjoying his newfound ol' man status. The notion of having a woman, one woman, who cared about him as much as Shell cared about Copper was so foreign to Rocket, he could barely imagine himself in Copper's place. Emotionally speaking. Physically? Yeah, he could imagine that pretty well. Closing the door while his woman stalked toward the desk, losing clothing along the way. Maybe she'd drop to her knees right there behind the desk. He could sink his fingers into all that auburn hair as he disappeared between plump pink lips. All the while, those green eyes would drill into his—

Auburn hair? Green eyes?

Shit, his fantasy woman bore a striking resemblance to Chloe.

CHAPTER NINE

Chloe managed to trick Scott into hanging around the house for three days. They lounged around in their sweats, ate junk food, and spent more quality time together than they had in years. Of course, during the day she'd had to work some. Her accounting business couldn't survive without some effort. Clients still needed her despite her plans, but she'd had plenty of time to devote to her brother. On the fourth day, Scott couldn't stand it anymore, and begged to go hiking.

Hiking, as it turned out, was a fantastic activity for her. Not once did they run into another soul while traipsing through the gorgeous mountain terrain. For the majority of their five-mile trek, they didn't even speak, just absorbed the peace and quiet of nature around them. Chloe wasn't certain, because he was even more tight lipped about his problems than she was, but she was pretty sure Scott benefitted from the healing calm as much as she did. Maybe even more.

But now, it was Friday and Scott wanted to check out some festival at a local winery. Since when did her brother give a shit about wine?

"I don't. You know I'm more of a beer or whiskey man, but I heard from a buddy of mine that the place was worth checking out. So we're going." He narrowed his eyes, practically daring her to disagree.

Rocket

"Okay," she said. "Sure. Sounds fun." Hopefully that came off as light and interested instead of dreading every second of what was sure to be a room jam-packed with people.

He strode past her and helped himself to a bottle of water from her fridge. The light gray T-shirt he wore was soaked with sweat from his forty-five-minute run. Chloe watched as he tipped his head back, guzzling the ice-cold liquid. Objectively, she understood why all her high school friends had flocked to her house whenever her big brother was home on leave. He was a good-looking guy. Charming too, when he wanted to be. Of course, as a sixteen-year-old, she'd been horrified and disgusted by her friends' interest in him. The memories made her chuckle.

"What? Am I dribbling?" He asked wiping his mouth with the back of his hand.

"Yes, but that's not why I was laughing." She sent him a sassy grin then drained the last of her own bottle of water.

He rolled his eyes and ruffled her hair like she was still six. "Smartass. What's so funny?"

"I was just remembering how my girlfriends all went gaga over you back in high school."

His brown eyebrows wiggled up and down. "Couple of those girls were easy on the eyes too, once they turned eighteen."

Laughing, Chloe tossed her empty water bottle at him. It bounced right off his hard chest as though the plastic had hit a brick wall instead of flesh. That had him flexing in all sorts of ridiculous poses, making her laugh even harder.

Her heart clenched. Damn, she'd missed laughing. Missed him. Maybe it had been a mistake to isolate herself from her family these last few months. Well, poor choice or not, it's what had to be done to keep her promise to the man who'd rescued her.

"Oh, hey, I forgot to tell you I won't be around tonight. There's a guy I met in boot camp who lives about ninety minutes from here. I'm gonna meet up with him and probably crash at his place."

Chloe froze. Friday night and she'd be all alone. The unexpected development had her insides twisting. She could do it. Head to the bar, pick someone up, and find some peace.

"You're welcome to join me if you'd like." Scott's voice snapped her out of her stupor.

"What? Oh, uh, maybe." No way in hell would that be happening. She'd never get a lick of sleep in some random man's house. Not to mention they'd probably want to go out drinking and pick up women. She almost laughed again. They'd probably do the very same activity she engaged in every weekend, but this time the thought of it had her ready to run for the hills.

What the hell was wrong with her?

A psychologist would probably tell her it was a control issue. Her routine was very regulated, controlled, precise. Going out with Scott and his army buddy, she wouldn't be in control of the situation. Probably why the encounter with Logan had thrown her for a loop.

Oh, no. Not doing it. Nope. Not thinking about Logan. Again.

"Great," Scott said. "The wine tasting starts in an hour. I'm gonna grab a shower then we can bug out." As he walked by, he ruffled her hair again.

Chloe snapped to attention and gave her brother a dramatic salute. "Sir, yes, sir!" she barked like she'd seen soldiers do in the movies.

His chuckle followed him out of the room. "You're such a little shit," he called out.

Chloe smiled. She may be a fully-grown adult, but she was still a younger sister. Being a *little shit*, was a rite of passage.

Two hours later, it was seven PM, and Chloe was seconds away from crawling out of her skin. Literally, her flesh felt itchy and too tight. She rubbed her right forearm again and again until the skin practically screamed at her to stop. Glancing down, she caught the bright red track she'd left on her arm from too many forceful scours with the heel of her hand. And why had she worn this damn dress? A few weeks ago, when she'd worn this to the bar, she'd felt sexy, confident, proud. Now she just felt exposed and vulnerable. Two things guaranteed to ramp up her anxiety.

"You having fun, sis?" Scott asked, a huge grin on his face. He was loving this. The large crowd was full of buzzed, socializing post-work folks just looking to let loose for a few hours. Neither of them drank much more than sampling a few of the wines. They'd driven in separate cars so Scott could continue on to his buddy's place and Chloe could head home afterward.

Seeing him so happy and relaxed had guilt gnawing at her. Here he was wanting to spend time with her in a setting that she'd have loved last year, and she could think of nothing beyond watching the minute hand creep toward closing. Plastering a smile on her face, she said, "Definitely, Scott. You know me and wine. This is right up my alley."

His grin grew even bigger, and pride shown in his eyes. It was then she got it. This wasn't about him. He'd suggested this for her. Because the Chloe he knew would have eaten this kind of event right up. Poor guy probably thought he was giving her exactly what she needed. Drawing her out of the hole she'd buried herself in. Healing her.

She didn't have the heart to tell him how miserable she was. How her chest was tight, her heart pounded, and her insides shook like a vibrating bed. Problem was, if this kept up too long, she was bound to slide into a full-blown panic attack.

"I'm starved," Scott announced. "Want me to grab us something from the counter?"

"Sure, I'd like that." The pangs in her stomach had nothing to do with hunger, but again, she couldn't let him down.

"All right. Be right back. You good?"

"Of course." The moment he turned his back on her, Chloe rested her head against the high-top table and tried to control her breathing.

"You're fine," she muttered against the polished wood. "Scott's here and you're fine."

"Looks like I'm not the only one who finds this to be a snooze fest, huh?" A male voice said from not far above her bent head.

"What?" Chloe shot up nearly clipping the newcomer's chin. "Oh, shit! Sorry!"

He chuckled. "No worries, you missed by a hair. Were you taking a nap?"

Light blue eyes full of teasing and laughter met her gaze. He was an attractive man. Golden hair, clean shaven face, full lips, smartly dressed in the suit he'd worn to work. His smile turned a bit cocky as he noticed her checking him out. Probably assumed she liked what she saw. Not that she didn't, but she wasn't remotely interested. There was only one way she could feel a flicker of interest in a man and it wasn't in this uncontrolled environment.

"Uh, no, just having a moment." Her laughter was definitely of the nervous variety. Again, this guy probably read it wrong. Probably thought she was flustered by his attention in the tee-hee-hee way, not in the freak-out way.

He stepped even closer, until he was officially too far into her personal space. "Mind if I join you for a few? A woman who looks as beautiful as you should never sit alone."

Chloe's gut clenched and her throat felt drier than the Sahara. "Um, well, I—"

"I promise I'll behave," he said with a wink as he dragged the empty chair around the table directly next to her before sliding into it. His thigh brushed hers. "At least for a while."

She made a sound that could have been a laugh but was probably more a choke.

"So what's your name?" he asked.

Words wouldn't come. Not only had her mouth dried up, but her throat seemed to constrict to a pinpoint. Just enough to drag in enough air to survive. She was rapidly losing control of the situation and couldn't handle it. The rational, intellectual side of her brain knew exactly how ridiculous she was being. Sure, he was a little assertive, but he hadn't done a damn thing wrong.

Hadn't touched her inappropriately, hadn't been creepy, hadn't crossed any lines. He was just being a typical male looking for some female company. But the side of her that had been violated still had jagged open wounds.

And she was internally freaking the fuck out.

His blonde brows narrowed. "Your name?"

She opened her mouth, and nothing came out but a wheeze.

Shit.

Shaking her head, she turned so her back was to him. Hopefully he'd get the message and just leave.

"What the hell?" he said.

Chloe just shook her head again. Now her breath was coming in choppy gasps that made the room waver before her eyes. She bent forward, resting her head between her knees. Some of the pressure in her chest eased. "Please just go," she managed to gasp out.

"Shit, you don't have to be a bitch about it," he growled. "You aren't that hot, anyway."

"What the fuck is going on here?"

Oh great, now Scott had joined the party.

"You harassing her, man?" Scott said, aggression coming off him in waves.

Chloe lifted her head. The room spun so bad she grabbed the edge of the table for support. "I-it's…fine…Scott." She was still panting like she'd just run circles around the room.

Immediately her brother's attention jumped from the guy to her. He abandoned the near-fight and wrapped her in his arms. Her cheek pressed against his chest, the steady beat of his heart helping to return hers to a normal rhythm.

"This is too fucking weird for me. I'm out." The guy said, lifting his arms in surrender.

"He hurt you?" Scott asked practically growling the words.

"No."

"Scare you?"

"No—I don't even..." Chloe sighed. "I just freaked out. I'm sorry."

Releasing her, Scott sat in the chair the guy had vacated.

Chloe turned away. How could she look him in the eye after he'd witnessed her lose her shit over nothing?

"Hey, don't do that." Scott grabbed her chin and turned her face his way. "Don't hide. I'm your brother, Clo. You're favorite brother." While she appreciated the attempt at levity, she couldn't muster so much as a huff of laughter. "I'm not going anywhere, sis. You think I don't understand psychological pain? You think I haven't seen some of my brothers in arms lose it over even less? It's nothing to be ashamed of."

"It's embarrassing," Chloe whispered.

"Nah. Who gives a fuck what these clowns think." He winked.

She was able to give him a small smile though her heart felt like it was resting on the floor.

"Come on," he said, tugging on her arm. "Let's get you home. We can watch one of those cooking competitions you love so much."

The plan sounded nice, but she'd never forgive herself if he missed time with his friend over this little setback. "No. You go to see your friend. I'm good to get myself home."

Scott frowned. "I don't know, Chloe."

Sitting a little straighter, she said, "Seriously, Scott. I'm fine now and I'll be even better once I'm home."

Ten minutes later after a hug goodbye and a promise to text Scott as soon as she was inside with the doors locked, Chloe was cruising down the highway.

Only she wasn't going home. There was only one thing that would right what happened tonight. One way to get her head on straight.

She needed to take back some of the control she'd lost at the winery.

Rocket

Pulling off the highway, Chloe steered her car toward one of her favorite bars. As soon as she arrived, she'd call and reserve her room for the night.

CHAPTER TEN

Without fail, Friday and Saturday nights Rocket could set his watch by Chloe.

With calendar precision, she rotated the bars she patronized, and always arrived at seven in the evening. Not once in the months he'd been tailing her had she deviated from the almost ritualistic process.

So why the hell was he sitting in a darkened parking lot at nearly eight at night twiddling his fucking thumbs?

Screw why he was waiting so long, why the fuck was he there in the first place? He fucked her. Now, he had indisputable knowledge she was screwing the men she picked up. And he even knew why she was doing it. Had a better understanding of the internal workings of her damaged psyche. He'd gotten the information he'd been after, yet here he was, one week later, still tracking her like some obsessed stalker.

All evening, he'd tried to fool himself his interest in her nocturnal activities was straight-up for her safety. For all she knew, Chloe was luring a crazed ax murderer to her hotel room to fuck. Rocket was just tailing her to ensure she didn't end up in pieces in a killer's trunk.

And yes, the irony wasn't lost on him. He'd killed more men than anyone he knew.

Rocket

The convincing worked, too. To his mind, he was there to keep her safe. Not at all because the thought of another man sticking his cock in her made his trigger finger twitch.

So where the fuck was she?

Just as Rocket was about to call the motel and verify she did indeed have a reservation for the evening, her little navy Honda rounded the corner and veered into the parking lot.

Interesting.

Once again, she wore that curve-hugging purple dress that had driven him batshit a few weeks ago. Rocket couldn't tear his gaze away as she exited her car and swung those sexy hips toward the entrance. Even though her appearance suggested the night was a typical weekend one, something was different, off with the way she carried herself. Gone was the confident woman who owned the room each week. In her place was a fidgety, nervous Nelly. The real Chloe. The woman who'd been violated and had been treading water for months. Made sense her limbs would tire at some point. Was tonight that night?

Had something happened? Did someone spook her? Hurt her? Fucking *touch* her?

Inhaling through his nose, Rocket fought to stamp down the rising anger. Whatever it was that set her back tonight, he needed to know. Needed to discover what put her off her game.

And needed to vanquish her demon.

There was a way to get it done. A way to work the information out of her, but it would be the stupidest thing he'd done in years. So reckless, Copper would probably rip his patch off and eat it for lunch if he found out.

A man on his way out of the bar held the door for Chloe. Normally, she'd bat her eyes, engage in some banter, flirt a little. Tonight, she averted her gaze and slunk in the building.

For long moments, Rocket just stared at the door after it closed behind her. Right now, she was scanning the room, looking for a man to dominate.

A man to fuck.

And she wasn't in top fighting form, which meant she was more vulnerable than usual. The bar faded from his sights, replaced by the vision of Chloe riding some nameless, faceless asshole. A rumble vibrated through his chest. No fucking way was her hot pussy taking in a strange cock tonight.

Decision made, Rocket fired up his truck.

He had a plan to put in motion.

HER HEART WASN'T in this.

Neither was her freaking body, or even her mind. Usually the idea of dominating whomever she'd taken back to her hotel room got her at least a little turned on. Even if her body had trouble getting on board with her choice, her mind craved the control and power enough that she was eager to go through with it.

Tonight? Nada.

Chloe lingered outside the motel room with her key card poised above the slot. She should bail. Plead a headache or an upset stomach. This guy seemed dumb enough to believe it.

But then, she might not get this chance again until Scott left. And she needed it. Needed to feel the power of having the upper hand for at least a little while. She needed to right her world and remember that she was in control of some things. It'd be the only way to erase the winery incident from her mind.

So, she stuck the card in the slot and grabbed the metal handle when the light blinked green.

God, she was so fucked up.

With a sigh, Chloe pushed the door open only to have her stomach drop and her eyes bug out of her head. "Holy shit," she said on a shriek, jerking backward and slamming the door shut as she did so. Her heart hammered so hard against the inside of her chest she was bound to have trauma to the vital organ.

"What's wrong?" Pizza-guy—as she'd been referring to him all night because he owned an Italian joint in New Jersey—asked.

"Wh—uh, nothing's wrong." She volleyed her gaze between the closed door and the man whose black hair was pulled back in a low ponytail, his matching eyebrows arched in confusion.

Nothing, except a very sexy man was already handcuffed to her motel bed.

A man she'd met.

A man she'd fucked.

A man who made her come.

Clearly, it wasn't going to happen with pizza-guy now. "You know," she said, lifting an unsteady hand to her temple. "My head is pounding." She squinted her eyes. "Gosh, I think I'm getting a migraine. I'm so sorry, but I'm not sure this is a good idea tonight." She tried to send him a sweet smile while her nerves were going berserk.

What was Logan doing?

How did he know she'd be there again?

Was he following her?

Was he a danger?

He was cuffed to a bed. How much of a danger could he be?

Pizza-guy frowned and crossed his arms. He seemed to grow three inches. "'Scuse me? You bailing? Now?"

Oh shit, he wasn't happy. She had a split-second to choose between three options. Stand there and try to pacify pizza-guy. Make a run for it and hope to reach her car before a pissed off pizza-guy caught up with her.

Or slip into the room.

Where a possibly crazy stalker was waiting to fuck her.

Mouth in a thin line, pizza-guy took an aggressive step toward her.

Decision made.

"I'm sorry," she rushed out as she shoved the key card back in the slot. "I really do need to lie down." *Maybe on top of the really sexy man in the bed.*

With that, she used both hands to shove the door open a foot, ducked in the room, and forcefully closed the door behind her before resting her back against it. One loud smack against the door had her jumping, but then the heavy plod of pizza-guy's footsteps faded as he left.

Her gaze met Logan's.

"That fucking dress." Logan said shaking his head as his heated gaze traced her curves.

She did a little visual assessment herself. Jesus, he was buck naked and sprawled on her bed, having somehow arranged himself exactly as she'd done last week.

And had she mentioned he was naked? Naked and very buff with a smooth chest, rippling abs, a few scattered tattoos, and—

Oh, my God.

Naked and growing by the second.

She gaped at his rapidly expanding erection before raising her gaze back to his stubble-covered face. The man didn't have a beard, but seemed to live by the it's five o'clock somewhere ideal. Always looking just a few hours past overdue for a shave. At least, the two times she'd met him he appeared that way. For all she knew, in his normal life he shaved once an hour and just reserved the scruffy look for times he followed unsuspecting women to their hotel rooms and tied himself to their beds.

Naked and hard.

Logan shrugged as though the organ in question was functioning completely independent from the rest of him. "The dress is hot."

The dress is hot? That's all he had to say?

"H-how did you get in here?" She clutched her purse against her chest almost as a shield in case the man magically broke free and advanced on her.

With a wink, he said. "I have my ways."

Yeah, he had his ways all right. He probably flexed one of those biceps and the damn room key tumbled right out of the receptionist's hands and into his pocket. Though he seemed fully at ease with the situation, Chloe wasn't prepared to let her guard down until she got answers to the five hundred questions pinging around her mind.

"How'd you get out last time?"

"A buddy uncuffed me."

It made no sense. "How did he find you?"

"My iPhone was on the night stand there," he said turning toward the night table. "I yelled for Siri, and she called my guy for me."

Oh, huh. That actually made sense. She wasn't sure if she'd have been so innovative were the positions reversed.

"I'm sorry about that," she said in a low voice as shame washed over her. Convinced at the very least he wasn't about to spring from the bed and attack her, she lowered her purse and let it drop to the ground. Ten steps brought her to the foot of the bed.

"Are you?" He tilted his head, studying her. She had the distinct impression he could see straight through her skull to all the fucked-up messiness swirling around inside. That had to stop. No one was allowed to know what went on between her ears these days. Way too scary.

"Why are you here? Are you stalking me?" Would someone admit to being a stalker if they were in fact a stalker? Good thing she wasn't a detective, she'd be out of a job in no time.

He grunted out a laugh. "I'm not stalking you. I've seen you out a few times on the weekends. You seem to do the same thing every time. You come in, have one drink, find one man, stay until the drink is gone then leave with your new…friend. It wasn't too far a stretch to think you went to the same motel room as well."

Jesus, she hadn't realized using a routine would make her so predictable and easy to prey on. A chill ran down her spine. She needed to be more careful. More observant of her surroundings. He'd seen her more than once? Shit, she'd never even noticed him. Last week she would have thought it impossible to miss someone with his strong presence. Apparently, she was dead wrong. Still…

"That doesn't explain why you're here."

"You intrigued me last week." Not one note of apology in his tone.

"I thought I'd have angered you."

He snickered. "I wasn't thrilled to be stuck here, chained to the bed with my dick hanging out, but I admired your lady balls for doing it. I broke your rules, you made me pay. I like a woman who's not a wilting flower."

He liked her? She forced herself to ignore the part of her that warmed at his words. "And you're here because? It's not exactly normal to sneak in a woman's hotel room and handcuff yourself to her bed. Especially a woman you've only met once."

Now his laugh was loud and full of real amusement. "And it's normal to tie random men to your bed and fuck them?" Despite the words, his tone held no judgment. As abnormal as he might have found it, he seemed totally at ease with her. "Told you, you intrigued me. You walk in the bar all full of sass and confidence, like you own the damn place and every man in there. It's sexy as fuck. But there's something behind your eyes that contradicts your actions. I wouldn't say you're broken, but maybe bent pretty far out of whack."

He had no freaking clue, yet he'd hit the nail way too close to the head. Chloe swallowed a golf ball sized lump in her throat, suddenly feeling as naked as he was.

"Top all that off with the tightest pussy I've ever worked my way in and, well, here I am. Game for round two. Ready and willing to follow your rules this time. See?" He jangled the cuffs above the bed. Even when he was slightly playful, his face still held a seriousness that would make most uncomfortable. Not exactly resting bitch face, but maybe resting growly bear face. Still, somehow, it fit him and didn't quite scare her as much as it probably should have.

"What makes you think I want a second go-around?"

"I made you come. Hard," he said in a manner that would have been arrogant from anyone else, but from him it was just a statement of fact.

"S-so?" she asked, mutant butterflies flitting around her stomach. Her damn body betrayed her as well, softening and aching for what he'd provided last time. "That makes you special?"

"It does."

"What makes you think I don't come every day?"

He shrugged. Not much else he could do, all bound to the bed. "I don't. But I know you put on an Oscar-worthy performance at first and were gonna leave it at that. Then, when the real thing happened you looked completely shocked and jumped off my cock like it was on fire. Guessing it's been a long time for you. Guessing you might have even had some kind of problem coming in the recent past. That makes my last guess that you want it to happen again. And again."

He was some kind of wizard. Had to be. Otherwise, how could he know so much? Like the fact that she'd relived that orgasm at least two hundred times throughout the week. And how very badly she wanted it to happen again. But this was so far from her usual routine, she wasn't sure she could go through it. No matter how much her body craved release.

"You said you didn't live around here." What else had the man lied about?

"So did you."

Well, he had her there. Guess those lies canceled each other out. Chloe blew out a breath. "Now what?"

"You're here, I'm helpless, the way you like your men. Whatever dipshit you picked up for the night seems to have taken the hint, tucked his tail between his legs, and left. Why don't you climb on board and we'll see if we can get you off again? I've thought of nothing but your pussy all week."

Chloe stared at him, her riotous body completely on board with his plan. Under the heat of his gaze, her nipples beaded, and her thong grew damp. Frozen in place, she clenched and unclenched her hands at her sides.

Logan, who'd spoken more in the past five minutes than he had the entire time last weekend, lifted his right hand. "I'm cuffed. The key is in the top dresser drawer. I'm totally at your mercy, gorgeous. All I ask is that you don't leave me here this time."

Chloe's face would have heated with embarrassment if her entire body wasn't already hotter than freakin' fire. Still, she couldn't get herself to make a decision.

Then Logan's cock twitched, and she swore she could feel it inside her. "It's Chloe," she said. "My name is Chloe, not gorgeous." There went the last thread of her sanity. Snapped by a sexy man who now wore a smug grin. Before she could talk herself out of it, she ripped the deep purple dress over her head, leaving her in a matching baby blue lace bra and thong. "I've got condoms and the lube in my bag."

She took a step back toward where she'd dropped her purse just as Logan's barked, "No," cut through the room.

Chloe halted, her gaze meeting his. "No?"

His mouth curled up in a sinful smile that had her pussy spasming. Damn, the man was something to look at. But she'd still need the lube. Even though Logan had her wetter than she'd been since she started this DIY form of *therapy*, experience told her she'd dry up shortly after penetration. Just a side effect of not being overly into any of the men she took back to the hotel. That and the fact that the most horrible night of her life was always lurking somewhere in her subconscious.

"Just a condom. Then how about you climb up here and straddle my face? We'll see if we can't get you lubed up the old-fashioned way."

Faltering mid-step, Chloe nearly fell on her face. His request stole her breath. Deep down, she knew if this man got his mouth on her, it'd be mind-blowing.

But it was against the rules. The rules she set up to remain in control and avoid a panic attack. The rules that kept her sane and moving somewhat forward in life. Even if the thought of it had her wetter than she'd been since long before she was kidnapped, she couldn't do it.

Could she?

He was restrained. He couldn't steal her control. Couldn't take over and dominate her.

Couldn't hurt her.

CHAPTER ELEVEN

Chloe was gonna bolt. She had that wide-eyed panicked look a deer got when staring into the headlights of a truck barreling down at seventy miles per hour. Any second now, her fight or flight juices would shoot through her system and he'd be left staring at the smoke rising from the skid marks where she once stood.

She blinked, her chest rising and falling in a rhythm slightly faster than normal. Rocket's attention fell to her tits as they moved with her breath. Both nipples were puckered to tight points. The room wasn't cold. He dropped his focus even lower, to the swatch of lace at the juncture of her thighs. Right where the fabric was slightly darker than the rest of her panties.

Because it was wet. Which meant her body liked his offer, but her mind was too afraid to reach out and take it.

She swallowed, shoulders straightening a hair as though she was injecting some starch in her spine. Maybe she wouldn't flee. Here he was thinking he'd pushed too hard and too far when maybe what she actually needed was another nudge. "Come on," he said, issuing the challenge. "Bring that pussy to me. I've been dying for a taste of it since I felt you come on my cock last week."

Her breathing grew even more ragged, and she licked her lips. Damn, she had no idea how sexy that tiny action was.

Rocket

And Rocket had no clue why he'd made Chloe's pleasure his number one goal in life. But there he was, tying himself to a fucking bed for a woman when all he wanted to do was toss her on her back, dive between her legs and not come up for air until she was screaming for mercy. The good kind of screams.

"I-I don't think so. That's not what I like."

They were a long way from his fantasy scenario. Not that they'd ever get there. This was it. Had to be it. Not only could his association with her put his club at risk, it was utterly insane to form any kind of attachment with her. Rocket's past was too fucked up to bring a woman, any woman, too deeply into his life. Esposito hounding his ass was a reminder of that fact.

"You don't like it? Which part don't you like? Having a man tongue your clit? Suck it? Straight up fucking you with their tongue?" The idea of another man doing any of those things to her had murderous thoughts he had no business thinking trying to worm their way to the forefront of his mind.

"No, I—" She blinked, opened her mouth to say something else but snapped it shut again. Yeah, she hadn't expected him to call her bluff.

Come on, baby. You know you want it.

Chloe might be playing the part of a dominant ever since she was assaulted, but Rocket was almost certain the role wasn't who she was pre-kidnapping. He'd bet his fucking Fat Boy, before her safety was shattered, she'd preferred a man to take charge in the bedroom, maybe even needed it to get off. Nothing about their previous encounter was actually about sex. It was strictly Chloe needing power over men. She just knew no other way to capture that feeling than fucking. Take the same act used against her and turn it on its head. She was doing it to survive, to heal. Yet the only time she'd been able to come was when he stole that control and fucked her into oblivion.

"I've been in agony all week wondering if your pussy would feel as incredible around my tongue as it did on my cock. Put me out of my misery and bring that soaking wet cunt over here."

Her eyes flared. She was practically panting at this point. The order he issued was wrapped in a layer of false submission. Let her think he was begging for what he wanted, what she had the power to grant him, when really, she was submitting to her own desires. Allowing him to give her what she needed.

Rocket was no psychiatrist, but he'd guess Chloe would only find true peace and healing in the renewed ability to surrender. That desire had been ripped from her, turned into something ugly, horrifying, and painful. Now, rightfully so, she was petrified of the prospect. Many, possibly even most women in her position would be paralyzed by that fear. Unable to be with a man until they found a method to deal with the trauma. At first, Rocket assumed Chloe's weekend activities were her taking the trauma and facing it head on. Getting naked, touching, fucking, proving the bastards hadn't damaged her sexuality and needs as a woman.

Now he knew different. She was just the same as the others. Terrified, scarred, dealing with a pain so deep it changed the core of who she was. Because Chloe was just as afraid of being with a man. Just as petrified to be trapped under a man, to have her control taken, to be hurt again. He was pretty sure she didn't even count what went down in this motel room as sex.

Hence why she never orgasmed. Never found physical pleasure in the act.

Until him.

And damn if that didn't make him even fucking harder.

Slowly, she closed the distance to the foot of the bed once again.

Rocket held his breath, the pulsing ache in his cock a match for his pounding heart.

"Y-your mouth stays between my legs," she said, one knee landing on the bed to the side of his foot.

"Deal."

She wasn't done. "You don't try to see if your hands can reach any part of my body." The other knee hit the mattress. She was officially straddling him, although a good few feet south of the end goal.

"Yes, ma'am."

Not even so much as a flicker of happiness. In fact, her spine was so straight and her body so rigid, she'd probably snap in two if a stiff breeze blew through the room. What he'd mistaken for a steel spine was clearly anxiety and fear.

Normally, he wouldn't push a terrified woman so far, but he was pretty damn sure she wouldn't be feeling anything but fucking bliss in the next few minutes.

"And if and when I tell you to stop, you do it. No questions asked."

He almost snorted. No way in fucking hell would she beg him to stop. Not once he got his tongue on her clit. She might beg, but it'd just be for more. "Understood. Anything else?"

Chloe stared a minute then shook her head.

"Then scoot on up here because as skilled as I am, even I can't get you off when your pussy is that far away."

She did, inching her way up his body as though making her way to the end of a plank instead of an orgasm. Had the reason for her trepidation not been so sad, the situation might have been comical. As it was, Rocket felt a strange urge to wrap his arms around her and shield her from anything else the world might throw her way.

When she reached his shoulders, she had to widen her legs to continue given the slightly awkward positioning of his bound arms. But they made it work. Finally, she was where she needed to be.

Chloe gripped the headboard, her arms visibly trembling. To keep from embarrassing her, Rocket shifted his focus to her pussy, hovering right above his mouth. Not that it was any kind of hardship to stare at her. She was wet, pink, and shaved to just a small triangle of neatly trimmed auburn hair.

A beautiful sight.

"W-why aren't you doing anything?" she asked, voice quivering with each word.

"Shh, can't rush a master."

A strangled laugh escaped, and he flicked his gaze to her face.

"A master, huh?" Her right eyebrow was arched high into her forehead. "Think pretty highly of yourself, don't you?"

Rocket couldn't keep the smile off his face if he was paid to frown. This was the first sign of any playfulness she'd exhibited since he'd met her. Hell, since he'd been tailing her. And it made her even more striking. Even harder to resist.

"Guess you're about to find out."

With that. He darted his tongue out, making a quick swipe directly over her clit.

Chloe gasped, her hips bucking at the shock of sensation.

"Just making sure you're paying attention," he quipped right before taking a quick nip of her thigh.

This time her laugh was shaky at best, but she widened her knees ever so slightly bringing herself closer to his mouth.

That's my girl.

A girl. Not his girl. To curtail the outrageous direction his mind was veering, he put himself to work getting Chloe off. He licked straight through her folds before circling her clit once, then once again in the opposite direction followed by a slow slide back down to her pussy. Again, and again he repeated the pattern until Chloe was squirming and practically grinding herself on his face.

With her eyes still open, gaze fixated on the wall above the headboard, she hadn't fully relaxed, hadn't lost herself in the sensations.

That was about to change.

This time, instead of ringing her swollen clit, he wrapped his lips around it and sucked enough to make her yelp.

"Oh, my God," she cried.

Still sucking, he glanced at her face once again. Now they were getting somewhere. Head tipped back, cheeks and chest flushed a pretty pink, eyes closed, she shamelessly bore down on his face.

The taste of her had completely overwhelmed his senses and fuck if he didn't want to drown in her essence. Sweet and spicy, he imagined it was a direct reflection of her personality if she ever let the real Chloe out to play anymore.

"Fuck, baby, you taste so good."

She moaned, finally lost in the act. "More." The command was soft, uncertain, but heard and understood.

Rocket wanted more too. Time to take this to the next level. Abandoning her clit, he went straight for her pussy. His tongue slid in with ease and he went to town fucking her with it.

"Shit," she whispered as she canted her hips to receive more. Whimpers and moans flew from her with increasing volume as her hips picked up speed. Chloe was fully immersed in the experience and aiding him by fucking herself on his tongue.

As she thrust forward, her clit bumped his nose causing her to cry out and jolt so hard she lost the rhythm.

God, what he wouldn't give to have access to his hands. To be able to grab the soft flesh of her hip and help her find her tempo once again. Maybe pump two fingers into her sex while his lips returned to her clit.

Chloe didn't seem to need much assistance though. She got right back into the groove, this time making sure her clit got some action with each roll of her hips.

She was getting close if the gentle fluttering of her walls was any indication. Rocket kept up the assault until she groaned a frustrated sound.

"Logan," she said, squeezing the headboard so hard, the underside of her palms was a stark white.

She was fighting it. Afraid to allow the monster orgasm to consume her.

"Let go," he growled against her. "I'm cuffed, just how you like it. You've got the upper hand here. I'm bound and at your mercy. Let. Go."

His words combined with the tongue lashing he gave her clit seemed to be exactly what she needed to free herself from the chains of uncertainty.

Her head fell back as her body started to tremble above him. Wanting nothing more than to feel it from the inside out, Rocket shoved his tongue deep inside her. Sure enough, her pussy went wild, squeezing and rippling all around him.

It lasted a while, her near shouts fading to soft whimpers as her body calmed. After a few moments, she gazed down at him, eyes hazy with satisfaction and something else.

Interest.

His little redhead wanted more. Thank fuck. Rocket couldn't remember a time he'd been this hard. His cock had been leaking since the moment she lost the damn dress. "Climb on my cock," he said. The command sounded far more like a plea than an order. Probably the only reason Chloe scrambled off his face. She snatched the condom she'd dropped next to him as she made her way down the bed. This time, she swung her leg over him like she was mounting her favorite stallion.

"Still think you need any fucking lube?" he asked.

Chloe let out a short laugh. "Uh, no. I'm so wet it's practically running down my legs."

Rocket grunted. Yeah, she fucking was. He couldn't stop the surge of male pride.

Chloe rolled the condom halfway down his dick. The touch sent a shot of lightning through his body causing his back to arch off the bed. "Fuck," he shouted.

Eyes wide, Chloe stared down at his erection in her fist. "Wow," she said on an exhale. "Seems like you're in a pretty bad way, huh?" He didn't miss the teasing tone and he fucking loved it.

"Baby," he said, ignoring her sharp inhale at the endearment, "you have no fucking idea."

"Well," she said as she worked the condom down his cock. "Since you were so generous, I suppose you deserve a little something in return."

Goddamn, he fucking loved her like this. Light, playful, unafraid to bust his balls. If possible, his cock got even harder.

And then all thoughts ceased to exist because the incredibly tight heat of her slid down him one inch at a time.

Rocket drew his knees up, putting her in the same position that got her off last time. She gifted him a sweet smile.

"Lose the bra. Want to see those gorgeous tits." How his mouth managed to work was a mystery he'd never solve. Pure determination and desperation.

Chloe reached behind her. A small snick sounded through the room seconds before she tossed the garment to the ground.

Fuck yes. Not too big, not too small, with hardened nipples he'd give damn near anything to feel in his mouth.

Another time.

What? There were not going to be other times. Too risky for his club no matter how goddammed good she tasted or hot she felt. And the club had to come first. He was already skating on thin ice.

"Ready?" Chloe asked. Gone was the timid woman of twenty minutes ago. In her place a fucking seductress held the reins.

"Do your worst."

And she fucking did. Riding him with complete abandon. Head thrown back, nails pricking his chest, she worked her hips on his cock like she was born for it. Thank God it didn't take more than a few minutes for her to go stiff and bite her lower lip as she came again because he was only two seconds behind. The moment her pussy clamped down on him, he was a goner.

With a primal shout, he gave into the hardest orgasm he'd had in recent memory. When his brain regained the ability to function, he stared at the woman smiling down at him.

Two orgasms looked fucking amazing on her. Hell, if he didn't want to see what she looked like after a few more. After she was too fuck drunk to do anything more than curl up against him and pass out.

These thoughts were beyond dangerous. Chloe had no idea who he was. No clue he was directly tied to her greatest nightmare. If she found out, she would not only kick him out of her bed, she might kick him straight to hell. Then there was the other matter. The issues she could cause for his club. All she'd have to do was snap and the cops would come running if they thought his club was somehow involved in what happened to her.

They weren't. Not directly, but Lefty's attack on her had been a message for the Hell's Handlers.

Even though he wasn't responsible, the guilt of that night had torn Rocket up for months.

This had to end. He couldn't destroy Chloe's world any more than it was already by telling her the truth yet he wasn't sure how much longer he could lie to her.

No matter how happy she finally looked.

With a radiant smile he'd have forfeited his life savings to keep on her face, Chloe rested her ass on his thighs. "Tomorrow?" she asked. "Do you t-think we could m-meet here a—um again tomorrow night?"

What must it have taken for her to squash her fear, break protocol, and ask for a repeat? Had to be a good sign. She was so hopeful, so over the moon to have found a little pleasure that Rocket's chest ached. That smile was going to disappear the moment he declined. But what choice did he have? Risking his club wasn't an option.

"Yeah, baby, tomorrow."

Apparently, his mouth no longer followed the command of his brain.

Her face lit like he'd offered her the stars. Made him feel ten feet tall.

He was officially fucked.

CHAPTER TWELVE

Chloe hummed along with Katy Perry as the singer belted out some lyrics about fireworks. Pretty appropriate choice considering what had gone on over the past few hours. Staring out her kitchen window at the darkness of night, she whisked the brownie batter for probably five minutes longer than the recipe called for.

What could she say? Being with Logan half the night made her hungry. And she currently had an intense chocolate craving. One indulgence begetting another or something to that effect. Plus, it gave her something to do. Something besides obsess over the fact that she'd completely broken her own rules and fucked the same man four times. The man who made her come and anticipate coming again all through the week. Well shit, so much for not thinking about it...

"Where the fuck have you been?" Scott's furious voice spoken directly beside her cut through her musings making her jump and fling the whisk. Gooey batter splattered in an arc across the granite countertop and onto her brother's arm.

"Shit!" she said on a gasp. "You scared the hell outta me." Chloe rested her hands on the edge of the counter and let her head drop as she tried to control her runaway pulse. Not since before her kidnapping had she been so unaware of her surroundings. These days, nothing got the jump on her. She was hypervigilant to the point of pathologic. And Scott knew that.

Logan wasn't only messing with her body, he was melting her brain.

Scott's scowl deepened. "Sorry, sis. I didn't realize you were zoned out. Usually you know what's happening in a five-mile radius around you."

"Yeah well, you're paying the ambulance bill when they have to cart me in for a heart attack." With a shrug, she lifted her head. "I was thinking about something."

Narrowed eyes joined his frown. "Thinking about what?"

She chuckled as she grabbed a handful of paper towels from the roll. "Nothing important. Didn't realize you were home. How was your date?"

Miracle of miracles, Scott had stayed at his buddy's house through Sunday evening the weekend before, giving her a chance to meet Logan for a second time without having to make up some story about where she was headed on a Saturday night when she barely left the house during daylight. Midweek, he'd met some chick as he ran through the park and planned to take her out Friday, which happened to be tonight. Another chance to have a few more of those stellar orgasms without having to account for her time out of the house.

That left tomorrow night. Was there a way she could pull off another night of Logan, cuffed to the bed and ready to eat her until she screamed? Just thinking about it had her shivering in anticipation and remembering the three times she'd come that evening. The most recent just an hour ago.

"What the fuck, Clo?"

"Huh?"

"I said my date was good." He bobbed his eyebrows, some of the pissed off expression morphing into a dirty smirk. "And how did you not notice I was here? My truck is parked right out front."

She really was off her game. Best to let that question go unanswered. Otherwise she'd have to admit to her own dates. Ha, dates? More like unconventional sex appointments. "Good, huh? How good could it have been? You're home before midnight." Her face flamed as the words left her mouth. Didn't take all night to send someone into the stratosphere. She damn well knew that.

"Good enough I'm not giving details to my little sister."

Chloe smacked his arm. "Works for me. I'm in the mood for brownies. If you make me vomit, I won't be able to eat them, and then I'll have to kill you. Here." She handed him a wad of paper towels.

"Don't need it. Use it on the counter." Scott lifted his forearm and licked the glob of chocolate from his inked skin.

"How is it?" she asked as she wiped the mess off the counter.

"Fuckin' delicious."

Chloe snorted. Guess fuckin' delicious was better than plain old delicious. "They'll be done in a little over half an hour." As she spoke, she scraped the batter into the prepared pan then popped them into the oven. "I'll let you know when you can have one."

Scott's laughter had her stomach twisting. He stepped in front of her, blocking her path out of the kitchen. Damnit. She'd been so close.

"What's going on? You're spaced out, fucking humming Katy Perry, and you weren't home when I got in. You never go out at night alone. What gives?"

If he only knew. Wait... "You listen to Katie Perry?"

With a roll of his eyes, he folded his arms over his broad chest. "Nice try. Don't change the subject."

It wasn't so much a subject change as a stall to give her a few more seconds to come up with a believable story. Saying something along the lines of—"I was out with a guy I met at a bar a few weeks ago. I like to tie him up and have sex with him after he makes me come with his mouth"—probably wouldn't go over too well.

Chloe waved him off, shooting for unaffected. "I was at a girlfriend's house. Someone I haven't seen in months. She guilted me into coming over for a glass of wine. Just one," she said when he opened his mouth. "I'm not stupid, *Dad*. I knew I wasn't staying long and had to drive home."

He didn't so much as crack a smile at her quip. In fact, he looked like he was in Ranger mode. Working as a human lie detector to find a crack in her exterior. Chloe swallowed and fought to maintain eye contact. A good liar she was not. "That's bullshit," he finally said.

"What? No it's not. That's where I went." Damn him and his training.

"No." He stepped closer and pulled her into a bear hug. Warmth and the scent of her childhood surrounded her, making her want to burrow deeper. "Not what I meant. You shouldn't let anyone guilt you into anything, Clo. She can't begin to understand what you've been through. None of us can, which means we have no right to judge the way you handle it. If you're not up for visiting her, she can either come here or fucking wait until you're ready. You hear me?"

Well, there went her desire for a midnight snack. Talk about a guilt trip. She wrapped her arms around her brother and squeezed him back, hard as she could. Her throat thickened with emotion. "You're the best big brother ever, you know that?"

He grunted and rubbed her back. "Of course, I know that. But feel free to drop that bomb next time you talk to our other brothers."

Her laugh broke the tension. Getting the four of them together was always a hoot. Each insanely protective, she'd always been a very well loved and taken care of sister. And cue the guilt for mostly ignoring her other two siblings the past few months. "How about this?" he said. "I'll cancel my date tomorrow night. We can have a movie fest and finish off whatever brownies we don't devour tonight. Sound good?"

He had another date tomorrow? Meaning she could meet up with Logan again and he'd never know it. Sure, Scott's offer sounded great, but she'd already had a much better one. Junk food and hanging with her brother was all well and good, but let's face it, orgasms from Logan trumped carbs and sibling bonding any day. "Have I mentioned you're the best brother ever?"

He snickered.

"But seriously, don't cancel your date. Canceling this early in the game makes you look like a huge a-hole."

More guilt. Selfish as it was, she wanted the night with Logan more than she could express.

He drew back, staring down at her as though assessing her authenticity. "You sure?"

"Totally sure."

"Well, then..." He ruffled her hair like only a big brother could do. "Don't wait up for me tomorrow night. I have a feeling I won't be making it home." He held up his hand for a high-five and Chloe shoved it away.

"Oh gross, that poor woman." She made gagging sounds like she'd done when she was eight and Scott seventeen. At the time, she'd spied on him kissing his date on their front porch. The entire experience had grossed her out beyond belief. It'd been like someone forgot to tell him he'd be passing along his boy cooties to the poor girl. Clearly, she'd grown out of that idea.

"Ha," he said, playfully shoving her away. "Trust me, the girl will not be gagging." He started to walk out of the kitchen, then paused, calling over his shoulder, "Well, actually she might gag if—"

"La la la, not listening," Chloe yelled, fingers in her ears as he walked out of the room laughing.

"Yeah, yeah," he yelled from halfway down the hall. "Come get me when those brownies are done. Need to start building up my energy for tomorrow night."

Two seconds later, Chloe realized she was standing in the middle of her kitchen with a big, goofy grin on her face. She felt lighter and more at peace than she had in a very long time. Since her kidnapping, to be exact.

The combination of physical release at night, and family time during the day was soothing her soul in a way she hadn't expected. And the best part?

She'd be with Logan again tomorrow night.

They'd exchanged numbers for the sole purpose of being able to contact each other if one wasn't going to be able to meet up. Neither had made contact beyond their standing Friday and Saturday night hook-up.

The radio silence was completely fine by her. In fact, it was preferred. This wasn't a relationship, they weren't dating. Hell, they weren't even friends. In the four times they'd been together, they hadn't shared any personal information or insights into each other's lives. She knew nothing more about the man than she did that first week. In fact, aside from the occasional, "fuck yeah" and "give it to me," Logan didn't talk much at all. The most verbal he'd been was the night he convinced her to ride his face.

And boy was she glad he had.

Just as she was about to head to the den and plop down in front of the television while she waited for the brownies to bake, her phone chirped.

Snatching it off the counter, she frowned at Logan's name on the screen. Seriously? Had he heard her thinking about their lack of contact?

Oh, God, what if he couldn't make it tomorrow night? What if he could make it but decided her fucked-up way of having sex and the fact she could only do it in that one manner was getting old? The guy was downright delicious. Women probably threw themselves at him everywhere he went. Why the hell would he spend his weekends with a head case like her?

Her thumb hovered over the screen, but she couldn't make herself open the text message. She'd been living in a fantasy of good sex and safety this past week, and she was far from ready to give it up.

Rocket

With a snort, she rolled her eyes. Thank God Scott was in her guest room or he'd be all over this, trying to find out what she was hiding. Might as well open it. Ignoring it wouldn't change the facts. If Logan was bailing, she'd find out soon enough, and it'd be much more mortifying to find out if she opened an empty motel room door than seeing his text in the privacy of her own home.

"One, two, three, now," she whispered then swiped the phone and held it up for the facial recognition to kick in.

Skip the dress next time I see you. Wear jeans. Been dying to see that ass wrapped in denim since the first night.

Chloe swallowed around a suddenly bone-dry throat. Though her throat seemed to be the only part of her that was dry. She shifted, trying to find a more comfortable stance now that her panties were damp.

Logan liked her ass? Part of her was surprised he'd even noticed it. It wasn't like they engaged in flirting, touching, or much ogling of each other. Sure, she'd gotten to soak in the sight of his body as he laid there unable to escape, but she pretty much got naked and hopped on board without giving him any kind of a show. The fact that he'd even taken note of her ass was shocking. And sent heat rushing through her. She could wear jeans. Some ultra-skinny ones that showed off her legs and butt.

Tomorrow night, she texted back.

I'll be the one cuffed to the bed.

The reply was instantaneous.

She couldn't help the purely feminine smile that curled her lips.

Logan liked her ass.

CHAPTER THIRTEEN

With one last groan, Chloe climbed off Logan and flopped next to him on the bed. When his well-used dick slipped from her body, he hissed as he did every single time. Chloe smiled, letting her eyes drift closed as she floated on a cloud of post-orgasm bliss.

Damn, she felt like she could leap over the building with ease.

"Hey," Logan said, laughter in his voice. "Don't go falling asleep on me. I'm still all trussed up here."

Chloe's eyes flew open. They never spoke after sex. She just dressed, uncuffed him, and they went their separate ways. She also never laid down beside him. "Shit, sorry," she said as she scrambled up and over to the dresser where the key rested. "Guess I'm more tired than I realized."

Thirty seconds later she had him uncuffed. Ever since the first night, he'd followed her rules—the new rules they seemed to make together. She now trusted him enough to release him at the end. It took his molten hot gaze on her breasts to realize she hadn't covered herself. Her face heated so quickly, she got dizzy. What the hell was wrong with her tonight? "Shit," she said again. "Sorry. Let me get my clothes."

Logan laughed for real this time. "Not sure what you're apologizing for, but it better not be keeping those gorgeous tits uncovered."

"No, um, well, maybe. They're kinda small. But it was more for almost falling asleep." Where the hell was her bra? She scanned the floor, far too embarrassed to look at him. And too shook by how much of her guard she'd let down a few seconds ago. Almost falling asleep? Shit, she needed to get her head back in the game.

"Hey," he said softly, as though she were a frightened kitten stuck under the couch. "Come here."

She obeyed without thought strictly because the gentle tone and the fact that he was chatting at all had her startled. Oh, there was her bra, lying next to the pillow. As she reached for it, Logan's hand circled her wrist and stopped her motion.

The moment his skin touched hers, she froze, and her vision tunneled.

"Hey," he said again, dropping her hand. "I'm sorry. Did I hurt you?"

Relief was instantaneous once the physical contact was gone. "Uh, no, just surprised me." She snatched up the bra and stared at his chest so she wouldn't have to see the questions in his eyes.

"Come here," he said again, now sitting on the edge of the bed. "I'll keep my hands to myself." He lifted them so she had a full view of each palm then tucked them under his thighs. He had to think she was crazy. She let him eat her out and fuck her, but he couldn't touch her wrist?

Chloe chewed on her lower lip. She was being ridiculous. The amount of chances the man had had to harm her if he desired were in the hundreds by now. Not once had he done anything threatening, or even aggressive. She stepped closer.

"More."

Another step.

His eyebrow rose.

One more step had her standing between his spread legs, close enough to wrap her arms around his back.

"First of all," he said. "The fact that I fucked you to near unconsciousness is not at all a problem for me. Actually, it's kind of my goal. Take you so good you can't think of walking that sexy body out of the room. This way I can do it again after you take a little nap."

Her eyes widened and her mouth dropped open, but no words came out. What was there to say? He wanted her to stay longer?

"And second," he continued. "Your tits are fan-fucking-tastic. About six times this week, I jerked off to the memory of them bouncing while you rode me."

Holy shit. Holy shit.

Her nipples puckered to hardened points under his attention.

"Just one problem."

"W-what?" she whispered.

"I need another fucking taste," he said on a growl. "The quick suck I had that first night hasn't been nearly enough to carry me through until now." He leaned forward, capturing a nipple between his lips and pulling it into his mouth with a hard suck.

Chloe moaned. Her head dropped back and she arched her spine and pushed her breast into his face. He tongued her nipple then pressed it to the roof of his mouth, ripping a sharp cry from her.

There weren't enough functioning brain cells to feel panic or even care she'd taken a huge step toward breaking their routine. All she could think about was how badly her other breast needed some attention.

"Logan," she said, practically begging with just one word.

"I've got you, babe," he said, kissing a path to her other breast. "Christ, I could live on these tits." Then the other nipple was in his mouth and she was moaning once again. This time, he scraped his teeth across the sensitive bud, making her entire body jolt like she'd been hit with a live wire. The entire time, his hands remained anchored to the bed, non-threatening.

After a few minutes, the need for release started to build in her again. She'd already had three orgasms that night and was getting close to demanding a fourth from him.

But he was free, not bound to the bed and that lightbulb was a big bucket of ice water on her arousal.

Logan must have felt the shift in her. He released her breast and sat back, looking her straight in the eye. "Thank you. That'll hold me a few days."

His cock was fully erect once again. Looked like she wasn't the only one to enjoy that. She was just about to offer to cuff him back up for another round when her stomach decided to let out a very loud rumble.

Logan chuckled. "Hungry?"

Ravenous. Sex with him always worked up an appetite. "Well, would you believe me if I said no now?"

"Nope. Let's go grab something to eat."

Chloe froze. Something to eat. Like a date? Like she was a normal woman. "I don't kn—"

"Come on," he said as though she hadn't even spoken. "I know a twenty-four-hour place around here that makes the best damn pie you'll ever have. They usually have at least five kinds, too. I can't let you drive home with an empty stomach. What if you pass out from low blood sugar and crash your car, who would I fuck next weekend?"

The ridiculous scenario had her laughing. "Pie does sound good," she said. "Last night I ate three brownies after I got home. If we keep at this, I'll need bigger clothes."

He snorted. "Nothing wrong with a little cushion, babe. Less likely to hurt you with a rough fuck that way."

Her eyes widened. They stared at each other as the seconds ticked by.

"Okay," she said. "I'm in."

His words were crude but sent a thrill through her. A rough fuck. Maybe someday she'd be over her issues enough to experience that. She almost laughed. Not that Logan would be around that long. He'd wise up one of these days. Which was why she should grab onto what he was offering.

"Good." He stood from the bed, muscles at play while he stepped into his jeans. "Hate to see you cover that body, but you better put some clothes on before we leave. Though I gotta say, your ass in jeans is even hotter than I'd imagined."

Chloe gasped as she glanced down at her body. She was still stark naked. Standing around talking to a man who was also naked like it was no big deal. Without even a hint of nerves or panic.

Maybe there was hope for her after all.

CHLOE COULDN'T SIT still. She fidgeted, drummed her nails on the table, tapped her foot, shifted her eyes around the small twenty-four-hour diner. If he didn't know better, Rocket would think she was overdue for a good fuck.

"Hey," he said, reaching across the table and placing his large hand over her jittery one. "You okay?"

"What?" She gaped at their joined hands. Yeah, he was pushing her. Or at least trying to nudge her along without totally freaking her out. Gave him an excuse for touching her besides the fact that he wanted his hands on her in some way nearly all the damn time.

"Yeah, of course. I'm great."

He gave her hand a squeeze. "You're nervous."

All her movements stopped as though someone flipped a master switch. "Sorry, I'm a little out of practice—"

"With what? Eating?"

That had her at least huffing out a half laugh. "No, being around other people. T-touching. I don't go out very much." Her face turned an adorable shade of pink. "Well, except for Friday and Saturday nights."

"How come?" Would she tell him? Mention she'd had a traumatic experience a few months ago?

"Oh, um, I'm just a homebody." Clearing her throat, she wiggled her hand out from under his and dropped it onto her lap. He immediately missed the soft skin under his. "So, uh, what do you do?"

Rocket leaned his back against the torn vinyl of the booth. "I'm a contractor. I own a construction company in Townsend."

Her mouth turned down. "Townsend?"

"Yep. Something wrong with Townsend?" He took a sip of the watered-down coffee the place kept flowing. Was it his club? Or some other connection to Townsend that had her looking like a scared rabbit once again.

"Huh? Oh, uh, no." She rubbed her bare arms below the short sleeves of her shirt as though chilled though the restaurant was pleasantly warm. "Of course not. I'm not over there very often. I hear the town has a pretty high, um, population of criminals."

Population of criminals? He almost spit the coffee across the table. She was fucking adorable. "What? You mean the bikers?"

Her face paled. What was that? Sure, he hadn't expected she'd welcome any of them with open arms, but her face showed genuine terror.

"Uh, yeah," she said. "I guess that's what I mean." She was practically whispering.

Rocket scratched his chin. Was she curious about the man who rescued her? Odd, she seemed almost fearful at the mention of bikers. Was it just the association with that night? Shit, maybe he'd done too good a job of convincing her not to go to the cops and made her afraid of the club. He had to tread carefully here. Seemed as though he had the power to turn her in favor of or fully against his club. "Run into them from time to time," he said, casual as he could manage. "Had a few work for me over the years." He shrugged and rested his palms on the table.

She quickly glanced down at his hands, then back at him.

"Never had a single problem with any of 'em. They're not angels," he said with a slight chuckle. Understatement of the year. "No one would argue with that, but they're sure not the devils some think they are." He made sure to give her his full attention, tone serious, in an attempt to convince her his club was no threat to her.

She snorted. "I'm sure they're a bunch of teddy bears."

Well, that was sarcasm if he'd ever heard it. His eyes narrowed. At what point had she decided his club was the enemy? And why? Not only had they been the ones to rescue her, but Maverick's woman even visited her at her house after Chloe was released from the hospital. The two had chatted and Stephanie never once reported a seeming hatred of the club.

"You have a bad experience with one of them?"

"No." She answered too quick. "Just not a big fan of people who think the law doesn't apply to them."

It was Rocket's turn to scoff. "Clearly, you haven't had much experience with the law dropping the ball more often than not." The moment the words were out of his mouth, he knew the error of them.

Chloe had been expressly asked not to cooperate with law enforcement regarding her kidnapping and rape. Was that why she hated the Handlers? Did she feel there was a lack of justice or punishment for her rapists?

Two of her rapists were already dead, killed by the club when rescuing others, young girls, who'd been kidnapped and sold to the highest bidder. As for Lefty, he'd get what he deserved and more. Maybe once Lefty was no longer breathing Chloe would be able to take a breath.

And not hate the idea of his club.

Not that her opinion of the MC should matter. It didn't matter. This wasn't a thing. Wasn't a date or a relationship. It was two wounded souls who fucked and got hungry.

Simple as that.

The waitress took that moment to arrive with their pie. Chocolate crème for Chloe and good old-fashioned apple pie for him.

Rocket

At the sight of the sweet treats, Chloe's face lit up. "Oh, man, those look amazing." She leaned across the table and inhaled deeply. "Do you smell the cinnamon in yours?"

Hand on her hip, the middle-aged waitress rolled her eyes. "Y'all need anything else?"

"I'm good," said Chloe. "So, so, good."

Rocket chuckled and picked up his fork. "We're all set, thanks."

"Mm-hmm," she said as she clacked away on small heels.

He couldn't help but notice the way Chloe kept eyeing his pie as she unfolded her napkin across her lap.

After picking up his fork, Rocket slid it through the pie with ease, gathering a huge mouthful onto the tines. Before lifting it, he dragged it through the mound of vanilla ice cream piled on the plate. He could practically hear the saliva shooting out of Chloe's glands. "Here," he said holding up the fork.

Her eyes were bright and shining. Any unpleasant talk of outlaw bikers forgotten. "For me?" she asked as though he was presenting her with diamonds.

"Yeah, babe. You're practically drooling over there."

She cocked her head, a flirty smile playing across those tempting lips. Lips he still had yet to kiss even though his mouth had sampled her pussy many times. "Don't you want the first taste?"

"Considering it can't possibly be sweeter than what I've already had my mouth on tonight, I'm more than willing to give you the first bite."

Her eyes flared with blatant interest, and Rocket had an insane vision of the two of them leaving together and heading to his place. She wouldn't make it past his foyer before he had her clothes torn off and his dick buried inside her.

Dangerous thoughts.

"Well," she said, licking her lips.

His cock jumped.

"If you insist."

Transfixed, he watched as her lips closed around his fork, then dragged down the tines until the pie was gone. As she chewed, her eyes rolled heavenward, and she let out a low moan. "Oh. My. God," she said around the generous bite. "That's amazing."

Goddamn right it was amazing. Rocket's cock was angrily protesting the confining fit of his jeans. He shifted on the bench seat. Thankfully the table hid his secrets.

"Want to try mine?" Chloe asked.

"Fuck yeah," he said. "I'll try anything you have to offer me."

She giggled, actually giggled, as she held out a much smaller piece of her chocolate pie. The sound was gorgeous coming from her. Happy, carefree, untortured. Just as she should always be.

Jesus, he was getting fucking sappy.

"You seem to be shorting me on my taste," he said as he brushed his fingertips across her wrist. She tensed for just one second before meeting his gaze. Slowly, he wrapped his fingers around her wrist, holding the fork in place. Chloe stayed loose but wary.

Progress.

Of course, they were in public and fully clothed.

"It's chocolate," Chloe said. "I'm no dummy."

With a grunt, he licked the pie off the fork then released her hand. After that, they both dove into their respective desserts and conversation flowed light and natural. Rocket couldn't remember a time he talked so much. With Chloe it just felt right. She asked a question and he answered. She was open, an attentive listener, and never seemed to pass judgment on whatever it was he told her.

Then again, he was completely lying about who and what he was. So there was that. If she found out he not only knew exactly what happened to her five months ago, but he was the assassin-turned-biker who rescued her, and he'd been practically stalking her since then, there'd be a trail of fire behind her.

Before he knew it, their pie was gone, and coffee cups drained. Silence fell, thick and heavy as they watched each other across the table. He wanted her, again. Seemed he always wanted her. This couldn't go on for much longer, but he also couldn't force himself to walk away. Not yet. Not when she was making strides toward recapturing who she was.

"Friday?" he asked.

Chloe tilted her head. Her eyes shifted to the diner's vacant counter before returning to his. "Logan, I have some issues," she said in a small voice.

If he was smart, he'd take that and run with it. Use it as an excuse to walk away from her now, before his club became involved. Once Lefty was dead, he could give her that peace and she'd be able to move on with her life.

But he was an idiot.

"We've all got fuckin' issues, Chloe."

Her smile was sad. "Mine are pretty big."

"Look," he said, reaching across the table for her hand. Once again, her attention was drawn to their connection, a small divot appearing between her eyes and matching the slight frown on her lips. But she didn't pull away. Rocket had to work to keep his smile at bay. Damn, it felt good to slip past her defenses, even an inch at a time. He kept his voice low so they wouldn't be overheard. "Pretty sure I figured that out already. It's not exactly every day you meet a woman who wants to tie random men to her bed and fuck them."

She dropped her head. "I'm pretty fucked up."

"Well that makes two of us then, babe, because I'm having a fuck of a time walking away from you."

Lifting her head, she blinked at him. "Really?"

"Really."

"I'm not sure I'll ever be able to do...things, differently than we do them. I'm not sure I'm capable of anything more than what this already is."

"Okay. Then it is what it is. Friday?"

One nod. "Friday."

Why did he feel such relief at that one word? "Come an hour early. I'll order pizza. Maybe if we feed you first, we can keep your stomach from going crazy."

She fell silent, those pretty green eyes hiding a whole room full of fear. "O-okay."

He gave her hand one last squeeze before releasing her. "Come on." He stood and dropped a twenty on the table. "I'll walk you to your car."

The tense set of her shoulders relaxed at his offer.

Once outside, he threaded his fingers through hers. As before, she flinched at first but slowly relaxed by degrees into his innocuous touch. The pressure-free caresses and handholds were all part of his master plan. Baby steps. She was like a wounded animal. Humans often reacted similarly to animals following trauma. While overseas in Iraq, one of his Marine brothers found an abandoned dog that had once been severely abused. At first the mutt snarled and snapped whenever they went near. Over time, with treats and soft words, the old boy let him and his team creep closer. It took months, but eventually they were able to pet him, and one of his brothers in arms finagled permission to return the dog to the states.

His strategy with Chloe was much the same. Get her used to a man's touch in a safe way. Maybe then, once she no longer reacted with fear, he'd finally be absolved of the guilt that had settled in his gut the moment he saw her beaten and brutalized. And maybe he could shake the iron grip she seemed to have on his balls.

"Thank you," she said turning to him.

The gratitude was for more than accompanying her to her car. He nodded. "Trust me, every second of this evening has been my pleasure." He stepped closer to her. Then closer still, until his body was flush against hers. What he wanted to do was crowd her against her car, but he didn't want her to feel trapped or forced into anything.

"W-what are you doing?" she asked as she lifted her hands to his chest, neither pushing him away nor pulling him closer. Did she even know which action she preferred?

"Friday's a long way away. That's six nights I have to lie in my bed remembering the taste of your pussy, the feel of it on my cock, and the way your tits felt in my mouth. Six nights of remembering and not being able to do a goddamn thing about it. Give me one more memory to add to my list. One more thing to torture myself with. Give me something I haven't had yet." As he spoke, he moved in until his lips where brushing hers with every word spoken.

He paused with nothing but millimeters separating them. She had to give the final okay.

"Yes," Chloe breathed.

That was all he needed to claim her mouth with a hunger that had been building for months. She was sweet, thanks to the pie, and warm from two cups of coffee. Her small whimper allowed him to deepen the kiss, slipping his tongue into her mouth. As he absorbed her flavor, she finally decided what to do with her hands. Those fingers curled into the fabric of his T-shirt and held on for dear life.

He fisted his hands at his side, fighting the urge to fully crush her to him. Making her feel trapped or reminding her of her nightmares wasn't an option. Rocket absorbed every sensation, the soft brush of her nose as it bumped his. Her curious tongue tangling with his and making him want nothing more than to feel it stroking the length of his dick. The near purr vibrating from the back of her throat when he nipped her bottom lip. Each and every sensation ramped up his need to have her hard, fast, and with screaming satisfaction.

One day soon. He could feel it in his bones. He'd get her there. Back to the woman she was before his club's business destroyed her life.

Maybe then he could move past this obsession and get on with *his* fucking life.

CHAPTER FOURTEEN

Rocket slid the heavy ladder into the bed of his pick-up then wiped his sweaty brow with the hem of his filthy T-shirt. These days, he didn't do nearly as much of the manual labor as he used to—owning the company had some perks—but there were certain things his anal-retentive self had never been able to completely relinquish control of. And one of those tasks was checking over every damn inch of the work before any type of inspection. He tended to whip out his fine-toothed comb afterhours to avoid raising his men's hackles. He trusted them to do quality work, wouldn't have hired them otherwise, but it was his name on the business card, and he'd be damned if he didn't stand behind every nail and screw.

His need for perfection was the reason he was at a jobsite by himself on a Saturday afternoon. Monday, a city inspector would be coming by to ensure the gas hook-ups had been installed properly in the massive kitchen of a restaurant his crew was renovating. Before the inspector came out, Rocket wanted one last peek at the work so there would be no surprises come Monday morning. As he'd expected, everything was perfect. He only hired the best and most meticulous of workers.

After another wipe of the perspiration, this time on the back of his neck, he checked his phone.

A message was waiting from Chloe.

7 work for you?

Rocket

Fuck yeah, seven worked. Fuck, he'd head there now if he could. Chloe was making and bringing him dinner to their motel room. That meant time together without him shackled. And that meant her trust in him was growing. They'd be alone in the motel room for a meal. Rocket wouldn't be shackled for the entire meal or for a few other things if he had his way. A huge step in whatever this odd friendship/sex buddy thing they had going on was.

"That from the sexy redhead I saw you with last night?"

Fuck! Shit! Rocket's blood went from ninety-eight to two hundred and twelve degrees in under three seconds. Just the thought of Esposito breathing the same air as Chloe had him homicidal.

He whirled around, doing his best to school his expression. Of all the ways to be approached by Esposito, being caught off guard was the worst. "Fuck you doing in my town, old man?" he asked in a bored voice that disguised his angst.

Esposito smirked. The man had been around the block too many times to fall for Rocket's shit. "Didn't mean to startle you." Older than Rocket by at least twenty-five years, his once black hair had dulled to a dingy gray and the flat abs he'd sported for years had pooched out since Rocket last saw him. The guy was getting too used to living the high life. Forgetting what hard work consisted of.

"Need this?" Esposito tossed an icy bottle of water Rocket's way.

He hated to take a thing from the guy, but he was thirsty as fuck and needed to pick his battles. Pitching a fit over the offer of water wasn't a good way to start this conversation.

"Why you here, old man?" Rocket asked as he caught the bottle one handed. He twisted the sealed cap off and took a long drink. When half the bottle had been drained, he leveled his gaze on Esposito.

His former boss chuckled with a shake of his head. "You always did have a way of looking at people that made them feel like you were melting their insides with your stare. You're a hard fucker, Rocket. And you know why I'm here. Told you, you owe me." He held out a manila folder.

Rocket didn't budge.

"Take it." When Rocket still didn't move, Esposito rolled his eyes and closed the fifteen-foot gap between them. "Just take a fucking look."

Rocket stared at the file as though it were covered in anthrax. One thing was for sure, he'd regret opening it. Another thing was for sure, he'd regret not fucking opening it. Esposito was good that way. The master of creating a damned if you do, damned if you don't situation.

Suppressing the growl of frustration clawing at his throat—he wasn't showing fucking weakness for a second—he snatched the file. "Doesn't matter what the fuck's in here. I'm not doing it."

"Just fucking look."

Sure enough, regret. The instant he flipped to the first paper in the file. An image of a beautiful young woman stared up at him. She was side by side with a smiling young man who had his arm slung across her shoulders. The rage, disgust, and hatred were instant. Copper had been fucking right. Rocket lived for protecting others. Eliminating the scum of the earth. Esposito knew it too and wanted to make a mockery of it.

"The fuck is this, old man? Ward and June here don't exactly look like terrorists or blood thirsty leaders of a cartel."

A smirk curled Esposito's lips. "No, but you're not far off. They don't run the cartel, they fight them."

What?

His old boss stepped closer. "This lovely lady and her husband here are your classic save-the-world do-gooders. They've been funneling illegals out of Mexico for the past three years. Specifically, people on the cartel's hit list." His smirk turned positively evil. "You have any idea how much the cartel is willing to pay to rid themselves of this annoyance?"

"No," Rocket said, impressed with how disinterested he sounded while his mind was whirling with a million what-the-fuck thoughts. "I have no idea what the going rate for one's soul is these days. I'm sure you're about to tell me, though."

"Five million," Esposito said, his greedy eyes gleaming with money lust.

Jesus.

"Per body."

No wonder the old man was so intent on having this done and done well.

In the last few months of Rocket's employment, he'd gained firsthand knowledge of Esposito's less than moral business dealings. When he let Rocket go all those years ago with a promise of being owed a favor, Rocket should have known this day would come.

Ignoring the primal part of him yearning to jump to the couple's rescue, he flipped the file closed, and held it back out.

"Not interested."

"You're mistaken if you think I care about your level of interest."

Rocket clenched his teeth. "Get lost."

Propping his arm on the side of Rocket's pick-up, Esposito smirked again. "No can do. I need this job done and I need it done by you. Yesterday. Come on, Rocket, shouldn't take you more than a few weeks. You zip on down to Mexico, do some recon, take the fucker out and done. Payment fulfilled. You'll never hear from me again. Hell, I'll even throw in a hundred grand to sweeten the deal."

So, all it took to get out from Esposito's thumb was the destruction of what was left of his soul.

"Fuck off."

"You can't refuse," he said with a laugh as though it was the most obvious fact in the universe. Esposito hated Rocket for the way he'd left the company. Esposito had probably been salivating after this for years. Get his big money maker job done and ruin Rocket in the process. No skin off his back. His company would thrive. The only thing the bastard cared about.

"I can," he said, slamming the tailgate closed.

He rounded the truck then slid behind the wheel. Before he had the ignition fired, Esposito appeared at his open window. The smug fucker folded his arms on the window frame. "You always did prefer the hard way, didn't you, Rocket?"

"Fuck off." Rocket leveled him with a glare so deadly, Esposito squirmed.

But his discomfort only lasted for the blink of an eye. "Pretty little thing, your redhead. Though all the women who seem to be attached to your club are. Maybe not that tall one with the braid, she looks like she could kick my ass. I'm partial to the little curly blonde. You know the one, with the cute little girl of her own."

Shell. Copper's woman. Copper would rip Esposito limb from limb if he so much as sniffed in Shell's direction. Might be kind of fun to watch. Rocket curled his hands around the wheel. It was either that or reach through the window and slam Esposito's head against the side of his truck. The goddamn motherfucker'd had eyes on his truck for who knew how long. The thought of him watching all the women, Chloe especially, was enough to make him lose his mind. He fired up the truck. Chloe had to be protected. If that meant confessing what he'd been doing with her to Copper, so be it. Esposito couldn't get his bloody hands anywhere near her.

Rocket revved the engine causing Esposito to back away from the vehicle, arms raised. "Think about. I'll be in town for a few days." He took another two steps back as Rocket shifted the truck in drive.

Copper was gonna shit a brick.

"See you soon," Esposito called out as Rocket's truck kicked up a cloud of dust in its wake.

He hung his arm out the window, flipping Esposito the bird with one hand. The other dialed Copper while he used his knee to steer.

"What's up, Rocket?" Copper answered on the second ring.

"Esposito's in town."

"Shit. You on your way in?" Something crashed in the background. Probably the brick falling from Copper's ass.

"Ten minutes."

"Make it five."

A grunt was the only reply he gave his prez before he hit the end button and floored the gas.

Seven minutes later, he was seated in the chapel with the rest of the executive board. Bringing trouble to the club's doorstep was the last thing Rocket ever wanted. First off, he hated being the fucking center of attention and second, he was the SAA. His job was to keep the club orderly and prevent any internal or external strife. And here he was, the one hand delivering a pile of shit. Copper ought to rip the title from him.

And he just might.

Since he was last to arrive, Copper began the moment his ass hit the chair. "Okay, Rocket, thanks for getting in so fast. I haven't had a chance to fill everyone in yet, so why don't you get the guys up to speed. And use actual full sentences please."

He shot his prez a look then took in the room. "Guy I used to work for, name's Esposito, wants me to do a job for him."

"What kind of job?" Zach cut in, all ears. As the club's enforcer, he lived for anything that allowed him to bring out his meaty fists.

Well shit, looked like it was time to bleed his past all over the clubhouse. His brothers probably wouldn't be able to stomach the sight of him by the time he was done with his tale. "He's top dog of a private defense contractor. I was his lead operator."

The room grew quiet as the men digested that information and read between the lines.

"Well, none of you have ever known me to keep my mouth shut, so I'll be the one to ask. Is lead operator code for badass assassin?" Maverick asked. His inked arms were folded across the table top, and the pierced eyebrow had arched high into his forehead.

"It means I was lead operator."

"Got it. So badass assassin it is. Why'd you leave?"

Copper cut in. "The real question here is how did he leave. Rocket started noticing some inconsistencies with their contracts. Turned out Esposito was taking on contracts that were questionable if the price was right."

Questionable. Rocket almost laughed. The contracts Esposito favored were downright fucking wrong. The face of the last man Rocket killed for Esposito floated through his brain. A cop in Russia who'd taken too much of an interest in putting a stop to the mafia. Esposito had been hired to take him out. Gave the job to Rocket complete with a thick file full of years of terrorist activity and affiliations.

All lies to manipulate Rocket into carrying out the execution.

The last hit of his career.

The mission that haunted him for over five years.

"Shit," Mav muttered as Jig grunted. Zach sat silent, but his fists curled.

"Rocket walked and—"

Rocket blinked himself back into the present. He may not be a chatty Cathy, but this was his story to tell. Time to man up and own it. "I got this, Cop. Esposito let me go with the condition that I owed him. Think he knew all along I'd catch on at some point. Figured if he let me walk, at least he'd get something out of me in the future. He's tried to collect a few times." Rocket shrugged. "I always turn him down."

"Let me guess," Zach said. "He's not taking no for an answer this time?"

"Something like that."

"He gonna send someone to take you out? Come after the club?" Zach asked, face hardening with displeasure. This got his enforcer hackles rising.

Rocket

"That ain't his style. He's a sneaky shit. More likely to go after an ol' lady than come for us guns blazing."

The tone of the room turned deadly serious. Each of his brothers wore expressions of varying disbelief and rage. With all their anger directed Rocket's way, he struggled to keep his head high and meet their solemn gazes.

"How likely are we talking here?" Zach asked.

Rocket folded his hands on the table, leaning on his forearms. "He's in town. Popped up at my jobsite right before I came here."

"He make any threats?" Jig's eyes were sharp, fully engaged and ready for action. He'd lived through the devastating loss of his first wife. As independent and capable of taking care of herself as Izzy was, any kind of threat to her or around her set Jig off.

"In a roundabout way. Told me the club has some beautiful ol' ladies. Let me know he's had eyes on us."

"Fuck," Mav said. "Let's go get the ladies." He looked to Copper who nodded. "They're all together. They have a girls' night planned for tonight. Drove out to Pigeon Forge to check out that new café, and then were gonna stock up on wine and junk food."

"Let's do it." Zach popped up and followed Mav out the door with Jig and Viper not far behind. Rocket remained seated for a moment as did Copper.

"He know about her?"

Rocket could play dumb. Ask who was the *her* Copper was referring to. But why waste his energy? The clock was ticking and he was itchy as fuck to make sure Chloe was protected.

"Yes. Mentioned seeing me with her a few times."

Even through his full beard, the thinning of Copper's pressed lips was evident. As was the angry glint in his eyes. "What happened to just following her to make sure she was safe?"

"It started that way, but...shit." He ran a hand down his face.

"Fuck, Rocket. You know you gotta bring her in now, right?"

He almost laughed out loud at the thought of asking Chloe to come to the clubhouse. That was going to fly as high as a lead balloon. But it didn't matter. Nothing mattered beyond keeping her safe. She could hate him and his brothers all she wanted, she was coming to the clubhouse and he'd protect her. Esposito was capable of things that made what happened to her before look mild. Just being on Esposito's radar put her in great danger. And nothing would touch her on Rocket's watch. He'd happily take out any man who made her so much as stub her toe.

"I know. I already sent a prospect to watch her house until I got there. I'll call her on the way. Might be a little bit. She's not exactly a fan of the club."

Copper's snort was full of disgust. "Good luck with that, brother. Better you than fucking me."

As he left the clubhouse, Rocket dialed Chloe's number. No answer.

Two seconds later his phone rang. "Yeah?" he said when he saw Thunder's number. He'd been a prospect for a few months and was proving his worth.

"She ain't home, Rock."

Well, shit.

"Thanks, Thunder. Stick around a while and let me know when she shows up."

She barely went out during the day. Where the fuck was she? Could Esposito have her already? No, he'd make Rocket look over his shoulder for a few days before trying something. It was all part of his mind games. Let the club sweat knowing he could pop up any place at any time.

Chloe was probably meeting with a client. Hopefully she'd show in the next few minutes. In the meantime, Rocket fired up his bike and rode off after his brothers to collect a group of ladies who were not going to appreciate being on lockdown.

Though the ol' ladies were going to react a hundred times better than Chloe would.

CHAPTER FIFTEEN

Chloe navigated the shopping cart through the bakery section without really seeing the loaves of bread she'd intended to choose from. She was too busy trying to combat the swell of panic.

She was having dinner with Logan.

Logan. A man. A man she'd been sleeping with, and had formed an unconventional but strong emotional bond to. To a normal person, cooking dinner for an interesting man wasn't exactly a newsworthy event. For Chloe?

Well it might as well be the headline of the year. Not the dinner part, not even the fact that he'd have to be uncuffed for them to share the meal. There was something else she had planned for the evening.

Tonight, she wanted to try something with Logan without handcuffing him to the bed. She wanted him to touch her. Put his fingers on her and in her, and make her come that way.

She had to try it if there was any hope of ever having a semblance of a normal sex life. And she was pretty sure she'd never find a man who made her feel safer and more protected than Logan. Without even knowing what had happened to her, he was extremely protective. She'd never felt better than when Logan was with her. Those feelings had bolstered her confidence and given her the ability to venture out on her own a time or two without panic attacks. Hence this solo shopping trip.

Chloe laughed out loud drawing a few curious stares from fellow shoppers. It was one thing to be crazy in her own head, but completely another thing for the world to see her insanity. With a sheepish smile for an elderly gentleman, she scurried out of the bakery, search for French bread forgotten.

She eyed the wine section and veered her cart in that direction. Liquid courage might be the only thing to quell her nerves. As she turned toward the reds, feminine laughter had her turning toward a group of women loading a cart with bottles.

They seemed close, heads together as they looked at a bottle one of the women held. At first guess, she'd have wagered they were sisters, but the differences in their looks were too vast to make them related in that way.

"Put it in the cart," the tallest of them said with a pout. She had a fierce look about her. A long black braid hung down the center of her back, nearly brushing her backside. "Can't believe you all get to float away on wine while I have to drink freakin' chocolate milk." She patted her stomach while another of the women, this one short with curly blonde hair, rubbed her back.

Pregnant, maybe.

A smile spread across Chloe's face. Must be nice to have a close group of girlfriends like that. Even before her kidnapping, Chloe hadn't had a group of girls she was quite that tight with.

"All right," another of the women said. Her back was to Chloe. "Let me grab a second bottle of this one. I think I'm gonna like it." She turned toward the display, hand outstretched and froze statue still the moment her gaze landed on Chloe.

Shit.

Shit.

Everything inside Chloe screamed *run, go, move*, but she was rooted in place as though bolted to the ground.

Stephanie.

Wife, or girlfriend, or—what had she called it—ol' lady to one of the Hell's Handlers bikers. Not the one who'd rode her away from her personal hell, but a biker all the same. A few weeks after Chloe had been released from the hospital, Stephanie had paid her a visit. Checking in on her to see how she was handling the ordeal. Apparently, Stephanie had also been a victim of the Gray Dragon's cruelty. At least that's what she'd claimed. Chloe had the impression the visit was more to check on whether she'd run her mouth to the cops, or her family, or a shrink. Even though the messenger was a cute and friendly woman who could somewhat relate to Chole's experience, she had always wondered if the visit had a more sinister undertone. Did they have eyes on her? Would something mysteriously happen to her if she disobeyed their order of no police?

You can thank the Handlers for this. She'd never forgotten Lefty's last words to her.

Stephanie's visit was the one and only time she'd heard from or seen anyone associated with the Hell's Handlers and she was more than happy to keep it that way. But here Stephanie was. In Chloe's town. One of the women laughing with her girlfriends as though she didn't have a care in the world. White hot jealousy joined her dread. Why couldn't that be her? And more importantly, why the hell were they in her grocery store?

Stephanie broke from her stupor first. Gently setting the bottle of wine in the cart, she said something to her friends that led to the other three sets of eyes turning her way. Each had a curious, but kind look on their face.

With a welcoming smile, Stephanie made her way over to Chloe. "Hey," she said softly. "This okay? Me talking to you?"

Clearing her throat, Chloe found her voice. "Oh, uh…it's fine. I guess."

It's so not fine.

Stephanie let out a quiet laugh. "You don't sound very convincing."

Chloe ran a hand through her hair, cursing internally when her fingers shook. "I'm just surprised to run into you."

"Me too. You look good," Stephanie said. "How are you doing?"

"Thank you. I'm doing pretty good." Ahh, awkward small talk. Who didn't love it?

The women stared at each other for a moment then laughed at the same time.

"Okay, so this is uncomfortable, huh?" Stephanie said, wrinkling her nose.

"Yeah, it kinda is."

"Hey!" Stephanie brightened. "We're about to check out then grab a drink at that hipster coffee shop next door. You should join us."

If it was possible for someone's heart to completely stop beating without killing them, Chloe would have sworn hers did. Hang out with them? While a bunch of biker ol' ladies stared at her and wondered how the poor girl who was gang raped was coping. "Um, I'm not sure." What she wanted to say was, Hell no!

Had the club sent her? Would she be walking into some kind of ambush? No, it was broad daylight in a crowded shopping center. Maybe she should go. Maybe if they saw she was of absolutely no threat to them, the MC would leave her alone. Or, maybe this was a total coincidence and Stephanie was genuine.

"Look," Stephanie said, leaning close and dropping her voice "None of them know who you are. I promise."

She stared at the blonde woman who was either sincere or deserved an Academy Award for her performance. God, she hated how she had no choice but to question every word out of the woman's mouth.

"I'll say we know each other from when I lived in DC. We're a fun bunch. Take a load off for an hour and have a calorie bomb disguised as a fancy coffee with us. I promise no one knows anything."

Glancing up, Chloe couldn't stop her puff of laughter, nervous though it may be. Stephanie's three friends all stared at wine bottle labels like they held the secret to eternal youth. "They aren't very good at being stealthy."

"Yeah, they're a nosy buncha bitches," Stephanie said but her tone was filled with affection. "Love 'em like sisters though."

"Um, is your...uh, sorry, I forget his name. Is your boyfriend with you?" Chains and a monster truck couldn't drag her into the coffee shop if the bikers were around.

"Nope just us girls today. I promise it'll be a biker free zone."

One more peek at the other women who weren't even pretending to hide their eavesdropping anymore and Chloe sighed. They all waved at her and made their way over, smiles on their faces. "All right. Thank you. Coffee sounds good." She'd go, show them their club was safe from her, and maybe gather some information of her own.

"Yay!" Steph said as she gave Chloe a quick hug. "Guys, this is Cl—Claire. We know each other from back in the day in DC."

Man, Stephanie could act like no one's business. Something to remember if they continued to hang out. Which they would not. A new friendship wasn't worth running into any of the Hell's Handlers.

"Hi!" Chloe said with a small wave and all the smoothness of gravel.

"Claire, these are my girls. That's Izzy," Stephanie said, pointing to the tallest woman with the badass braid. "And this is Shell and Toni." She pointed to the curly haired blond and then the final girl, just a few inches taller than Shell with brown hair. "Toni owns the diner in Townsend. Have you been there?"

"I have! It's been a few years, though. And, I'm sorry but I don't remember seeing you there."

"Yeah," Toni said. "I've only been at the helm for about a year. So, we checking out or what? I need some caffeine."

And just like that, the women accepted Chloe. Twenty minutes later, still missing the bread she'd planned to serve alongside her steak and potato meal, she found herself having a blast with four biker chicks. She'd expected thinly disguised questions about her attack designed to ferret out what she'd told the police. But the conversation never ventured close to her kidnapping. True to her word, Stephanie had the girls believing they were friends from a while back.

Chloe discretely checked her phone. She'd give it a few more minutes before she'd beg off and head home to prepare her meal for Logan. Placing the phone down, she tuned back into the conversation at hand.

"Please don't make me tell the story," Shell begged, face buried in her hands.

"Oh, you're telling it," Izzy replied as she took a bite of a giant chocolate chip cookie. The woman was in fact pregnant, though you could barely tell, a fact Shell seemed to hate her for. "If you don't tell it, I'm telling it and you don't want me to do that. I'll probably throw in some extra stuff I make up for shits and giggles."

Chloe snorted. Izzy was a trip and it'd be hilarious to witness her raising a baby. Hilarious for these women. She sure wouldn't be around them after this coffee break. This hanging with the bikers' women was a one-shot deal. It's not like she had plans to go to Townsend in the next ten years and one of the women mentioned they didn't make it out this way often. Just came to check out this newish coffee shop.

"Okay, fine." Shell dropped her hands and stuck her tongue out at Izzy, which had the table giggling yet again.

Chloe sipped her frothy drink that tasted more like a warm chocolate milk shake than coffee, but it was delicious.

"So," Shell began, "Beth, my four-year-old daughter," she said to Chloe. "Beth keeps coming in our room in the middle of the night. Ever since Copper moved in, she's totally fascinated with him being in the house and sleeping in the bed with me." She rolled her eyes and turned to Chloe again. "We're getting ready to move out of my itty-bitty house into something bigger. If you knew Copper, you'd know nothing about him was small."

The other women snickered.

"Hey," Shell said with a shrug. "What can I say? I'm blessed."

"Will you get on with the story already?" Toni said, tossing a crumpled napkin at Shell.

"Sorry, sorry. So we've had to start locking the door when we"—she waved her hand around—"you know."

"Fuck. When you fuck." Izzy said.

"Seriously?" Shell fired back.

"I don't know, it's your story." Izzy was doing a terrible job hiding her laughter which had the rest of them starting up again.

Man, Chloe would love to be part of this group. Too bad they were involved with a bunch of criminals who may or may not have something to do with her kidnapping. She frowned. Something didn't quite sit right. These women were strong, independent, not any kind of beaten down or degraded possession like she'd heard of ol' ladies. Hard to imagine any of them being with men who abused women. But Lefty clearly told her the Handlers were to thank for what he did to her. Could men treat *their* women okay but order the kidnapping and rape of others? If she didn't have the horrifying memories as proof, she might not believe it possible.

"Okay shut up and let me finish. So the other night we were —"

"Fucking," Izzy said.

Everyone glared at her.

"What? I'm not saying making love. That shit's not happening."

"Okay, fine, we were fucking," Shell said way too loud, drawing the attention of a stern-faced older woman reading at the table next to them. With a grimace Shell lowered her voice. "We were *fucking* and there was a pounding on the door. It was Beth and she was mad. I mean hopping angry at us. She just kept screeching about how it was unfair, and how we didn't like her, and how we were mean."

The table had quieted as they all waited for the outcome of the story.

"She pretty much killed the mood, at least for the moment, so I tossed on some clothes and unlocked the door. She marched her sassy little four-year-old self in the room, looked at the television then at us, and said, 'What did you do with it?'. Neither of us had any idea what she was talking about. Then she said, 'I know what you were doing in here.' By now, Copper was laughing his ass off, and I thought I was about to have to call a therapist for my scarred child. When I asked her what she thought we were doing, she said we were watching the Lion King without her and she was very angry at us."

Toni's forehead drew down as she blew on the black coffee in her oversized mug. She made up for the low-calorie drink with that plate sized chocolate chip cookie. "The Lion King?"

"Yep," Shell replied, popping the *p*. "She said could hear all the wild animals from her room. There was a lion growling, a hyena laughing, and a monkey going 'ooo ooo, ahh ahh.' She then crossed her arms and demanded to know why we turned off the TV."

"Oh, my God," Toni said, trying so hard not to laugh that she snorted quite loud.

Izzy's face was turning red and her eyes leaked.

Stephanie held her napkin over her mouth but her shaking shoulders gave her away.

With a roll of her eyes, Shell said, "Go ahead. Laugh your asses off."

And they did. Even Chloe.

"Wait, wait!" Stephanie said waving her hands in the air. "Which one were you? No, let me guess. You were the hyena, right?" They all dissolved into hilarity once again.

"She totally was!" Toni said, tears leaking from the corners of her eyes. "And Copper—oh, my God I can hardly breathe—Copper was the monkey! Ooo ooo, ahh ahh." She lost it in a fit of hilarity.

"Holy crap," Chloe said once she was able to breathe again. "You guys are hilarious. I'm so glad I joined you." She bumped Steph with her shoulder. "Thanks for the invite."

As Steph smiled at her, she found she truly meant the words. Aside from her time with Logan, this was the most fun she'd had in ages.

"Anytime, sister, anytime."

Chloe scooted her chair back. "I should probably get going. I've got a dinner thing I'm cooking for tonight, and I need to get my groceries home." Just as she was about to say her goodbyes to the women, the bell over the door jangled.

"Mav!" Steph said with a beaming grin.

For one quick flash, Chloe felt a sharp pang of envy. How wonderful it must be to have a man who could make her light up just at the sight of him.

Oh shit...Stephanie's man was...Maverick. One of the Hell's Handlers. Chloe's hands started to shake and her breathing sped as though she'd run miles. She gripped the edge of the table to keep the group from noticing.

Still grinning like a loon, Stephanie said, "Mav, what are you —uh oh, that's not a good face. What's wrong?"

Chloe's head snapped up, and her gaze landed on four very large, very serious, and very sexy bikers making their way to the table.

The Hell's Handlers. Shit. She stood on rubbery legs, prepared to flee until a fifth biker came through the door. "Let's get moving," he barked to the group.

Chloe's jaw dropped and a strangled sound fell out. Everything she'd experienced during those horrifying forty-eight hours came stampeding back to her from the moment she woke up in her trunk, to the assault, to the agonizing motorcycle ride to the hospital. The burden of pain and shame returned as though the kidnapping happened minutes ago instead of months.

"Shit," Stephanie said. She'd turned away from her ol' man and was biting her lip as she stared at Chloe. "Chloe, I had no idea they'd be here. I swear it." Her eyes widened. "Chloe? Are you okay?"

She couldn't answer Stephanie to save her life. Her mouth had gone completely dry and her throat had constricted so tight she couldn't even squeak.

The late-coming biker approached the table. Chloe could barely process what she was seeing. He was out of the dress shirt and pants, and wearing faded denim and a leather vest. A chain hung around his neck and rings adorned two of his fingers. Gone was the polished look, replaced by a far more casual style. Almost grungy.

He was one of *them.*

A biker.

Logan was one of the Hell's Handlers.

Her entire body began to tremble like a leaf in a category five hurricane. Try as she might, she had no control over the convulsing of her muscles.

"We good?" he asked as he reached the table. His gaze hit her then a wide-eyed expression of shock that should have been comical crossed his face. He let out a harsh curse. Last weekend she'd have said Logan was unflappable. Right now, the man was beyond flapped. "Chloe," he said, blinking and looking to Stephanie as though she would provide the answer to why they were in the same place at the same time. Oh, and with all his biker buddies present, of course.

Logan was a biker.

Like gears slamming into place, Chloe heard the pieces of the puzzle connecting in her head. From the very first time she'd laid eyes on Logan in the bar, something about him was vaguely familiar.

Even though she'd never seen her savior's face, she knew it then. Logan was the man who had rescued her from the hotel room.

He'd seen her at her very worst.

He knew who she was all along. Knew who she was when he approached her in the bar. He'd lied. She'd broken every one of her rules, leapt outside her comfort zone, and given the man her trust. And he'd lied to her at all stops along the way. The sense of betrayal and mortification was almost suffocating. She had to get the hell out of there.

"Chloe—" he started.

"No!" she shouted as her stomach churned like a washing machine. She backed up, holding her hands out toward him off. When her next step had her chair crashing to the ground, she stumbled around it and spun. Two running steps had her nearing the side exit. Her knees wobbled, her vision went fuzzy, her breath came in ragged gasps, but she focused on that exit sign with nothing but the thought of escape in mind.

As she continued toward freedom, she thought she heard Stephanie call her name.

With only a few feet separating her from the exit, a strong hand closed around her upper arm at the same time a familiar scent invaded her senses.

Logan.

How could she have been so stupid?

"No!" she yelled again as he jerked her back around. Why wasn't anyone helping her? She was being attacked in the middle of a coffee shop and not a damn soul was helping.

She had to get away. She struck out wildly, aiming for whatever she could hit, but he wrapped her in a bear hug from behind, ending her pathetic attempt to fight him off. "Please, don't," she said as he started to walk her toward the others.

"Jesus, Chloe, I'm not going to fucking hurt you. I would never hurt you."

But he had. The pain cut so deep it nearly sliced her in two.

Chloe could barely process what was happening. Her brain screamed with so much fear she couldn't think. All she knew was she needed to get away. She tried to suck in a monster breath, prepared to scream the place down, but the air got stuck in her throat. It was then she realized how dizzy she was and how shallow her breaths had become.

"I can't..." She wheezed a whistling sound. "I can't b-breathe."

Logan's hold immediately slackened, and the next thing she knew a chair hit the back of her legs and he was shoving her down into it. A gentle hand clasped the back of her neck, guiding her head between her knees.

"Slow your breathing, baby," Logan whispered in her ear causing her to focus on slowing the choppy, rapid gasps.

"P-please l-let me g-go," she managed to get out around the gasps.

"I can't do that." Logan said, and she'd swear she heard sadness in his voice. But that didn't make sense.

You can thank the Handlers for this.

She hadn't thought it could get any worse than the kidnapping. But with the group of scowling bikers frowning down at her, she had the feeling shit hadn't gotten anywhere near the fan yet.

CHAPTER SIXTEEN

"You need to move," Rocket growled down at Stephanie where she stood sentry outside his own goddammed room. It'd been three hours since Chloe arrived at his clubhouse. Three hours since he witnessed her lose her mind with panic at the mere sight of him. Weeks of progress undone in a matter of seconds, all because he was trying to protect her from a threat she had no idea existed.

Fucking Esposito deserved to die almost as much as Lefty.

"Look, Rocket, I don't know what the hell is going on here, but she took one look at you and freaked. You have any idea how hard it was to convince her to come back here? I thought I was going to have to get Izzy to slug her and drag her unconscious body here, which given her history would have probably made her have a complete breakdown. After begging for a half hour, Izzy and I were finally able to make her understand there was a credible threat to the club and her association with you put her at risk. I swore on my life no harm would come to her here and that this is the safest place for her. Don't you dare break my promise and hurt her further."

"She's stronger than you think," he said, giving her his most lethal glare.

A former FBI agent, Steph didn't cower easily. She glared right back up at him.

"Swear to fucking Christ, Stephanie, if you don't move I will toss your ass—"

"Wanna tone it down a bit, brother?" Mav's furious voice broke through Rocket's red haze. Shit, his brother was gonna rip him a new one for trying to intimidate his ol' lady like that. And rightfully so.

Rocket stepped back, running a hand through his hair. Ever since he'd walked in that damn coffee shop and spotted Chloe, he'd been spiraling out of control.

Mav's shoulder slammed into Rocket as he made his way to Stephanie. It was the least he deserved for speaking to her the way he had.

"You good, babe?" Mav asked.

"Totally fine. He's not as scary as he thinks."

Mav grunted, clearly not ready to join Team Rocket.

"Shit. Sorry, Steph. I just need to talk to her." This time, Rocket tried for genuine instead of asshole.

She cocked her head. "I don't get it, Rocket. You said she never saw your face. She shouldn't have known who you were on sight. What's going on?"

Mav may have been shitty over the way his ol' lady was being treated, but he was smart enough not to let that interfere with club business. "Hey, babe, why don't you go downstairs and hang with Izzy and Shell? I think they're making some food."

Folding her arms, she turned her displeasure on her ol' man. "Seriously? You're sending me off to the kitchen?"

Mav whispered something in her ear that had her rolling her eyes, but she nodded then gave him a quick hard kiss. "Don't fucking scare her," Steph warned, jabbing her finger in Rocket's face. "You look like you're about to rip the heads off a bunch of puppies."

Scare her. Shit, there was only one person scared and it was him. Terrified she'd order him out of her life forever. Not that he'd listen. No matter what, he wasn't stepping away from her until Esposito had been dealt with and Chloe reclaimed her life.

Even if today set her back. Now that he knew what her skin felt like against his, what she tasted like, and how her face glowed when she came, his obsession with Chloe had morphed into a full-on addiction. One he couldn't walk away from.

"You gonna stand in my way too?" Rocket asked Mav who now stood in Steph's place, arms folded, and legs spread.

Lifting his hands in surrender, Mav shook his head. "I ain't looking to get a bullet between my eyes, brother. Just didn't like the way you were talking to my woman. Want to make sure you get that. Have at her." He stepped away from the closed door. "Be warned, if you upset Chloe, Steph will probably recruit Izzy to go for your balls. My woman's like a mother hen around that one." He inclined his head toward the closed door.

Rocket winced. Steph would unman him if he hurt her friend. Izzy would do it for fun. Hell, she'd probably bronze his nuts and wear them around her neck. The woman was positively bloodthirsty now that she was carrying Jig's spawn.

Mav whistled a cheerful tune which faded down the hallway until Rocket was completely alone. Church started in an hour, so he needed to get his ass downstairs soon, but he couldn't leave things with Chloe so fucked up.

After two sharp knocks, he entered without waiting for an invite.

Chloe sat on his bed, huddled in the corner with her chin resting on drawn up knees. Her face was pale, making her auburn hair and green eyes even more striking. Resting just beyond her feet, a sandwich sat untouched as did the glass of Bourbon Stephanie brought her.

This was the second time he'd walked into a room to find a defeated Chloe. Sure, the first incident was a million times worse than this one, but he fucking hated the pattern forming here.

She lifted her head, eyes shrinking to slits as he stepped into the room. He gave her a moment to take him in. This was the first time she was getting a full-on view of who he really was as opposed to the role he'd been playing in her presence. Her narrowed gaze traced every inch of him, lingering on the patches covering his worn cut. "Rocket," she stated, the name sounding like a revolting taste in her mouth.

He nodded. "My road name. A nickname," he added when her forehead wrinkled.

"Why?"

"Leftover from my days as a Marine. I had a knack with weapons. Explosives especially." He shrugged. The name hadn't been his choice, but the club liked it, so it stuck.

She huffed out a bitter laugh. "So that much was true? You really were in the Marines?"

Ouch.

Her tone was heavy with accusation. Any ground he'd gained over the past weeks had been obliterated in the blink of an eye. One look at him, at who he really was, and Rocket fell even further back than square one.

"I was."

"Am I a prisoner?" she asked in a flat voice, staring out the window at the woods that stretched for miles behind the clubhouse.

What? A prisoner? "Fuck no. I thought Steph explained it to you. You're here so the club can protect you." He balled his fists to keep from reaching for her, though denying that need made his insides coil into a tight knot.

"Protect me?" she asked with another harsh laugh as though being helped by his club was the most foreign concept imaginable. "Please, after all the other lies, you can at least spare me this protection bullshit."

Well, shit. He deserved that.

He could see her walls erecting, blocking him out. Well that wasn't happening. He wouldn't stand for it. In two long strides, he reached the bed. The moment his ass hit the mattress, Chloe curled in an even tighter package. Her eyes were so guarded, so wary, Rocket's chest ached.

Rocket

Death was too good for Lefty. Though he couldn't blame everything on the motherfucker. He'd done plenty himself to fuck her up.

"Chloe."

Once again, she fixated on the woods outside the window.

"Baby, please look at me."

She did, her angry expression doing nothing to alleviate his conscience. "Don't call me that," she said with heat. "I know who you are now. The fucking charade can stop."

Damned if he knew why that word set her off, but that was a conversation for another day. They had a larger mountain to scale before they could get to his use of endearments. He could see he wasn't getting anywhere until they addressed the elephant in the room. "You know I'm the one who rescued you."

This time her laugh was empty, a hollow sound. "Rescued. That's fucking rich. You can thank the Handlers for this," she said, robotic and monotone as she turned away again.

"What?" Thank the Handlers for what?

"That's what he said." Her gaze never left the thick forest, green now that spring had returned to Tennessee. "The very last thing he said to me. While he was..." She swallowed, then cleared her throat. Now she was looking at him. Straight on, gauging his reaction. "When Lefty was raping me, he said, 'You can thank the Handlers for this.'"

Lefty. His eyes fell closed as he absorbed the impact of her statement. No wonder she lost her shit when the lot of them waltzed into the coffee shop like they owned the fucking place. This entire time she'd thought the Handlers had a hand in her assault. The thought of her fearing him in such a way, of her thinking he condoned Lefty's actions shattered the remaining pieces of his heart.

Fuck death. Lefty wouldn't be getting death until Rocket was good and done with him. He was going to revel in each scream, each plea for mercy the motherfucker made. And he'd scream.

They always did.

"Then you showed up, Rocket." Again, she said his road name like it was poison on her tongue. "I had no idea why you took me out of there and to the hospital. Still don't. But you did. You saved me. And I gave the police a bogus story, like you asked. Mostly because I was afraid your club was involved. Even though you were so gentle with me. And as much as I was hurting and terrified, for those few moments on your bike I felt safe. But Lefty's words were right there. Whispered in my ear over and over." She shivered and Rocket fought the desire to hold her. "I didn't want to know what else could happen if I went against the big bad bikers. Her voice hitched and Rocket swore his hardened insides softened to mush. He wanted to gather her in his arms and promise no man would touch her as long as he was fucking breathing. But she'd probably gut him at this point.

"Chloe, I never would have hurt you. I'm not like him. The Handlers are not like him," he said.

It was as though she hadn't heard him speak. "And then Stephanie came to see me." Her recounting was flat, emotionless without a flicker beyond a neutral expression on her beautiful face. "It didn't make sense. If you guys wanted to scare me into keeping my mouth shut, why send a woman who was sweet and kind? I had no idea what to think, so I just kept to myself and avoided Townsend for all I was worth. I didn't know how the MC was involved, just that you were. Then I met a man named Logan. A man who—" Her voice grew wistful right before a sob caught in her throat. "A man who turned out to be a fucking liar."

Rocket hung his head. "Shit," he ground out. Every word grated on his brain a million times worse than nails on a chalkboard. Though any of the Handlers would have given up their patch to keep a woman from suffering what Chloe endured, it was at least in part the club's fault. Chloe deserved the truth, as much as it killed him to speak it. "The club got word through a contact that a woman, you, was kidnapped. Lefty had been up to that shit for a while, so we were on the lookout for any abduciton reports. The club was able to get our hands on footage of the guys abducting you from the parking lot." He ran a palm down his face as the memory of that recording played through his mind. He'd been drawn to her. Even then. That tape was the reason he'd been the one to rescue her. He'd practically begged for the job. "I'd give anything to bring the two fuckers who kidnapped you back to life. I'd love nothing more than to rip them apart with my bare hands. Won't even tell you my plans for Lefty."

She snorted. "Get in line."

His lips twitched. There she was. The feisty woman who'd left him cuffed to a bed a few weeks ago. "I'm going to kill Lefty," he said to her startled expression. Cards were falling all over the table now. Before this day was over, she'd know exactly what kind of man she'd been sleeping with the past few weeks.

"Lefty's gang, the Gray Dragons, were enemies of my club." Every ounce of Chloe's attention was trained on him and now it was his turn to avoid eye contact. Admitting his club's role in her fate was harder than he ever imagined. "Our president, Copper, took a few guys to meet with Lefty. See if he could convince him to release you. At the time, Copper was trying to avoid a bloody war. Lefty didn't want war either, so he claimed. He'd just taken over the Gray Dragons and was working to build up the gang. Copper gave him until the end of that day to deliver you to the motel room completely unharmed or we'd rain hell on him."

"Lefty delivered you. Had no choice. Copper would have gone after him, but he hurt the fuck outta you before he did it. It was a big fuck you to Copper. Because he knew Copper wouldn't start a war if you were in the motel and alive."

Her lips rolled in and her head moved up and down as understanding set in. "Even though he didn't do exactly as your president said, I was alive and your club wasn't going to start a war just because he beat and raped me."

He winced. Christ, it sounded so heartless. Shame washed over him. He'd done some heinous shit in his day, much justified in his mind, but plenty that didn't live up to even his own loose moral code. Nothing though had ever made him feel shame, until he had to admit to Chloe his club had failed her. "I didn't agree with his decision," he said. "And maybe had the others seen you that night, they'd have sided with me, but I was out voted. We called getting you back alive a victory and let Lefty go about his business until we found out he had a barn full of underage girls."

"So your club didn't order him to kidnap me?"

"Fuck no. Copper would strip the patch off any member who harmed an innocent woman. Trust me, that's a fate worse than death for any of my brothers."

Trust him. Like that would happen anytime soon. All he could do was hope and be forthright.

"Has the club been keeping tabs on me ever since you found me?" She was still tucked tight into herself, but a bit of color returned to her cheeks. She no longer looked like a light breeze would take her out.

"We did at first. For a week or two. To make sure the cops bought your story."

"Oh."

Admitting this could be a huge mistake, but after all she'd been through, the least she deserved was the unvarnished truth. "But I've been watching you on my own."

Her eyes bugged wide and she let her knees drop down, ending up in a cross-legged position. "Y-ou've been following me?"

He nodded.

"For how long?"

Their gazes connected. Something crackled between them. Rocket had no fucking clue what to call it. He'd never experienced it before. It was some kind of magnetic pull. A need to protect her, to be near her, to comfort her. He felt compelled to answer honestly even if she wouldn't like his response. "Since the beginning. I'd drive by, make sure your car was there. When you started going out on Friday and Saturday nights I tailed you."

She gasped. "You followed me to the bars? How many times?"

He just stared at her.

"E-every time?"

"Yes."

"W-why? I assumed you ran into me by accident that first time."

"Because I couldn't stay away."

He saw her lips begin to form the word why once again, but she changed her mind with a sharp shake of her head. "Fuck all this. I want someone to take me home. Stephanie or Izzy."

His heavy sigh caused her eyes to narrow once again. "I can't force you to stay here, but I'm asking you to give the club a few days to work some things out. The threat Stephanie mentioned is very real."

"Lefty? Because I'd love a shot at that piece of shit."

He worked to hide his grin as he shook his head. "No. Someone from my past wants something I'm not willing to give him. He was spotted in town and isn't above using people I care about to get what he wants from me. Club's just making sure all the ol' ladies are safe. He saw me with you, so I'm asking for a few days to deal with it."

"People you care about? Guess I'm off the hook then." She rose to her knees, hands on her hips. "I'm going home if I have to walk the whole goddamn way. Now get the hell out of this room."

She had questions. Was curious. Her curiosity was there in her searching eyes and the way she chewed her lower lip in frustration, but she was fighting the urge to ask him. Whether because she didn't want to have to deal with a story she might not believe or because she just plain hated his guts, he may never know.

He scooted off the bed, rose, and stared down at her. "I fucking care, Chloe. You think I'd let just any goddammed woman tie me to a bed and ride me like a damn stallion? And knowing how sweet that pussy is? Knowing how hard it squeezes my dick as you come? You think I'd give up taking control of that if I didn't fucking care? Don't fucking think so." *Let her chew on that for a while.*

Chloe's mouth dropped open and she hopped off the bed.

She shot forward, going toe to toe with him as though he couldn't snap her in half with his pinky finger. "Fuck you," she growled.

"Any time you want. Hell, I'll even bring the cuffs."

"Screw this. I'm leaving," she marched past him, heading for the door.

Shit! Could he have handled that any fucking worse? The woman drove him out of his mind. He caught her wrist as she was halfway out the door.

She spun, spitting fire with her eyes. Her mouth opened, no doubt to blast him once again.

"You can leave," he said. "But I'll follow. I'll stay out of your way, but I can't let you walk when there is a chance you could be hurt again."

Her chest heaved with the force of her fury.

"The club needs me here to help with this threat. If I'm gone, that's one less man around to make sure the problem is solved, and the rest of the women are protected. You may hate me and the men who run this club, but you don't hate the women. They're strong, and fierce, and have all overcome tremendous obstacles. They're good women who don't deserve this danger."

She didn't relax, but her shoulders slumped in defeat. "You play dirty."

"I'll do whatever I need to, to get you to stay."

"Fine," she spat out still facing the door. "A few days. That's it. And you stay the fuck away from me."

Shit. Guess that meant he wasn't going to be able to sweet talk her into letting him sleep beside her.

"If you make a list of some things you might need, I'll swing by your place and grab them for you."

Looking him straight in the eye, she said. "Don't bother. I don't need anything from you."

With a nod and a pit in his stomach, he walked around her and out the door. What else could he do? She'd left him no options.

She was done with him.

The question was, for how long?

CHAPTER SEVENTEEN

On the morning of the second day of wallowing in whoever's room she'd hijacked at the Handlers' clubhouse, Chloe was officially sick of herself, and ready to rejoin the real world.

Or the biker world as it would be.

Okay, the whole being ready part wasn't entirely true. Although she spent hours on end obsessing over every hour spent in Logan's presence, she hadn't come to terms with a few things.

The lies.

The fact that he'd been following her for a long time.

The fact that he'd slept with her. Repeatedly.

None of his actions made sense. Was she a charity case? Were his actions a product of guilt? Then, there were her personal feelings. A jumbled mess of conflicting emotions. Her rational brain was so furious over the lies, she couldn't see a way to move past them. Then there was the irrational side of her that spent every moment since she'd kicked him out wondering what he was doing and who he was with. Basically, she was a hot freaking mess in the head.

Aside from the few times Steph and Izzy brought her food, everyone had respected her insistence on being left alone. Until now. The slightly scary, pregnant Izzy had barged into the room a few seconds ago, following one sharp rap on the door, and pretty much dragged Chloe off the bed by her ankles. "Okay, princess, no more hiding out in the castle." She tossed some clothes Chloe's way. Declining Logan's—or rather Rocket's—offer of clothing had come back to bite her, not that she'd admit it to him. A few fumbling grabs kept the garments from landing on the rug. "You got five minutes to put that on and meet me in the room next door."

Chloe bristled as she dressed in the sports bra, tank, yoga pants, and running shoes. Princess? The last thing she was, was a freakin' princess. With a near snarl, she yanked the door open, stormed past Izzy, and into the room next to hers. It took everything in her to ignore the snickers from the Amazon warrior trailing behind her.

"Whoa," Chloe said as she stepped into what she'd assumed was going to be another bedroom. Instead, the large space had been cleared of all furniture save one overstuffed chair in the corner. Plush gym mats covered the floor from end to end. Someone had hung a heavy bag in one corner and a much smaller punching bag in the opposite corner. Izzy's ol' man, Jigsaw, was standing in the center of the room, also dressed for a workout.

"What's all this?"

"Your first lesson," Izzy said.

Jig gave his ol' lady a stern look then pointed to the chair. "Sit that tight ass down, baby."

Scowling, Izzy stomped to the chair and plopped down. "Happy?" Jig's back was to her, so she stuck her tongue out in a childish gesture Chloe never would have expected from her.

In a failed attempted to mask her chuckle, Chloe hid her mouth behind her hand.

"Love you too, babe," Jig said as he winked at Chloe. Behind his back, Izzy opened her mouth again.

"Uh, what am I doing here exactly?" Chloe rushed to say. The well-timed question had probably saved Jigsaw's life.

"Iz thought you might benefit from learning some self-defense."

Izzy cleared her throat—loudly.

With a roll of his eyes and a smirk for his woman Jigsaw said, "Sorry, Izzy likes to call it self-offense."

"Damn straight. Someone comes after you, you're not gonna defend yourself, you're going on the offensive to take the motherfucker out. We're not just gonna teach you how to break holds so you can run away. Forget that shit. We're going to teach you how to incapacitate a motherfucker so you can cause some serious fucking pain."

"The mother of my child, ladies and gentlemen," Jig said in a dry tone.

Chloe chuckled then a huge grin stretched her cheeks. Something deep within her soared at Izzy's description. Yes! The idea of taking someone out sent a rush of endorphins thorough her system. This was it. What she'd been missing. These skills would give her the same high she chased when dominating men. Hell, maybe she'd experience even more of a rush. She could already feel the promise of euphoria flowing through her veins like a drug.

"Before we get started, let me show you how to wrap your hands." Jig said. "I'll do one and you can try the other after you watch me. Okay if I touch your hand?"

Her gaze flew from where he held the wrap, up to his face. By now, everyone in the club probably knew precisely what had happened to her. For a split-second, shame and embarrassment shot through her. Who needed to give permission for someone to touch their hand in the most innocent way possible, while their pregnant significant other looked on no less? Oh yeah, she did. The girl who'd been violated.

But what she saw in Jig's face washed away all those negative feelings. There was nothing. No pity, no sorrow, no awkwardness or judgment. Just patience while he waited for the go-ahead to gear-up her hands. While she knew he only asked in deference to what had happened to her, the nonchalant way he acted made it seem as though he'd ask the same to anyone. He was so nonchalant, he might as well have been asking her to pass the salt.

Jig's chill attitude immediately set her at ease. "Yeah," she said. "Go for it." And she only felt one microsecond of discomfort when his hand first grazed hers.

Progress.

After he'd wound the wrapping around one hand, and she did a fairly decent job with the other, Jig ran her though a few warmup exercises. Izzy barked the occasional order from her throne, clearly not accustomed to being sidelined. Jig was patient and didn't seem to mind the interruptions.

"Okay, time to get down to business," he said, sliding big cushioned gloves onto her hands. Once he was done, he slipped his palms into black pads. "Without me teaching you any kind of technique at this point, I just want you to go to town and wail on the pads. Hard as you can. It's amazing for tension relief."

Chloe rotated her wrists, getting used to the feel of the gloves. "What if I hurt you?" She'd never done anything more that swat her brothers when they pissed her off. Punching someone was a foreign concept that didn't quite sit right.

"Trust me, girl, he can take it." Izzy's eyes gleamed, and Chloe had the distinct impression she wished they could change positions. "You won't hurt your hands either. Try whacking your fists together."

"I can do that." She banged her gloves into each other, barely noticing the impact. Huh. This could be fun. Turning her body sideways, she held up her gloved fists. "Like this?"

"Just like that. We'll worry about perfecting your form later." Jig lifted the pads. He was a handsome man. Dark brown hair, the same color beard, ink, and muscles galore. He'd be a perfect physical specimen if it weren't for an intricate scar on his cheek. There was a story there. A person didn't get that kind of extensive damage from a fingernail scratch. Chloe's scars may be on the inside, but they were there, and just as prominent as Jigsaw's. He looked into her eyes. "Let it fly, darlin'."

Chloe stared at his scar for one more second. She may never discover exactly how he got it, but knew in her soul he'd been where she had. He'd been helpless, at the mercy of a sadist, suffering through unimaginable pain. This, what he was offering her right now, he was doing it because it'd worked for him. Succeeded in helping him become what was obviously a man no one fucked with anymore.

That's what Chloe wanted. What she craved. The power and strength to keep others from ever thinking they could harm her. "Okay," she said. "Here goes." She cocked her arm and let her gloved fist collide with Jig's pad. "How was that?"

Izzy snorted. "Called you princess for a reason, didn't I?"

"Iz," Jig said, frowning at her. She just winked back at her man.

Chloe stared down at the fire-engine red gloves. Maybe they should scrap this whole idea. Just because the notion of being able to fight sent a surge of exhilaration through her didn't mean she was cut out for it. Wouldn't she have been able to fend off Lefty a bit better had a battle-drive been engrained in her?

Izzy's voice cut through her musing. "Sometimes it helps to picture someone's face on the pads. Someone you hate. Someone you want to hurt. Someone who hurt you." Gone was any teasing. All that remained was a serious recommendation that also reeked of personal understanding. But then she smirked. "Or someone who straight up pissed you off," she said with a sparkle in her eye. "I don't know. Maybe someone tall, growly, who doesn't say much. Rides a motorcycle."

Jig grunted and rolled his eyes.

Pressing her lips together, Chloe managed to keep from smiling. Mad as she was at him, Rocket's face wouldn't conjure the type of rage she needed to fuel this exercise. She shifted her focus to the pads. Lefty had a face she wouldn't forget any time soon. Or ever. It haunted her nightmares and lurked in every dark corner she walked past. Here was her chance to demolish him, if only metaphorically.

A tingling started in the base of her spine and crawled its way up to her shoulders. She rolled them, loosening the tension in her neck and straightening her posture. Crackles of energy flowed through her limbs making her feel strong, invincible.

There it was. The illusive high she chased on Friday and Saturday nights. The same buzz she experienced handcuffing a man to her bed and taking control. She smiled. Good thing there wasn't a mirror in this room. She had a feeling her grin was a bit evil.

Power. Dominance. Command. The upper hand.

Her drug of choice.

Lefty's face appeared on Jigsaw's pads.

Game on.

With a warrior's cry, Chloe hurled everything she had into beating on those pads. For long minutes, she threw punch after punch, as hard as her not very toned arms possibly could. Jig staggered on his feet, absorbing every single blow. Not once did he or Izzy speak. No encouragement, no critique. They just let her get it all out. With a final cry, Chloe connected with the pad one last time as her knees gave out. Breath heaving, she dropped to the mat. She rested her forehead on the cool vinyl, hands on either side of her head, enjoying the gallop of her heart.

Both Jig and Izzy remained quiet, giving her body and mind time to quiet. She had no idea how long she stayed curled up like a child, but when she got herself together, and rose to her knees, both her new friends were smiling at her with proud grins. Jig was right. That was some damn good tension relief.

"More," she said, rising on trembling legs. "I want to do more."

"Maybe tomorrow. You're going to be sore enough as it is." Jig started to remove one of the punch mitts.

"No!" Chloe bounced on the balls of her feet, pounding her gloves together. "I feel so good, so full of energy. Like I've had three Red Bulls in the last half hour. Teach me how to do this right."

Izzy threw back her head and laughed. "She caught the fever, babe. Looks like our girl won't be a princess for long."

Chloe locked eyes with Izzy, giving her a nod. A silent thank you, to her new friend for yanking her out of her funk and giving her an emotional and physical outlet for the fucked-up thoughts in her head.

"Let's do it," Jig said, but his attention was on something behind her.

Chloe glanced over her shoulder at the open door, and could have sworn she caught a glimpse of Logan passing by. But it couldn't be. He had made himself completely scarce in the time since she asked him to scram.

She missed his presence. Missed the intense way he looked at her and the feeling of safety when he was around. She also missed his body and the pleasure she'd found in him.

And that was terrifying. Because he wasn't Logan anymore, not really. Now he was Rocket. And she didn't know Rocket. She knew Logan, the sexy, brooding contractor who let her use his body to work out her issues. Rocket, the biker who told her he had fantasies of murdering Lefty was a mystery to her. And he hadn't been kidding. He was capable of killing, and she had a feeling Lefty's wouldn't be the first life he'd taken. Rocket lived in a world she was ignorant of, where women were kidnapped, and clubhouses put on lockdown.

Jig walked her through a series of strikes with occasional interjections from Izzy. Each time he touched her, a hand under her arm, a shift of her shoulders, the discomfort grew less and less. After a short time, she was able to completely ignore the fact a man had his hands on her and view it from a totally educational standpoint.

Chloe worked for hours with the couple, until she could barely lift her arms. Then, after a well-deserved shower, she spent a few hours with Shell and her adorable daughter Beth while the majority of the guys were out of the clubhouse. Felt good to leave her room, and even better to know she wouldn't run into Logan. Shell had assured her he was gone until the following day. That night, exhausted from the intense activity and emotionally drained, Chloe fell into a deep sleep right after dinner.

The next morning, as sore as if she'd been in a car accident, she returned to the makeshift gym an hour and a half before she was scheduled for another training session. She ran through everything Jig and Izzy had taught her again and again.

Once the badass duo joined her, Chloe pushed herself to the limit, reveling in everything they showed her. After another few hours, her muscles cramped with a fury, sweat ran in rivulets down her face, and she felt ready to collapse in the very best way. Her soul was soaring, and for the first time since she'd been kidnapped, she was too wrung out to feel fear or anxiety. Even when she had a man cuffed to the bed, she didn't have the peace she did now. Not only was she free from the grip Lefty had on her, she hadn't thought about Logan for the past few hours. Her mind was clear of everything but the combinations and deadly strikes Jig and Izzy taught her. That and the fantasy of sinking into a hot bath to ease her aches and pains.

"All right, hon, I think we need to call it a day. You're not gonna be able to fucking crawl out of bed tomorrow." Jig said, pulling off the punch mitts.

Panting, Chloe tried to wipe a damp lock of hair out of her eyes with her gloved hand. All she managed was to plaster the strands across her forehead. Whatever, didn't matter what she looked like. This was about impressing with her skills not appearance. "I'm good. I want to go a little longer."

Jig and Izzy exchanged a glance. Didn't matter if they wanted her to stop. Her body, her decision. And she wanted more. More of the burn, more of those delicious endorphins making her feel invincible.

"She's done."

The deep timbre of Logan's voice had her whirling around. He hovered in the doorway wearing a black T-shirt under his leather cut. Dark wash jeans covered those thick thighs and giant motorcycle boots housed his feet. Arms crossed and shoulder propped against the door, his assessing gaze drank her in. Today, she'd left off the tank and wore only a sports bra and tight workout leggings. It had been a few days since his laser-focus attention had been on her and she'd nearly forgotten how it made her feel stripped bare both emotionally and physically.

And damn him for looking so sexy. Now along with slapping him, she wanted to grab him and demand he bury his face between her legs.

It had been way too long since he made her come and her traitorous body didn't seem to care that he'd lied and betrayed her.

"Logan," she said as if he didn't know his own name. Heavy on the sarcasm, she added, "Sorry, I guess I need to get used to calling you Rocket."

He pushed off the wall and stalked toward her, his focus never wavering. There was a startling contrast between the man approaching her and the man she'd met as Logan. Rocket was scary as hell. The stare she felt like a caress when she'd first met him in the bar now seemed like an irritable glower. The tense way he held his body seemed as though he was one harsh word away from throwing down with whoever dared cross his path.

Chloe stood in the center of the room, limp and exhausted arms dangling at her sides.

"Uh, we're gonna jet," Izzy said, coming up behind Jig. "You really rocked it today, girl. Same time tomorrow morning?"

"Yeah," Chloe said unable to break away from Rocket's stare.

"Make it an hour later," Rocket said.

"How come?" Izzy asked in the most fake innocent voice Chloe had ever heard.

Jig snorted. Out of the corner of her eyes she saw Jig propel Izzy out the door with an arm around her shoulders. "When we get home, I'll show you exactly what he has planned for that extra hour," Jig murmured to her as he passed by.

Rocket

Izzy giggled. Actually giggled like a schoolgirl instead of a badass who could take a man out with the tail of that wicked braid she wore like a uniform. "Don't take any shit from him, Chloe," she called out as she slipped out of the room.

The two disappeared, leaving Chloe alone with Logan—er, Rocket—who she hadn't laid eyes on in days.

When he reached her, he lifted one of the gloved hands and moved as if to help her remove it. "To the club, I'm Rocket. You can call me whatever the fuck you want."

She yanked her arm out of his grasp. Despite her anger and the oppressive feeling of betrayal, her traitorous body still reacted to him as it always did. With lust and need. But they had shit to sort out and she couldn't afford the distraction of his hands on her.

He ran a finger down her arm leaving a trail of goosebumps. "When we're in bed, I'm Logan." His voice was smooth, warm liquid drizzling down her spine. For a split-second, her brain short-circuited before his words registered.

When they were in bed?

When they were in *bed together*?

The nerve of this asshole.

He'd lied to her. Tricked her. Deceived her. The one man she'd been beginning to trust, beginning to let her guard down around, took that gift of her trust and tossed it in the trash. He was out of his freakin' mind if he thought she'd be crawling into bed with him anytime soon.

Or ever.

Suddenly, her energy returned in the form of rage. It breathed new life into her tired limbs, chasing away the soreness, and giving her the need to dominate. The need for that high she'd been riding moments ago.

"Why are you here?" she asked, rising onto her toes and getting right in his face. "I said I didn't want to see you."

He remained calm though his eyes widened at her near snarl. "We have shit to work out."

Chloe laughed. "Shit to work out? Oh, you mean how you lied to me? Let me believe you were someone else. A harmless business owner."

His Adam's Apple rose and fell as he swallowed. "That's part of it."

"Or maybe you wanna talk about how I fucked you, what? Six? Seven times? Giving you more trust each time, and yet you still lied your ass off about who you were!" She was breathing heavy now, shouting the words at him. "You're no better than Lefty!" she yelled, knowing the words were both cruel and untrue as they left her mouth, but she was too far gone to take them back.

Logan however wasn't as inclined to let it roll off his back. He surged forward, towering over her, using his size to show her who really had the upper hand here. "You have no fucking idea the shit I'm capable of. The shit I've done." His nostrils flared and she was surprised he didn't breathe fire in that moment. "You'd have nightmares for a month if you knew. But don't you ever compare me to that motherfucking piece of shit."

She should have been terrified, would have been were it anyone else but him, but she wasn't. Because she trusted him. Despite it all she trusted him, and she believed everything he'd said to her a few days ago. She believed Lefty was an enemy of his club. Believed the Handlers didn't have anything to do with her kidnapping and rape. And she knew deep in her heart, he suffered over what she experienced. She may be a damn fool, but she wasn't afraid of the growling man who loomed over her.

And that infuriated her even more. Because she should hate him for lying to her. Those deceptions should have killed her faith in him. Her attraction to him.

But they didn't. He cared and wanted to protect her. Which made the deceit cut that much deeper.

And that made her angry.

Irrationally, pull-out-her-hair, howl-at-the-moon, blood-rushing-in-her-ears angry. With her two gloved hands, she shoved him out of her personal space. A small surge of power ran through her.

Logan smirked, his blue eyes sparkling. "You wanna hit me?"

Shoulders bunched, fists itching to do exactly as he asked, she took a step back. "Get out."

He shook his head. "Do your worst."

"Logan, get out."

He shook his head again.

"Log—"

He stepped forward. "No." There was a taunt to the calm word. An unspoken *come and get me.*

"Get out!" she cried as she charged forward, fists raised. Exactly as she'd done yesterday when she let loose on Jigsaw's punch mitts, she lost her shit on Logan.

On Rocket.

Over and over her gloved fists connected with him as he stood there absorbing the blows without a word or without fighting back.

Bam! Shot to the shoulder.

Bam! Jab to the gut.

Bam! A hook to his upper arm.

Again and again, she wailed on the man who'd given her the first hint of pleasure she'd experienced since being attacked, only to take it away with his untruths.

"You lied!" she screamed each time her fist bounced off his hard body. "You lied, you lied, you lied."

After what felt like hours, her screams turned to sobs. Without a thought for the techniques she just learned, Chloe drove her exhausted right arm forward, missing Logan by a mile. The momentum of her traveling arm unbalanced her and were it not for Logan's quick reflexes, she'd have crashed to the ground.

Instead, she found herself cradled against his chest and on the move.

"Put me down," she ordered. Damn her voice for sounding so weak in that moment. But she couldn't help it. She was tired. Completely drained from the intense physical activity.

And from days of holding onto her anger.

Months really. Ever since she'd been kidnapped, she'd had a knot of anger and hatred swirling just beneath her sternum.

"I can't do that," Logan said, moving freely as though she hadn't just punched him a hundred times.

"Where are we going?"

"My room," he said as they exited the makeshift gym and entered the room she'd occupied the last few days.

He set her down on the edge of the bed then sank to his knees at her feet. "W-what are you doing?" she asked as he lifted a gloved hand.

He didn't answer, just worked the glove off her hand, tossed it on the ground, then began unwinding the wrap.

Chloe had no idea what to do in that moment. The anger of moments ago had faded. Sailing out through a barrage of fists and accusations as she pummeled Logan. All that remained was a hollow emptiness in her chest.

Oh, and questions. So many questions. But in that moment, she wasn't sure she had the reserves to start firing inquiries at Logan. So she watched the gentle, almost tender way he held her hand as he unwound the rest of the long wrap.

"I'm sorry," he said as he lifted her hand, stroking his thumb over her reddened knuckles. "Sorry I lied and sorry I hurt you." He pressed his lips to her knuckles. "You overdid it. They'll be sore tomorrow."

As the rough pads of his fingers stroked over the back of her palm, she shivered. She searched his face, his eyes, looking for what, she wasn't entirely sure, but all she found was sincerity, remorse, and even pain. "Why?" she asked in what sounded more like a croak than her normal voice.

He sighed as he repeated the process on the second side, starting with removing the glove. "I'd been following you every

Friday and Saturday night. Watched you leave the bar with a different man each time." His gravelly voice filled with displeasure.

Unease slithered over her. Shit, what must he have thought of her, seeing her head to a motel with man after man?

"The first few times, I had no idea what you were doing, or why. I thought you were out of your fucking mind. After what you'd been through, to leave with men you didn't know?" He was tense as hell. Muscles bunched, his fists curled on his thighs. "Pissed me the fuck off."

Both hands free now, Chloe rubbed them together and swallowed. This man was dangerous. In the literal sense. If he wanted to hurt her, he could. And there wasn't a damn thing she could do to protect herself. Hell, chances were high the handcuffs she'd used to secure him to the bed were child's play to him. He probably could have snapped those headboard slats in two any damn time he wanted.

Yet, she didn't feel so much as a niggle of unease around him. Even now as his mood trended toward a darker side.

Rolling his shoulders, he seemed to calm somewhat. "I ran through every scenario in my head. Maybe you were dealing drugs, maybe it was a work thing I didn't understand. Maybe some kind of off-the-wall therapy. And of course, I wondered if you were fucking them. You became an obsession I eventually couldn't resist. So, I became one of your guys."

"It was only supposed to be the one time," he plowed on. "I vowed it would only be once. To find out exactly what you were doing. So what did it matter who you thought I was? You would have run from me had I been truthful." His gaze never wavered from hers as he gave her a truth she had no idea how to handle. "And then I had you. And you were so fucking brave. So fucking beautiful when you came. There was no way in hell I couldn't do it again. So I kept going. With you and with the lies."

Chloe's heart plummeted to the ground. It shouldn't have. Whatever this screwed-up relationship had morphed into, it started with her using him and him lying to her, not any kind of romantic notion. She had no right to be upset about his reasons for leaving the bar with her. But it still irked her. The woman in her wished he'd left with her because he wanted *her*. Not because he was curious about her odd behavior.

She was left with questions gnawing a hole through her gut. How was he not disgusted by her actions? By what she'd become since she was kidnapped?

CHAPTER EIGHTEEN

"I don't understand," Chloe stated, voice heavy with fatigue. "You've known the whole time. Every time we've been together." Water spilled from her eyes. Rocket rose from the floor, taking a seat next to her on the bed.

She didn't kick him off. That had to be a good sign. Chloe had paid attention to what Jig was teaching her. Her cathartic punch-fest might have been sloppy and wild, but it wasn't without some skill. He'd bear bruises for a good few days.

"Known what? What happened to you? I know how you were when I found you, but even I don't know the details of what happened." They'd never discussed it. But he knew she'd thought all her encounters with the men were anonymous. That the guys she took to that hotel room had no idea why she derived pleasure in dominating them. That they would assume it was just a kink. She never had to worry how they viewed her because they were clueless to what she'd been through.

But not him. Not only did he know what Lefty did to her, he was the one and only person, besides the medical team, who knew exactly how badly her body had been treated. Exactly how battered and abused she'd been.

Rocket caught the tears before they could track all the way down her cheeks. He cradled her face between his large palms, holding her head still so she couldn't turn away. She let him, and he sent up a small prayer of thanks for small favors. "Baby, I'm not going to say it doesn't matter or it's okay, because it matters and it's so far from fucking okay. Finding you that way fucked with my head. And yes, had it not been for that night I wouldn't know who you are or felt compelled to follow you, but I don't do shit I don't want to do. I'm a mean motherfucker, ask anyone. I followed you because I was drawn to you, and I was with you in that hotel room all those times because I wanted you. Because I think you're gorgeous, and I love your hands and this sexy as hell body all over me."

Her eyes fell closed and a strangled sob erupted from her. "But everything else," she whispered, shaking her head between his palms.

Rocket frowned and skimmed his hands down to her shoulders. He rubbed at the rock-hard tension bunching her small muscles. "What do you mean?"

"I mean you know what I did with all the men." She swallowed and stared at a point somewhere on his chest. "You know how many men I've been with. You know what a slut I've become. Jesus, Logan, I was raped and beaten. Now I go out and pick up random men to fuck twice a week. And I've been doing it for months. That's a lot of men. Even if I hadn't been raped, even if you hadn't seen what they did to me, everything that happened afterward makes me dirty, used. My head is so fucked up I've basically become a whore to scrape up some sense of peace for a few moments each week."

"Stop!" he barked. Christ, her own mind was beating the hell out of her worse than Lefty had. Rocket gently placed a palm over her mouth to halt her growing frenzy of self-loathing. Every one of those words was a knife stripping his soul bare. He wanted nothing more than to take every ounce of pain from her. Copper was right. He was a damn protector. This impotent feeling of being unable to save Chloe from the agony of what happened to her was akin to the helplessness he encountered when his friend's wife Elena killed herself. But the difference here was he still had a chance to help Chloe heal and find herself again. Never had he felt the desire to shield someone like he felt for Chloe. It was as high on his needs list as water, air, or shelter.

"Yes," he said. "I know the exact number of men you walked out of that bar with. And that means I know the exact number of men you cuffed to the motel bed. And yes, I'd like to rip the dick off each and every one of them. But never once did it even cross my mind that you are dirty, or easy, or a slut. Not because you were violated, and not because of the way you've coped since then."

Her red-rimmed, puffy eyes gazed at him with hope. Even sweaty and tear-stained, she was beyond beautiful to him. "But —"

He shook his head. "You need to get those thoughts out of your pretty head."

Chloe licked her dry lips nearly making him groan. The action shot straight to his dick. He was a sick fuck who couldn't even give her this serious conversation without wanting to feel that damn tongue lapping at his cock. "Logan, the number of men I've been with in the past few months would shock most people in polite society." As she spoke, she again averted her gaze as though too embarrassed to face him.

Snorting, he captured her chin between his thumb and forefinger. When she was once again facing him, he said, "First of all, fuck polite society. My brothers and I haven't lived in that world ever. I couldn't give a fuck about what anyone thinks of you, and I have no problem introducing anyone who gives you lip to our enforcer, Zach. He and Louie will make them wish they'd never been born."

Unable to turn away since he still held her chin captive, Chloe frowned. "I haven't met Louie."

"He's a bat. A Louisville Slugger to be exact. One Zach uses to help people see things from his perspective."

Chloe gasped, her eyes growing huge. She was so goddamned pretty.

"Baby, what you endured after Lefty kidnapped you would break most people. There's not a damn person alive who has the right to judge you for the way you're handling shit now."

"Logan," she whispered, scooting closer.

It was then he realized he'd had his hands on her for the past few moments. One on her face, the other still resting on her shoulder. He'd touched her more since they entered his room than he had the entire time he'd know her. And she seemed to be okay with it. Maybe because she was too distracted to notice.

"You think I don't get it? You think I don't understand what you're doing isn't about sex? You were raped," he said, pretending her flinch didn't gut him. "You were tied up, and men touched you against your will." Saying this and witnessing her pained reaction wasn't easy, but necessary. She had to understand that he didn't blame her for the way she'd been living recently. It was a product of trauma. Not who she was.

"The only time I've been able to breathe lately is when I have that feeling of control. Of power. It only lasts for a few minutes, but it's become vital to my surviving each week without completely breaking down."

He nodded. "I get it. You know I was in the Marines. When I separated, I was recruited by a private defense contractor because of certain skills I possessed. Babe, you wouldn't believe the shit I've seen. Worst of the worst. Fuck, you wouldn't believe the shit I've done. There's no script for how people are going to react when their ship is blown to fucking bits. All you can do is grab the nearest floating object and hold on for dear life. And that's what you've done."

"Even though I've always used protection that I've purchased myself, what I'm doing is not exactly a smart or healthy decision." Her fingers played with the patches on his cut. Over and over she traced the Sergeant at Arms patch below his name. She shrugged. "I know how risky it is. I just can't seem to stop myself."

He nodded. "You stopped over the past few weeks."

She stared at him. "Not really. Yes, I was only with you, but I was still handcuffing you to the bed. I've barely let you touch me at all. You have to admit it's still been more about me taking control than us having some kind of mutually pleasurable sex."

"You come though. Every time, multiple times." If he sounded smug, he couldn't help it.

Her face turned an adorable shade of red. "There is that."

"And you like it. Want more of it. More orgasms, not just psychological relief. Can you tell me the past few weekends have only been about the power and control?" Hell, he didn't give a shit if she wanted to tie him up and ride him every single time they were together. They both came. Him hard as hell, and for her, it was happening easier and with more abandon. Their sex may not have been about mutual pleasure in the beginning, but she was lying to them both if she didn't think what burned between them wasn't straight up desire for each other.

Slowly her head moved side to side as her forehead crinkled in thought. "No. I can't say that."

"What else has it been about for you?"

She swallowed. "Pleasure. When I'm with you, it's about pleasure for the first time since I was kidnapped."

There's my strong girl. His girl? Shit. There was no his anything. As evident by the manipulative asshole in town gunning for him, Rocket's life wasn't conducive to him having any kind of claim on a woman for longer than a few nights. But that was an issue to conquer after he helped slay Chloe's dragons. "So, you're having orgasms. I'm having orgasms. You can stand being in my company, right?"

A ghost of a smile tilted her lips. "Yeah, you're all right."

He grunted a laugh. "And you left all right in the dust miles ago. You're pretty fucking amazing. Sounds like a healthy sex life to me. You like to tie me up? Big fucking deal; everybody's got their kink."

Chloe snorted and rolled her eyes. "Somehow I don't think being tied up every time you have sex is *your* kink. Hell," she said, throwing her arms up. "It's not even my kink. I certainly never liked it before. I just can't do it any other way right now."

"Well, clearly it's still getting me off, so no worries there, babe. I'm good to keep going as we are."

She tilted her head. "Seriously? You're okay letting me continue to tie you up?"

"Yes, babe, I am. But know this, my body is yours to experiment with in whatever way you want. You feel ready to change things up, let me know. If it works, fuck yeah. If not, at least we know we both get what we need the way we're doing it." He meant it. He'd take her any way he could get her. Handcuffs, ropes, fucking chains if that's what she needed.

"So you want this to continue? With us?"

Like he wanted to keep living.

"Don't see a reason to end it, do you?" It sure wasn't a declaration of love, but it was something he had a feeling she'd appreciate more. Security. Safety. Someone she trusted to help her past her issues. When she was ready and able to return to the woman she'd been before the attack, he'd just have to hope he was ready to let her go.

"No," she said. "I don't." Reaching out, she smoothed a hand down his chest. He had to clench his teeth as a line of fire traveled straight to his dick. That's all it took. One innocent over the clothes touch and he was hard and aching for her. "Can I tell you something?"

"Of course, babe. Anything."

"That feeling I get." Her face turned pink as she traced the patch with his road name. "When I have some guy at my mercy, that feeling? It's kind of like a drug in my system. Like a high. I felt the same way when I was fighting with Jig."

"Knowing you can defend yourself, that someone can't hurt you is pretty fucking empowering." He frowned as something akin to jealousy surged through his veins. Jig may be a better fighter than Rocket, but he'd be taking over her training. She didn't need to be getting any kind of high from another man. Not while Rocket was the one in her bed.

"Yeah. Maybe it's a better way to work out my issues." She chewed on her bottom lip then said, "You know, before I ran into the girls at the grocery store, I was thinking of maybe trying some stuff without you handcuffed."

"Some stuff, huh?" He raised an eyebrow. Shit, he wasn't sure he'd survive whatever *stuff* she had planned for him. He was starting to think keeping him handcuffed was a smart move. Kept him from becoming a complete rutting animal in her presence. But damn if he could deny her anything in his power to give when she looked at him with that mix of courage and vulnerability. "Just let me know what you need and I'm game."

She lifted her arms, reaching for him, then winced. "I think what I need right now is a bottle of Motrin and a hot bath."

He stood, not bothering to try and hide the bulge in his jeans. If they were going to continue spending time together, she'd have to get used to him in this state. Her eyes widened then she licked her lips causing him to groan as he imagined that pink tongue on the head of his dick. "I think that can be arranged." With six large steps he was in the bathroom and turning on the tap. "I'm the only one who ever uses this shower and I had one of the Honeys scrub it before you got here," he called out above the sound of rushing water.

"Honeys?"

Oh right, she wouldn't know who they were. Chloe appeared at the door of the bathroom wearing only her sports bra and black bikini panties. Her stomach had a slight roundness to it that flared into hips he'd fantasized about countless times. He'd give anything to sink his fingers into the soft flesh as he fucked her long and hard.

They'd get there.

"Club girls."

Her frown was adorable. "That's not making it any clearer."

Ugh, he was going to have to spell it out for her. "They help out around the club, shit like cleaning, cooking, servicing the guys, in exchange for a place to crash, protection, and basically a family."

"Service the guys?" Chloe's chuckle was unexpected. He'd kind of expected her to be disgusted. "Sooo basically, they clean and fuck you for a place to stay."

He grimaced. People outside the club culture always made it sound so much worse than it was.

They stood there for a few moments, watching each other, the air thick with steam and something he refused to look too closely at. Chloe wouldn't want a biker long term. Hell, she'd had a near violent reaction to finding out he was in the MC. She was stuck with him now, and willing to sleep with him because she, at the very least, trusted him not to hurt her, but that's as far as it could go. His life was too fucking messy and hers was just beginning again.

The disappointment was a new feeling. His entanglements with women were limited to short term flings. In the Marines, his frequent deployment schedule made meeting someone difficult. Afterward, working as a hired gun for a private defense contractor kept him living a very solo life. He hadn't been willing to bring a woman into the world he'd existed in. A world full of lies, danger, and the very real possibility he wouldn't come back from one of his many missions.

By the time he joined the MC, he'd grown accustomed to living and being alone. Becoming close with his brothers had been a struggle. Hell, he still wasn't known for hanging out much and definitely not for being any kind of conversationalist.

He'd had a number of women throughout the years, what single man didn't? But it never lasted more than a few encounters. Once they started asking questions about his life he tended to flee. Unlike many of his brothers, he wasn't much for one-night stands, and wasn't into any of the Honeys. Sure, he'd accepted a blow job or two over the years, but the club girls never held his interest much beyond that.

Now Chloe was in his life and he had no idea what he wanted from her. The only certainty was the gut-punch he felt at the thought of her walking away right now. For Christ's sake, he was willing to be tied up and fucked just to keep her close.

"Think that's enough water," she said, humor in her voice.

"Shit." He'd been totally lost in his head. Not something that ever happened. Years as a paid assassin had honed his ability to be aware of his surroundings at all times. And now he'd nearly overflowed the bathtub, fucking daydreaming. He released the drain and once the water was at an appropriate level, stopped it back up again. "All set. I'll leave you to it," he said as he started past her.

"Wait." She reached out and curled her slender fingers around his arm. "Maybe...um...would you mind staying in here?"

His cock jerked at the thought of her soaking naked within touching distance. He balled his fists. He'd have to sit on the damn things to keep from reaching for her gorgeous body. This was going to take willpower of epic proportions. But he couldn't fucking say no to her. "Hmm, watch a gorgeous woman take a bath or go play pool with a bunch of smelly bikers?" He winked. "No contest."

Her smile grew. "You're different here. More relaxed. Chattier."

His brothers would lose their fucking heads over that one. It wasn't the club that made him different, it was her. He talked more around her than he had anyone in ages. "You gonna hop in?"

"Yeah." She bit her bottom lip as she worked the sports bra over her head. Rocket almost swallowed his tongue. Had she been any other woman, he'd wonder if the little strip tease was some kind of manipulation, but with Chloe he had no doubt it wasn't. She was nervous as a drenched cat.

And so damn brave. Baring her body before a man who could overpower her in the blink of an eye.

Her hands trembled slightly as she dropped them to her panties. To help set her mind at ease, Rocket sat on the edge of the tub and rested his hands on his thighs in plain sight. Two seconds later she was naked. She straightened; uncertainty clear on her face.

"Jesus," he said, feeling like he'd swallowed a mug of sand. "Your body is out of control, woman."

She smiled. "Thank you." She walked toward him then braced a hand on his shoulder as she stepped into the tub. The smell of her, something subtle and fruity combined with clean sweat from her workout hit his nostrils. All her smooth, pale skin was so close. Wouldn't take more than a lift of a hand to feel her flesh sliding beneath his palm. But Chloe needed to know she could trust him completely, so he swallowed his desire and kept his paws to himself.

Inch by inch, she sank into the tub until she was covered to her neck. Being a guy who hadn't taken a bath since he was probably six, he didn't have any bubbly shit for her to use, so there was nothing to hide her tits from his view.

Thank fuck.

She rested her head back with a satisfied groan.

Rocket's cock twitched. The damn thing ached from the pressure of his tight denim.

Following her groan, a soft sigh left her lips. Eyes closed, she wore a small smile of complete contentment. She extended her arms, allowing them to float on the surface of the water.

"This feels so good." Another freaking groan.

Rocket wasn't going to survive this. Well, he may not die, but he'd make a mess of his pants like a fourteen-year-old boy who'd just discovered his older brother's porn stash.

"You know what would make it even better," she asked in a drowsy voice, eyes still closed.

"What?" Christ, he sounded like there was a hand wrapped around his throat.

Her eyes opened and connected directly with his. "You could touch me."

Just like that everything took a back seat to her request. Copper, Esposito, Lefty.

All that mattered was getting his hands on this woman and making her cry out in pleasure.

CHAPTER NINETEEN

Somehow, her request came out sounding strong. Confident. Sensual even.

Completely in contrast with the nerves running rampant just below her skin. Her mind and body were driving her absolutely crazy. The internal war between desire and fear, need and dread, aching and trembling, couldn't go on. She'd lose what remained of her sanity. Something had to give, and leaping off this cliff seemed the way to push forward.

"You want me to touch you?" His voice had grown so gruff it was nearly a growl.

Chloe nodded, unable to do more than stare at the handsome man perched on the edge of the tub with his expression so fierce. Were it anyone else, she'd have thought he looked angry with his narrowed eyes, flattened mouth, and assessing glare. But she'd learned that was just Logan. Severe, yet not a threat to her.

He shifted, sliding from the tub to his knees on the small navy-blue bath rug. "How do you want me to touch you?" he asked as he shrugged out of his cut then tossed it on the vanity.

"Y-you decide." Where this brave woman emerged from, Chloe would never know. Inside, her fear screamed at her to leap from the tub and tear out of the clubhouse, nudity be damned. But part of her had an acute memory of what it felt like when Logan made her come, and the distant memory of being with a man before she'd been assaulted, back when she wasn't afraid and had far fewer inhibitions. She was learning that woman still remained, not as buried below the surface as she'd feared, and that woman craved a man, this man, pressing her into the mattress and dominating *her*. But those memories were now twisted around the disgusting recollections of being violated and injured. Getting back to the woman who was willing to surrender would be impossible if she couldn't even let Logan touch her. This was the first step and she had to take it. No matter how apprehensive the notion made her.

"Hmm," he said, drawing the sound out so it became a caress. Chloe shivered. With a knowing smile, Logan slid his hand into the warm water. The apocalypse couldn't have torn her attention away from the sight of that strong, callused hand disappearing into the water and advancing toward her. He cupped her inner thigh, lifting her leg out of the water. Then he draped her knee over the side of the tub. "You want me to make you come?"

God, hell yes! "I d-do."

Logan ran his fingertips up and down the inside of her thigh, changing direction when he was just inches from her sex. All the while, his piercing blue eyes were trained directly between her legs, a look of hunger transforming his face.

Chloe swallowed. With his fiery gaze and ticking jaw, he looked more like he was about to launch an attack on a terrorist cell than finger her. Once again, he coasted his palm up her thigh, but this time, he brushed the tips of his fingers through her folds. She jumped at the contact, her hand going to his forearm.

Logan froze. "Stop?"

"No. I'm good."

His features softened as he gave her a smile. "Relax, the only thing that is going to happen here is you digging those nails into my arm as you cry out in pleasure. Yeah?"

"Yeah," she said on an exhale. Damn, that sounded good.

"Rest your head back. Close your eyes."

Did she dare? It required a level of trust she'd have denied she could ever achieve last week, but now, it seemed within reach.

"The door to my room is locked. It's just you and me. Swear on my life I will not hurt you, baby."

So much sincerity in that one statement. How could she not believe him? But it wasn't a matter of believing him. It was being able to conquer a powerful internal wound making her afraid despite her belief in Logan. "I know you won't."

Over the past month, he'd had the opportunity to bring her harm countless times. Instead, he'd selflessly let her use him for her own healing and unconventional therapy. Maybe it was time to give him something back. Give him the gift of trust. With a shuddered sigh that was as much desire as fear, she let her head tilt back against the tub, and closed her eyes.

"That's my girl," Logan murmured as his hand kicked up its journey once again. This time, he ran his fingers through her sex on each pass. Instead of jolting in surprise, Chloe was squirming with unsatisfied need by the third swipe of those digits.

"Logan," she said though it sounded more like a moan.

"So wet," he said back.

Chloe couldn't stop the small giggle. "I'm in the tub."

"No," he said, and she imagined him shaking his head with a stern expression. "It's different." As if trying to demonstrate his point, he worked one thick finger inside of her.

Her back arched off the slope of the tub, upsetting the water. She gasped. God, that felt good. Her nipples immediately hardened to tight points. Water sloshed over them, intensifying their sensitivity.

"That's it, baby. Feel good?"

"Shit, Logan. Yes, it feels good. Really good. Amazing."

"You have any idea how beautiful you look right now?" his gravelly voice asked.

Chloe smiled. There was something to this eyes-closed thing. She had no idea what was coming or when, but it was bound to rock her world.

"Your tits are gorgeous. Your pussy is sucking at my finger just like it does my dick. Can't wait for it to be on my dick again. And those nipples poking out of the water are just begging for some action, aren't they?"

"Yes," she said, and God help her, she sounded like she was begging. "Touch them."

"Think I can manage that." There was laughter in his voice but also an edge of desperation. He had to be hard as a lead pipe. Chloe should probably offer to do something about that, but her body was sliding into a state of languid ecstasy where she could do nothing but absorb the sensations he piled on.

All at once, he pinched her left nipple and slid a second finger inside her. Chloe cried out. Her eyes flew open and locked on his. As predicted, her fingers curled into his forearm, nails gouging his skin with a strong pressure. Just as she was about to apologize, she caught his nostrils flare and his eyes darken to a deeper shade of blue.

He liked it. The prick of pain letting him know how much the pleasure affected her.

Rolling her nipple between his thumb and forefinger, he fucked her with his fingers, gently at first, then with increasing speed and purpose. Each time he pulled those long digits back, he stroked over her g-spot. Before long, Chloe was writhing under the sensual assault. He alternated between nipples, pinching, tugging, and twisting until she was a whimpering mess of need.

"Logan," she whined. He was killing her. One erotic finger pump at a time.

"So fucking beautiful, baby. Ride it out. Take what that sexy body wants."

She still held his arm. Hell, the poor guy was probably bleeding by now, but she couldn't release her grip. Even though she knew instinctively he wouldn't stop, wouldn't tease her in this moment, her hands acted of their own accord, holding him in place between her legs. The water sloshed as though she were caught in the wake of a speedboat instead of reclining in a small tub only half full.

All of a sudden, his thumb tapped her clit with a heavy but brief pressure. Once, twice, a third time. The lash of pleasure was so intense, she nearly came right there. "Logan," she screamed out. "Oh my God, I'm so close. Do it again."

A strained chuckle was the only auditory response, but he complied, driving his fingers deep into her, squeezing her nipple, and pressing her clit all at once.

Chloe's back bowed and she let out a wail she'd be embarrassed about in a few minutes. Her eyes screwed shut as she rode out the orgasm, wave after wave of delicious pleasure crashing over her. "Holy shit," she said once she finally slumped in the tub. Thank God Logan was still there. He could save her life—again—if she grew boneless and slipped beneath the surface of the water.

Hadn't she said something about sore muscles not too long ago? Logan certainly found the cure for that. Man, he could make millions marketing his relaxation technique to top athletes all over the world. Chloe giggled.

"You find my work funny?" Logan asked as he withdrew his fingers from her pussy.

She gasped then groaned at the loss of fullness. "No, not funny at all." Popping one eye open, she stared, enraptured as he licked his fingers.

"Fuck, the taste of you."

Their gazes met. Logan gave her a crooked smile that was so sexy she almost jumped out of the tub and tackled him.

It hit her then, the magnitude of what she'd just accomplished. Not the orgasm, though it was certainly stellar, but the fact that she had a man's hands on her. In her. Bringing her pleasure that led to an orgasm. Plus, she'd closed her eyes. Surrendered not only to the incredible feelings Logan brought her body, but to him.

She trusted him, plain and simple.

And maybe, just maybe she trusted him enough to try even more with him. Another laugh almost escaped. Good thing she wasn't seeing a therapist at the moment. They'd probably have her committed. Here she was, contemplating the possibility of sleeping with someone she'd already slept with a number of times.

The manner in which they had sex was the question of the hour. Could she trust him enough to have sex without tying him up?

Logan sighed and the smug look disappeared from his face. "Shit," he said running a hand through his hair. "Wish I could watch you soak all afternoon, but Copper wants to meet with you. It's the real reason I came looking for you during your workout. He wants to fill you and the rest of the ladies in on what exactly is going on with the lockdown and what the plan is from here."

And *pop*. There went the bubble of happiness, burst by the sharp point of reality.

Fuck reality.

Chloe sat forward, shivering as she left the warmth of the water.

Logan rose and vacated the bathroom. Fifteen seconds later, he reappeared with an oversize towel. Well, oversize for her, probably just right for most of the giants in the MC. He reached out to her then hauled her up when she placed her hand in his. Before she'd even stepped out of the tub, she was engulfed in soft terrycloth. "I'm gonna run down and let Cop know you'll be ready in few. You okay to get dressed and meet us down there?" As he spoke, he rubbed his large hands up and down her towel covered back. Worked wonders for chasing away the post-bath chill.

Chloe nodded. "Am I late?"

"Nah, you're good. No rush."

"Okay."

With that, he gave her one of his infrequent genuine smiles. She filed it under *rare and precious* in her memory. Right up there with unicorns and fairytales. "Take your time. Copper can wait." Then, to her complete and utter shock, he pressed a lingering kiss to her forehead.

She blinked, stunned by the intimate move. It was such a loving gesture; one he'd never come close to doing before.

Wait...holy shit...they'd had sex half a dozen times, he'd made her come twice as many and they'd only kissed that one time in the diner. Their relationship was seriously fucked up.

Long seconds ticked by before she realized she was standing alone in the bathroom, shivering beneath the towel.

Might as well get dressed and head down to see what the head honcho wanted from her. Her stomach twisted. Copper couldn't be pleased she was hiding out in his clubhouse. She was the girl who was supposed to stay far, far away from his MC. Not land at his doorstep engaged in some kind of complicated relationship with one of his men.

Silently, she worked a pair of black leggings up her slightly damp legs then shrugged into one of Logan's Hell's Handlers T-shirts. The thing was too large but smelled of him and gave her the childish impression she was wearing some kind of shield.

Depending on Copper's mood, she might need it. She was a TV watcher. She knew the president of an outlaw motorcycle club could be ruthless, lethal, and cold as ice.

After sliding her feet into her favorite Toms, she reached for the door only to stop dead in her tracks.

"Oh, my God," she said aloud. She was a first-rate bitch, worrying only about herself and wondering if the big bad president was going to growl at her.

Rocket was the one who'd been a step away from stalking her for the past few months. There was no way Copper would condone their relationship. What the hell would his punishment be?

Rocket

Pins under his toenails? Balls in a vice? Cleaning the clubhouse toilets?

She wrinkled her nose and opened the door, stomach twisting and turning around on itself. As much as she feared the wrath of the MC president, she wasn't about to let Rocket take the blame for her being there. She was going to stand up for her man.

Her man? If by her man, her brain meant the man who pity fucked her, then she guessed he was her man.

Sounded kinda nice.

Her man.

Crap, she was in so much trouble.

CHAPTER TWENTY

The moment Chloe entered the room, Rocket's senses popped and fizzled, making him acutely aware of her presence. Not something he'd ever attempt to unpuzzle. He simply accepted that he seemed to have developed Chloe-dar. It wasn't a tangible or explainable concept. Just a feeling. A tingle arose at the base of his spine and along the back of his neck, alerting him to her presence. Sounded like voodoo shit he'd have busted a gut over should any of his brothers have claimed the same thing with regards to a woman, which meant he'd be keeping his trap shut about it. He glanced at her and had to swallow a groan. Did she have to wear his T-shirt? Now all he could think of was his scent coating her skin, sinking into her pores the way he wanted to sink into her body.

And, big surprise, he was hard again. Touching her in the tub, watching her yield to him, feeling her hungry pussy squeeze the life out of his fingers had been unreal, but he'd been left with a monster of a hard-on that only faded after he remembered Copper's demand to speak with Chloe and the other ol' ladies.

The ol' ladies. Period. Not *other* ol' ladies. Chloe wasn't an ol' lady. Wouldn't ever be an ol' lady.

All eyes in the room shot to her as she slunk in the room, lower lip tucked between her teeth and hands wringing the T-shirt at her waist.

"Uh, hey," she said, lifting one hand in a stationary wave. Her red hair, still damp from her bath, was secured high on her head in a long ponytail that fell halfway down her back. She had the best hair. Long, thick, auburn silk. Mark his word, one day he'd wrap that tail around his hand as he plunged into her until she screamed, but not for mercy, never for mercy. Chloe's screams would only be for more.

"Hi, Chloe! Come on in. We saved you a seat," Toni said, indicating a vacant chair at the table where she sat with Zach, Maverick, and Stephanie. Steph was perched on Mav's lap while Toni had arranged her chair next to her ol' man. Jig and Izzy occupied the next table with Viper and his ol' lady. Her name was Cassie, but everyone had called her Mamma V for as long as Rocket had known her. A few additional members were scattered throughout the room, waiting on Copper. Church had been held only hours after Esposito dropped in on Rocket, but they'd waited to fill the ol' ladies in until Chloe felt up to joining.

"Oh, thanks." Chloe's gaze shifted to him, uncertainty as to how to act reflected clear as day. Any benefit she'd gotten from the orgasm he'd given her ten minutes ago seemed to have left her, if the tension in her shoulders and stiff walk was any indication. On top of being sore from her balls-to-the-wall workout, she had to be nervous as fuck about this meeting.

Shit, he should have done a better job explaining what they were gathering for. Not a damn thing she had to worry about. Now, because he was a dipshit, she probably assumed she was in for an ass chewing or worse.

Without caring he was laying his cards on the table, he shoved away from the bar, and lumbered toward the empty chair Toni had marked for Chloe. He dropped onto it, ignored Toni's huff and frown, then pulled Chloe onto his lap the moment she was within reach.

"Oh," Toni said, blinking like an owl. "Ohhh." Her face lit, mouth curling into a wicked grin as she winked. "Guess you guys worked things out." From the other side of the table

Stephanie gave Chloe two thumbs up while Maverick made a blow job motion with one hand and his tongue in his cheek.

Rocket froze. Had Chloe not been on his lap, he'd have reached across the table and yanked Maverick up by his scrawny neck. The fucking bastard, cracking crude jokes around a woman who'd been raped. The asshole needed to grow a fucking filter.

But of course, Chloe snickered. Why did everyone find Maverick so fucking funny, females especially? Any other man would get a slap to the face or slammed with a sexual harassment suit. Mav got giggles and dropped panties. Damn tatted asshole.

Worst part of it was he wasn't so much as a bit remorseful. He sent Rocket a smug grin and threw in an eyebrow waggle for good measure.

"Watch your back," Rocket said in warning.

Stephanie's eyes widened, but Mav just mock shivered. "Ooh, I'm so scared."

Rocket didn't get the chance to reach across the table and knock his brother upside the head because Copper chose that moment to limp into the room—minus his crutches—holding Shell's hand. He lifted her—against doctor's orders—setting her on the bar, then stood next to her, one arm around her back. It had taken Copper years to finally admit his feelings for the much younger Shell, but now that he had, the two practically needed a surgeon to separate them. "All right, we waiting on anyone else?" Copper asked in his customary Irish brogue.

"Nope," Mav said. "All present and accounted for, prez."

Copper nodded. "Thanks for coming. Know all you ladies have been real patient the last few days. Think I've only been hounded for answers maybe a hundred or so times. And that doesn't count Izzy's constant threatening text messages demanding to know why the hell she couldn't open her shop."

A handful of the men snickered. At least Stephanie, Toni, and even Shell had the good sense to look sheepish. Izzy couldn't have given less of a shit. She just shrugged and said, "If you'd just told me what the fuck was going on, I wouldn't have texted so much."

Jig shook his head, doing a shitty job of hiding his smirk as he cupped the back of his woman's neck. It was a possessive move that would have earned any other man a trip to the emergency room, but, wonder of wonders, Izzy often deferred to Jig when around the club.

The rest of the room erupted in laughter with a few comments about Izzy being a ball buster thrown in for good measure.

"All right settle down. Gotta get serious for a few minutes here," Copper said as the crowd grew quiet. "We got a credible threat we had to look into. I wanted to fill you all in because I realize I can't keep you locked up here forever. It's been a few days and the guy we were worried about has been spotted leaving town on a private jet. That means you're all free to go about your business."

The women immediately began chattering about how relieved they were to be released from "MC prison." Chloe remained quiet but had relaxed against Rocket as Copper spoke. Unfortunately, Rocket had a feeling her languid state wouldn't last.

"Hey, I ain't finished," Copper said, clapping his meaty hands to get everyone to focus back on him. Shell rolled her eyes and patted his arm.

Rocket tensed. There was nothing he hated more than being the center of attention and here it fucking came.

Shifting on his lap, Chloe peered down at him. "You okay?" she asked low enough he was the only one who heard. "You just got all stiff." Her cheeks pinked. "And not in *that* way."

Leave it to her to get some sort of laugh out of him when he wanted to tear the room apart. "I'm good, babe. No worries." He gave her a gentle squeeze as he spoke.

Her eyes narrowed and one auburn eyebrow arched. Yeah, she didn't believe that.

"Okay," Copper said. "Try to keep your yaps shut until I'm done, yeah?"

Izzy snorted and Copper sent her a death glare. Of course, the woman didn't so much as bat an eyelash.

"You all know Rocket is a former Marine. After he left, he was recruited by DarkOps."

Now it was Chloe's turn to go rigid. Fuck. Looked like the cat was out of the damn bag now. Too bad he couldn't have killed the furry beast. His life prior to the MC wasn't a secret, per se, of course ninety percent of the missions were classified to the nth degree, but the fact that he worked for DarkOps wasn't. However, he fucking hated the reaction when people found out who he worked for. So he kept that shit to himself. Until today.

"I said, shut your fuckin' yaps," Copper bellowed, and the few whispered murmurs ceased immediately. Unfortunately, that meant it was pin-drop quiet as everyone in the room stared at Rocket with open curiosity.

Nosy motherfuckers.

Rocket trained his gaze on Copper. The goal was to keep himself from noticing the way his brothers gawked at him. Didn't work. He could feel each and every one of their stares like hot pokers against his skin. Hear each and every one of the questions hurling silently through the air.

Chloe rested her hand on the top of his where it lay on her thigh. She linked their fingers and gave a comforting squeeze, not letting up the pressure as Copper began talking again.

"I ain't gonna get into details about what he did there, that's Rocket's private fucking business, but I'm sure you can figure out the gist of it." Copper sent an apologetic look Rocket's way.

He got it. The prez had no choice. Esposito could approach any one of his brothers or their ol' laides. They had to know who he was and what he was to remain vigilant and safe. In his typical manipulative style, Esposito was likely to approach and scare the fuck out of one of the women with a blackmail scheme. He'd dig up something they'd rather remained buried and threaten to out them if Rocket didn't complete the mission. Everyone in the room had at least one dancing skeleton in their closet. Sure, he'd left town, but who the hell knew when he'd be back and the clubhouse couldn't stay on lockdown forever.

Rocket would peel the skin off Esposito's breathing body before he let the fucktard anywhere near Chloe.

So, while he understood why Copper had to air his dirty laundry all over the damn clubhouse, he hated the fuck out of it.

"Bottom line, folks, Rocket walked when shit started seeming hinky. Again, I ain't getting into details. They're his to share if he wants, and I think it's been made pretty clear he's not interested. Anyway, they want him back, and aren't above playing dirty to get him." He lifted a photograph from the bar. "Want you all to keep your eyes peeled for this fucker. Tracking?"

Murmurs of assent could be heard around the room. "Pass this around for me, babe," he said, handing the photo to Shell. She hopped off the bar and dropped the photograph on Izzy and Jig's table.

Izzy lifted with photo with a snort. "I could take this guy with one hand tied behind my back. Even knocked up." She rubbed her belly as everyone laughed. The brief tension relief was greatly appreciated.

Too bad Rocket had to ramp the seriousness back up. "He's not someone to mess with," he said, breaking his silence for the first time. All heads swiveled in his direction. There were about a million things he'd rather be doing than sitting under the nosey stare of the majority of the club, including pulling out his own toenails. "Might not look like much, but he's a lethal bastard. And I mean bastard. He's not above snatching one of you ladies and blackmailing you to get to me. He runs DarkOps so he's got the best hackers and contacts backing him. Trust me when I say by now he knows every damn secret you keep."

His stomach cramped as the look on Toni's face turned to one of discomfort. Zach's ol' lady would be a perfect target for Esposito. She had shit in her past she'd much rather leave there.

Things that would be devastating should they find their way onto social media. Zach circled his arm around her shoulders and pulled her in for a quick kiss to her temple. After pulling back, he whispered something that had her nodding and her shoulders losing some of their starch.

Rocket shifted his attention to Chloe. She was gazing down at him with a look of concern on her face, still clinging tight to his hand. "It's okay," she whispered as she lifted her free hand to his face. That soft palm cupping his three-day unshaven face was the last straw. He rose, careful not to send her to the concrete floor.

Being a burden to his club was fucking bad enough. Having them wonder what kind of heinous deeds he'd committed in the past and whether they were going to be the ones to pay for his past sins cut to the bone. Copper was right. He was a protector. As SAA, he looked out for the club. Anticipated threats and trouble before it arose and did what he needed to neutralize it before it touched any of his family.

Being the one to disrupt that family sickened him. And now Chloe felt the need to comfort him.

Fuck that.

"Izzy and Steph picked up some clothes for you. Get whatever shit you might need for a few days and meet me at my bike in ten minutes," he said.

"Oh. Uh, sure." She blinked, clearly caught off guard by his sudden command and change of attitude. "Where are we going?"

He needed space from the club. Needed to purge the poison from his mind without feeling like the thousand-pound chain dragging everyone down. But he refused to let her out of his sight, so she'd be tagging along. "My house."

"Holy shit," Shell whispered which was followed by Copper's low chuckle.

"What?" Chloe asked, flicking a glance at Shell.

"Oh, uh, nothing." Shell's eyes were comically wide.

Great, now he was bound to be the topic of conversation for a host of brand-new reasons.

Fuck it all. He needed a goddammed break.

"Ten minutes," he said as he spun on his heel and tromped outside where at least the trees wouldn't be digging into his private shit.

CHAPTER TWENTY-ONE

Arms limp at her sides, Chloe watched Rocket's back as he practically fled from the clubhouse. The urge to chase after him was strong. She wanted to wrap her arms around him and give back some of the support he'd shown her. But she resisted. The most important thing she'd learned about him in the recent past was his absolute need for privacy. He hated people prying in his business. Went hand in hand with him not loving conversation. If he kept quiet, didn't draw attention to himself, people wouldn't ask questions and delve into his affairs. Most likely, he wanted, or needed, some space at the moment.

"All right, you all can scatter now," Copper said. "Talk to you for a second, Chloe?"

Uh oh. Even though he hadn't come down on her as she'd expected when she walked into the room, he intimidated the crap out of her. He'd probably scare just about anyone. At well over six feet with a thick beard not too far off her own hair color, bulging muscles, and plenty of ink, he was a threat just by sight. Chloe shivered. Better Shell got to be the one to deal with him on a daily basis than her.

Swallowing her nerves, she closed the ten-foot distance to where Copper stood holding Shell's hand. "Sure, uh, what's up?" She shifted, feeling like a bug under a microscope.

Copper studied her until she could no longer stand the intense scrutiny. Thank God for his observant woman. "Copper, stop scowling at her. You're freaking her out." She elbowed him then smiled brightly at Chloe. "Sorry, Chloe, he's just growly because he's working through this new threat to the club."

"It's all right." God, she wished she had something to do with her hands besides play with the hem of Rocket's T-shirt.

"I can't believe Rocket is taking you to his house. None of us have ever been there." She looked up at her man who was still staring at Chloe. "Well maybe this lug has, but no one else. It's actually become somewhat of an urban legend among the guys. Rumor has it he lives in a mid-century castle complete with a dungeon and tall towers."

Copper made a sound close to a snort.

"What?" Shell blinked up at her man, giving him an innocent smile. But her lips betrayed her. They twitched with the effort not to laugh.

"What the hell are you going on about? A fucking castle in the Smokey Mountains?"

Shell just shrugged, lifting her hands. "Just what I've heard."

With a roll of his eyes, Copper pulled her close to his side. He might pretend to be annoyed, but his eyes now sparkled with mirth, making him a much less menacing character. "You know what a Sergeant at Arms is?"

Hello topic change. "Uh, no, I don't have a clue."

Nodding, Copper said, "It's an officer position within the MC. Basically protector of the club. No one better for that job than Rocket. He's held the position for the past few years."

Copper hit the nail on the head; she couldn't imagine a man better fit for the job. Logan was nothing if not protective. Warmth filled Chloe's chest. After suffering through what she had, the idea of having her own personal protector was very appealing. Not that she didn't want to learn to defend and guard herself. Standing on her own two feet was vital, but having someone in her corner who would always try to step between the evil of the world and her made her heart soar.

"This shit with his past is fucking with his head. You get what I'm saying?"

Like a crate full of bricks, Copper's underlying meaning slammed into her. Shit, she should have seen it earlier. Her only excuse was that she was still learning about the man who'd come to mean so much to her in a short period of time. "I think I do. Lo—uh, Rocket feels as though he is failing in his job. He feels responsible for bringing danger and trouble to the club."

Copper nodded and his eyes softened. "The man might put some distance between you. It's not personal. Just how he deals with shit."

"I understand. I can give him the space he needs." After all he'd given her, she'd pay him back with every cent she'd ever earned if it was what he needed.

For the first time, Copper cracked a smile at her. "I ain't saying it's what he needs. In fact, I think he needs someone to blow through his solitary nature."

Chloe pondered that. Sounded like Copper was giving her his stamp of approval. Sure, she could keep Logan from disappearing into himself. But should she? She was already in so deep with him. When the threat was gone, and she returned to her home, life would be hard. She'd be hurt. There were no two ways around it. Feelings had developed for Logan. What those feelings were had yet to be fully fleshed out, but they were the kind that fucked with a girl's head as well as her heart. And in Chloe's case, her body.

Shell bounced on the balls of her feet. She looked two seconds away from squealing and clapping her hands. "He wouldn't be bringing you to his secret castle house if he wanted space from you. Go get him girl!"

"Jesus Christ," Copper said, running a hand down his face. "You women are fucking nuts."

Now it was Chloe's turn to laugh. Maybe the big bad MC president wasn't so big or so bad after all. Okay, that was a lie, he still was the last person she wanted to cross, but he seemed to be okay with her, so she'd take it.

"Well," she said taking two steps backward. "I better get going."

Shell released Copper's hand, rushed forward, and gave Chloe an exuberant hug. "You're just what he needs," she whispered then drew back. With her hands on Chloe's shoulders, she said, "And I think he's the same for you."

He just might be. "Guess I'll see you guys soon?"

"You bet, girl. I'm working at Toni's diner the next few days. Stop in for breakfast if you two can come up for air." With a wink, she stepped back until she bumped Copper's chest. The prez just gave Chloe a nod as he wrapped his thick forearm around Shell.

"Sounds like a plan. Bye." With a lame wave, she turned and hustled to Logan's room.

Come up for air. Ha. That meant she had to dive in to the deep end first. As she threw some things in a bag, her thoughts drifted to Logan. Sexy didn't come close to describing the sculpted body he seemed to maintain without much effort. Tanned skin, a smattering of tattoos, muscles that rivaled any male fitness model, he was everything that turned her on physically. Even standing there holding a pair of leggings, her body began to respond to thoughts of him. Her stomach fluttered, nipples tightened, and mouth watered at the idea of licking all those ridges and valleys.

Logan was a protector. Even his brothers knew it. A feeling of peace and clarity settled over her. She was safe with him. At least her body was. He certainly had the potential to obliterate her heart, but that was something she couldn't worry about right now. One issue at a time and right now, her body was clamoring for top spot.

She was ready. Ready to try for some semblance of a healthy sex life.

But first she had to see what she could do to help Logan battle his own monsters.

Packing took only four minutes plus another two to hightail it outside to Logan's bike. He sat astride it, dark athletic sunglasses hiding his piercing blue eyes. His attention was on her the moment her foot hit the compacted dirt of the parking lot.

"You okay to wear you backpack? Might be too big to fit in my saddle bags."

"Yeah, that's no problem," she said as she stepped close to the motorcycle.

He held out a helmet. Probably his only one as he wasn't wearing one. The thought of him riding without the protection of a helmet had her hesitating to reach for it. Not that he'd ever let her go without, but maybe there was a spare hanging around the clubhouse somewhere.

One look at his face had her scrapping that thought. He'd probably laugh her out of Tennessee if she made a big deal of it.

"You been on a bike before?" he asked as he batted her hands out of the way and clasped the helmet himself.

Chloe blinked and frowned. Was he serious? "Um, yes." She swallowed around a constricted throat. "Just one time." The words were practically whispered. Damn her voice for quitting on her now.

Logan's expression darkened. "Shit. Fuck. I can't fucking believe I forg—"

"Hey." She lifted his sunglasses to the top of his head as she stepped into him. "Shh, it's okay. You forgot. No big deal."

Charcoal storm clouds darkened in his eyes. "There's nothing okay about this. Don't let me off the hook."

All right, being sorry for the slip-up was one thing. Self-recrimination was a whole other issue. "Logan," she said with a small laugh. "You think I'm going to complain about you forgetting that the one time I was on a motorcycle was when I was battered and bloody after the worst two days of my life?"

"I'm an asshole."

She cocked her head which was the wrong move. Unused to wearing the heavy helmet, she felt like she was going to keep going until she hit the ground. She quickly unclasped it and yanked it off.

"Here's the thing. When I'm with people who know some version of what happened to me, like my family and now your club, I wonder constantly if it's all they see. If I'm now the girl who was raped and beaten. I can't stop questioning whether I'm pitied or looked at differently than I was before. You are the only one I spend time with who knows exactly what I looked like that night, because you are the only one outside the hospital who actually saw me. I've asked myself a million times whether you see that version of me every time you look at me. So yeah, I'm pretty damn happy that you forgot about it, even it if it was only for thirty seconds. I didn't get to enjoy my ride that night. This ride, I plan to savor." She injected as much seduction as she could into her voice. Let him wonder if she was hoping to savor a different ride.

Because she was. It was time.

He growled. Quick as lightning, his hand came around the back of her neck and yanked her forward. When his mouth crushed against hers, she nearly lost her footing. Clinging to the flaps of his cut for dear life was the only reason she remained upright.

Holy hell, the man could kiss. If she had any lingering worry he only saw her as a victim, it evaporated the moment his lips captured hers. There wasn't a hint of restraint in his kiss. The moment boiled down to nothing more than a man and a woman who wanted to devour each other. No past baggage, current complications, or future uncertainties tainted the perfection.

Logan raked his teeth across her bottom lip, eliciting a deep shudder and a low moan from her. Before she had time to react to the aggressive move, he was plunging his tongue into her mouth and sampling her from within. God, he tasted so damn good. His lips were firm and demanding as he stole her sanity.

She wanted to be bold. To launch her own attack on his mouth, but he controlled her so masterfully she could do nothing but absorb his sensual assault. Finally, when her lungs practically screamed for oxygen, he ended the kiss. Of course, he didn't just draw away. No, he once again took her lip between his stark white teeth, pulling it out before releasing it. The moment her lip sprung back, she licked the sting away.

Panting, they stared at each other before he finally said, "When I look at you, I see a woman I want to bury myself in so deep I might never find my way out." He grabbed her hand and placed it over the iron rod tenting his jeans.

Holy shit. How had she missed that?

"I can't be in a room with you and not be ready to fuck you. You are one hundred percent sexy-as-fuck woman. I do not see you as a victim."

Her fingers curled around the bulge beneath her palm as her eyes widened. His words...she didn't know how to describe what they did to her. There was only one thing left to say. "Take me to your house, Logan. I want you." She was ready to be with him. Ready to leave the safety of other people and be alone with Logan all night. A huge step, but one that felt right.

His eyes narrowed and he seemed to understand the unspoken plea. She wanted him in a way she hadn't had him before. Tonight, he wouldn't be cuffed to a bed, and she wouldn't be riding him with the sole purpose of ridding her mind of demons. Tonight would be about pleasure.

"Fuck," he rasped out. "Get on the bike before I lose my mind and take you right here."

Chloe shivered before throwing one leg over the bike, then donning her helmet for the second time. Once she was settled behind him with her arms snug around his waist, he hit the throttle and made his way toward his home.

The ride was euphoric, something she didn't have the opportunity to experience last time. Two minutes in, Chloe completely understood the fascination with motorcycles. Rocket handled the winding mountain roads and switchbacks like he was born to it. The first few times he made a nearly ninety-degree turn, her heart lurched into her throat, but it wasn't long before she realized his skill as a rider and relaxed into the ride. The day was picture-worthy. Crystal clear blue sky, warm sun, slight breeze, mountain view. Damn near perfect.

After fifteen minutes, the scenery grew even more mountainous. They had to be fairly high, elevation-wise. Were they heading toward his house or was he just riding through the mountains to clear his mind?

A few moments later, she got her answer. They pulled up to the most stunning house Chloe had ever seen. "Logan," she breathed as she hopped off the bike before he'd even killed the engine. Taking two steps toward what could only be described as a log cabin on steroids, she stroked her hand down his arm. "This is where you live?"

He nodded. If only those eyes weren't hidden behind dark glasses. He was watching her, assessing her reaction to his home, but she was at a disadvantage. His reaction to her impression of his home was obscured.

"It—" she swallowed as an emotion she couldn't name rose in her throat. "It's magnificent." She'd been right, they were fairly high in the mountains and the view from his wraparound porch had to be remarkable. A two-story home made entirely of long logs. The second level also had a balcony winding around the sides of the house. A set of French doors on the second level led inside from the balcony. Was it in the master bedroom? God, how incredible must it be to open those doors and watch the sun rise or set?

Heavenly.

"Did you build this?" Any other time she'd have been embarrassed about the reverence in her voice, but come on, the man was an artist.

Again, he only nodded. Made sense. Her presence was the ultimate invasion into his private life. She understood. Since her kidnapping, Scott was the only one beside her parents she'd allowed into her home. Too intimate, having someone in her personal space. Logan's standard defense mechanism was silence. His impenetrable wall always kept people out. Right then and there it became her mission to infiltrate and stay behind that wall. She'd dipped down a few times, but as evident by his sealed lips, she hadn't remained there.

"You are incredibly talented, Logan. This house is truly beautiful."

Finally, he lifted the sunglasses, perching them on his forehead. Keeping that arctic blue gaze on her, he slowly dismounted the bike then strode her way. Was he going to kiss her again? The dominant way he had before? A shiver skittered up her spine as she prepared for another mind-blowing kiss.

When he reached her, he took her hand in his and pressed a quick but intimate peck to her lips. "Let's go in."

Her lips tingled from the sweet gesture, but something else burned for more.

Still holding her hand, he guided her into the house. There was no stopping the gasp that left her mouth. Immediately upon entering the home, she was in the great room. On the far wall, a gorgeous stone hearth running straight up to the ceiling surrounded a wood burning fireplace. Oversize plush furniture filled the space around a giant flat screen television. To the right, a large kitchen complete with dark oak cabinets, stainless appliances, and a black and tan granite countertop beckoned. At once, Chloe could imagine herself here, relaxing with a glass of wine after a delicious meal, fire crackling, and Logan's strong chest beneath her ear as they held each other on the couch.

A sweet fantasy she'd better shake out of her head before she journeyed straight to heartbreak city.

Logan still hadn't said anything beyond inviting her into the house. Arms folded across his chest, he lingered behind her and let her take in his place. All well and good, but it was time to get him talking again. To tease out the man who'd made her come only hours before.

Hours? Felt like days ago.

"Logan, this is seriously one of the most gorgeous places I've ever seen. I'm blown away by your talent and skill."

It took him a few tense seconds, but finally he spoke. "Thank you."

Okay, looked like this getting-behind-his-walls plan might not be as easy as she'd anticipated.

CHAPTER TWENTY-TWO

"How long did it take you?" she asked, an open smile on her pale face. That complexion of hers was something he'd have to remember if she was on the back of his bike frequently. Riding for hours could fry anyone, especially a fair-skinned redhead like Chloe.

Rocket closed his eyes and rubbed at an ache throbbing against his temples. Felt like someone was taking a hammer to the sides of his head. Fuck, he was losing his mind. Planning to buy a woman sunscreen so she wouldn't burn on the back of his bike? Chloe was the first woman who rode behind him ever. Full stop. Not a single ass had touched the second seat. Who even knew why the hell he had it? But he wasn't gifting her permanent real-estate back there. "Few years working on and off. Was never able to give it full time hours."

"Let me do that." Soft but surprisingly strong fingers batted his hands away, then landed on either side of his head. Gently, much more so than he'd been, she pressed in and rubbed soothing circles on his scalp. The pain evaporated almost instantly, replaced by a comforting pressure that nearly made his eyes roll back in his head. The feel of those fingers, and the awareness of her close proximity had him losing sight of the big picture. His body tightened, muscles contracting, dick hardening, stomach tensing as he fought the need to tackle her to the ground and pillage.

Chloe was making progress, but an overtly aggressive come-on could send her back into her shell.

"Talk to me," she said, voice low and calming as though she fretted over making his headache worse. Rocket was a mean motherfucker. His kill count was higher than most people's bank balance. Yet he was fucking putty in her hands, ready to spill whatever she wanted to know. The CIA could use her, hell DarkOps could employ her to uncover any host of national secrets from the country's enemies.

"Talk about what?"

"Why you were upset today. Your life before the club. Anything. Give me a piece of you no one has." Her hands smoothed down his scruffy face, over his shoulders and down until she circled his wrists. The woman had no idea. Something no one else had? She was fucking standing in it. Copper was the only one of his brothers to ever enter his home, and that was one time, three years ago.

The club had Rocket's loyalty above all. There wasn't a thing he'd do to betray his brother's trust or turn against them. Despite it all, he kept so much of himself private. Copper once suggested he was punishing himself for his violent past and Elena's suicide by cutting himself off from any kind of deep relationship. Rocket had no idea about all that psychotherapy shit, but he did know he'd given Chloe more of himself than any other person.

And by doing so, he'd made a mistake. Gave in to a dumb idea in a weak moment of stress. Sharing their secrets, surviving trauma, and battling enemies was binding them together in a way he couldn't allow. DarkOps would always feel he owed them. Could come for him, guns blazing, at any time. Not to mention the number of enemies he'd racked up over the years. Yes, he'd been careful with identities and aliases, but none of it meant shit if someone or some government figured out who he was. Bringing a woman into that kind of risk wasn't just stupid, it was cruel.

Had nothing to do with punishing himself or whatever bullshit Copper wanted to spew. It was just logic.

Easiest way to break the hold Chloe had on him was to shatter her illusions of what kind of man he was. What kind of man she'd allowed inside her. He wouldn't even have to pretend to be an asshole to push her away. Sharing the story of his life would be enough to make her leave. But she'd be safe from whatever ghost may come for him, including the ones in his head.

"You want to know what my life was like before I met Copper and prospected with the club?" Even he recognized his hostile tone was over-the-top, but he couldn't stem it. Powerful emotions he'd never dealt with were fucking with his head day and night. Something had to give and telling it to her straight would be the swiftest rip of the band aid.

"Yes," she said, gorgeous green eyes shining with sincerity. "I want to know."

He backed an extended step away from her, rubbing his knuckles. Something to pound would have been perfect right about then. That's who he was. A violent bastard. Born to it. Trained for it. Excelled at it. Not the kind of man a woman stayed with long term.

"I separated from the Marines at twenty-three when I was recruited by DarkOps. They scouted me out due to my skill with weapons. Pistol, shotgun, bombs, sniper rifle, you name it, I made it my bitch."

"Okay," she said folding her arms across her chest as though she didn't know what else to do with them. The move closed her off, and he immediately missed the open and warm connection from earlier.

"Spent five years working directly under Esposito. All my operations were off-the-grid classified, no back up, solo missions."

She blinked, waiting for the punch line.

Fuck it. Beating around the bush would take too damn long. Wasn't his style anyway.

"I'm a fucking killer, Chloe. Best assassin in the company. You know, I don't even keep a kill count anymore. Number got too damn high."

Her naked lips pressed together so hard they turned white at the same time a deep furrow appeared between her eyebrows.

He turned and paced the length of the room, rubbing at the back of his neck. First time he'd said those words out loud in over six years. Why did experts recommend getting shit out in the open? Was spilling his guts supposed to be cathartic? Because it fucking wasn't. With each word, Chloe's light had dimmed a little more. Granted, making her despise him was the point, but he felt like complete garbage in the process.

Turning to face her, he let the frustration and self-loathing take control of his tongue. "Esposito wouldn't hesitate to grab you, or Toni, or Shell and dangle you like a fucking carrot to get what he wants. And what he wants is me. His killing machine. Back under his thumb. That's what I bring to the table, babe. That's what I tossed on your doorstep and brought to my club. Fucking death and danger. Don't you think you've been through enough in the last few months?"

He'd expected the sharp crack of her palm to connect with his face. The least of what he deserved for who he was.

"Why'd you walk away?" Chloe asked instead, voice calm though her body still portrayed a strong hands-off vibe with her crossed arms, hunched shoulders, and flat eyes. "I'm assuming the people Esposito sent you to…uh…eliminate were pretty bad people. Terrorists? Murderers? Evil dictators?"

This conversation needed to end. He had to walk out of the room and away from Chloe before he lost his resolve. But he opened his mouth instead. "At first, I vetted the missions myself. Researched the targets. Yeah, they were the worst of the fucking worst. Did shit you couldn't dream up in your nastiest nightmares. Over time, I trusted the information Esposito gave me and stopped doing my own investigations." He turned away, staring at the cold, unlit fireplace. Having Chloe in his private space felt nice. Too nice. Imagining her dozing on the giant sofa with her head in his lap while a fire roared a few feet away was too easy a picture to paint. Ridiculous fantasies for a different type of man. One that worked nothing more than a nine-to-five job, whose worst habit was leaving day old grounds in the coffee pot, and who would never bring psychotic mercenaries to her world.

"My last mission, something didn't add up. When I looked into it, I found my mark was basically nothing more than a fucking mob hit. Some asshole wanted someone who'd pissed him off taken out. Esposito was the highest bidder, so we got the job. I was seconds away from wasting the guy when my gut started ranting at me. I bailed and dug into the situation. What I found made me sick. Some family man with a gambling problem owed the mob a boatload. He couldn't pay and the boss wanted to make an example of him. I walked on the spot and Esposito let me go. Think he knew he'd lose me if I ever found out what he'd been up to. But there was a catch, of course. I owe them because I had years left on my contract. So far, I've staved off all their attempts to collect. Doesn't seem to be working this time."

"Hmm." She said, cocking her head as she rested her hands on those curvy hips. Where her eyes had a dull, shocked glaze to them a few moments ago, they shot fire now. "So, the second you found out the company you worked for was less than honorable, you left. Pardon me, Logan, but I'm not seeing the problem here. Sure, you had an atypical job that required you to do something most couldn't imagine doing, but, come on, I'm not naive. I recognize that type of work is necessary to prevent acts of terror, wars, and other horrible atrocities."

Rocket snorted. What the hell was she playing at? She was way too understanding. Why wasn't she walking away? Seeing him for the monster he was? Chloe was supposed to make this easy on him because fuck if he was strong enough to tear himself away from her.

He stormed toward her. As he breached her personal space, towering over her, Chloe's eyes widened. Fear flashed. Just for a fraction of a second before it gave way to concern once again, but it was there.

Rocket deserved to be shot for this. Even if the ends justified the means. "That's the thing, babe, I didn't walk because they violated my moral code. I don't have one. There's not a goddamn thing I wouldn't do under the right circumstances. I walked because I won't be used."

Chloe's mouth dropped open and her eyes flared so wide he almost laughed despite the sickness in his gut. Let her chew on that while she's thinking about what kind of man she wanted in her life.

"Master's at the top of the stairs. It's all yours," he said as he brushed past her. He had to get the hell out of there before her shocked gaze turned to one of disgust.

"Logan," she called out as he was halfway up the open staircase. He didn't answer. Just trudged on, ignoring both the plea in her voice and the sharp pain behind his ribs.

WHAT THE HELL had happened?

Chloe had asked herself that question at least a hundred times in the past—she rolled over and glanced at the bedside clock—eight hours. It wasn't even that late, only ten p.m., but Rocket had disappeared shortly before four, leaving Chloe on her own and confused as hell. After the kiss at the clubhouse, and Rocket taking her to his gorgeous and apparently secret home, she'd been sure their relationship was taking a step forward. Where exactly that step would have led, she didn't have a clue, but she'd been ready and excited for it. Turned out they took a step all right. Two of them. Two giant strides backward.

"Argh!" She rolled over, planted her face in the pillow and let out what would have been an ear-piercing scream had the feathers not absorbed the sound. For good measure, she threw in a few fist pounds and kicks to the mattress.

It didn't help. She was still frustrated beyond words. Both emotionally and physically.

With a huff, Chloe sat up. Trying to sleep was a giant waste of time. After puttering around the first level for a while, she'd scrounged up something to eat, watched a movie on Netflix, then had given up around eight-thirty. Ninety minutes of ceiling-staring and obsessing later, she'd had enough.

What bothered her most, was the line of bullshit Logan fed her at the end. That nonsense about not having a moral code. Serious bull. The man had a very strict moral code. Sure, it might not be in line with everyone else's or even with the law, but she didn't believe for one second he only quit DarkOps because he felt used. No, that man walked away from a dangerous job with a deadly company because he discovered his employers were evil. And Logan vanquished evil, he didn't condone it.

He'd not only rescued her from hell, but he accepted her idiosyncrasies—if you could call tying random men up and screwing them nothing but an idiosyncrasy—and reminded her not all men were out to harm her.

Yeah, she'd take him. Warts and all. Or at the very least she'd try. There was still the question of whether she'd freak out having any kind of *normal* sex life. Only one way to find out.

Chloe slid her legs over the side of the bed, shivering when the air hit her bare skin. Only thing she had on was her skimpy panties and a T-shirt of Logan's she'd pilfered from his dresser. Smelling him all around her was too tempting to resist.

Quiet as can be, she tiptoed barefoot down the hall to the only closed door. Not that he'd ever admit it, but Logan was hurting. His past caused him shame, and the fact that his past was interfering with his present sent him spiraling.

He needed to know she didn't blame him. None of his brothers or their women blamed him. And not a single one of them, her included, would hold his history against him. Hell, no one would even think less of him for it. In fact, she'd bet he'd been able to use his skills to benefit the club on more than one occasion.

Six months ago, those thoughts would have scared the hell out of her. Violence of any kind hadn't been a direct part of the life she lived. Then it found her, transforming her world. And if she were honest with herself, the idea of having a trained killer sleeping under the same roof was more a comfort than a deterrent.

She came to a stop outside his door. After a quick prayer that she could give Logan what he needed, she stepped into the quiet room only to stop dead when his piercing blue gaze drilled into hers.

CHAPTER TWENTY-THREE

Spending countless nights in hostile territory had honed Rocket's ability to maintain awareness of his surroundings while still catching some sleep. Wasn't really something he could teach or explain. Just a skill his body developed as a result of exhaustion combined with fearing for his life. His body demanded sleep but had an innate sense of self preservation, so it found a way to rest while staying alive. As such, he woke the second Chloe padded within three feet of his door.

Expecting her to knock, he sat straight up in the bed. The sheets only covered his lower half, which was buck naked and already reacting to the thought of her nearness. Nothing he could do about all the skin on display up top unless he wanted to dart across the room naked and risk her walking in. Not that she hadn't seen it all before. Still, she was skittish and probably not expecting to walk in on him naked and hard.

Seconds ticked by with no movement beyond the closed door. Had she changed her mind? Decided whatever she'd needed from him wasn't worth the effort? He wouldn't blame her after the bombs he'd dropped earlier. Or the way he'd abandoned her in his house without so much as a "here's where the bathroom is."

He was torn, split down the middle by greed and selflessness. The altruistic half—okay, maybe one third—of him hoped she'd just turn around and scurry back to the safety of her room. Lock the door for good measure. The other side, the side that was a selfish, horny bastard wanted to call out to her, pull her into the room, and have her in all the ways he'd imagined since he started following her around.

A soft snick sounded through the room immediately before a sliver of light appeared by the door. The crack grew until the door was open, illuminating Chloe standing frozen with wide eyes.

Rocket stiffened—everywhere. Goddamn, there wasn't a single piece of lingerie for any amount of money that was sexier than Chloe standing there in nothing but his worn T-shirt. He swallowed, adjusting the sheet in a lame attempt to hide his boner. All he could think of was whether she had anything under the shirt or if the soft fabric rested directly against her tits and ass.

"You okay?" he asked, voice noticeably strained.

She stared for a few seconds before starting forward. Step by step those long, sleek and very bare legs ate up the gap between her and the bed. Being held close by those silky thighs while her ankles crossed behind his back was a vision he had both awake and asleep.

"Can't sleep," she finally said as she reached the bed. "I have a few things to say to you."

Fuck.

Here's where she informed him what fucking scum he was.

As if he didn't already know. Most days he was good with it. Good enough to keep his past from the forefront of his mind. But ever since he'd met Chloe, he felt dirty.

Without being invited, she slipped into the king-sized bed next to him. Rocket clenched his jaw so tight, his teeth squeaked.

Don't fucking look. Don't fucking look.

He looked.

Of course.

Curled on her side with one hand under her head, she peered at him. The goddamned T-shirt had ridden up, exposing her creamy thighs and the three fucking freckles that drove him nuts. Saliva pooled in his mouth at the thought of running his tongue over the trio. If this was his punishment for the sins of his past, it hit the fucking mark. One lick. That's all he needed. Just a hit of her flavor to slate the hunger.

Okay, that was a fucking lie.

A sample would never be enough. If she gave him a taste, he'd devour the whole fucking meal.

"Chloe, you need to cover the fuck up." The words came out harsh.

One half of her mouth curled up in a semi-smirk. He was around painted up women daily at the clubhouse, yet the sight of Chloe's naked mouth was sexier than any shade of lipstick he'd ever seen.

"I don't believe you," she said.

He snorted. "No?" Grabbing her hand, he pulled it across his body until it rested right over his hard-on. "That make you a convert?"

Her soft chuckle did nothing to ease his desire. Her hand curled, giving him the slightest squeeze.

"Fuck me," he said on a groan as he stared up at the ceiling. Yeah, there most definitely was a God and he was in full-on smiting mode.

"While I appreciate the warning, that's not at all what I was referring to. I was talking about the bullshit you spouted earlier."

Rocket couldn't help it. She was too fucking cute with her nose wrinkled and her pissed off expression that didn't quite take away her cream-puff look. "What bullshit are you talking about?"

"The bullshit about you leaving DarkOps because they were using you, not because you had a problem killing an innocent man. Or if you don't want to call him innocent, a man that didn't deserved to be killed." She fell silent, just stared at him with those emerald eyes that seemed to see clear into his soul.

Rocket

Why couldn't she just buy the damn story, walk away from him, and let him suffer in peace? He steeled his expression. Looked like he was going to have to fall back on plan B: being a total dick.

Her hating him was far better than Esposito getting his filthy mitts on her.

"Little girl," he practically growled as he loomed over her. Fear flashed for just one second before she schooled it, but it was enough to make him want to vomit. If hell wasn't his after-life plan before, he'd made it so now. "You think you fucking know me? You don't know shit about me. I've done shit that would make Lefty look like a fuckin choir boy." Let her chew on that for a while.

Expression so calm it was almost serene, she reached a hand up and covered his mouth. Rocket flinched, the initial contact like fire and silk all at once. "Stop," she said, but her voice held no fear. More like a teacher scolding a disobedient student. "I don't know everything there is to know about you. Not even close. And I don't know the details of your work with DarkOps, but I've gathered it's dark and probably twisted."

Understatement of the century.

"I've spent a lot of time with you recently. My past may be bright and shiny, but my present is pretty damned dark and twisted. Yet there is only one man I can say with one hundred percent certainty I trust to keep me safe. One man I know without a doubt will not hurt me no matter how vulnerable I make myself. And it's you. I *know* you, Logan. Your name and Lefty's should never be spoken in the same sentence, unless it's to describe the ways you plan to make him suffer."

He froze, the breath in his lungs seizing. A slow, yet powerful thump sounded in his ears in time with each beat of his heart. She was right. He'd die before hurting her, physically at least. Before this was over, both their hearts could end up flayed.

"So why don't you try again. Tell me what really eats at you about your time with DarkOps. Tell me why you were upset today. You know my deepest shame and are the only one who has seen me in the very lowest moment of my life. Let me see you in yours. I will not betray your trust. And I will not walk away from you because of it."

He didn't dare blink. If he did, the angel lying next to him would surely vanish. How could a woman who'd been raised by a loving, supportive family, one that sheltered her from life's ugly side, accept him so easily? Sure, she'd gotten an up close and personal view of hell recently, but she should only be more critical of him because of it.

"Please," she whispered. With a tender touch, she nudged his chest until he was also lying. He faced her, propping up on one hand. Her long auburn hair spilled down her back and over her shoulder, beckoning him to touch. If he was about to crack his soul wide open and lay it bare before Chloe, not touching her no longer seemed an option. Hair was safe. Hair was non-sexual. He fingered a lock, lifting it and letting it sift through his fingers. All at once a powerful image of all that red silk wrapped around his fist as he fucked her popped into his head.

So much for non-sexual.

Chloe seemed as eager to touch him. She inched closer, then closer still until only inches remained between their mouths, and her legs were able to tangle with his. "You've made this easy since you're totally naked," she said.

Rocket groaned. "And you're only wearing fucking panties."

She chuckled. "Yep." Once again, she grew serious. "Please give it to me."

Jesus, if that wasn't a phrase to be misinterpreted, nothing was. Chloe had given him so much of herself. She'd walked miles out of her safety zone and trusted he wouldn't hurt her. He could give her this—he owed it to her.

Still playing with her hair, he stared straight into her eyes. The patience and understanding he saw shining back at him allowed him to speak. "Discovering the details of my last mission was a fluke. For almost two years, I took the jobs they assigned me without question. Without looking beyond the surface. Esposito knew that. Probably used it to his advantage."

"You trusted him. Trusted the company."

Like a fool. "Yes."

Chloe shifted her thigh. Her buttery soft skin whispered across the head of his cock. Rocket bit back a shouted curse.

"Sorry."

He huffed out a laugh. "I'll take any touch from you I can get. Even if it kills me."

"Keep going. I think I know what you're going to say, but you need to say it, Logan. You need to purge it."

The only light was the dim glow shining from a nightlight in the hallway. Rocket always kept some form of light in the halls for security purposes. Never know when he might need a quick getaway.

Old habits died pretty damned hard.

A troubling thought popped into his head. "You never got a chance to purge your demons, did you? Because we asked you not to speak to anyone about what happened."

She gave him a half smile. "And see what happens when you let things fester? You develop really risky behavior like picking up strange men at the bar."

Risky wasn't tame enough a word. Fucking idiotic fit better.

Chloe poked his side. "Logan, I was kidding. It was a joke."

"Someday I want you to tell me. All the details, no matter how ugly."

"Okay," she said softly. "But today we're working on unburdening your soul. Tomorrow we can do mine."

Rocket inhaled until his lungs were at capacity. He held it, then said the words he'd never dared to utter. "How many innocent people have I killed because I was too damn complacent to question my missions?"

Silence met the question until he almost begged her to say something. Anything.

"You never went back and dug through the details of your old missions?" she finally asked.

He shook his head. "No. I couldn't."

Chloe captured his hand in her much slenderer one. After working her hair free from between his fingers, she placed his hand over his heart, anchoring it there with her own. His heart thumped steady and strong beneath their palms. "Feel that?" she asked.

"I feel it."

"In there lies the heart of a protector. I may not know all of you, but I know that much is true. You are a man who guards and defends. You've built your life around it."

Nearly the same words had come from Copper's lips only days before. Apparently, this was the image Rocket portrayed. Not a bad one, but he'd always thought of himself more as an angry vengeance seeker. Not a protector.

"Of course, the idea of harming an innocent got to you. It goes against the very heart of who you are as a man. But, Logan, you have to realize you are as much of a victim here as any innocent person Esposito targeted. You were used, tricked. The details don't matter." She pressed harder against his chest. "This does. And it's not the heart of an evil man. An evil man wouldn't give a shit. An evil man wouldn't be torn up over the notion of bringing danger to his family. An evil man wouldn't give a shit about anyone but himself. And from what I see, the only one you aren't protecting well enough is you. So I'll do it for you."

"Chloe…"

"No," she said, voice firm and unyielding. "I want you to listen to me. And listen good."

Despite the heavy conversation, his lips quirked. So feisty.

She leaned in, breathing right against his ear. "You are a good man, Logan. Nuh-uh," she said when he started to argue. "I'm going to tell you this a lot. Until you start to believe it. You're a good man. You're honorable, strong, and you'd do anything for the people who matter to you. You're a really *good* man."

He swallowed. How could one woman's softly spoken words have the power to break him?

"You don't believe it, do you?"

He shook his head, afraid if he spoke, he'd beg her to tie herself to him forever. A good man. A good man would have taken better care of his dead friend's wife. A good man wouldn't have let her become so depressed, she killed herself.

"Then let me show you," she whispered, then shocked the hell out of him.

Soft lips pressed against his. At once, he opened for her, allowing her to explore his mouth. And she did, kissing him with more tenderness than he'd have thought possible. But it didn't remain that way. Seconds into it, her tongue became insistent, her lips firmed against his, and her tits pressed into his chest, pebbled nipples driving him wild.

Chloe canted her hips, dragging her soaking wet pussy into direct contact with his dick.

"Fuck," he cried out. She was out of her mind if she thought he was strong enough to endure this.

"Touch me, Logan," she pleaded against his mouth. "Put your hands all over me. I need you, now. I need your skin on mine. I need to be close to you. I need you inside me."

And with those six sentences, Rocket was sunk. Chloe owned him. If she thought he'd do anything for those he cared about, she was dead wrong. For her, he'd fucking blow up the moon. Too bad the only explosion was going to be his heart when she was healed enough to realize she didn't want an outlaw biker in her life.

CHAPTER TWENTY-FOUR

"Straddle me," Rocket bit out, desperation bleeding through the command.

Chloe grabbed his shoulder, holding him on his side. "No," she said.

He grew still. "Sorry," he said as he started to scoot away.

"No!" she said again. "Don't move away. That's not what I meant. I don't want to cuff you. I don't want to be on top. I—can we stay like this. Facing each other?" Her cheeks burned so hot, she was beyond grateful for the minimal lighting.

"I want nothing more than to feel you all pressed against me, Chloe. We can do anything you want."

"I want you like this."

His erection lay trapped between them, so hard and heavy, Chloe's sex clenched. Soon it would be inside her, bringing her the pleasure she craved.

Every word out of her mouth was genuine. With her entire heart, she believed Logan was a good man. Sure, he didn't follow the letter of the law, but his worth couldn't be judged only by the fact he was in an outlaw MC.

"Can I touch you? I've been dying to run my hands all over this gorgeous body."

"Yes, please," she breathed out, already anticipating his callused hands coasting over her skin.

Rocket

He started slow, and so gently tears came to her eyes, but she refused to let them fall. This was the time for pleasure and connection. He stroked down her shoulders, over her stomach, and up the sides of her breasts. Everywhere he touched fizzled where electricity remained, reminding her she was alive.

She was so wet, her juices had coated his thigh as well as her own. Chloe rubbed her slit against him. Tiny shocks of pleasure shot from her pussy all through her body.

"All that cream for me?" Logan asked.

"Yes. Just you. Always for you."

A rumble sounded in his chest seconds before he smashed his mouth against hers. She met him head on, fighting for control of the kiss. Logan's hands were everywhere with much bolder pressure than before. Squeezing her ass, stroking her thighs, and running up and down her sides until he finally palmed her breasts. Her nipples ached with a fierce need for attention. Logan must have sensed it. He chuckled into her mouth then pinched both nipples, twisting as he did. "This what you need?"

"Yes," she said on a groan as she arched into his touch. He didn't let up, tugging her nipples and rotating them between his thumb and forefinger. His mouth no longer on hers, he trailed a path of hot kisses from her jaw to her shoulder. Chloe's mind spun at the onslaught of pleasure. Even though she'd had sex with Logan, even though he'd made her come at least once every time, something had been missing. This was it. The connection of two minds and bodies fully engaged with each other. Intertwined and losing themselves in the magic of touch. No handcuffs, no rules, no worry about control. Just need and want.

"More," she said, running her hands over his abundance of muscles. Rounded shoulders, corded bands along his spine, ridged abdomen. Her fingers dipped into that V of his hips that drove all women bonkers. The man was physical perfection. Unable to resist the tempting offer so close at hand, she curled her fingers around his length and gave a few strong strokes.

Rocket grunted. "So it's like that, huh?"

His hands immediately left her breasts. The grin he gave when she whimpered was nothing short of wicked. And then he was there, those very talented fingers gliding through her slippery folds. He worked her like no one else had ever come close to doing. Fucking her with his fingers, strumming her clit, teasing her opening, he drove her straight up at lightning speed.

And then his mouth closed around her nipple. When he'd moved to her breasts, she had no idea. Her brain could barely process the combined sensations coming at her from every angle.

"Logan," she cried out as his teeth scraped over her. Between her legs, his fingers still played her like a treasured instrument. She speared her fingers into his hair, holding him against her. Still, he had so much strength on her, he easily licked his way to the other breast. All at once, he shoved two fingers deep inside her, pressed her clit with his thumb, and sucked hard on her nipple. Chloe bowed into him, a ragged yell leaving her as she came.

Logan gave her no time to recover. He palmed her cheeks, kissing her again and again, as though praising her for being brave enough to let him touch her. "I wanted to make you come at least one more time before I fucked you. Goddammit, I wanted to eat that pussy until you came all over my face."

With no chance to recover from the hard orgasm, her head was already spinning. The erotic words only made her eyes glaze over more as renewed desire crashed over her. "You can do anything you want," she said. It wasn't really true. She wasn't ready to take his weight on top of her, but Logan was a good enough man to recognize that and respect it.

"I can't," he ground out. "I have to be inside you. Right now. I'm gonna fucking lose my mind if I can't feel that pussy on my cock. I'm clean. Swear it on my life."

"Me too," she said. "Tested." He'd gone back to playing with her nipples and one to two words were all she could string together at once. "IUD."

"Fuck, yes," he said as he grabbed her top leg. In one smooth motion, he lifted her thigh over his and entered her, hard and deep.

"Ohmygod," Chloe cried out as he filled her to capacity.

Logan stopped moving. "You okay?"

She shook her head. "Would be better if you'd start moving."

"Pretty sure I can manage that." He hiked his hand higher up the back of her thigh, holding her in place as he started to slowly withdraw. Chloe glanced down her body. Even in the darkened room, she could see just how damn sexy his tanned hand looked on the pale skin of her thigh. He gripped her hard, five fingers denting into her flesh. Chances were, she'd have marks tomorrow. One could only hope. Something to remember the significance of the night. Because it was so freaking significant. She didn't know how to label it, or if she should even try, but something had shifted between them when Logan opened up to her. It went far beyond just her physical progress. They were connected now. Bonded by their mutual pain and trauma.

"Ready for more?"

She looked at his serious expression most would describe as mean. Funny, she'd never once thought of him that way, even though he hardly smiled. "I'm ready for all you got."

And there it was. A rare Logan smile. "You got it, ma'am," he quipped as he started to fuck her with real power. Teasing stopped. Talking ceased. The only sounds in the room were those of their bodies coming together and her frequent mewls of pleasure. His hand moved to her ass, fingers scoring the tender flesh as he held her exactly where he wanted her for his pummeling.

It was then, Chloe realized he was completely in control. Okay, sure, if she yelled "Stop," he'd drop her like a hot potato, but at that moment, *he* was fucking *her*. Not the other way around. And damn did it feel unbelievable to let someone else take the reins for a little while.

"Finger your clit," he said. His nostrils flared, jaw ticked, and his eyes were slits as though he was fighting like hell to maintain control. "Not gonna last," he said. "Riding you goddamn bareback is too fucking good. Do it now."

She complied at once, hand diving between them until she reached her clit. One feather light stroke was enough to make her cry out and her body jolt. Rocket pounded into her, his cock dragging ruthlessly over the sensitive nerve endings in her sex. "You there?" he asked, never breaking from the brutal thrusts.

God was she ever there. "Y-yes."

"Come now."

He thrust hard, three more times, before slamming deep and shooting inside her. As he did, he batted her hand away and pressed his thumb to her clit. Chloe went off like a whole display of fireworks.

Without meaning to, she dug her nails into the backs of his arms as she groaned through the epic climax. Her entire body shook, out of control for long seconds. With anyone else, she'd have been fearful of the vulnerable state, but not with Logan. After he roared out his own climax, he wrapped his strong arms around her and held her until the shaking subsided. Even after the most intense tremors died down, an occasional aftershock rippled through her. Might have something to do with the not completely soft cock still inside her.

"Thank you," he said. The words were gruff and spoken into the top of her head. Chloe tried to look up, but he held her too tight. Perhaps he just wasn't ready to bare more of himself tonight. Which was fine. He'd already given her more than anyone else, even his brothers.

"For what?" she asked.

"For giving me you."

She smiled against his damp pec. With her eyes as heavy as they were, it didn't take long before she was nodding off. The sound of Logan's voice jerked her back to reality. "My life isn't built for a relationship." Pain lanced her heart, all the more agonizing for the fact she'd been soaring only seconds ago. Of course, he believed that. He still didn't fully believe he wasn't a monster. But they'd get there. As for their relationship?

She wasn't built for one either. At least not anymore. She still had issues out the wazoo.

"Shh." She put her hand over his mouth. "I don't want to have this conversation. Not now. Maybe not ever. Can we just enjoy each other until it's done?"

He was silent for a moment, then his soft lips caressed her palm. She pulled her hand back to allow him to speak. "Yeah. We can do that." He kissed the top of her head. "You gonna be able to handle me or one of my brothers being your shadow until this shit with Esposito's been resolved?"

"Pretty sure I'll handle it better than Izzy."

He grunted and tightened his arms. Right there, wrapped up in him, she felt invincible. There wasn't a thing in the world that could touch her as long as Logan was around. They were a mess of sweaty post-sex stickiness, but neither moved. Logan's shower wasn't going anywhere and neither was he, at least not for the moment. She wasn't going to risk missing this intimate moment to clean up. Later, they could shower together and hopefully she could talk him into another round.

He rubbed up and down her back in long, soothing strokes. Chloe's eyelids drooped once again as a pleasant lethargy flowed through her. Finally, for the first time in months, she was going to sleep feeling completely safe and protected.

Still inside her, Logan started to thicken again. She must have made a noise of disbelief because he chuckled. "Can't help it, baby. You're too damn hot. But sleep for a bit. I promise he'll come around again five seconds after you wake up."

Safe. Protected. Happy.

She fell asleep surrounded by his warmth and crossing her fingers this would last longer than the niggling in her gut warned.

CHAPTER TWENTY-FIVE

The following two weeks sailed by. In the daytime, when Logan was required to visit various job sites, Chloe completed her own work from his breathtaking house. They'd grabbed her laptop and a few paper files from her place the day after she arrived at his house.

Along with the French doors leading to the balcony, his master bedroom boasted a large arched bay window overlooking the mountains. After she'd spent twenty minutes gushing about the view, Logan had dragged a buttery soft leather recliner from an upstairs loft area over to the window. She spent hours at her computer managing her client's accounts and occasionally getting lost in the scenery.

All in all, she hadn't left the house much. Whenever Logan worked, another biker was parked outside, keeping an eye on things. Anything she needed, one of the prospects was tasked with fetching for her. And when Logan returned home each evening, she'd had no desire to leave him.

Home.

She ought to be careful throwing that word around so comfortably.

Bottom line, she'd spent a blissful fourteen days getting to know Logan on all levels. And she'd learned quite a bit about him. The man was a coffee fiend. Drank at least a pot of the stuff before noon. He was also neat. Crazy neat. Wouldn't-leave-a-glass-in-the-sink neat. And he slept buck naked every night after making her lose her mind with pleasure. She still hadn't ventured into any territory where he laid directly on top of her or caged her in, in any way, but they'd gotten creative with a myriad of other highly enjoyable positions.

Chloe also had a few chances to hang with the ol' ladies of the MC. Once at the clubhouse, and twice at Toni and Zach's place. She was officially as smitten with them as she was with Logan, though in vastly different ways. Not one of the women pressed her to talk about her kidnapping, yet there was a kinship and understanding between them. Each woman was a pillar of strength in her own way despite having some triggers due to past distressing experiences. Izzy's triggers tended more toward a rage-filled reaction as opposed to fear or panic, but none had made it to the stages they were without some form of traumatic ordeal.

Despite the fun two weeks, reality still existed, mostly in the form of Chloe being sick of the few outfits she'd brought to Logan's and needing some additional files on a new client. That meant a trip to her neglected little house.

Rocket swung home after work on Friday evening and picked her up, which meant she got to ride the thirty-minute trip to her house on the back of his bike. An activity she'd totally fallen in love with. Not much surpassed the feeling of freedom and euphoria she experienced wrapped around Logan as he cruised the mountain roads.

"Man, that gets better every time," Chloe said as she tugged off the helmet. Smoothing a hand down her long braid, she tamed the flyaways that sprung out no matter how tight she worked the strands. As much as Logan proclaimed to love her hair down, she refused to wear it that way on the bike. She'd made that mistake only once. It'd taken her hours to work the tangles out of her thick strands. Hours she'd much rather spend naked in bed with Logan. Once she'd presented that argument, he no longer gave her grief about riding with a braid. If only all their disagreements were that easy to win.

"You're a natural," he said with a swat on her ass.

She giggled and swatted him right back.

"Hey!" he said as he lunged for her.

With another laugh she tried to jump out of the way, but was no match for his speed. In the blink of an eye he had her over his shoulder, his palm cracking against her ass once again. "Only one of us is allowed to do any spanking. You hear me?"

"Hmm," Chloe said. Despite the blood rushing to her head, she couldn't really complain about the position he had her in. Not when she had an up close and personal view of his very fine ass. "I hear you. I'm not allowed to spank." Her braid swung back and forth like a pendulum, only inches from the ground. A smirk curled her lips. "Guess I'll just be doing this instead." Before he had a chance to react, she pinched what she could grab of his ass. It wasn't much; the damn man had a damn hard ass, but she managed to elicit a grunt and a jolt from him.

He dropped her back to her feet and growled as he caught her in a loose head lock. "Whatcha gonna do now, smartass?"

The playful side of Logan came out so rarely, she treasured every second of it. As it was, she'd never seen him act this way with anyone other than her. Warmth filled her chest. He might not be one to give her flowery words every day, telling her how he felt about her, but his actions showed the depth of caring he felt toward her and never failed to make her feel like the most special woman on the planet. At least in his eyes.

"This work?" she asked with an impish grin and she reached back and pressed the heel of her hand against his balls.

"Shit," he cried out, releasing her at once. "You win." His genuine and also rare smile meant the freaking world.

"Come on." She grabbed his hand and towed him toward the door. "This place looks itty bitty compared to your castle," she said with a huff. She'd taken to calling Logan's house a castle, which never failed to make him roll his eyes and curse Shell's name.

Just as she slid the key into the deadbolt lock, her front door jerked open and Scott barreled out. His face was a facade of murderous fury. Before she had time to process his presence, she was yanked behind her brother and away from Logan.

"Who the fuck are you?" Scott yelled in a venomous tone she'd never known was possible from him.

"Scott..." She peered around him only to shriek, "What the hell are you doing? Get that gun out of his face." Held in Scott's hand as though it were nothing but an extension of his arm, was a deadly black pistol. "Scott, please!" she tried again as a cold sweat broke out all over her body.

"Is this him?" Scotty snarled, thrusting the gun in Logan's direction. "For Christ's sake, tell me this is not him, Chloe."

Logan lifted his hands. Chloe sensed rather than saw a change in him. He wasn't scared, wasn't surrendering by any means. Scott may be a Green Beret, but Logan had dangerous skills she did not want to see in action. At least not in this case.

Chloe tried to take a step to the right only to be locked in place by Scott's free hand. "L-Logan," she called out from behind her brother's broad back, words quivering. "T-this is m-my brother, Scott." *Please don't hurt him* was the unspoken request.

"Babe," Logan, said, eerily calm for having the business end of a powerful weapon inches from his face. "You need to tell him to stand down." *Or I will hurt him.* His unspoken message was as clear as hers.

"Don't you fucking give her orders," Scott said, still in attack mode. "Babe?" he asked in a way that sounded like Logan had insulted her instead of using an endearment. "Jesus Christ, you tell me this motherfucker is him and I swear to God I'll gun him down on your porch."

"Scott," she said, gently placing her hands on her brother's back. He didn't so much as twitch. Tension coiled his muscles so tight they felt as though they could snap beneath her palms.

"Please put the g-gun down. You're s-scaring me. L-let's go inside and t-talk. One of my neighbors is going to see you and call the police."

"Maybe they need to be called. Tell me who this fucking biker is, Clo and do it now."

"His name is Logan. And he's—"

"Is. It. Him."

Again, she tried to step around the wall of her brother, but Scott had a fistful of her sweatshirt.

"Do not move, Chloe." Logan said.

"Shut the fuck up," Scott sneered.

This situation was going downhill fast. "Okay, okay, I'm not moving." Chloe said to Scott's back. "Is he who, Scott?"

"Is he the motherfucking boyfriend who raped you and beat you bloody?" he snarled like a panther seconds from pouncing.

Well, fuck.

"The hell is he talking about?" Logan asked.

"I told you to shut the fuck up." Scott stepped forward, dragging her with him. God, he was so close to Logan now, the gun had to be pressed right between his eyes. Chloe knew deep in her gut Logan could get away if he wanted. And he was only holding back for her sake.

"You've got thirty seconds to get that water gun out of my face," Logan said in a deceptively tranquil voice. Shit. He wasn't going to hold back for long.

Damnit, Logan.

Scott seethed. He'd do it. He'd shoot Logan right there if he really believed he was protecting his baby sister.

Diffusing this ticking bomb fell to her, which meant giving up information that Logan's club didn't want circulated. But what alternative did she have? Logan's dead body on her stoop? Scott in jail for the rest of his life?

She shuddered.

"Scott," she said as though talking to a frightened animal. "I lied to you about what happened to me. I wasn't assaulted by a boyfriend."

"Ahh, fuck," Logan said as clarity must have set in. She'd never informed him of the tale she'd woven for her family and the authorities. They didn't speak of that night.

"Don't defend this biker piece of shit, sis," Scott said, but he'd lost some of his vehemence.

"I'm not defending anyone, trust me. You know me, Scott. I'd never go anywhere near him if he'd done that to me. I swear on Grandma's grave I'm telling you the truth."

His shoulder relaxed a hint. Had he lowered the weapon? She couldn't see a damn thing. Why did he have to be so freakin' big?

"Can we please go inside now? I promise Logan is no threat to me. And we will explain everything to you, but we need to get off the porch before someone sees you and calls the cops." She poked her head around him and this time he let her. "Please?"

"Fine," Scott said. The gun lowered and Chloe blew out a long breath.

Logan kept his hands at shoulder level.

"But I'm keeping this out until I'm convinced," he said, showing her the gun.

With a painful swallow, Chloe met Logan's gaze. His blue eyes had darkened to the shade of the sky seconds before a hurricane. A barely perceptible dip of his chin was all she got. It was enough for her. He had her full trust to run this show and keep all three of them safe. "That's fine."

The hand at her waist finally released her clothing. Chloe immediately stepped toward Logan. "I don't think so," Scott ground out, catching her by the back of her sweatshirt. "You're staying away from him until I'm satisfied with this situation."

Jerking out of his hold, Chloe scowled at her unreasonable brother. Enough was enough. "Will you stop grabbing my clothes?" With a frustrated sigh, she smoothed her shirt then shoved her brother toward the open door. "Get inside."

Walking backward, he stepped over the threshold into her home without taking his suspicious gaze off Logan. Though he was at least two feet behind her, Logan's presence at her back took away the hysteria she'd have felt were he not there. Of course, if he weren't there, she wouldn't be in this situation in the first place.

Details.

"Sit," Scott barked.

Logan strode to her couch all confident and full of swagger. Like this entire get together had been his idea in the first place. Rolling her eyes, Chloe moved to sit next to him.

"Don't fucking think so," Scott said with a slightly sinister laugh.

"Scott, this is getting ridiculous."

"Sit," he said to her, pointing to the opposite end of her couch with his gun.

She narrowed her eyes. "You need to put that thing away or I'm going to tell mom you pulled a gun on my boyfriend," she muttered as she stomped to the couch. As a kid, she'd been a wicked tattletale, losing her brothers countless privileges as revenge for their antics.

Logan snickered but Scott didn't so much as blink. "Talk," he said.

After clearing his throat, Logan opened his mouth.

"Not you," Scot spat out. "Her."

With a glare for her brother, Chloe folded her arms across her chest. Prepared to blast him for being an idiot, she caught Logan's gaze. As small as the nod he'd given her outside, he shook his head.

Chloe's heart plummeted. Looking at this through Scott's perspective put an entirely different spin on the scenario. Here he was, coming to surprise her when he found her with an outlaw biker after she'd been raped and beaten by who he thought was a vicious boyfriend. No wonder he went all alpha on her.

She opened her mouth, but suddenly the words weren't there. Reality of what she'd experienced was far worse than the story she'd told her family. Shame washed over her. No one really knew exactly what had happened in that motel room. Not even Logan. Now, not only did she have to bear her humiliation for her brother, she had to show it to her lover as well.

"It's okay, baby," Logan said in a soft voice as though privy to her internal struggle.

She blinked at him as tears flooded her eyes.

"Fuck it," Logan said. "Shoot me if you gotta, man." He scooted down the couch and pulled her onto his lap. At once, she curled into him, soaking up the warmth and safety only he could provide. Glancing at Scott, she expected to see him with his finger on the trigger again. Instead, he had a profound look of sadness on his face. All their lives, he'd been her favorite big brother. Her best friend, her protector. Couldn't be easy to see himself replaced. And by a man he didn't trust.

"All right," he said, laying his weapon on her end table. "You win." He took a seat on the side of the couch Logan had vacated. "Tell me."

Logan looked to her and she gave as much of a sad smile as she could muster. "Your sister had stopped at a Subway to grab some dinner one night," he began. He must have sensed how difficult it would be for her to rehash it all on her own. So he took the burden from her. Despite how much he hated talking to people he didn't know. Just one of the many reasons she loved—

Holy shit.

I love him.

Chloe swallowed. There was no denying it. She'd fallen in love with the man. How could she not?

"It was late. The parking lot was dark as fuck. She was nabbed right by her car. Tossed in her trunk. Kidnapped."

"Christ." Scott hung his head. "I should have given you Mace. I should have given you a fucking gun."

"It wouldn't have helped," she said, her heart heavy. "They clocked me from behind. It happened too fast for me to react. I was careless, not paying attention to my surroundings."

"Who was it that took you?" her brother asked, running his fingertip along the barrel of his gun where it rested on her end table. She had the distinct impression he was imagining using it on whoever had hurt her.

"It was a gang," Logan answered. "Led by a guy by the name of Lefty. Real motherfucker."

"Why?"

"Trafficking."

"Fuck." Scott's curse was whispered.

"Lefty is an enemy of my club. We got wind of what happened and my prez had a meeting with him. Demanded he release her or we'd set the full power of the club on ending him. Gave him orders to leave her in a motel room unharmed." His voice grew thick, pained sounding. "I'm the one who found her."

"Not unharmed," Scott said.

"No."

The only thing keeping Chloe from losing her shit was the steady thrum of Logan's heartbeat beneath her cheek as she listened to him recount the events leading up to her rescue. As much as she appreciated him taking on this task, it was time for her to speak up. Horrifying as it was, she needed to own what had happened to her. How could she move on with Logan or any man—though the thought of trying to be with another man made her stomach hurt—if she didn't face what had happened head on?

Straightening on Logan's lap, she looked her brother in the eye. "No," she said, pleased with the strength of her voice. "They beat me. Badly. And..." Just breathe. "And they raped me," she said as she looked Scott square in the eye.

Anguish flashed across his face, impossible to miss. "They?"

242

Chloe swallowed. "Three of them," she whispered.

Logan's arm tightened almost to the point of uncomfortable. She risked a glance at him. His jaw was like granite, nostrils flared, eyes shooting sparks, but he held himself in check despite the fact the information was new for him as well.

Scott did not. "Fuck. *Fuck!*" he screamed as he sprang from the couch. "Tell me these fuckers paid. Tell me you've got their dicks in a jar in your closet."

What the...

"Scott," she began.

"No, Sis." He paced the length of her small living room, hands clutched in his hair. "Christ, are you...shit! I don't even know what to ask."

"I'm all right, Scott. Now anyway. Physically, I'm all healed and I'm working through the mental stuff." She glanced at Logan who gave her a much softer squeeze. His facial expression was still as serious as she'd ever seen it. This had to be almost as hard for him as it was for her to recount. Remembering her in the state he'd found her couldn't be easy. "Logan's helping me more than you could know. He's a good man." She said for his benefit as much as Scott's.

The groan that left her brother was tortured. "He's an outlaw biker, Chloe. Not what you need."

After pressing a quick kiss to Logan's flat mouth, she focused on her brother. "I told you the truth. Gave you what you asked for. My relationship with Logan is not up for discussion. You do not get a say in anything related to him."

"Aww, isn't that sweet. Had no idea you had such a champion in your corner, Rocket," said a man from Chloe's now open doorway.

In a flash, Logan had deposited her on the couch and was standing between her and whoever had entered her house. Her whole body locked up at the thought of an uninvited male in her house.

Shit, was it Lefty? Chloe forced herself to breathe in an even in-and-out pattern. No. She'd recognize Lefty's voice anywhere. She'd heard it in her head daily for months after she was rescued. This wasn't Lefty.

"Who the fuck are you?" Scott asked as he reached for his gun.

"Don't," Logan barked. Gone was the calm façade he'd shown all morning. In its place was a predator.

Scott froze.

Chloe leaned to her right. Her heart pounded as she took in the newcomer. She gasped then covered her mouth as recognition set in.

"You crossed a fucking line, old man." Logan advanced toward him but Chloe grabbed his arm, holding him back. He'd left his weapon in his saddle bag, thinking they'd be in and out in under five minutes. Knowing Logan as she did, she knew he'd beat himself up over that for a long time.

The menacing grin that crossed the man's face told them all he didn't care how many lines he crossed. A shiver raced down Chloe's spine.

However crazy the evening had already been, it'd just gotten a whole lot worse.

CHAPTER TWENTY-SIX

"You made this so easy it was almost boring," Esposito said in a droll tone, as though he really was bored when Rocket knew he was fucking elated by this turn of events.

Icy rage surged through Rocket's veins.

How could he have been so goddamned oblivious?

Beside him, Scott tensed, as prepared for action as Rocket.

"Let me reach for my gun," Scott muttered so low he almost missed the words. "I think he's unarmed."

From talking with Chloe a few weeks ago, he'd learned Scott had been serving as a Green Beret for over a decade. Meant the man was more than capable of handling himself and protecting Chloe. Though if anyone was going to stick near Chloe, it'd be Rocket.

"Tell him," Esposito said after a few seconds of silence ticked by. Of course he heard Scott's murmuring.

Over the years, Rocket had learned the quiet could be his best weapon. People often hung themselves if he gave them enough rope. But Esposito wasn't a naive fool who'd fall for his psychological warfare. Still, Rocket fell back on old habits.

"He's always armed," he finally said.

"Who the fuck is he?"

"Esposito," Chloe whispered from her spot on the couch.

Dammit, Rocket had nearly forgotten Copper had passed Esposito's photograph around the clubhouse. Though Chloe was clever enough to figure it out without visual aid.

"Esposito, huh?" Scott said, letting some bravado enter his voice. "That supposed to mean something to me?"

"He runs DarkOps," Chloe said while Rocket remained mute.

"Ahh, I see you told your pretty lady about me," Esposito said with a wink for Chloe.

"Eyes on me, old man." Rocket growled. So much for not talking. One glance at Chloe and he was ready to pounce.

Scott snorted. "Showing your hand a bit early there, man," he said form the corner of his mouth.

Didn't matter. Esposito already knew Rocket was deeply involved with Chloe. No point in pretending otherwise.

Scott ran a hand through his short hair. "DarkOps." He shook his head. "Jesus, you got my sister mixed up in some shit, didn't you?"

"I see my reputation precedes me." Esposito extended a hand in Scott's direction. "Nicholas Esposito. And I'm not as old as Rocket likes to think."

Rocket resisted the urge to roll his eyes. The old man could be charming as fuck when he wanted to be. That's how he drew so many unsuspecting suckers into his company.

Scott ignored the outstretched hand. "Why don't you just tell us why you're here. Doesn't much seem like you're wanted."

Esposito's eyes shifted to Rocket. In his early sixties, Esposito no longer resembled the man Rocket knew, a man who kept himself in tip-top shape. Looking at him was almost a comical paradox. Faded ink ran down both forearms which were thinned with waning muscle and covered with wrinkling skin. Yet Rocket had no doubt he was as deadly as always despite the softening of his body over the years.

"I need him." He jerked his thumb in Rocket's direction. "Got a complicated job and I need the best."

Rocket grunted. Complicated job. More like he needed someone he could manipulate to perform an unsanctioned kill.

"You work for him?" Scott asked.

"No," Chloe said, the word ripe with finality. "He doesn't."

She stood, and Rocket wanted to knock her back to the couch. But damn if she didn't look sexy as hell, all indignant on his behalf. "This is my house, and you're trespassing. You need to leave now, or I'll be forced to call the police."

Like DarkOps didn't pull the strings of law enforcement all across the country. Hell, the world. Chloe wouldn't be aware of that, though. She still believed in a universe where those who vowed to protect and serve actually did so.

Esposito smirked. "Got a live one there, huh, Rocket? Pretty thing too."

"What'd I say about your fucking eyes?"

The smirk reappeared; this time accompanied by a shrug. "All right," Esposito said as he lifted his hands. "I can see I'm not welcome here. Just wanted to check in one last time before I head back to South Carolina."

"You made your offer. Now leave," Chloe said as she took a step closer to Rocket.

Rocket reached out and tagged her around the waist, bringing her flush against his side. Without so much as a flicker of resistance, she melted into his side, circling her arm around his back. The contact pacified him somewhat. Confirmation she was safe despite the shitstorm of the evening.

Esposito flicked a glance her way then focused back on Rocket. "Actually, I haven't made my offer yet. But I do have one."

Rocket clenched his fists. Shit. Unease slithered down his spine, twisting his gut. Whatever Esposito was about to lay out, he had a feeling it was the ace the man needed to get what he wanted.

"One job," he said to Rocket as though they were the only two in the room. "Couple weeks max."

Rocket rolled his shoulders, breathing slow to keep from reaching out and wringing Esposito's neck. Next to him, Chloe flinched subtly. Shit, he'd been squeezing the life out of her waist. Rocket forced his grip to slacken. "And?"

"And in return, you get this." Esposito lobbed his phone to Rocket.

With one hand, he snagged it out of the air.

"Open it up. No passcode. There's a video on screen. Go ahead and give it a look."

Rocket met Esposito's gaze. Dread filled him, almost to the point he didn't swipe the screen open. Whatever the video contained, it was the key to Rocket's compliance. Deep down in his gut, he sensed Esposito was about to dangle a carrot he'd be forced to chase.

The room fell eerily quiet. Only the soft sound of Chloe's shaky breathing registered.

Watching the video was a fucking mistake of epic proportions, but what choice did he have? He just prayed Esposito hadn't abducted one of his brothers or their ol' ladies. He'd never be able to live with that guilt. Careful not to let his discomfort show, he swiped up. On screen was the image of a dark room Rocket didn't recognize. The camera had been angled toward a corner that appeared to be empty.

"What the fuck is this?"

"Play it," Esposito ordered.

Chloe rested her cheek against his bicep as she peered down at the screen with him. As the recording began to play, the camera panned across a dimly lit room. After only five seconds, Chloe gasped. Rocket's head snapped up.

"Oh my God," Chloe breathed. "How did you...it's him." Next to Rocket, she started to tremble.

Esposito grinned at him. "Check mate," he said then spoke to Chloe. "I'm sorry for what you went through, Chloe."

The motherfucker.

"Fuck you," she yelled, lunging forward out of Rocket's grasp.

Rocket

Scott caught the waist band of her jeans, dragging her back to him. She seethed, struggling against her brother, but he held firm, wrapping her in his bulky arms and whispering in her ear.

Though Scott still restrained her, Rocket slipped his fingers through hers. At once, she settled. After he was certain she wouldn't be committing murder, he focused on the video. There it was, right there. The goddamn winning hand.

On the screen, Lefty sat on the floor in an empty room, clearly a prisoner. The grainy feed didn't allow for details, but he appeared to be slumped against the wall, injured. Esposito wouldn't have been able to resist taking a bit of fun for himself.

"You give me what I want," Esposito said. "And I'll give you what you want. Hand delivered to your club alive and kicking. Simple as that."

Christ, he could taste the thrill of killing Lefty. And it was delicious. "I'll do it," he said, tossing the phone back before the clip ended.

"No!" Chloe cried out, once again struggling against her brother's hold. "No, Logan, you can't." Her voice cracked. She squeezed his hand until her knuckles whitened. Horror was scrawled all across her pale face. "It's not worth it."

Not worth it? She had no clue exactly how worth it getting his hands on Lefty was. "I have to," he said.

She stared at him, eyes watery and lips pressed into a thin line. After what felt like five minutes of watching her heart bleed, she sagged against Scott, and nodded. "I know you do."

"One of you better tell me what the fuck is going on," Scott said from behind Chloe.

"The old man's got Lefty." Those five words were all it took for understanding to cross Scott's face.

Rocket should have known Esposito would pull a trick so dirty he couldn't refuse. Lefty was literally the one prize he'd never walk away from under any circumstance.

Scott released Chloe and charged forward. He hovered over Esposito, snarling and snapping like a junkyard dog. "You fuck him up?"

"A little." Esposito shrugged. "Not enough. Figure Rocket wouldn't agree to my terms if I took away his fun."

"Scott, calm down." When her brother turned and began pacing the room like a caged animal, Chloe faced Rocket. "Logan," she said, yanking on his arm to get his attention. "Please don't do this. It's not worth it. It's not worth whatever he's going to make you do."

Esposito was going to make him kill an innocent man and woman.

The soft plea was a knife, carving into his heart. Chloe would rather sacrifice her chance at getting justice for the atrocious crimes committed against her than have him live with one more DarkOps mission tainting his soul. He'd been wrong, there was one scenario where he'd walk away from Lefty. If Chloe truly asked him. If the night passed and she woke, unable to live with him taking on this task, he'd leave Lefty to Esposito. But, fuck, he hoped it didn't come down to that. Part of him would never feel fulfilled.

"When do you want me?" he asked Esposito. It took nearly everything in him not to crack under the weight of Chloe's despair.

"I'll send a driver for you in the morning. About five."

Rocket nodded once. "You got what you wanted. Now get the fuck out of my woman's house."

After giving him a two fingered salute, Esposito turned to Chloe. "I really am sorry for what happened to you. DarkOps is glad to have a hand in doling out punishment to the man who orchestrated your kidnapping. And I'm sorry it had to go down this way, but I need him. And this time, I can't take no for an answer."

"You show up here again, I'll shoot you myself," she snapped.

Despite the gravity of the situation, Rocket smiled. Man, she was something else when she got all feisty.

After Esposito left, Rocket, Chloe, and her brother stood staring into space for a few moments. Eventually, Rocket sighed. Esposito would be back for him in less than twelve hours and he had a shit ton to get done before then. Starting with...

"You sticking around?" he asked Scott.

"Fuck." Chloe's brother ran a hand through his hair. "Just through the weekend. I'm shipping out Wednesday morning for a few months. Need to report back no later than Monday. Fuck!" He turned and slapped his palm against the wall, making Chloe's floral oil painting crash to the ground.

"Sorry."

"It's okay, Scott," Chloe said, moving to rub her brother's back.

"Maybe you should go stay with Mom and Dad for a while," he said, hands resting on the wall above his head.

Fuck that. "My club will keep her safe. She's not going anywhere."

Chloe frowned. "I can't go stay with our parents. They'll ask too many questions. Besides, my home is here."

"But, Clo—"

"My club will keep her safe," Rocket said again, this time with force. He held out his hand, giving Scott the respect of full eye contact.

With a nod, Scott gripped his hand. They shook, bonding over their need to protect Chloe.

"You can have her this weekend. She's coming home with me tonight."

The sigh that left Scott was full of resignation. "A goddamned outlaw biker," he said with a shake of his head. "You hurt her, and I'm warning you, neither your ninja skills nor your club will mean a damn thing. You'll be a fucking dead man."

A throat cleared. Both men turned to find Chloe frowning with her hands on her hips. "Seriously, guys? Did you forget I was here? I hope so. Because if you didn't, then you're just being jerks and deciding my fate for me while I stand around like an idiot."

Rocket pressed his lips together to keep from grinning. Looked like Chloe hadn't quite gotten out of feisty mode yet.

"Shit. Sorry, sis. You're right. We should have asked you what you wanted to do instead of deciding for you." He had the decency to look sheepish, hands in his pockets, shoulders shrugged to his ears.

Fuck that. Chloe wasn't going to her parents' place. She was spending the night with him. And if she didn't like it, too damn bad. He had no problem hog-tying her to the back of his bike to get her where he needed her to be.

"Thank you," she said with the haughtiness of a queen.

"So what are you thinking. You want to get out of town?"

"Oh…well…um, no I definitely want to stay. Logan's club will keep me safe."

Fighting the urge to snicker, Logan lost the battle to keep his smirk at bay.

Scott's face screwed up in confusion. "Okay, well what do you want to do tonight? Stay here?"

Her face pinked. "No, I'd like to go to Logan's."

Now Scott looked thoroughly baffled. He looked between Chloe and Rocket. "I don't get it. Isn't that the same shit we just said?"

"Yes," Chloe responded.

"So…"

She jammed her hands on her hips. "So you two Neanderthals didn't have to decide it for me. You could have asked me what I wanted."

"But you want what we decided," Scott said.

Chloe threw up her hands and growled. "Yes, but I didn't want you to tell me that. I wanted to tell *you*."

"Dude, help me out here," Scott mumbled. "What the fuck is going on?"

Rocket chuckled. Scott was all right. Clueless about women, but a damn decent guy. "Don't have time to educate you, man. Got a woman to take care of." He winked.

Chloe stared at him, cheeks growing redder by the second. Her two jade-colored eyes stared at him with a combination of worry and adoration. The first was certainly warranted, though he'd try like hell to keep her from spending the entire night anxious for him. The second emotion? Yeah, he didn't deserve adoration from anyone. But he'd fucking take it as long as she was willing to dish it out.

"Christ, Rocket, that's my baby sister you're talking about. Keep that shit to yourself."

Chloe rolled her eyes then stuck her tongue out at her brother in a move that seemed second nature.

While this was entertaining and Chloe was obviously trying to distract herself from the shittiness of the situation with her sibling antics, it was time to get down to business. "Grab what you need, babe," he said right before he gave her a quick hard kiss.

She grabbed him before he drew fully back. "I'm terrified for you," she whispered.

Rocket pressed his lips to her ear. He wouldn't make her promises he couldn't keep, such as coming back in one piece or without an extra black mark on his soul. But he could give her what he knew without a doubt. "It *is* worth it," he whispered. "*You're* worth it. You're the only thing that is."

CHAPTER TWENTY-SEVEN

It was clear by the unhappy Honeys milling about and the mess of bottles strewn all over the clubhouse that Rocket's call for emergency church had interrupted the MC in full-on party mode.

After squaring away Chloe's plan to return home with him, Rocket spent a solid twenty minutes convincing Scott he'd be better off remaining at her house. Chloe had gone off to grab what she needed to set up the guest room for her brother. Scott was pissed and out for blood, but there wasn't a damn thing the man could do short of going AWOL, and Uncle Sam didn't take kindly to deserters. Copper never would have let him sit in on church, so there wasn't any point in him tagging along. After some yelling and choice phrases, Scott finally agreed with the caveat he'd murder Rocket with a big fucking smile on his face should something happen to his baby sister.

Once that problem had been solved, Rocket placed a call to his prez. Despite Copper's ranting threats, Rocket hadn't given up the details over the phone. What he had to say was an in-person conversation and one for the entire club. After much bargaining, Copper agreed to call an immediate emergency church. Only problem, some of the guys were getting an early start that Friday night which meant barely dressed club girls were hanging all around and many of his brothers were well on their way to being blitzed before the sun had even set.

Rocket

He and Chloe stepped into the clubhouse just as Copper's thunderous voice rang out. "Get your asses in the chapel."

"Think the girls are in the kitchen," Rocket said to Chloe.

"Seriously? You're not expecting me to cook or something while we're here, are you?"

With a chuckle, he kissed her lips once. "Of course not. We'll grab something on the way home. Cop said they were in there sucking down wine like water."

She was trying, Rocket had to give her that, but her brightness and perky smile were too cheery to be believable. "Okay. See you after your meeting." She kissed him this time, grabbing the flaps of his cut and fusing her mouth to his. Her sassy tongue swirled around his then was gone before he had a chance to lock her against him. "Don't be long," she whispered. "I need you tonight."

He groaned. Not only was he going to be the last one to walk into church, he'd be doing it with an obvious hard-on. Though the way the club girls were dressed, the majority of his brothers were probably at full chub by now.

He waited until she disappeared into the kitchen before joining the rest of the club in church. All eyes zeroed in on him the moment he opened the door. Being the center of attention was getting old real fast. Time to end this shit once and for all.

Mav was the first to speak. "What the hell is going on, brother?" he asked, which sparked a barrage of questions his way.

"All right, rein it in," Copper yelled when the noise grew too loud to discern what any one man was saying.

Rocket curled his fists. "Can you all shut the fuck up?" he yelled over the rumble of his brothers' curiosity.

The room fell deathly quiet. Completely unused to any kind of outburst from him, he had the attention of each of his brothers. "Esposito has Lefty," he said.

The silence lasted for exactly two point four seconds before mayhem erupted. Each of his brothers shouted questions, insults for Lefty, and general exclamations of disbelief.

Rocket's gaze met Copper's. The president blinked at him, clearly as caught off guard as the rest of them. With a jerk of his head, he shook off the stupor and banged his giant palm on the tabletop. "Shut the fuck up," he roared. "Explain yourself, Rocket."

He sighed. What he wouldn't give to have someone else tell the story. "Took Chloe home to grab some of her shit. Her brother was waiting there, freaked out as fuck because he couldn't get a hold of her. When I showed up, he flipped even more, came barreling out of the house guns blazing. Literally."

"Shit," Jigsaw muttered. "You good?"

Rocket waved away the concern. "Yeah, it's all good. Turned out Chloe had told her family an ex attacked her, and her brother thought I was that fucker."

Mav snorted. "Musta been a few tense moments."

"You have no idea. Thought the guy was gonna fill my skull with lead a few times. He's a Green Beret." Respect for Chloe's brother shot through the roof. More than a few of his brothers had served and each knew what was required to be a special forces soldier of Scott's caliber.

"How's Esposito fit into all this?"

"Getting there." Rocket rubbed the back of his neck. He was starting to feel twitchy without Chloe nearby. Even though she was perfectly safe and happy getting tipsy with her girlfriends, he preferred to keep her in sight. "I was distracted." He shook his head. "Off my fucking game after explaining shit to Scott. Esposito waltzed right the fuck into the house like he'd been invited for a beer."

"Guy's got cojones," Zach said. "I'll give him that." He leaned back in his chair, arms crossed, and feet propped on the table. As usual, his hair looked like a freaking Ken doll.

Rocket

Rocket grunted. "He said he was there to ask me one more time about this bullshit mission." With a shake of his head, he stared at his palms resting on the table. "Knew the second he asked, he had something for me. Something that would keep me from telling him to fuck off."

"Lefty," Jigsaw said.

"Lefty."

"Goddamn," Copper muttered. "How'd he get 'im?"

"No fucking clue. Don't give a shit, either. Esposito has friends in high and very low places. Anyway, he had a video of Lefty so I know he's not lying."

"Would he lie?" Zach asked.

"He'd do anything to get what he wants."

Nodding, Zach looked at Copper then back at Rocket. "Guessing you agreed to the mission."

"Mmm-hmm."

Copper blew out a breath. "Fuck."

"How's Chloe?" Mav asked, his customary snark absent.

"Freaked but hanging in. She's tough as shit, but I know this is killing her. She feels responsible. Knows the hard-on I have for Lefty is because of what he did to her." No one spoke for a moment. With those four sentences, Rocket had shown more of his insides to his brothers than he had since he joined the club. Surprisingly, it wasn't as torturous as he'd thought. More spikes under his nails than skinning flesh.

"She ain't the only reason," Screw added. He was a newly patched member of the club. One who'd been working closely with Zach, learning the role of enforcer. Took a hot minute for Rocket to warm up to him. For the first six months he prospected, he was nothing but a screwball, hence his name. But at some point, a switch had flipped, and he was proving to be a reliable and loyal brother. "Lefty is a scum sucking bottom feeder who's hurt God knows how many women. Women...shit, he's hurt girls. We'd be gunning for him even if it weren't for her."

A few of his brothers grunted their agreement.

Sure, but Rocket wouldn't be jumping into bed with Esposito if it weren't for Chloe. He knew it and so did she. His task for the night would be to show her just how damn worth it she was.

"When are you bugging out?" Copper asked.

"Tomorrow. Ass crack of dawn."

"All right," the prez said with a nod. "You need us at any point, you get in contact."

As each of his brothers nodded their agreement, some of the dread left Rocket. It was damn good to have his family at his back. "Might be doing that, Cop."

"Whatever you need, Rocket. Now, get out of here. Be with your woman. And when it's time to collect, Lefty comes to me. You hear me?"

"Yeah, Cop. I got you." He stood, nodded to all his brothers before heading for the door.

"Rock?" Copper called before he'd gotten halfway to the exit.

He turned.

"Your woman will be safe while you're gone. We'll look out for her real close. Both us and the ol' ladies."

His gaze met Copper's and a wealth of understanding flowed between the two men. Rocket might not have voiced his feelings for Chloe, but, without a second thought, he was marching into hell for a chance at the asshole who'd harmed her.

If he could ease just a fraction of her pain, he'd sell his soul to the highest bidder.

Of course, she didn't want him to do it. She was selfless, not once thinking about revenge or justice for what happened to her. Only worrying over what this assignment would do to him.

The woman was perfection. Gorgeous, kind, selfless, loving. It was no wonder he...

Christ.

It was no wonder he loved her.

Well goddammit.

Copper got it. He'd protect her as he'd protect his own woman.

And that was the one and only reason Rocket would be able to leave her behind.

"SO HOW MUCH trouble am I going to be in for blabbing all that to you ladies?" Chloe asked after sucking back the last of her wine. More than half a glass in three point two minutes. Had to be some kind of record. Unfortunately, the tension relief she'd hoped to achieve wasn't happening. Instead, she sat at one end of the long banquet table surrounded by Toni, Shell, Steph, and Izzy. Mamma V was rummaging through the walk-in pantry for something to sop up the alcohol.

"We won't say a word," Shell said, waving her wine glass around like it wasn't about to slosh all over the table. Apparently, they'd already downed a glass or four by the time she and Rocket showed up.

Izzy snorted a second before stuffing a dinosaur-sized bite of powdered donut in her mouth. "What?" she said with white tinged lips and a full mouth as all the girls turned to stare at her. "I'm hungry."

Chloe couldn't put words to how much she appreciated how hard they were trying to keep the mood upbeat and distract her from what was to come, but she could see the worry in their eyes despite their smiles and attempts at normalcy.

"Excuse me, hungry hippo," Shell said. "I can totally be trusted to keep my mouth shut."

After taking a minute to swallow the sugary goodness, Izzy rolled her eyes. "Sure you can, from us. We all know Copper tells you shit we couldn't pry outta you with the jaws of life." She took a long drink from the laughably large glass of milk in front of her. Setting the glass down she shuddered. "Fuck, milk is disgusting. Freakin' Jig," she muttered. "Anyway," she said as the rest of the girls snickered, "All it'll take is one smoldering look from that giant who warms your bed and one, 'Shell if you don't tell me what you know, I'll take you over my knee,' in that sexy Irish brogue, and you'll be spilling your guts all over the place," Izzy said with a pointed look for Shell.

"Wouldn't be so sure about that," Shell mumbled as she buried her face in her wine glass.

"What was that?" Izzy asked.

Chloe blinked, volleying her head between the players as she tried to keep up with the byplay. Despite her sky-high stress level, they'd managed to wring a smile from her with their banter.

"I believe she was saying something to the effect of not being deterred by the threat of Copper's hand on her ass," Steph broke in.

Mamma V dropped a giant bowl of tortilla chips and a smaller one filled with salsa on the table. "Best I could do, ladies. Looks like I'm going grocery shopping tomorrow. Dammed if one of these fool men would do it themselves."

Chloe opened her mouth to thank the surprisingly maternal older woman just as Izzy said, "Shit, Shell, I had no idea." Her lips curled in a snarky grin. "Bet you're gonna dangle this over his head to get a spanking on purpose, aren't you?"

Shell turned cherry red.

"I would," Steph said without looking up from her position of refilling her glass. When she'd finished giving herself a generous portion, she held it out to Chloe who shook her head no. Logan was leaving tomorrow for a mission she knew nothing about. A mission that could be dangerous to both his physical and mental health. They had the night to spend with each other. There were a few things she wanted to say to him and needed a clear head to do so.

"I'm good, thanks," she said, unable to keep the strain out of her voice.

Steph squeezed her hand.

"Guys," Toni said, snatching up the wine bottle. "They already know Chloe's gonna tell us everything." She shrugged, watching the red liquid fill her glass. "We're sisters. It's what we do."

"Here, here," Steph said, raising her glass. The rest of the women did the same. "You too Clo," she said, gesturing to Chloe's empty glass resting on the table. "You're one of us, babe. And we're gonna get you through this shit."

The moment Logan agreed to Esposito's terms, Chloe's stomach had twisted into a hot ball of tension. She felt it still, burning its way through the lining of her gut. Her entire body vibrated like a pressure cooker, rattling around as the force of the steam grew to threatening levels. If someone didn't open the valve soon, the seal was going to burst, only instead of boiling steam and water spewing every which way, it'd be a messy explosion of her emotions.

"Thanks, you guys," she said, not even trying to hide the choked quality of her voice. The women clinked their glasses together just as the door to the kitchen opened and the men invaded their female bonding.

"Guess it's too much to hope you ladies don't already know exactly what's going on," Zach said as he moved directly toward Toni.

"See," she said, tipping her head back to accept a kiss most would have found too hot for mixed company. Not this group.

"You know," Maverick started as he literally lifted Steph straight out of her seat. He plopped his own ass down in it then drew his woman onto his lap. "Every time—"

With a roll of her eyes, Steph said, "We do know, Mav. Every time you walk in a room where we are, you get a little flare of hope that we'll all be naked and rolling around on the table, moaning, and getting each other off. Then you have to face the crushing sting of disappointment when time after time it doesn't happen."

Chloe's eyes widened just as the warmth of Logan's hands landed on her shoulders. She blinked. Not a single person in the room seemed stunned by Steph's outburst.

"Well…" Mav said before nipping at her jaw. His hands freely roamed over her, not even pretending to avoid her breasts.

Steph shuddered, her eyes darkening as she glanced back at him.

"Well, what?" Izzy asked. Jig sidled up behind her, in much the same position as Logan was with Chloe. Copper just crooked a finger at Shell who rose and went to him immediately. He lifted her to the counter where she rested her head on his large deltoid.

"Well if you ladies all know what I want, why the hell won't you give it to me?" Mav whined. "You're supposed to support my dreams, Steph." He mock growled and she giggled.

The room erupted in laughter and a few raunchy yet encouraging comments from the men.

Above her, Logan remained silent much as she did. Maverick's in-your-face sexuality and humor were a little out of her realm of experience. As time went on, she'd probably find him as hilarious as the others, but for now, most of what came out of his mouth stunned her to silence.

Logan's thumbs stroked along her collar bones. The gentle touch soothed her in a way nothing else could have. It also drove up her need to be alone with him. She zoned out a little, the hypnotic repetition of him stroking her skin lulling her. Next thing she knew, warm breath was tickling her ear. "Let's roll. I need time with you before I gotta leave."

"Yes."

They said a quick good bye to the group who seemed to completely understand their need to be with only each other. The walk to Logan's bike was made in silence. Chloe felt as though a weight was dangling from her heart, dragging her entire body down as she moved. Never chatty, Logan was even quieter than usual, but he held tight to her hand. The silence was just him processing the day's events, and the physical contact was his way of making sure she knew he wasn't neglecting her. Just working things out in his head.

Rocket

When they reached his motorcycle, Chloe climbed on behind him after donning her helmet. The temp had dropped, so she snuggled closer to his back than usual. Oh, who was she kidding? She needed full-body contact. Skin on skin would have been better, but she'd take what she could get, so she held him tight, pressing her torso, thighs, breasts, and even helmet against him. He seemed to need her just as bad, frequently taking a hand off his handlebars to stroke it alone her jean-covered thigh.

The ride to his home passed in a blur of worst-case scenario thoughts bombarding her. By the time they arrived, Chloe was a mess of nerves. She needed him. Needed some kind of assurance he'd come back to her, in one piece—both his body and his mind. But he wouldn't give it to her. Because he wouldn't know for certain, and one thing Logan would never do was bullshit her with false promises and platitudes.

"Come on, baby," he said.

Chloe started. Logan stood next to the bike, arm extended. Shit, she'd really been lost in her own head if she hadn't even realized he'd climbed off the bike. With a heavy sigh, she removed the helmet and joined him, sliding her palm against his. Immediately, strong fingers close around hers, holding her in an unbreakable yet gentle grip.

Logan shortened his stride, matching hers as they climbed the walk to his house. Chloe felt like she was trudging through quicksand. Each step was heavy with resistance stemming from her absolute dread of the following day. The slower she walked into the house the longer it would take for Logan to leave, right?

Wrong.

After unlocking the door, Logan stepped aside so she could precede him into the house. Always looking out for her. Never would he leave her with her back unprotected. Suddenly, Chloe had the overwhelming urge to send him off with something to make him feel special. To make him remember what was waiting for him back at home.

Midway through the foyer, Chloe spun and dropped to her knees. Her hands went straight to the button of his jeans.

"Chloe, shit, babe," Logan started but it turned into a growl when she freed his cock from his boxer briefs without even pushing his pants down. "You don't have to—oh fuck," he said as she licked his slit. Immediately, he stiffened from the attention, going from semi-hard to full-on lead pipe in about two seconds.

"I do, Logan. I do have to." She licked him again, loving the way his hips jerked and he ground out a string of curses. "I need your taste on my tongue. Need to send you off that way. To give you something. Something you can think about when you're away."

He looked down at her, lust burning in his gaze as he gave her a single nod. Chloe turned her attention back to the rigid erection in her hand. "Just so you know," he said as she opened her mouth over the head of his cock. Chloe paused, mouth wide, and canted her gaze up to him.

"Fuck," he whispered. "Sexiest fucking thing I've ever seen." He reached down to cup her jaw. "Just so you know, you don't need to do a goddamned thing for me to think of you while I'm gone, Clo. You being you is enough to keep my mind occupied all the fucking time."

Her heart swelled until it felt too big for her chest.

God, she loved him. Loved this man who had pulled her back into the real world when she'd been drowning under the strain of her issues and engaging in behavior that was sure to end in more harm than good.

Yeah, she loved him.

She just hoped she'd get the chance to tell him.

CHAPTER TWENTY-EIGHT

Chloe's gaze met Rocket's, and for one second, he thought she was going to say something. There was a sadness in her eyes, not completely eclipsed by the lust, and he knew no matter what he did, he wouldn't be able to dispel it tonight. The despair was a product of the circumstances, and he felt it as deeply as she did.

Giving in to Esposito's demands was the last thing he ever wanted to do. Actually, it was the second to last thing. The absolute last, was to let Lefty get away with what he did to Chloe. And that was the one and only reason he'd be taking this job that would destroy what was left of his humanity. He could no more fight against his need to make that cocksucker pay than he could stop breathing. So the sadness would remain, for both of them, until he returned.

And he'd fucking return to her, even if his soul was in shreds.

The moment Chloe's piping hot mouth closed around the tip of his dick, Rocket's eyes crossed.

Shit, that felt fucking good.

He shifted his stance, widening his legs and locking out his knees to keep the weak fuckers from giving out.

As she sucked the tip like it was some kind of lollipop, her tongue found its way back to his slit. "Christ, Chloe, that mouth." Curling his fists to his sides, he prayed to a God that had never listened to him before that he wouldn't grab her head and fuck her mouth like his instincts begged. Last thing he needed was to freak her the fuck out when she was doing something he'd wondered if she'd ever be willing to do, given what happened to her.

"Hmm," she hummed as her lips slid in a slow, torturous glide to the base of him. After holding the position for a few seconds, she backed off just as slow. Her cheeks hollowed and the suction ramped up, tugging at the skin of his cock until his hands were fisted so hard, his knuckles ached. Rocket groaned. Surviving this might be more hazardous than what Esposito had waiting for him.

She repeated the action at least a half dozen times, the same snail's pace glide up and down, only each time she sucked him back, he edged a bit farther down her throat. Just as he was about to open his mouth and beg her to move faster, she took him all the way to the back of her throat and fucking swallowed.

"Shit!" Rocket shouted and her throat muscles clamped down on the tip of his dick.

Chloe chuckled and his eyes rolled back. Who the fuck knew the woman was so damned devious? Without warning, she finally picked up the pace. Rocket stared down at her, watching his length disappear between her glossy, swollen lips again and again. After she swallowed another time, he gave up on trying to be a gentleman. He could hold her hair gently without ramming himself down her throat...maybe.

He scooped up the tail of the braid Chloe always put her hair into when she got on his bike. After working the thick band off the end, he let her long wavy locks flow down around her face. It obstructed his view, which was unacceptable, so he gathered it up in a man-made pony tail, making sure to massage her head a little as he did it.

Chloe moaned and sucked him even harder. She smoothed her hands up his thighs. Sneaking one around back, she grabbed his ass and squeezed, making him shout another curse. The other hand moved slower but was no less devastating. She cupped his balls, giving a gentle pressure that had him clenching the strands of her hair far tighter than he'd planned. Chloe moaned again. The same damn sound she made when his tongue was on her clit.

Goddamn, she fucking liked having her hair pulled, didn't she? He tightened his grip, taking just a hint of her control for himself as he held her head still and eased his cock back in her mouth.

Let's test that theory, shall we?

With her mouth stuffed full of his cock, her gaze met his and she nodded around him. It was all the encouragement he needed.

He didn't dominate her in the way he may have had she not been assaulted, but he held her head and kept his thrusts shallow. She allowed it, groaning around his cock and fondling his sac the entire time.

At one point, she growled a frustrated sound and swatted at the hand in her hair. Rocket released his hold immediately even as the vibrations from her throat nearly made him shoot off. Just as he was about to apologize for being a dick, the hand on his ass gripped him so hard her nails pierced his flesh in a pleasure pain that made him grunt. A second later, his dick hit the back of her throat, she swallowed again and tugged his sac.

"Holy fuck," he shouted as the orgasm bowled him over. He pumped down her throat in spurts that seemed to last far longer than ever before. Chloe stayed with him, her throat working reflexively as she took down every drop.

His eyes closed as waves of pleasure shook him to his core. He'd never come like that before. Usually there was an obvious build up. A tightening in his balls and coiling in his stomach that timed with a tingle in the base of his spine. This time, he was feeling fucking good and then wham, he was exploding.

Chloe released his ass and his nuts then rose to her feet. With his eyes still closed, enjoying the few remaining tremors, he heard rather than saw her lick her lips.

Fucking goddess.

He smiled as he opened his eyes. Chloe stood before him with —what the fuck? Tears rolling down her face?

Motherfucking asshole. "Chloe," he said in a voice that sounded like he'd been chewing gravel. "Shit, baby, I'm sorry. I'm a fucking asshole. I was too rough."

What the hell was he supposed to do now? Hold her? Would that scare her? Back away? Would she feel rejected? Foregoing both of those options, he stood there like an idiot with his arms dangling at his sides and his words failing him. No surprise there.

Chloe's head shook side to side rapidly. "No, no." She sniffed and he wanted to kick his own ass. "That wasn't it at all. I loved it, Logan." She looked him straight in the eye, obviously seeing his disbelief of her statement. "Loved. It."

"So, why…"

She swallowed as fresh tears fell down her face. "I'm scared, Logan. I'm scared as hell."

For him. Jesus, his heart actually hurt. "Baby," he whispered as his arms closed around her. "Shh, I'm a mean motherfucker, Clo. And I'm damn good. It's why Esposito came for me. I don't fuck up. You don't need to worry about me."

"When I was, uh, on the floor," she said, cheeks pink, eyes glistening and focused on his chest. "When I was on my knees, I almost begged." Her voice was barely a whisper. "Instead of going down on you, I almost begged you not to go. To stay here with me and forget all about Lefty."

His eyebrows drew down. "Why didn't you?"

"Because you would have listened. You would have stayed. Am I right?"

Had he seen her on her knees begging him to say, would he have given up a shot at Lefty? His sigh dragged out of him by the weight of her words. He captured her chin between his thumb and forefinger, tilting her head up to meet his gaze. "I would have."

She nodded. "Thought so." A sad laugh left her as her hands circled his waist. "And as much as I want that, I know you. Letting him slip through your fingers goes against who you are. You'd do it for me, but it would kill a part of you. And I need all of you, so I can't do that to you. So I didn't ask. But you have to promise me—"

He kissed her then, still holding her chin. A kiss of gratitude, devoid of the hunger and fury circulating in his blood. There'd be time to indulge in that later. Now, he needed to show her what he could never express with words. Show her how much her sacrifice meant to him. She was willing to endure weeks of hell worrying and being clueless as to his wellbeing because she knew he had no choice but to do whatever it took to get Lefty within reach. To let this go would be to deny the man he was at his very core.

"I promise," he said as he broke the kiss and rested his forehead against hers.

"You don't know what I was going to say," Chloe said with a half-hearted grin.

"I promise to come back to you." He released her chin but she didn't look away. Instead, she nodded.

"You better," she whispered.

He kissed her again, cupping the back of her head. This time, their mouths nipped and explored as heat exploded between them. Still holding her head prisoner, he used his free hand to unbutton her jeans just enough to slip on in. "I promise." And he only said it because it was true. Nothing would keep him from returning home to her.

"Logan," she moaned against his mouth as he worked his fingers in her pants.

"Need to see you come," he said, lips still dueling with hers. "Should drop to my knees and eat you till you're screaming, but I need to watch this beautiful face tip over the edge. When I'm gone, I want to close my eyes each night and see yours dazed with pleasure." He pressed the heel of his hand against her clit.

With a jerk, she arched into his hand. "Knowing I can come home to this will be the reason I get through this fucking shit show. So that means you get my fingers and you keep your eyes wide the fuck open. You good with that?"

"Y-yeah, I'm so good with that. And you're much better with the words than you think."

His lips curved and he gave here one more quick, hard kiss as he closed the hand at the back of her head. Hand full of her silky hair, he had her just where he wanted her. Unable to break from his hold. Unable to focus anywhere but on him.

Without letting up on the pressure, he slid his fingers farther into her jeans. Chloe moaned as he caused the heel of his hand to drag along her ultra-sensitive clit. Ridding her of the garments would take too damn long, so he hooked a finger around her— goddamn, he'd love to see her in noting but this, and maybe some fuck me heels—thong. He eased two fingers into her drenched heat. Being unable to spread her legs due to her jeans, she felt even tighter than usual. Her pussy clenched as though trying to suck him as far as his fingers could reach.

He didn't move, just held them still wedged deep inside her. "Got pretty fucking wet sucking my cock, didn't you, baby?"

Chloe nodded as best she could without having control of her head.

"Guess you liked it. Having me buried in your throat. Hearing me moan your name. Swallowing my cum. You like that, Chloe?"

"Jesus," she whispered. "Yes, Logan, I freakin' loved it. You're killing me. Please move your fingers."

He chuckled. "Please move my fingers? Hmm, what do you mean?"

The cutest fucking scowl he'd ever seen appeared on her face. "Logan," she said, probably going for stern but it came out far too breathy and needy.

Damn, he liked her this way. On the knife edge.

Apparently, she grew tired of waiting for him because she began rocking her hips, shamelessly fucking herself on his hand. He gave her a few minutes to work herself over, mesmerized by the lip tucked between her teeth and the soft mewls that vibrated her throat. Leaving her tomorrow was going to gut him in a way he'd never experienced before. Through countless dangerous missions, he'd never left someone he cared about behind.

And he cared about Chloe with a ferocity he'd never thought possible.

Trust in his brothers was the only reason he'd be able to leave.

Arousal coated his hand, warm and slippery as she moved faster. "It's not enough, please." Her eyes were growing heavy lidded, but she did as he commanded and kept them open.

Time to reward her.

"Tell me what you need, baby. Say it."

"I need you to fuck me with your fingers, Logan. I need you to make me come before I lose my mind."

"Oh," he said with a chuckle. "Why didn't you say—"

"Logan," she growled.

He chuckled again but this time gave her what she wanted. He curled his thick fingers, dragging them along the wall of her pussy as he withdrew. She gasped, fisting his T-shirt.

They stared at each other as he fucked her, plunging deep and grinding his palm against her clit with every forward lunge. Chloe met him with heavy thrusts of her hips. She whimpered, cursed, and moaned all the while keeping her gaze fixed on his. As predicted, her eyes grew hazy and unfocused the closer she got to coming.

"Logan," she cried as her legs began to tremble. "God, I'm close. More, more, more." She was babbling now, a combination of words and sounds making less sense by the second.

God, she was beautiful. Trusting him to take care of her. Something passed between them as they stared at each other. Something powerful he'd never be able to walk away from despite the many reasons he should.

He fucking loved her. And the love was returned. She was shit at keeping her feelings off her face. But neither said it. Words weren't necessary. The emotion was palpable between their locked gazes.

He'd give her the words too. But not until he put Lefty in the ground. Lefty was the last tether to what had happened to her. And once that rope was cut, she'd be free to live again.

"Oh, my God," she shouted as she grabbed his hand and held it deep inside her. He pressed hard, letting her grind down on his hand for all she was worth. Her eyes fluttered as her pussy did the same.

"Eyes open," he growled, rotating his palms as best he could in the small space.

Rocket crooked his fingers hard inside her, hitting that rough bundle of nerves that had her screaming his name.

She flooded his hand as her pussy squeezed him again and again. Chloe's entire body quivered with the force of the orgasm rocking through her. "Holy shit, holy shit," she chanted again and again.

They stood there for a long while, Chloe occasionally shuddering and Rocket with his hand buried inside her. When she finally sagged against him, he released her hair and held her close.

"I'm gonna be okay, baby," he whispered as he slowly inched his hand out of her pants.

Chloe shivered as she nodded against his chest.

"Come on, let's get a little sleep."

The moment they crawled into his big bed, Chloe curled into him, wrapping one arm and leg over top of his body. She held the back of his T-shirt fisted in her hand. Even enough distance for air to flow between them seemed too much. The orgasm helped, and within minutes, her breathing evened.

Rocket remained awake throughout the night memorizing the feel of her soft body molded to his. She held tight, even in sleep, as though afraid he'd disappear before she woke. Part of him was tempted to slip out in the a.m., but she'd be devastated if she woke alone.

As it turned out, Chloe sat up in bed just as he was loading his tactical bag. Sleepy eyes followed him around the bedroom while he gathered the small amount of supplies and clothing he planned to take. The rest would be provided by Esposito. Except his rifle and a few other weapons of choice. Those he kept in a safe beneath his home and he wouldn't be traveling without them.

A horn honked outside. The driver Esposito sent. Even though she couldn't see the driveway from where she sat on the bed, Chloe turned toward the window. Her throat worked as she swallowed what was probably tears.

"Clo," he said. Sure enough, her eyes were misty when she turned back.

"Logan," she said, voice cracking. "You promised."

He moved to her, catching her face between his palms. "I sure as fuck did. I'll be fucking back." Then he kissed her with a desperation he'd never felt before, trying to pour all the love, all the words he couldn't yet say into her.

She clung to his shirt, tears wetting both their cheeks.

The horn blared again, popping the bubble that had surrounded them for a few seconds. Rocket ripped his mouth from hers and grabbed his bag. Without another word or glance in her direction he strode straight out of the room, down the stairs, and out to meet his fate, leaving his heart behind. He couldn't have so much as spared her another glance. Had he seen the tears or the attempted bravery in her eyes, he'd have caved and told Esposito to go fuck himself.

And he'd have lost his shot at Lefty forever. Because Esposito wouldn't just let the bastard go. He'd take Rocket's chance at vengeance for himself.

The idea of Chloe lying in his—their—bed, tears staining the pillow nearly made him turn around, but he forged on and climbed into the black Escalade idling in his driveway.

Once seated, he shot a quick text to his president and then Scott, letting him know he was out and to get his ass to Rocket's house to pick up his sister. Then he turned off the device, slipped on his dark sunglasses, and transformed into the role of operative.

He had shit to do and a woman to return to.

I promise.

CHAPTER TWENTY-NINE

At exactly two-fifteen a.m., sixteen days after Rocket left home, the same black Escalade he drove off in rolled up his quiet driveway. He'd never been so damn glad to see his house. And he wanted nothing more than to crawl into bed and wrap himself around the woman who'd been on his mind non-stop for the past two weeks.

An agitated restlessness zinged through him, making the journey home seem twice as long as it should have. The entire time, he'd felt like a caged animal, first trapped on a plane then hours in the damned Escalade wondering if in fact Chloe would still be at his house. Seeing her car parked at the top of the driveway tamped down some of the nerves, but actually finding her in his bed and getting his hands on her were the only things that would finally pacify the rabid beast inside him.

He blew out a breath trying to get himself in check, but it was useless. Until he touched his woman, he was going to be riding the line of sanity. The past two weeks had been far worse than advertised. He wouldn't have believed the job could get shittier than murdering an innocent man and woman, but throw in a child and it was a million times worse.

The kid had been conveniently left out of the file Esposito presented him at the construction site. Once he arrived in Mexico, and received the full dossier, his mind had been blown by the absolute evil of the man he used to work for.

As the SUV came to a complete stop, Rocket ran a hand down his face. He was tired. So damned tired, and the atrocities that he'd been asked to commit on this mission would stick with him for a long time. Probably forever.

Without so much as a word for his driver, whoever the brooding fucker was, Rocket grabbed his bag and hopped out of the large SUV. He winced as the landing jarred his sore body, especially the brand-new knife wound on the back of his calf. The one that came dangerously close to severing his Achilles tendon. And what a fucking mess that would have been.

Walking slowly in deference to the multitude of bruises and aches he'd garnered this trip, he made his way toward the door. The Escalade sat idling behind him. What the fuck for? It's not like he needed a babysitter to make sure he got in the house okay. God, he couldn't wait to be in an actual bed. With a soft, warm, sleepy woman.

"I hear your objective was completed successfully. I suppose our business has concluded. For good this time," Esposito's voice came as no surprise. In fact, he'd expected the asshole much earlier. Seemed the old man enjoyed showing up uninvited to peoples' homes.

"*My* part's done. You still have a delivery to make." Rocket made a dramatic show of looking around. "In fact, where is my package?"

"On its way. I expect it to arrive within two days. You'll be contacted about a delivery time and location." The motion lights attached to Rocket's three car garage illuminated Esposito enough Rocket could see he wore black jeans and a black sweater.

Rocket took a step forward. "You fuck me on this, old man, and—"

"I won't."

The front door flew open and Chloe appeared on the porch. "Logan!" she cried as she started running down the four steps. When she reached the walkway, she came up short, her gaze bouncing between him and Esposito. "What's going on?" she asked as though she could feel the thick tension.

God, she looked good, though perhaps a little thinner and exhausted. Rumpled from sleep or at least attempting to sleep, her hair hung long and disheveled down her back. She wore another of his T-shirts over a pair of stretchy black leggings.

Esposito smirked at Rocket before addressing Chloe. "Just congratulating your man on a job well done. Kinda surprised he had the balls to pull it off. Especially once he found out there was a kid involved."

Chloe gasped then sent a horrified look his way. With her hand covering her mouth and another on her stomach, she looked like she was going to vomit.

"L-logan?" she asked. "Please tell me that isn't true. You couldn't have killed a child."

Fuck. Fuck. Fuck. This shit was not supposed to go down this way. He stared at her, willing her to remain calm and give him a chance to explain.

"Logan?"

He flicked a glance to Esposito. The fucker was grinning ear to ear as though the impending showdown was the highlight of his miserable life. Keeping his gaze on the barefoot Chloe, Rocket stalked toward her, stopping when he hovered just inches away.

"Please?" she whispered.

"It's true."

The wail of agony that fell from her lips just about broke him. Chloe's knees buckled but he managed to catch her before she hit the ground. The moment she was steady on her feet, she shoved out of his hold. "Don't fucking touch me," she shouted, backing away like he had the plague. "How could you?"

Rocket swallowed. His insides solidified to ice. It was the only way to survive the hatred in her stare.

Just as Chloe fled back into the house, no doubt to pack her shit, Esposito said, "Well, this has been entertaining. Sorry to say I won't be in touch anymore, but you will be receiving payment soon." After his customary two fingered salute, he climbed into the passenger seat of the Escalade Rocket returned in.

Rocket waited until the SUV was clear of his driveway and cruising down the street before entering his home. The place was tomb-quiet. Funny how with just a few weeks of having Chloe there, the silence he'd become accustomed to after living alone for so many years no longer felt comforting, but empty and cold.

Taking the steps two at a time, he ran upstairs and into his room. Chloe was stuffing as much as she could into the small suitcase she'd stashed under his bed.

"Chloe," he said placing a gentle hand on her shoulder.

She jolted like he'd touched her with a live wire. "Don't touch me!" Hands up, she backed away from him. Her eyes were wild, more yellow than green in that moment. "Don't fucking touch me."

He advanced. They had to hash this shit out and it had to happen now. In ten minutes, company would arrive.

"Chloe, you need to listen to me," he said, voice calm as he followed her retreating form.

"No," she said. "I don't have to do a goddamn thing, *Rocket*. Jesus, a kid? They wanted you to kill a kid? And you did it? This is all because of me." She pressed a hand to her stomach. "I think I'm going to be sick." Her back hit the wall and her eyes widened as she realized there wasn't anywhere else to go. She lifted her hands, warding him off.

Or trying to.

That sure as hell wouldn't stop him.

He crowded her against the wall as he grabbed her hands and lifted them high above her head. She fought him, wrenching with surprising power, and screaming curses at him. The strength required to hold her in place had his aching body screaming for relief. When she jammed her knee upward, he nearly lost his balls.

"Stop!" he shouted but the order either didn't penetrate or she didn't give a shit what he wanted. "Listen!" She struggled against him with all her might. To keep those wicked knees from unmanning him, he spread her legs and used his thighs to pin her to the wall.

"How could you?" she shouted over and over again.

He wanted to lean in and whisper the truth in her ear, but she'd probably take a chunk out of his neck, so he let her writhe until the fight began to dwindle. Even then, she used her fledgling energy to try and escape.

"How could you?" she choked out as her body finally sagged against the wall. Streaks of tears ran down her face.

Rocket leaned in until his mouth was directly against her ear. "I didn't." How could she believe he could commit such a heinous act? He thought they'd moved beyond her distrust of him and his club.

Her eyes flew open. "W-what?"

"I didn't kill the child. I didn't kill anyone."

Her chest rose and fell against his as she stared up at him. "I don't understand."

The sound of gravel crunching had him looking out the window to find another SUV slowing to a stop. "I know," he said. "Come on. I'll explain everything." He grabbed her hand and led her out of the room. She only hesitated for a second before following him. Still that one second was soul-crushing.

"You didn't kill anyone?"

"No."

"But Esposito thinks you did."

"That's right."

Chloe stopped and tugged his hand. He came to a stop as well before turning to face her. "You're hurt," she said as though actually seeing him for the first time since he arrived home.

"It's nothing. Bruises, a few cuts. I'm fine."

"I'm sorry," she said, gripping her hair with her free hand. "I lost my mind when I heard him say—"

No way in hell did she owe him any apologies. He cupped her face between his palms and cut her off with a kiss. "Shh," he said. "Not now. We need to get outside."

With a nod, Chloe grabbed his hand this time and led him out to the porch. Rocket and the club may not have near the contacts Esposito did, but that didn't mean they didn't have their own connections. Ones they now owed some mega favors to.

"Hey, Rocket," the tall dark-skinned man who exited the vehicle said.

"Johnson," Rocket replied. "Any issues?"

"Nah, the little one slept nearly the whole time and the mother dozed on and off." He rubbed his smooth head as his gaze drifted to Chloe.

Rocket slipped his arm around her shoulders. "Johnson this is Chloe. Clo this is a buddy of mine from my time with the Marines. Works for a competitor of Esposito these days."

"Nice to meet you," Chloe responded. "So what is this?"

"Special delivery," Johnson said with a smile. He opened the back door of the SUV and helped a thin woman who couldn't be older than early late twenties out of the car. With a baseball cap and dark baggy clothing, it was hard to tell exactly what she looked like, but she carried a sleeping child and had an air of sorrow around her.

Chloe gasped. "Is this—I mean—Were you…"

Rocket squeezed her hand. "Yes, this is Stacy and her daughter Rose."

"Holy shit." Chloe immediately stepped toward the terrified woman trying so hard to put on a brave face. "Your daughter is beautiful. How old is she?"

"Just turned three," Stacy said in a small voice.

"We're going to help you," Chloe said with a soft smile as she stroked her hand over the sleeping child's blonde head. "You have nothing to fear here."

And that was his woman. Not afraid for her own safety or wondering what it would mean to have this woman in the house, but open and welcoming without question. And without even understanding why Rocket had a strange woman in his house at two in the morning. No wonder she'd wormed her way so deep under his skin.

"I'm gonna bug out," Johnson said, handing Rocket a large duffle bag full of all the things Stacy and Rose now possessed in the world.

"Thanks man. I owe you one." Rocket said clapping his buddy on the back.

"Nah. You worked so hard to keep Elena from spiraling out of control after Evan's death. I'd say this almost makes us even."

The mention of Elena was like a shot to the gut. Rocket grunted "Some job I did."

"More than the rest of us." Johnson held out a hand.

Rocket shook it, then his buddy slipped back into the car.

Chloe was gaping at him with a million questions in her eyes. "Let's get these two inside and I'll try to explain."

She nodded. "Come on," she said to a wide-eyed Stacy. "I've got a great room you can use. And a fantastic shower."

It took about thirty minutes to get a snack for Rose and get the two settled in Rocket's guest room. The child was scared, but so exhausted sleep won out after a short bout of tears and asking for her father. Chloe took care of getting them settled while Rocket showered the filth of the past two weeks off of him. Their guests would be at his house for no more than a few hours before it would be time for the next leg of their journey.

When he returned downstairs, he found Chloe sitting on the couch with a glass of whiskey, staring at the darkness outside.

After taking a sip, she held it up for him. Rocket downed it in one gulp as he sat down next to her.

"Tell me," she said, turning to face him.

With a sigh, he let his weary head drop back on the couch and closed his eyes. He had no desire to tell the tale he'd have to repeat more than once over the next few days. What he wanted was to forget the whole damn mission ever happened. The next thing he knew, Chloe's soft weight was pressed all along him as she straddled his lap.

"Tell me," she said again.

He lifted a lock of her hair and brought it to his nose. It smelled of fresh peaches. "Stacy and her husband Allen are—were—missionaries in Mexico for about three years. While they were there, they became involved with a group that helps citizens escape from the cartel. Mostly people on the cartel's shit list. This group works to get them into America legally, and illegally in some cases. Whatever they have to do to ensure the safety of those needing to flee the country. The couple stayed after their missionary work ended, and basically took over running the organization. Cartel eventually discovered who they were and wanted them eliminated. Esposito won the very lucrative contract."

"Oh, my God," she said on an exhale as she laid her head on his chest. "That's so fucked up."

"Yeah."

"So…"

He slid his hands under her shirt and glided his palms up and down the smooth expanse of her back. She practically purred as she burrowed into him. "I never intended to kill any of them."

"I know."

Her faith in him was astonishing.

"I'm sorry for how I reacted earlier. I was just so shocked by what Esposito said. I know you. I trust you."

"It's okay," he said, ignoring the punch of uncertainty.

She lifted her head. The sincerity in her eyes obliterated any lingering doubt. "No, it's not. You need to know I have faith in you and know you would never kill innocent people." She tucked her head back under his chin. "So how'd you get them out?"

"Once I was able to explain to Stacy about the danger they were in, the three of us set a plan in motion. "Between my contacts, the club's contacts, and Stacy and Allen's surprising network of connections, we were able to stage their deaths by blowing up their home. Then we snuck them out of Mexico."

"Hmmm, somehow I think it was much more complicated than you're letting on."

She had no idea. In fact, the entire plan almost went south when they encountered a group of cartel enforcers before they'd even finished developing their escape plan. At first, Rocket thought Esposito had sent them to eliminate him, but the old man seemed convinced the targets had been eliminated.

"Where's her husband?"

Rocket looked at the ceiling, swallowing the lump of sadness that formed in his throat. Allen had been a genuinely good man. One who loved his wife, loved his daughter, and spent his life working to make others' lives better. "He didn't make it. We were attacked by members of the cartel outside their house and he was shot. Stacy and I dragged him inside and tried to save him, but he died quickly. We had to alter our plans and get outta dodge early, so we torched the house and fucking fled."

She brought her hand up to her heart, eyes full of grief. "That poor woman."

"Yeah, she has a long road ahead of her."

Chloe ran a soft fingertip over a cut on his forehead. "It was a close call."

He grunted.

"So what happens to Stacy and Rose now? Will they stay here with us?"

A small smile curled his lips. Had she even realized what she said? Stay here with *us*? Did that mean she wasn't planning to run back to her house now that the threat had been eliminated?

"I know someone who runs a women's shelter a few hours from here. The club has used them in the past when we retrieved some girls Lefty had been selling. Screw will be here in about ninety minutes. We're going to drive them up there."

"Should I come?"

He shook his head. "No. I'm pretty sure we're in the clear but I need you here to act as though everything is normal in case DarkOps has eyes on the house."

"All right."

"I'll be home late tomorrow night, but one of my brothers will be here all day. We're going to hit up various places. Throw off anyone who may be following."

"Do you think they are? Watching us?"

He shook his head. "No. Just being overly cautious."

She let out a breath. "I hate that you're hurt." Chloe leaned forward and ghosted her lips over the cut she'd been touching. Then she kissed the bruise around his eye. And the host of additional bruises on his face, neck, and arms.

The gentle touches were so in contrast to the two weeks of violence and stress. When she'd doled her affection on the majority of his injuries, she tucked her head under his chin and held him tight. "I love listening to your heart beat below my ear. It's the most soothing sound. So strong and steady, just like you, Logan. I was so worried while you were gone. But I shouldn't have been. You made me a promise and you kept it."

When the word love passed her lips, the heart she was listening to nearly stopped beating. For a second, he thought an actual profession of love would follow.

Maybe he was just projecting, because as she melted into him, he couldn't imagine a future where he came home and she wasn't waiting for him with her sweet smile and gentle touch. Nothing helped bandage his battered soul quite like having Chloe in his arms.

But he was a biker. And he would always be a reminder of the hell she endured. How could she possibly love him?

CHAPTER THIRTY

Chloe sat midway up the stairs, her forearms resting on bent knees with her phone between her hands. Despite the fact it'd been a warm day, Chloe had felt chilled since she woke up. The fire crackling away in the great room helped warm the lower level of the house.

Every so often she switched her gaze from the blank phone screen to the closed front door, willing the phone to light or the door to open. She'd been at this back and forth game for upward of an hour. Far longer than necessary since Logan wasn't expected for at least another fifteen minutes.

The few hours he was home that morning, long before the sun came up, seemed almost a dream at this point. She'd barely gotten to hold him or kiss him before he was out the door again with the woman and child he'd risked his life to save. The only communication she'd received since he drove off was a text an hour ago reporting him and Screw seventy miles out.

God, she missed him these past couple weeks. In a relatively short period of time, he'd come to mean more to her than anything or anyone else in her life. She ached to wake next to him each morning and hardly slept at night alone in his giant bed. More than once, she'd tried to sleep on a couch or in a guest bed, but those attempts were even less successful than the master. At least in Logan's bed she could smell him and fool her subconscious into thinking he was there in her dreams.

The lock on the door clicked and Chloe shot to her feet as though she were a marathoner and the starting gun had just blasted the race into action. "Logan!" she cried as he came into view and dropped his pack to the ground.

Much as he had in the early hours of day, he appeared battered and bruised. His handsome face actually seemed worse than when she'd last seen him, because he hadn't slept and had heavy fatigue circles under his eyes.

"Are you really here? For good?" As deeply as she wanted him in her arms, the sight of him seemed to have rendered her immobile. "It's over? Please tell me I'm not dreaming?"

He stood frozen midway between the door and staircase, his gaze soaking her in the same way hers was him.

"I'm here, baby. It's over."

Her eyes fell closed as she breathed out a prayer of thanks. "Stacy and Rose are settled?"

A smile tipped his lips giving his tired face a less severe look, but it disappeared as fast as it came. "They're in good hands."

"Good," she said, disgusted to find herself wringing her hands together. Shit, she wasn't this nervous the first time she had cuffed him to the motel bed. But everything was different now. She'd been living with him because of a danger that no longer existed. Esposito was out of the picture and Lefty would soon be the devil's problem. So where did that leave her? Where did that leave them?

"Chloe," Logan started.

"Wait." Still rooted to the step, she held up a hand. "Can I say something first?"

Logan nodded.

She fisted the hem of his T-shirt in her hands. Something to keep here from gnawing her nails to the cuticle. "I think you're amazing, Logan Carrera."

His eyes widened and he took a step forward.

"No, wait," she said, hand still out like a stop sign. "I know you have a lot of conflicting feelings about what you have and haven't done in the past, but the man I see standing before me, the man I know today, is a good man. He's a man who took an enormous risk to save an innocent woman and child. And don't try to tell me anyone would have done the same thing because that is complete and utter bullshit. Not only did you prevent them from being killed, you set them up with a new and safe life. You amaze me and I—"

"Can I say something now?" he asked, one eyebrow raised.

She let her hand fall. "Sorry, yes, of course. I'm rambling. I just wanted you to know—"

"I love you, Chloe," he said, and she almost choked on what she was going to say next.

"Y-you do?" She gaped at him, completely unable to do anything but blink in shock.

"I do." He wasn't smiling. In fact, his severe expression seemed even harsher than usual which was a feat in and of itself. A small laugh bubbled up, and she covered her mouth to keep it inside. Of course, Logan would declare his love with a scowl on his face.

"One more time," she whispered as her eyes drifted shut.

"I love you, Chloe."

She kept her eyes closed, savoring the incredible feeling of warmth blooming in her chest and spreading throughout her body. "Logan?" she said as she opened her eyes.

He tilted his head. "I love you too. I love everything. All of you. So much." Her voice caught on the last word.

As though a spark leapt straight from the fire and into the space between them, heat filled his eyes. A small, strangled sound tore from Chloe's lips, and in the next instant she was flying down the stairs toward him.

The sight of her in motion kicked his ass into gear as well. He shot forward, closing the distance with his longer legs pumping faster than hers. An all-consuming need to touch him, feel skin on skin burned her more than the fire ever could.

Chloe launched herself straight at him. They met at the second step, colliding against each other like two runaway trains. She wrapped her arms and legs around him and clung like a spider monkey.

"I forgot you're hurt!" she cried as he tried to hide a subtle flinch.

"It's fine. Can't feel a damn thing but the need to touch every part of you right now," he said right before he slammed his lips on hers.

She moaned. Normally, she went pliant in his arms, melting into him. Not tonight. Tonight, she fought for control of the kiss. Battled him for dominance. Their mouths dueled in a fierce lip battle full of nips, hard sucks, and plunging tongues.

"Skin," Chloe said as she ripped her mouth away. His lips were swollen and a thick bulge behind his zipper pressed right into her core. She couldn't help but rock against him, eliciting a harsh groan from both of them. With his hands on her ass and her legs wrapped around him, she was stable enough to use her hands. And, boy, did she use them. In a frenzy, she yanked his T-shirt up and off his body, scoring his skin with her nails as she went. Hers was next, tossed over her head without care.

His focus immediately went to her tits. With his hungry gaze on her, Chloe felt strong, powerful. He hefted her higher and closed his mouth around one stiff peak.

Shit, that felt so damn good.

Chloe cried out, clutching at his head for support as lightning shot from her nipple to her clit. She ground against him, humping at his abs, wild for some kind of friction to ease the ache.

"Shit, Logan, I need your cock." She was soaked, the thin panties not doing a damn thing to contain the flood of arousal leaking from her body into him.

"Fuck yes," he said as he released her panty-covered ass to undo his cargo pants. The moment he let go, she almost crashed to the ground.

Rocket

Chloe yelped and clung to him tighter while he tried to remain on his feet. All they managed to accomplish was another press of her drenched pussy against his abdomen which had him groaning and losing his balance entirely. There was no time to cushion her fall or for him to brace to keep from squashing her. They crashed to the steps, landing in a heap of tangled arms and legs.

Chloe grunted as her back made contact with the carpeted steps. The coarse fibers dragged across her skin in a burning trail that would certainly leave a mark. Her small grunt was the only indication either of them had even noticed the incident. Logan's gaze held a crazed hunger as she locked in with single minded focus on her target.

His belt.

She attacked it with a ferocity she hadn't thought herself capable of. In record time, his belt was undone, zipper down, and cock firmly in her hand. She stroked, loving the way his entire body bowed into her. "Fuck me, Logan. Now. You have no idea how bad I need you."

The second her hand stroked down his throbbing length, he fucking lost his shit. "No idea?" he growled near her ear. "I spent the last sixteen nights fucking dreaming of you with a dick so hard it hurt. Swear to Christ, woman, I've never wanted anything like I want to fuck you right now."

He was going to make her come with his words alone. "So stop talking and do it," she said, throwing as much sass into the command as possible.

Rocket grabbed her hand in a rough grip, ripped it off his cock, and pinned it to the step near her head. He aligned himself with her drenched opening, and without any finesse, powered into her.

"Shit, you're so fucking tight and hot." She was so wet he had no problem sinking to his balls on the first stroke. When he bottomed out, Chloe emitted a sharp cry. Her back arched off the steps, tits like an offering he didn't ignore. He scraped his teeth over one nipple.

"God, yes! Fuck me hard, Logan. So, so hard."

Hooking one of her legs over his shoulder, he hiked it high, opening her for an even deeper penetration. Their combined groans caused their gazes to meet.

Then it was game on.

Logan fucked her like an animal, without any thought to technique. With short, choppy, wild strokes, he slammed into her again and again, never pulling out more than an inch or two as though he couldn't bear to be anything but balls deep inside her.

It was the most exquisite experience of her life. Every choppy thrust brought his pelvis in direct contact with her clit, and since his strokes were so fast and hard, the nub took a pounding like never before.

Chloe clung to him as best she could as the bull rode her. Her nails dug into his back and her body absorbed every erratic push, coiling tighter and tighter until...

Kaboom!

Pressure exploded out of every pore in her body, replaced by a pleasure so sharp it was almost too much to tolerate. Chloe's spine bowed, her nails raked across Logan's back and she keened out a wail as a monster orgasm overtook her.

Rocket followed immediately. With one last brutal thrust, he planted himself deep and roared out his climax. It took several minutes for Chloe's head to stop spinning and her eyes to focus. Her arms and legs tingled with the aftereffects of coming so hard. The room had a hazy glow to it due more to her sated state than the glimmering fire.

She shifted. Logan's heavy weight crushed her into the stairs making her aware for the first time, that their positioning wasn't the most comfortable. She wiggled experimentally. Yeah, there was some serious rug burn on her back. Probably on Logan's elbows as well.

Rocket

That reunion almost, almost made up for the weeks of agony and loneliness.

As Chloe sighed with the simple pleasure of having Logan's weight pinning her down, her eyes flew open. Holy shit. Logan was pinning her down. *Pinning her.* As in his entire weight was on top of her and had been while he fucked her stupid.

A grin so huge it hurt her cheeks spread across her face. "Logan," she whispered, tears of joy clogging her throat. "Logan, you're on top of me."

He stiffened for a split-second, then shot off her like she was covered in fire ants.

"Fuck! Chloe I'm so sorry. Shit." He raked his hand through his sex-mussed hair. Guilt and despair were scribbled all over his face. She needed to put an end to it before he beat the hell out of himself misunderstanding her meaning.

Of course, that meant she had to move and her body was so limp and sated she wasn't quite sure that was possible. She lay, sprawled on her back, legs splayed, and painting quite the wanton picture.

"Christ, how far did I set you back? Did I hurt you?" His gaze roamed her as though looking for signs of distress or wounds. "Fucking hell," he grumbled before stalking to the kitchen.

Chloe frowned and struggled to sit and then stand. She walked on wobbly legs to the kitchen without bothering to cover up. Hopefully, the sight of her naked would help sway things her way.

"Logan," she said to his just as naked back as he poured himself a glass of Jack. A long, jagged wound on the back of his right calf caught her attention. It'd been stitched closed, and recently. Chloe swallowed and forced her gaze higher. He'd be answering her many questions later. For now, she had a pressing issue to deal with.

He spun around, softened cock resting against his thigh. It glistened from her wetness and the sight of it turned her on all over again. Something that didn't escape his notice if the way he stared at her breasts was any indication.

When he didn't speak, she stepped closer, until she was able to reach his glass. After stealing a long sip, she handed it back to him.

His poor face was a mess of bruises, and self-loathing.

"I fucked up." He ran a hand through his hair. The strands already stuck out every which way, and his restless hands only made it worse. "Was too fucking rough. Shit, I didn't even think about freaking you out. I was so fucking gone I'm not sure I'd have realized if you were panicking." Chloe closed the short distance until their bodies were flush. She reached, despite the way he stiffened against her, and not in the good way. With a soft chuckle, she smoothed his hair back in place.

"Well, I don't believe that last part for a second. As for the rest of it..." She shrugged. "I took one look at you and all I could think was 'Thank God he's home,' followed by 'holy shit he said he loves me,' and then 'he better fuck me until I'm screaming.' You were just giving me exactly what I wanted."

"Chloe—"

She held her palm over his mouth as she shook her head. "No. I can't believe I'm actually saying this, but don't speak. Just listen."

When he nodded, she removed her hand. "I didn't have a single moment, not even a flicker of panic or unease or discomfort." She grimaced. "Well except for this rug burn that's now screaming at me."

Logan scowled and spun her around. "Shit," he muttered. "I've got something you can put on that to take the sting out." His lips landed on the sore skin, making her shiver.

"Logan, listen to me, please. This is important." She turned back to him and placed her hands on his bare chest. "I trust you. Completely. One hundred percent. You and your club. I've been shown over and over these past weeks how much they love you and how far they are willing to go to keep your woman safe, happy, and well fed." She gave him a lopsided smile.

"I admit I had some reservations about your club. But they're gone. Any lingering doubt was completely obliterated when you and your brothers worked to give Stacy and Rose a second chance at life. I told you I love you, and I mean it. I wanted everything that just happened. In fact, I'm pretty damn proud of myself. Not once did I think about what Lefty did to me. I was just a normal woman who wanted her man desperately. You should be celebrating, not beating yourself up."

He huffed out a small laugh then hauled her against him for a bone-crushing hug. "Hi, baby," he said.

Chloe giggled. "Hi. I missed you so much."

He grunted which she took to mean he missed her just as much.

"Logan?"

Another grunt.

"Are you really okay? You look like shit."

Silent seconds ticked by. So many, Chloe assumed he wasn't going to give her more details, but then he said, "Got a little roughed up. Nothing serious."

Nothing serious. Just a giant gash on his calf.

"You must be exhausted."

His cheek came down to rest on her head. Chloe reveled in the closeness for a few minutes before pulling away. She refilled his glass then took it and one of his hands. "Come on, Logan. Let's go to your bed." She gave him a sheepish smile. "I haven't been able to sleep in it without you."

Renewed desire flared in his eyes, and his cock was now semi-hard. He kissed her then squeezed her ass. "Meet you there. Gonna deal with the fire."

Five minutes later, Logan slipped under the covers next to her. She handed him the Jack Daniels. After swallowing the entire contents in two gulps, he placed the empty glass on the night stand.

They lay facing each other, just absorbing the pleasure of being in the same space. Chloe traced the ink on his chest, and he ran his callused hands over her arms, her back, her ass. The urgency of earlier was gone. Now they were just exploring, reconnecting, and loving.

"Logan?"

A grunt.

"Thank you for keeping your promise. Even though I knew you'd do everything in your power to come back to me, I was so worried about you."

"I can see that."

Uh oh. He didn't sound pleased.

"Uh, what do you mean?"

He traced what had to be a spectacular circle under her eye with the coarse pad of his finger. "When is the last time you slept more than a few hours?"

"Um…" Damn the man for being so observant. "It's been a few days?"

"Yeah? How many?"

"Uh, sixteen?"

"Shit, Chloe. And have you lost fucking weight?"

Oh boy. "About ten pounds," she mumbled against his chest.

Logan stilled. "I'm sorry," he said into her hair.

Well that wasn't what she'd expected. She peered up at him. "Logan, you have nothing to be sorry for. You had to do this. We already had this discussion."

He grunted, causing her to smile. They'd probably revisit this a number of times over the next few days. Underneath the quiet growly exterior was a man who protected and cared more deeply than most. He was just cautious with revealing that side of himself.

They fell silent, the steady rise and fall of his chest lulling her into a near sleep state. Just as she was drifting out, Logan's rumbly voice spoke next to her ear. "Night, baby. Love you, Clo."

He could tell her that twenty times a day for the rest of her life and she'd never get tired of hearing it. Never grow weary of the surge of ecstasy the phrase created.

"I love you too, Logan."

He gave her a sweet lingering kiss, then gathered her close. All that remained was for the club to deal with Lefty. Then they could begin to put this part of their lives in the past and move forward. Hopefully together and with his big crazy club family.

"I'm home, baby," he whispered into her hair. "Won't leave you like that again. Time to turn your brain off and let me take on all the worries for a while."

The most amazing feeling of safety and love wrapped itself around Chloe, allowing her to fully relax for the first time since Logan walked out the door a few weeks ago. She put everything out of her brain and allowed herself to sleep, knowing the man surrounding her would keep the world at bay at least until she woke.

CHAPTER THIRTY-ONE

"Hey, brother, damn good to have you back." LJ held out a meaty hand. When Rocket grabbed it, LJ pulled him into a rib-shattering hug complete with a heavy back slap that stole his wind. And it damn sure didn't do any favors for his sore body.

Still, it meant he was home, alive, and done with DarkOps.

"Nowhere else I'd rather be." Well, maybe back in bed. Buried inside his woman. But, damn if it didn't feel good to be back in his cut and strolling into the clubhouse. Being absent so long really drove home where he belonged.

With his club family.

And his woman.

Chloe was off taking care of a few tasks at her house while Rocket met with Copper and the rest of the executive committee. Soon as the meet was over, he'd swing by and pick her up. Then they'd be heading to his place where he intended to barricade the door and keep her naked and satisfied for the next three or four days.

"How'd everything go in my absence?" Rocket asked the prospect he'd left in charge of his business for the past three weeks. LJ had been working for him almost two years now, and was personable, hardworking, and respected by everyone he came in contact with. He was turning out to be a perfect number two. The guy would make a great brother too. He was due to be patched in any time now. Actually, he was long overdue, but with all the chaos in the club recently, his patch-in had been delayed a few months.

Of course, LJ hadn't bitched once. He'd taken on every chore the club assigned him, shitty or not, and performed it like a rock star. About nine months ago, he'd suffered a nasty beating while trying to protect Maverick. Ended up in the hospital for a good few days. Never wavered in his loyalty for a second. There wasn't a brother in the club who wouldn't vote him in in a heartbeat. Which reminded Rocket, he was supposed to be on the fucking party planning committee. Once again, LJ's patch-in had been postponed due to club drama.

"Smooth sailing, Rocket. We're actually ahead of schedule on the bank renovation."

Rocket smiled. "Good work, man." He shook LJ's giant hand again. LJ stood for Little Jack which was pretty much the complete opposite of the six-foot-six-inch three-hundred-pound monster of a man. "Appreciate you stepping up."

"Thanks for trusting me."

"No one better for the job."

LJ beamed, the hulk looking more like a boy who'd been given a treat.

"Prez in?"

"Yeah, most of 'em are there. Think they're just waiting on you and—"

Maverick burst through the door.

"Maverick."

He strode into the room with a shit-eating grin on his face and a bandage on his neck. New tat probably. Seemed like he was gunning for Guinness Book status. "Yo, LJ, you seen the porn with that tall blonde chick with big tits? You know, she's sucking off that guy with the Godzilla dick, then he comes all over—"

"Seriously?" LJ cut in with a laugh. "The porn with the big-titted blonde and Godzilla-dicked dude? You pretty much described ninety percent of the porn out there."

"Hmm." Mav pursed his lips. "There was this thing in there I wanted to try with Steph, but I couldn't find it again. Oh well. I'll just have to get creative." He waggled his eyebrows then turned as though just noticing Rocket was there. "Hey, Rocket, glad you made it home in one piece, brother." Mav hugged him much the same way LJ did but without LJ's bulk, Rocket didn't feel quite so squashed by this one.

Still laughing, LJ said, "I don't know how that sweet woman of yours puts up with your perverted ass, Mav."

There went the eyebrows again. "That woman happens to love my ass. And my—"

"That your trap I hear running on and on out there, Maverick?" Copper's voice boomed out of the chapel.

"Looks like our master calleth," Mav said with a slap for LJ's back. "Let's roll, Rocket."

They joined the rest of the exec board which consisted of Zach, Jig, Viper, and Copper. Screw had also been sitting in lately as he was working closely with Zach as backup enforcer. He hadn't technically been patched long enough to hold an exec position, so he wasn't allowed a vote, but he'd been vital to Zach over the past few months. After taking a vote, it became clear no one had issue with him attending the meetings.

"Welcome back, brother," Copper said. He sat in his spot at the head of the table. Each of the men had a glass in front of them.

Jigsaw held one out to Rocket. "Prez broke out the good shit just for you."

He raised an eyebrow at Copper who was nodding. "Thought your return, the official end to your involvement with DarkOps, and the impending end of Lefty deserved the Macallan."

Damn, he really did dig into the good shit. Had he mentioned how fucking great it was to be home?

Cop lifted his glass and the guys followed. "Job well done, Rocket. Know this wasn't easy for you, and you look like complete shit, so it couldn't have been a cakewalk. This club owes you."

"Fuck no it doesn't," Rocket said, but he lifted his glass as the other men followed and sipped the expensive scotch.

"Cop's right. You're looking kinda worked over there, brother," Zach said from across the table.

Rocket narrowed his eyes at their enforcer. "Rough few weeks. You know who else was looking kinda worked over?"

Zach winced. "Shit, brother. We tried our damn fucking best. Short of drugging her, I couldn't force her to sleep. Toni started feeding her at the diner as soon as we realized she was dropping pounds. She doin' okay?"

Rocket nodded. She was now, and he'd make damn sure she stayed that way.

"Get everything settled yesterday?" Copper asked.

"Yeah. It's all good. We covered our tracks real well. Had a visit from Esposito when I got home. Seems to have worked. He's satisfied the marks are dead. Even congratulated me on having the balls to whack a kid." Rocket's stomach soured at the memory.

"Fucker," Jig muttered.

"Agree with you there, brother. You think he's done with you?" Copper asked with a concerned expression.

Rocket nodded. "I do. He said as much, and he may be a piece of shit, but he'll stick to his word."

"And our payment?" Copper's eyes now gleamed with a familiar need for vengeance.

"Will be delivered tomorrow at the latest. Just waiting on communication via text."

"I want to hear as soon as you do, get me, Rocket?" Copper pierced him with a laser stare.

For a split-second, it seemed as though Copper could sense the plans for Lefty's death and dismemberment rolling through Rocket's brain. "I get you," he said though the words cost him.

Handing Lefty over would take a feat of internal strength he might not possess.

"No going off half-cocked. No vigilante shit. No solo shit. I'm to be kept in the loop the entire fucking time. Know it was your ass out there doing the dirty work, and you'll be compensated for your time and trouble, but Lefty belongs to the club." He leaned across the table offering his fist to Rocket. "You have my word, you can be the one to pull the trigger, but you're not doing it until I get some time with him." There wasn't an inch of wiggle room in his tone. Absolutely no room for argument or even discussion.

For the first time since he patched in, a part of him wanted to tell Copper to fuck off. Lefty was his. Motherfucking his. He'd raped and beaten Rocket's woman. If Rocket had his way, he'd keep Lefty locked up and at his mercy for weeks. Slowly carving away at his body until nothing remained but a bloody mess begging for death. Even then, he might not grant the bastard's wish. But that wasn't how Copper wanted it done. The club had been after Lefty for months. As much as it burned his ass to share the spoils, Cop would make Lefty pay and only then would Rocket end him.

And Chloe's demons would be vanquished.

That was the end goal. Not Rocket's insatiable thirst for vengeance. Though he'd still get to feed his bloodlust. And enjoy every fucking second of it.

He bumped his fist against Copper's. "Said I get it, prez. And I don't want the club's fucking money. Lefty's death is payment enough."

With a nod, Copper scratched at his beard. The damn thing was getting downright scraggly. Only a matter of time before Shell started riding his ass about that. She probably gave him leeway due to his recent injuries. "Anything else?" He made eye contact with each of the men as they shook their heads. "Well if that's it, we're done here. Anybody sticking around?"

Rocket

"I got some shit to do in my office," Jig said. As club treasurer, and anal-retentive record keeper, he spent a fair amount of time glued to a computer screen.

Rocket nearly shuddered. Better Jig than him. Just the thought of dealing with the club's finances made him want to run screaming.

"I'm out. Gotta pick up Clo."

His brothers shared looks and smirks between them.

"What?"

"Rocket and Chloe sitting in a tree. K-I-S-S-I-N-G." Though Mav was the only one brave—or stupid—enough to taunt him, the rest of the assholes busted out laughing.

Rocket gave them all his best fuck you glare, which did nothing to stem the heckling.

"First comes fucking, then comes more fucking, third comes a baby in a baby carriage," Mav sing-songed.

Flipping him off, Rocket said, "First of all, you should be singing that to Jig. He's the one who's woman is knocked the fuck up. And second, fuck you all."

Of course, that did nothing to stop the singing. In fact, the whole damn lot of them busted out in Maverick's jingle. By the time they finished the second round, they were all howling like a bunch of fucking buffoons. "Jesus," Zach said as he wiped his eyes. "He's even using full sentences. Must be getting damn serious."

Copper was the first to get control of himself. No surprise there. "Hey, for real, brother, you thinking about making this official?"

Christ, had he known he'd be walking back into tenth grade, he'd have brought a trapper keeper and letterman jacket. They all stared at him, practically slobbering for his answer. God, how he hated being under the microscope.

"Hey, brother," Zach broke in. "We all fucking love that woman. In case that means anything to you."

As he scanned the room and the curious expressions on his brother's faces, he actually relaxed somewhat. Sure, they may tease the fuck outta him, but every single man in the room cared about him as though he was a blood brother. And he felt the same for them. He'd take a bullet for any of these fuckers without thought.

He had to admit it was a damn nice feeling.

"Making her my ol' lady."

Mav whistled and slapped his palm on the table while the rest of the guys broke out in applause. "Another one bites the dust, baby," Mav shouted.

Rocket rolled his eyes and started for the door, but he couldn't keep the grin off his face. Good thing his back was to the table full of jokers. Last thing they needed was more ammo.

As he stepped out into the sun-warmed air, his phone rang from his pocket. Without looking, he palmed it and brought it to his ear. Now that he was done with DarkOps, he didn't so much care about vetting each call. "Rocket," he barked into the phone.

The greeting was met with hitched gasps. Pulling the phone away, he glanced at the screen. His stomach took a dive.

"Clo?" Rocket said into the phone as he picked up his pace.

"L-logan?" The terror in her voice had him flat out running toward his bike. "I need you. Now."

"Baby, you hurt? Tell me what's wrong." His heart raced in time with his pounding footfalls.

Her next words rendered him momentarily immobile before he flung a leg over his bike, hit the throttle, and peeled out of the parking lot at breakneck speed.

CHAPTER THIRTY-TWO

If someone had told her in only a matter of weeks her house would no longer feel like her home, Chloe would have laughed in their face. Two years ago, when she'd purchased the little ranch style, she'd been elated and so damn proud of herself. Her first major display of independence. At the time, she'd imagined a man moving in with her one day. The little three-room abode would be their starter home. Maybe the place they'd have their first child. Start a little family. Make memories and traditions.

Now?

Now she couldn't pack fast enough, dying to return to the tranquility and safety of Logan's house. His place had become so much more than her boyfriend's—or whatever he officially was—house. His custom-built cabin had become her safe haven, her comfort zone, her...home.

Hopefully she wasn't a total fool for thinking along those lines.

Chloe rummaged through her top desk drawer, searching for a specific flash drive. The one with her biggest client's tax records—ah, there it was. After slipping it into her purse, she made her way through her small kitchen to the opposite end of the house where the other two bedrooms were located.

Clothes were the next necessity to be packed. At the rate she was moving belongings to Logan's, it wouldn't be long before she had more stuff at his place than she did at her own. She sighed as she dropped her purse on the kitchen counter. Perhaps it was time to have the dreaded discussion. The where-was-this-going talk. Ugh, that was bound to be awkward as hell with a biker who wasn't big on conversation.

Or, maybe she could just enjoy Logan being home and stop trying to organize her entire future. There was an idea.

Chuckling to herself, she stepped into her bedroom, and let out a blood-curdling scream. The room swirled, nausea swamped her, and her knees nearly buckled. A loud voice inside her head screamed at her to run, but her feet were rooted to the floor as though superglued in place.

"Hey, Chloe. Been awhile." Lefty stood at her dresser, a pair of her silky panties dangling from his finger. "These are nice." He stroked the soft material down his face, pausing to inhale, and Chloe almost vomited. "Too bad you weren't wearing them when we—"

The crude reminder of what he did to her was enough to shock her out of her frozen state. She spun, running out of the room and down the hall at full speed. Laughter followed her before the sound of pounding boots chased her down. She'd almost made it to the front door when a hand grabbed her ponytail and jerked her back against a hard chest. Tears leaked from the corner of her eyes from the pain of being held by her hair.

This was it. It was happening again. Her heart pounded out of control as she anticipated the pain to come.

"Where you going? We were just about to get reacquainted." He circled her throat with his hand, the pressure just enough to have her stilling, then trailed it down the front of her body, squeezing a breast as he went. She trembled as heart-stopping memories assaulted her.

She started to drift off in her mind, going to another place as she prepared for a repeat of the most painful and humiliating experience of her life. His hand began to journey downward, but just as the tips of his fingers brushed the waistband of her jeans, a voice sounded in her head.

Izzy's voice.

Someone comes after you, you're not gonna defend yourself, you're going on the offensive to take the motherfucker out.

Fuck this. Fire shot through her veins as she channeled the feeling of power she'd experienced fighting Jig. It might not work, he might overpower her and hurt her all over again, but this time she was going down fucking swinging.

Never again would she be a helpless victim tied to a bed as men assaulted her.

With a feral cry, Chloe lifted her foot and thrust it straight back with as much force as she could muster. Lefty never saw the attack coming, and when the thick heel of her biker boot slammed into his kneecap, he shouted and released her.

Instead of running for the door, Chloe spun and assumed the fighting stance Jig had taught her. With his attention momentarily on the pain in his knee, Lefty missed her next strike as well. A perfectly executed punch to his gut.

As he doubled over, Chloe straightened to her full height. A high that was positively electric shot through her. She bounced on the balls of her feet, grinning like a maniac. "What's wrong, fucker? Not exactly how you planned our reunion?"

Lefty growled and charged forward. Chloe dodged right, but not fast enough. His shoulder hit her hip, sending her crashing backward onto the floor, narrowly missing the corner of a coffee table. As she hit the ground, she cried out, stunned for a split-second by the pain in her upper back.

But it was long enough for him to be on her. His fist connected with her cheek in a punch so agonizing, her vision blurred and she swore her face split in two.

Like some kind of wild animal, Chloe fought his attempts to pin her arms above her head. A technique Jig taught her came to mind and she bucked her hips up. Hard. The move unbalanced Lefty, who went tumbling off her body.

Chloe flipped onto her stomach and crawled away as fast as she could. The blood rushing through her ears made it impossible to hear anything. Just as she was about to stand, Lefty's hand closed around her ankle. As if by instinct, she kicked back with her free leg, connecting with something that had a high-pitched scream coming from Lefty.

As she scrambled to her feet, she risked a glance over her shoulder and saw blood pouring from his lip. A sense of satisfaction fueled her desire to fight even harder. When she reached her kitchen, she stopped fleeing. She could have run, maybe should have run, but she turned back to him. "Come on, fucker." She pointed to her face which already felt swollen. "This the worst you can do?"

Later she'd probably regret taunting a psychopath, but in the moment with adrenalin coursing through her and the euphoria of finally getting a piece of the man who caused her so much agony, she wanted nothing more than to beat his ass to the ground.

Lefty lunged forward. In the three seconds it took him to reach her, a calm settled over Chloe, and Izzy's voice sounded in her head yet again. This time reminding her of the sensitive points of the body. The areas to focus on for maximum impact… aka maximum pain.

The groin.

The eyes.

The foot.

The nose.

She opened her hand flat and rammed the heel of her palm upward just as Lefty was reaching for her throat. When she connected with the underside of his nose, the most satisfying crunch reverberated through the room. She'd hit him so hard, his entire body propelled backward. Lefty cried out, his hands immediately flying up to his face.

He sailed backward. His head connected with her rock-solid granite counter top. The crack of his head hitting the stone was so loud she was surprised if her neighbors didn't come running. Chloe watched with a combination of horror and fascination as his body slumped to the floor in an unconscious heap.

She stood there for a moment, sucking wind and trembling as she stared at the man she'd knocked out cold. Funny, he didn't look so dangerous sprawled out on her tile floor, eyes closed and blood dripping from his nose and mouth.

After another moment of staring, her phone chimed with an incoming new alert. The sound ripped her from her trance.

Who knew how long he'd be out for? She could see the rise and fall of his chest, so she hadn't killed him, which meant he'd be waking at some point. There was no way in hell she planned to be around when that happened, but she needed to restrain him, or the fucker would be free to continue his reign of torment.

Suddenly feeling frantic to have him restrained, Chloe pulled open drawer after drawer searching for something to tie him up. Her handcuffs would work but she'd need something to secure him to and wasn't sure she could drag his heavy body through her house once she found something.

"Damnit," she yelled as she slammed her junk drawer closed. Her heart was thrumming so hard, it was hard to think above the pounding in her head. She forced herself to close her eyes and take a deep breath. As she did, visions of herself bound to the motel bed flooded her mind.

"Duct tape," she whispered aloud. "I have duct tape."

Ohh, sweet irony, using the same medium to restrain Lefty as he'd used to tie her up. She ran out of the kitchen, careful to swing a wide berth around his body as she ran for her office. A quick rummage through her closet had her emerging with a thick roll of duct tape.

After running back to the kitchen, she stood over Lefty's prone and bleeding body. Her fingers shook as she tried to peel an edge of the tape back. "Fuck," she grumbled as she failed for the fourth time. Her quivering fingers just wouldn't obey.

She inhaled a stuttering breath. "Relax. You can do this." After exhaling, she snuck her nail under the corner of the tape and peeled back the sticky strip. Her eyes fell closed. "Thank you," she whispered.

She tiptoed over to Lefty as though that would somehow prevent him from waking and crouched down by his feet. Reaching out a tentative hand, she touched his shoe and jumped as though she was electrified.

Nothing happened.

It was now or never, so she shoved his legs together then wound the tape around his ankles. Once, twice, and again until she was convinced he couldn't bust out of it should he wake. Lefty hadn't so much as stirred, which bolstered her confidence. After struggling for a few minutes, she was able to roll him onto his stomach. Not bothering to be gentle, his face clunked against the tile floor and she held her breath, but once again, he remained motionless.

Still breathing like she was being chased, Chloe gathered his wrists at the base of his spine. With quick hands, she treated them to the same overkill taping as she had his feet. Then she rose to survey her work.

A horn honked somewhere in the distance and she jolted so hard, the tape flew from her hands and landed on Lefty's back.

No movement.

He could still escape if he woke up. Yeah, she'd tied him, but he could work his way to a stand and hop. Blowing out a breath, she wiped her sweaty brow and knelt down near Lefty's feet. Bending Lefty's knees, she used her torso to press them toward his ass. When they were somewhat close to his hands, she wound the remaining tape in a loop between his hands and feet, securing them together.

Panting, she fell back on her butt. "Shit," she muttered as perspiration ran down her face. Tying up a sadistic asshole was hard work. She stood on unsteady legs and surveyed her work. Sloppy as hell, but Lefty wasn't going anywhere.

As she stood there gazing down at the damaged man who once held so much power over her, the realization of what just happened crashed down around her.

Esposito had let him in her house.

They'd fought.

She'd won.

Now that the immediate danger was gone, her face throbbed like a sonofabitch. She wiped her cheek and discovered what she'd thought was sweat was actually blood. He'd split the skin with his knuckles. As the adrenalin waned from her system, her body began to shake. Hard.

Her skin itched, and all of a sudden, she could not stand being in her house for one more second. Eyes on Lefty's prone form, she stumbled backward, crashing into her kitchen table.

With a yelp, she spun and sprinted outside. The day was truly beautiful. Seventy degrees, sunny, no humidity. There could have been a tornado in her driveway for all she took note. The only thing she cared about was getting outside the walls she could never live within again.

Once she was locked behind the wheel of her car, she pulled out her phone to call Logan. That task took longer than it should have. Her damn hands still hadn't quit trembling.

As she listened to the phone ring once, twice, then a third time, memories of the most horrifying night of her life assaulted her.

Lefty looming over her.

Lefty laughing and mocking her.

Lefty touching her.

Lefty hitting her.

"You got him," she whispered. "He can't hurt you. You won."

"Clo?"

"L-logan?" No matter how hard she tried, she couldn't keep the hysteria out of her voice. "I need you. Now."

He was all business immediately. "Baby, you hurt? Tell me what's wrong." He sounded frantic. She hated to do this to him.

The ride over would be hell on him, and he'd been through enough lately. They both had.

"I-I'm okay." Throbbing face notwithstanding. "He-he's here," she whispered.

"Esposito?" Confusion and anger came through in his voice.

"N-no. Lefty. He was in my bedroom. We fought." How she managed to get that out without stuttering, she'd never know.

"Motherfucker!" he screamed into the phone. "Where the hell is he now?"

She started to laugh, a slightly hysterical sound. Logan must think she'd lost her mind. "In my kitchen. Unconscious. I tied him up." She couldn't keep the smug note out of her voice.

"You tied him up." Logan said. "Fuck, baby, I'm so goddammed proud of you. Leaving now, Clo. Be there in fifteen."

"B-but you're half an hour away."

"I'll be there in fifteen minutes," he said with more force.

"Okay."

"Are you safe?"

"Y-yes. I think so. I'm sitting in my car with the doors locked. I don't think he can escape."

"Good, baby. That's good. Turn the car on just in case you need to get away. You did great. I'll take it from here, okay."

She breathed a sigh of relief. It was done. Logan would call in the club, they'd remove Lefty and it would be all over. The man who hurt her would finally pay. Best part, she'd gotten in some damn good shots. She'd forever have the pleasure of hurting the man who'd hurt her.

"Thank you," she said as she slid her key into the ignition. Just being on the phone with Logan had steadied her to the point she no longer trembled.

"Fuck, babe, don't thank me for that shit. Stay on the line with me, okay? Don't care if you don't talk."

"Okay."

Rocket

She had no clue how long it actually took him to arrive, but it felt like a lifetime. With the phone pressed to her ear, she stared at her house, and listened to Logan's even breathing. In some kind of trance, she didn't hear the rumble of his motorcycle approach. When he tapped on her window, she nearly flew through the sunroof.

"Shit!" she cried, slamming a hand over her heart.

"Sorry. Tried not to scare you," he called through the closed window.

"I don't care," she said as she shoved the door open and launched herself into his arms. They immediately engulfed her with crushing force. Exactly what she needed to feel safe. "He touched my things. I can't—" She swallowed as she shook her head. "I can't live in there ever again."

"Shh." He stroked the back of her head. "You don't have to. Hell, you don't have to step a fucking foot in this house again if you don't want to. I'll get him out of here. We might have to wait until the sun goes down." With his hands cradling her face, he drew back and assessed the damage. Rage darkened his eyes. "Fuck."

"I'm okay, Logan. Just some bruising and a cut. I've had worse." She gave him a wry grin but quickly realized mentioning how he found her was a mistake of epic proportions.

His face hardened to stone. A shiver ran down her spine as he transformed from a concerned lover to a merciless killer.

"I'm going to take you back to my house while I deal with him, okay?"

"Um, maybe I should stay with you."

"No. Let me just go in and see what we're dealing with. Wait here." He kissed her forehead as she nodded then he started for the front door. He walked like a jungle cat tracking its prey.

Unease washed over her. Though Logan hadn't said anything, Chloe knew Lefty wouldn't be leaving her house alive.

"Hold on," she called out. "Don't you have to call Copper?"

He looked her straight in the eye and she shivered. His deep blue irises were nearly black with a gaze that promised death. Never before had she seen that side of him. The side that could kill like a well-oiled machine. She wasn't afraid of him. He'd never hurt her. Even in the lethal mood he was in, she had full confidence he'd never so much as lay a hand on her.

But he was scary. Whatever he had planned for Lefty would probably give most people nightmares. Logan wouldn't bat an eye. He was on executioner autopilot. The night he rescued her, he radiated rage and fury. Today? Today there was nothing but cold calculation and acceptance of what was to come.

A killing.

"I'm not calling the club."

Oh, shit.

She shot off after him back into the house, no longer concerned about her home being contaminated by a sadist.

"Logan!" she said when she caught up to him in her kitchen standing over Lefty's body. He flicked her a glance over his shoulder then walked around the body toward her counter. She followed, grabbed his arm, and turned him away from...her knife set?

Double shit.

It took a monumental amount of effort, but she managed to ignore the fact he was now holding her butcher knife. "What do you mean, you aren't calling the club? Logan, you can't do this by yourself. That's crazy. Copper will flip his shit."

"Go back outside, Chloe," he said, voice hard.

"What? Go back outside? That's all you have to say?" She threw her hand up. "Logan, you told me what Copper said. Lefty belongs to the club. Now, I may not have been around your club much, but from what you told me, you don't ignore an order from your president."

"Chloe, outside."

She seethed; fists clenched at her sides. What the hell was wrong with this stubborn man? "Logan. He could kick you out of the club. Or worse!" Her stomach hurt all over again. She'd been completely wrong about Logan being calm and unaffected by Lefty's presence. He was affected to the point he was no longer thinking rationally. He was willing to toss his life away over this.

And Lefty would win. He'd die, but part of him would win if Rocket went against the club. Against his family. What the hell would happen to him without his brothers?

"Logan, please," she said as she grabbed his forearm. She absolutely had to stop him. Had to find a way to make him listen to reason. She'd do anything short of diving in front of the knife. "Stop and think for a second. You'll realize how reckless this is. You aren't reckless. You don't act without thinking."

He looked down at her with much the same ice-cold gaze he'd had in her front yard. "Go. Outside." Each word was punctuated with a narrowing of his eyes.

Chloe swallowed. It was a wasted effort. He wouldn't see reason.

"Fine," she said as she stepped back from him. Without another word she turned and walked outside. Once the front door had closed behind her, she sucked in a huge breath. She knew what she had to do. The one thing that would save Logan from himself.

Even if he'd see it as a betrayal.

Even if it might make him walk away from her forever.

CHAPTER THIRTY-THREE

He'd bruised her. Again. Cut her face.

And Rocket hadn't been there. Hell, he hadn't even checked the house. Just let her hop off his bike and go on her merry way. Guilt swamped him until it felt like a physical ache.

The motherfucker had touched her for the last time. In fact, Rocket twirled the knife by the handle, Lefty was about to breathe his last breath.

Rocket shoved the sight of Chloe's worried face from his mind as he stood over Lefty. She'd come around later, after the shock of finding Lefty in her house waned.

He was loyal to his club. Always had been. Never once had he been tempted to betray his patch or buck Copper's orders. Until the very moment he'd heard Chloe's fear-filled voice through his phone. Until he saw the angry bruises that would take weeks to fade. The club took a backseat to Rocket's need for retribution, and for the first time since he patched, he was willing to throw it all away.

From his spot face down on Chloe's kitchen floor, Lefty groaned and turned his head to the side.

A grin curled Rocket's lips. "Wakey, wakey, motherfucker," he said right before using his heavy boot to shove Lefty onto his side. A surge of pride in Chloe raced through him at the sight of Lefty's ravaged face. She'd fought like a wildcat and beat his ass.

Rocket laughed. "Damn, she did a number on you, huh? Guess you're not much without your little gang."

God, he'd waited for this for so long. Lived for this moment. He was going to prolong the execution as much as possible. Savor it. Soak up every ounce of Lefty's misery.

Fucking Esposito. The bastard must have suspected Logan didn't complete the mission. Otherwise why fuck with him this way? He was a problem that would have to be addressed once Lefty was on ice.

"Rocket," Lefty said, in a nasally whine due to the broken nose. "Been hoping you'd visit."

He grunted in response. Any other time he'd seen Lefty, the fucker looked like a knock-off version of Rambo. Wife beater, jeans, bandana around his head.

"How about you send sweet Chloe back in. I'd much rather look at her and remember the feel of her pussy than have to stare at your ugly mug."

Rocket breathed through his nose as he let the taunts roll off his back. Took a lot more than Lefty to get under his skin. Though he had to admit, each word out of the motherfucker's mouth inspired further torture.

"Not gonna bite?" Lefty asked with a smug as fuck grin. Hard to pull off with blood seeping from his mouth. "She still here?"

Rocket remained silent as he crouched down.

Lefty's grin was full of yellowed teeth. Looked like the sex trafficking and drug pushing industries didn't come with top-notch dental insurance. "How 'bout you call her back in. We could double team her. Hell, I'll even let you have her cunt. I'm more than happy to stick it in her—*argh!*" He gritted his teeth as his body arched off the floor.

Rocket had stuck the knife through the bindings at Lefty's back. With a sawing motion he cut through the tape connecting Lefty's arms to his legs. The limbs were still bound but now he could push the asshole flat on his back. "Oops," Rocket said as he *accidentally* sliced Lefty's hand with the knife. "Too vigorous. My bad."

Panting through clenched teeth, Lefty stared up at him. "You're nothing but a fucking joke," he spat out, not quite as cocksure as he'd been before a knife cut into his skin. "What do you think's gonna happen here? You think I'm gonna just disappear without any repercussions? My guys will be all over your ass before you can bury my fucking body."

Rocket rotated the point of the knife back and forth against his finger tip. "Hmm, I think you've been missing for two weeks and no one gives a shit. Not even a dingleberry. There's no loyalty among your men. Never has been. So I'm thinking I've got time and plenty of it. Hell, I'm thinking I could keep you for days. Maybe even weeks. As long as I can tolerate the stench." As he spoke he popped the button at Lefty's fly open then drew down the zipper. With rough tugs, he yanked his jeans down to his ankles.

"The fuck are you doing?"

"Commando, huh? Making this easy for me. I just wanted to get a peek at this thing between your legs you're so proud of. Had to see what makes it so special that it gets to fuck women without their consent."

"Fuck you."

Rocket lunged forward, pressing the deadly tip of the knife against the base of Lefty's dick. "No," he said. "Fuck you." He dragged the end of blade down the length of Lefty's dick, scraping hard enough to cut a shallow slice into the skin. A high-pitched shriek flew from his captive's mouth. The sound filled Rocket with a sadistic pleasure. This was what he'd been seeking for months. Not just Lefty's death, but his suffering. His fucking torment. "In fact, how about I take this," Rocket said as he returned the knife to the root of Lefty's dick, "right off your body and fuck you with it? Give you a little taste of what you gave to Chloe."

Rocket

Sweat beaded across Lefty's forehead. A few drops rolled down his face, mixing with the blood and pooling on the floor. His gaze was riveted to the knife as though he could somehow stare it away.

"Nothing to say now?" Rocket said with a laugh. "Too bad. I was so enjoying listening to you run your fucking mouth." He dug the knife in. "I'm gonna need to hear something or I'll go through with my plan."

"N-no. Don't." Lefty's eyes were wide, crazed as his legs started to tremble.

"Begging already? Huh, I'm kinda disappointed." He laughed again. "Thought you'd hold out a little longer. You pig shits are all the same. Think you're the top junkyard dog. Love to lord over those weaker than you. But the second a bigger dog comes on the scene; you turn into a giant pussy begging to let you keep this tiny thing you call a dick. Let me hear some more. I'm not fully convinced you don't want me to cut it off." He nicked Lefty again, this time in an arch over his cock as if he were going to cut a circle around it.

"D-don't do it. Don't cut it off." High-pitched again, almost as though Rocket had already rid him of his nuts. Ohh, he could take those as well. The cock and his balls. A perfect set.

"Why?" Rocket asked. "Because you need it to rape women?"

"N-no." Sweat dripped down his face in rivers now. He was uselessly bucking against the bindings, trying to get his arms and legs free.

"You sure? I'm having a hard time believing one would fuck you willingly."

"Rocket." Copper's bark hit him like the crack of a whip, jerking a response out of him.

He stilled, knife pricking the skin above Lefty's dick.

Fuck.

The bastard's fear evaporated, morphing into a smirk once again. Fury surged through Rocket's veins, but he steeled his expression. He tilted his head while keeping the knife gouging into Lefty's skin. Let the man think he was prepared to discount his president.

"Rocket," Copper said again.

For a flash, he was tempted to drive the knife forward, fuck his president's wishes. But he didn't. He tossed the blade onto Lefty's stomach. It landed with a thump against a bruise Rocket hoped came from Chloe.

Lefty hissed.

As Rocket turned, LJ and Zach entered the kitchen.

"Hallway, Rocket. Now," Copper growled. His stony expression gave away nothing about his anger, but make no mistake, the president was fucking pissed. About as furious as Rocket had ever seen him. That damn boot didn't hinder him a bit. At least not when he was rip-shit.

Zach and LJ stared down at Lefty. As he passed, Zach thumped Rocket on the back. Lefty's belligerent laughter followed Rocket out of the kitchen. Did the fucker think this was some kind of reprieve? Once in the hallway Copper speared him with a hate-filled look. He rubbed his beard and appeared to be choosing his words carefully. "Jig's gonna drive your woman to hang with Izzy. After you say goodbye to her you're going to ride to the fucking clubhouse. I'll meet you there. You're lucky I don't slice that brand off your arm right here and now. You hear me?" Copper was practically vibrating with suppressed rage. "Do you fucking hear me?"

Rocket stared his president down. "I hear you." No matter his punishment, he'd do the same thing again. Lefty had been delivered with a fucking bow—literally. Couldn't look that gift horse in the mouth.

"Fuck were you thinking Rocket?"

"He fucking touched her. Again." he spat out as fury surged once again. "How'd you know?"

Copper didn't answer.

"How. Did. You—Jesus." Like a smack to the face, it dawned on him. A soul-crushing sense of betrayal stole his ability to breathe. No. Not Chloe. She couldn't have. *Wouldn't* have. She knew exactly what this meant to him. Hell, she'd suffered through the past two weeks of his absence for this very moment. She'd told him she loved him for fuck's sake. But one look at Copper's face confirmed his fear.

Chloe had stabbed him right in the back. Taken away the thing that had driven him forward for months.

Revenge.

He turned, unable to continue talking to Copper without risking spewing some vile shit he could never take back. As he stepped outside, he caught sight of Chloe standing with Jigsaw. His solemn brother said something and pointed over her shoulder. She whipped around, scanning until she found him. Her cheeks were wet, eyes somber, but the moment they landed on him, she appeared lighter. After squeezing Jig's hand, she took off at a run.

"Logan," she said as she reached for him with outstretched arms. He sidestepped her embrace and just glared at her. He couldn't deal with her right now. He was too enraged. Too furious that his shot at Lefty had been interrupted. Because of her. He couldn't see anything past Lefty's smirk and Chloe's injured face.

Her expression fell. Crumbled to pieces right before his eyes. Despite it all, despite her disloyalty, he had to dig his blunt nails into his palms to keep his traitorous hands from reaching for her. The sight of her heartbroken tears had a power over him like no other.

"L-Logan?" She placed her hand on his arm.

"Not now." He shook her off, ignoring her shocked gasp.

"Please," she said, again reaching for him. She either wasn't aware or didn't care that a handful of his brothers witnessed her near begging. "I had to."

That may be true, but there were things he had to do as well, and killing Lefty topped that list.

"Logan if you're not gonna haul that woman into your arms and kiss her silly for saving your fool ass, then get on your bike," Copper said from behind him.

With one last scowl in Chloe's direction, he marched toward his motorcycle. After climbing on his bike and donning his helmet, he risked a peek at the house. Copper frowned at him from the front stoop. Screw hovered next to him, his bulging arms wrapped around a sobbing Chloe.

He knew he should go to her. Should be the one to hold her and comfort her. She'd been attacked and fought for her life, not to mention experienced the shock of finding her rapist in her house. But he couldn't. He was too fucking angry to think logically.

CHLOE'S HEART ACHED until tears clogged her throat and poured out her eyes. Two incredibly strong arms held her close, and a sweet man whispered soothing words in her ear.

But they were the wrong arms. And the wrong voice. And the wrong man.

So it did nothing to quell the heartbreak or ease her guilt.

He was so angry with her. Angry enough to end it? Of course, there was no screaming match. No hurled accusations or words of hatred. Words weren't Logan's style. But that look? That glare that conveyed what words never could? How she'd stolen something from him. That look would remain with her for the rest of her life.

She turned her head and watched him ride off through watery eyes.

When he was out of sight, she pulled out of Screw's embrace. Copper peered down at her. "You did good here today, Chloe. Your man doesn't agree right now, but he can't see past his hatred of Lefty. Club has rules, strict ones. Had he continued here today I'd have been forced to take his patch and worse. You saved his ass, girl."

Didn't feel like she'd done anything but turn her life upside down once again.

"Come on." He slung a heavy arm across her shoulders. "Let's get you to Izzy. If there's anyone who's good company when a man's being an idiot, it's Izzy."

Chloe cracked a smile because she felt he expected it, but her heart wasn't in it.

Worst part of the entire afternoon was that she'd make the same choices again given a do over. The club was Rocket's life. How could she let him risk it all to avenge crimes committed against her?

She *couldn't*. Simple as that.

Too bad that thought wouldn't keep her warm through the night.

CHAPTER THIRTY-FOUR

Rocket splayed his hands on the bar, head hanging as he fought for control of his emotions. Not a phrase he'd ever thought in reference to himself. On a normal day, emotional shit was easy. Turn it off. Compartmentalize. Shove it deep in the vault. Thanks to Chloe, he'd been bombarded by every goddamned feeling he'd refused to allow in the past.

But there were two he was achingly familiar with.

Fury and guilt. The two emotions that registered as soon as he heard Chloe's scared voice through the phone. They had taken over, clogged his brain and heart until nothing else could penetrate their thick walls. And the fury grew to epic levels once his chance at torturing Lefty was shot to shit.

The clubhouse door flew open, bouncing off the wall with a loud bang. Copper's body filled the space. "Everyone out!" he shouted. "Right fucking now."

As much as he'd love to hightail it out of there, Copper's order didn't extend to him.

Thunder, one of the newer prospects, froze mid-pour. He glanced from Copper to Rocket. He could obey the damn order after he finished getting Rocket his drink. With a wave of his hand, Rocket urged him to continue.

"Uh, yeah, man, here." He capped the bottle with one hand while pushing the not full enough tumbler across the bar. "I'm outta here."

Rocket

"The fuck is this?" Rocket asked lifting the glass which couldn't have held more than an ounce of whiskey.

With a snort, Thunder rounded the bar. "That is me obeying the prez. Something I hear you forgot how to do." His hand landed on Rocket's shoulder as he walked by. "Good luck, man. Think you might need it. The big man looks like he's been chewing bullets."

"Fuck you," Rocket said before downing the meager amount of alcohol. "I'll remember this shit when it comes time to vote you in."

Thunder just laughed and jetted toward the exit with a "Hey, Prez," on his way out.

The drop of whiskey he'd consumed wouldn't do shit to numb the fucking feelings he'd grown so he reached across the bar and helped himself to the bottle Thunder had abandoned. Fuck the glass. He unscrewed the cap and took a long drink, aware of Copper's hard stare the entire time.

"You done?" Cop asked as his heavy tread sounded across the floor. The boot he wore on his left leg thumped along making Rocket wonder how the hell the prez had managed to sneak up on him at Chloe's house. He'd just been that zoned out, intent on destroying Lefty.

"Just getting started." Rocket set the bottle down and turned to face his president. He wasn't stupid, he knew he'd crossed about a hundred lines this afternoon. He just wasn't sure he had it in him to be sorry. But one look at the fury on his president's face had him second guessing that theory.

Copper wasn't just pissed, he actually looked sad. And that gutted Rocket ten times worse than anger ever would.

"Here's how this shit is gonna go," Copper said, taking a seat at the bar. He faced Rocket head on and when he paused, the quiet room seemed to mock Rocket's thoughts. "I'm gonna talk and if you have any desire to hang onto that patch, you're gonna keep your fucking mouth shut. Think you owe me at least that much respect. Yes?"

Shit.

Shame washed over Rocket, far worse than any punishment Copper could dish out. So much of what the club stood for came down to respect, and Rocket had shown his president the ultimate disrespect today. Not intentionally. In truth, there wasn't a man alive Rocket respected more than the club's top guy, and he, as well as his brothers, followed a strict code which demonstrated respect for Copper.

At least until today.

Fuck, he was a royal asshole.

He gave Copper a single nod. If the man wanted him to shut up and listen, he'd do it. It was the least he owed him.

"All right." After stroking his beard, Copper grabbed the open whiskey and downed a gulp. "I get it, brother, I really get it." Copper thumped his chest. "In here." He patted a gentle hand on his still healing abdomen. "Here." Then he tapped a finger to his temple. "And here."

Rocket remained silent, his attention focused on Copper. Being called brother gave him a flicker of hope he hadn't completely destroyed Copper's faith in him.

"My woman was hurt by a motherfucker too. Yes, it was different than what Chloe went through, and it was a long time ago, so she'd had time to learn to live with it. But for me? It was all fresh fucking information. And if someone else hadn't gotten to the bastard first, you can bet your ass I'd have put a bullet in him."

Rocket shifted his eyes to the orthopedic boot covering Copper's leg from toes to knee. It had only been a few months since that all went down. Only a few months since he found out about the horrors in his own woman's past and he'd sure as fuck handled it better than Rocket had.

"So I get it, brother. The rage, the hatred, the need for revenge. Not justice. I didn't give a fuck about justice. Guessing it's the same for you. There ain't no such thing as justice for what happened to your woman. Nothing in the world makes up for it.

But it feels damn fucking good to make the fucker responsible pay, doesn't it?"

Rocket grunted.

"Easy to lose your head in that situation. I get that too. But Rocket, I swear to Christ if you ever go against the club again, I'll tear that patch from your cut, skin the brand from your arm, and kick your ass to the curb myself."

With a swallow Rocket nodded. Now that he was away from Lefty, rational thought returned. As did the magnitude of his fuck up. Christ, he'd nearly lost his club. Running a hand through his hair, he blew out a breath.

"Yeah," Copper said. "Crashing down on you now, huh?"

"Cop…" He rolled his shoulders back. Time to fucking grovel.

His president took another drink then shook his head. He slid the bottle across the bar to Rocket. "Don't need or want an apology. Told you I get it. Just need your word it's a one-shot deal."

"You have my word."

"That means something to me," Copper said. "Always has. You broke your word once. Do it again and it won't mean shit to me anymore."

Which would be the harshest punishment of all. Losing the trust and respect of someone who meant so much to him would make losing his patch that much harder. Chloe had tried to warn him, but he'd been too blinded by hatred to see past his own selfish need for revenge. She'd saved his stupid ass big time. And how did he repay her? With rejection.

Christ, he'd fucked up.

"Now," Copper continued. "Let's get down to the box so we can end this shit and let you get on to apologizing to your woman."

"Not sure an apology is gonna cut it."

Copper chuckled. "Yeah, you might have to resort to full-on groveling."

With a grunt, Rocket nodded. He took in his president, who really did understand what Rocket was going through. Shell's situation had been vastly different but just as devastating and something that would probably haunt Copper for the rest of his life. If there was anyone he could talk to about this shit, it was his prez.

"Shoulda been with her," Rocket mumbled so low he was surprised Copper actually heard him. "Shoulda checked the goddamn house at least."

"Ahh," Copper said before taking another swallow of the whiskey. "Guilt sure is a nasty motherfucker. Makes us do all kinds of stupid shit." He raised an eyebrow.

"Can you stow the Dr. Phil bullshit? This right here is why I don't talk to any of you fuckers." Rocket grabbed the bottle and downed three healthy gulps.

Copper was back to rubbing his chin. "All right. I'll give it to you straight. You couldn't have known what the fuck was going to happen today. Just like we couldn't have known Lefty was going to rape Chloe in the first place. And you couldn't have known your buddy's wife was going to kill herself after his death."

Rocket watched his president as he continued scratching his beard.

"Much as this is gonna fuck with how you think, it's gotta be said. You can't protect everyone all the time. Shit happens. And yes I know that's a cliché, but it's also the fucking truth. And when shit goes down, how you deal with it is what matters to the people you care about. No one expects you to be psychic, Rocket. But your woman expects you to be by her side no matter how pissed or guilty you feel.

"You were selfish as fuck. Disobeyed my orders and acted against your club because of what *you* needed. Chloe went behind your back to save your ass. You wanna feel guilty, feel it over that. Not because you didn't use your crystal ball to guess that Esposito was going to plant Lefty in your woman's house."

Rocket

With that parting shot, he grabbed the bottle and limped toward the exit. "I get thirty minutes alone with Lefty. Then you're free to join. I'll give you the kill, and you can take your time with it, but this ends today," he called over his shoulder without turning around.

Rocket scrubbed a hand down his face. He'd really fucked this day up no matter which angle you looked at it. He'd been so hot to make Lefty pay, he'd nearly lost the only two things that mattered in his life, his club and his woman. Actually, one of those things was still dangling in the wind. Or at least he hoped the tether hadn't been completely severed. If the situation weren't so screwed up, it'd be laughable. For years, Rocket functioned as an elite operative, working under staggering amounts of pressure. He'd been successful under fire, while being hunted, in the most hostile of territories, and never so much as cracked under the strain. But give him one woman with a tragic story, sexy-as-fuck body, and heart big enough to overlook his issues, and he lost his fucking mind.

"By the way," Copper said as his palm landed on the door. "You're taking LJ's collection runs for the next three months. And don't think I've forgotten you're planning his patch-in party. Just got delayed…again."

Huffing out a laugh, Rocket shook his head. There wasn't anything he hated more than collecting debts for the club's loan-sharking business. Copper nailed that punishment. As much as he despised the task, he'd suck it up and compete it without a word of complaint. It was the absolute least he deserved. Had he been in Copper's position, he wouldn't have been so lenient.

Twenty-seven minutes later, after being sent straight to voicemail, and receiving no response to four text messages, Rocket gave up on contacting Chloe for now. Once Lefty had been dealt with, he'd go seek her out, which meant getting past Izzy. Rocket had a sneaking suspicion Copper planned that as well. Izzy on a good day was a force to be reckoned with. Izzy full of pregnancy hormones was enough to make any man's balls suck back into their body.

Small price to pay to get his woman back.

As he trekked through the woods to the underground bunker affectionately known as the box, Rocket let thoughts of Chloe fuel his hatred for Lefty. He conjured the images of her beaten, naked, and bound to the hotel bed. She didn't deserve to be remembered that way, and it would be the last time he thought of her in such a manner. Chloe was strong as fuck and moving past what happened to her. He'd give her the respect of going forward with her. But for tonight? Tonight, he'd bathe in the memories of that night and use them to torment the man responsible for her pain.

When he reached the box, he yanked the heavy wooden door straight up, then descended. With each step, a whistled wheezing grew louder as did the sound of flesh hitting flesh and the weak grunts of a man who was so defeated he could do nothing but lie limp and accept the brutal punishment.

After a minute, Rocket's eyes adjusted to the dim lighting in the box. A single bulb dangled from the ceiling over Lefty's head. "Damn, Cop," Rocket said as he whistled.

His president grunted as he wiped the sweat off his brow with his shoulder. "Mighta got a little carried away."

It was Rocket's turn to grunt. "That's one way to put it."

Lefty slumped in a chair in the center of the room. He was out cold, completely unconscious with his head lolled back and arms sagging like wet noodles at his sides. There wasn't a single restraint holding him to the chair. He was beaten all to fuck and couldn't escape if his life depended on it—which incidentally it did.

"Just us?" Typically, Zach was in on this kind of thing. Sometimes Screw or one of the other exec board members. Not this afternoon. Today it was just Rocket and Copper, the two whose hatred for Lefty ran deepest. Rocket for obvious reasons and Copper for all the grief this man had caused his club.

Rocket

Copper would move heaven and earth for his club, and the demise of Lefty symbolized the culmination of nearly a year of shit.

"Yeah." Copper strode, as best as he could with a bum leg, to the wall where a hose hung on a large hook. He grabbed it with bloodied-knuckled hands. Shell would be giving him a lecture over that for sure. Unless he told her the reasoning behind it, which Rocket assumed he would. He had a feeling the prez didn't keep much from his ol' lady. Once she found out why his knuckles were torn to shreds, she'd probably drop to her knees instead of railing at him.

"You ready?" Copper asked as he aimed the sprayer Lefty's way.

Rocket nodded. Fuck yes, he was ready. He'd been ready for this shit since the moment he opened the motel room door and discovered an abused Chloe. With a smile that could only be classified as diabolical, Copper squeezed the lever and let loose a blast of frigid water.

Icy droplets sailed off the stream in every direction, pelting Rocket's face and arms like tiny needles. He didn't so much as flinch at the discomfort, welcoming it instead. The pricks of pain kept him grounded and present in the moment.

The water sprayed directly into Lefty's face, eliciting a shriek from a man who looked ready for a casket. He slapped at the water with his hands as though he could somehow stop the ice-cold assault. Copper let it go on for another thirty seconds before killing the spray.

"Welcome back," he said. "Brought someone to see you."

Lefty's head wobbled atop his neck like a bobble head doll. He coughed weakly, attempting to spit water from his mouth. The action had no power behind it, and the spittle just rolled down his chin. After the coughing fit subsided, he moaned and clutched his sides.

"Not much of a big man now, is he?" Copper asked.

Rocket grunted.

He took five steps forward, until he was just two feet away from Lefty. The man's eyes were hazy, but alert enough to recognize his fate. Shivers racked his body, bouncing him on the metal chair. He gave one last attempt to save himself by trying to push to stand. All he managed to do was flop to the wet ground in a wet, naked, quaking heap.

Both Copper and Rocket laughed.

"What do ya want? Gun? Knife? Wrench?" Copper asked as he pointed to a pile of tools on the ground. "I got it all."

Without a word, Rocket stalked to the goodies and selected a K-bar knife. A favorite of his. He walked back until he stood over Lefty's crumpled body.

"Want him back in the chair?"

Rocket shook his head. No, this would do nicely.

He took a deep breath and prepared to settle in for a long afternoon of making this man as miserable as humanly possible. But as he looked down, it wasn't Lefty he saw, but Chloe. And not the abused and traumatized version of Chloe, but the version who had given herself to him. The version that allowed him to touch her despite her fear and past. The version covered in sweat as she wailed on a heavy bag, determined to beat back every demon. The version who flew into his arms when he returned from Mexico as though she couldn't bear one more second of separation. The version who clashed with Lefty and won. And the version who risked losing him to save his worthless ass.

Suddenly, an urgent need to be with her clawed at him like a wounded animal trying to escape a trap. All of his priorities fell into place in that moment. Lefty's fate was set. Rocket was seconds from terminating him. But it didn't need to take all night. Didn't need to be drawn out into an elaborate torture session. All that would do was delay him getting to his woman.

And being with her was imperative.

Knife in hand, he crouched, careful to keep from resting his knees in the chilly puddle. "Sorry we were interrupted before," he said with a snicker.

Rocket

"F-fuck you," Lefty said but it came out as a wheezy whisper of words.

"Yikes, you're not sounding too good. And I'm pretty sure you're not up for fucking anything right about now." He placed the tip of the knife to Lefty's sternum.

Rocket leaned in close to Lefty's ear while dragging the knife down the man's body, making sure to score the skin in the process. Might as well have a little fun while he was at it. He stopped when he reached his prisoner's groin. Lefty's pitiful moan made him smile. "No one gives a shit that you're missing. No one's gonna give a shit that you're dead. Hell, I bet everyone you know will dance on your grave. But me and my brothers? We're strong as ever. Free to do whatever the hell we want. Fuck our women. Drink our booze. Make money. Live the good life."

As he drew in a breath, he spared half a second to enjoy what was about to happen. Then he pushed his arm down, sinking into the flesh of Lefty's groin and severing his femoral artery. "Enjoy your trip to hell," he whispered. As blood poured out of the two-inch-long gouge, Rocket withdrew the knife and repeated the process on the other side. Then he stood in silence with Copper while they watched twin crimson rivers run the life out of a psychopath.

Once the light vanished from Lefty's eyes and the flow of blood slowed to a trickle, Rocket turned to Copper and extended his hand. It was an apology, an affirmation of respect, and a thank you all rolled into one. Their gazes met as they shook.

"Shell expects you guys over for dinner tomorrow night," Copper said as though they hadn't just killed a man.

Rocket nodded, giving his president's hand a squeeze.

After one last glance at the dead man lying in a pool of blood on the cement floor, Rocket made his way up the stairs. Halfway there, he heard Copper on the phone. "Need a clean-up in the box," his president said. "Got some trash to dispose of."

It was done. The task he'd focused on for months, yet Rocket didn't feel one ounce of the relief he'd expected. That would only come after he'd laid claim to Chloe.

CHAPTER THIRTY-FIVE

"Christ, woman, you are going to make me go into labor with all the stress you're spewing my way," Izzy said as she intercepted Chloe's pace halfway through the living room. "Stop moving." She placed her hands on Chloe's shoulders and steered her toward the couch. "Sit. Look out the windows at the pretty view. Chill the fuck out, sister."

Chloe blew out a breath as her leg kicked up a bouncy rhythm. The scenery was nice. A lovely mountain view she'd have appreciated on any other day, but as it was, all she could think about was Logan. About what an ungrateful ass Logan was. Once she got her hands on him she was going to give him some of what she gave Lefty, earlier.

"Jesus, you can't help yourself." Izzy slammed her hand down on Chloe's thigh. "Stop moving! You're making me nuts."

"I'm pissed!" With a shake of her head, she flopped back against the couch cushions. "Okay," she said. "Give it to me."

Izzy looked down at the can of ginger ale now in her hand. "What? This? No way. You know where the fridge is. Get one yourself."

"Nice hostess, babe," Jig yelled from the kitchen. "Want a drink, Clo?"

Ugh. She'd probably vomit anything she tried to swallow. "No thanks, Jig," she called back. Then for Izzy, "I wasn't talking about giving me your preggers drink. I meant *give* it to me. Lay it on me. Tell me how stupid men are so we can bash them together and I can gear up to kick Logan's ass.

"Ahh," Izzy said.

What the hell? "Ahh? That's it. That's all you got for me? Aren't you supposed to be the tough one?"

"Well…" Izzy put the soda down on the coffee table, then turned, curling her legs under her. "Normally I'd be the first one on the men-are-pigs bandwagon, but seeing as how I'm also a violent offender, I can kinda see where he's coming from." She flinched and held her hands in front of her face. "Don't hit me. I'm with child."

With a grunt of laughter, Chloe rolled her eyes. "A violent offender? And I'm not going to hit you, bitch. I'm just going to call you a bitch."

Izzy grinned at her with a shrug. "I can live with that. Look, you gotta think about this like a man."

"Jesus," Jig said from out of sight. "Can't wait to hear this."

"Love you too, babe," Izzy called back. Her comment was followed by his laughter.

"Look, you know you did the right thing calling Copper. Rocket knows it too. He's just throwing a mantrum because he's pissed that Lefty got near you. I'm guessing he feels like it was his fault you were alone. You see what I did there? With man and tantru—"

Chloe waved her hand. "Yes, Iz, I see it. You're so clever."

"I like to think so." She rested against the couch with a smug grin.

"You always do," came Jig's reply.

Izzy scowled. "New subject. No more talk of Rocket, who I have no doubt will come crawling around soon. How's your face?"

Lifting a hand to her cheek Chloe winced when her fingers probed the sore skin.

"Well I didn't ask you to poke it," Izzy said with a roll of her eyes. "I just asked how it was feeling."

"Well I had to feel it to know how it was feeling," Chloe shot back. The two grinned at each other. "It's sore, but the Advil helped."

"Yeah and those butterfly bandages are holding it together well, but you may have a scar. Still say you should have gone to the ER so a surgeon could have stitched it up all pretty."

Chloe blew a raspberry. "Would you have gone to the ER?"

"Well, no, but I'm a badass." One of Izzy's perfect black eyebrows arched over her eye.

"Well after today, I think I qualify as one too. Plus, I've spent enough days in the hospital for three lifetimes. Not going back unless it's a matter of life and death." A shudder traveled through her at the memory of the days spent in the hospital following her attack. Being poked and prodded at all hours, no privacy but plenty of pain.

No thank you. Not even a few hours long ER trip.

"Well, you'll look cool with a scar. I could cover it with a tat."

That had Chloe laughing her first real laugh all day. "On my cheek?"

Izzy just shrugged as if to say, "What of it?"

"Not even Mav has ink front and center on his face."

They sat there for a while longer, shooting the breeze and sharing some laughs. There seemed to be an unspoken agreement to avoid further talk of Rocket, Lefty, or anything that had happened that morning. Fine by Chloe. The distraction went a long way toward leveling her out.

After more than an hour of chatter, her eyelids grew heavy. "You mind if I lie down for a bit? All of a sudden I'm zonked." Plus, she could use a few minutes alone to sort out what she'd say when she next saw Logan.

Izzy stared at her as though trying to decide whether it was a good idea or not. "Sure. Guest room is the only door on the right."

"Thanks, Izz." She leaned forward and gave her friend a hug. "Thanks for everything."

"Please do not thank me. Us ol' ladies need to stick together if we want to keep these bikers in line."

"Amen, sister."

She walked toward the room feeling like the air was made of thick goo. Without bothering to remove any clothing or pull back the blankets, she flopped back-first onto the bed. Softness enveloped her, a counter to the ache in her heart at the memory of Logan's anger.

God, the way he'd glared at her. She probably could have shot him, and he wouldn't have been as devastated. His eyes reflected just how much her actions gutted him. Whatever headway she'd made into his heart was completely obliterated by one phone call. Thing of it was, no matter how many times she replayed the incident in her head—and it'd been hundreds of times in the past two hours—she couldn't come up with a single alternate solution.

Bottom line, she loved Logan. Loved him so hard, she would do anything to keep him from suffering an ounce of pain. And she knew in her heart she'd done the right thing. He just had to come to the same conclusion somehow. Losing the club would have altered the course of his life in the most negative way possible. He'd be adrift. Floating through life without purpose or family. And that would have destroyed her right alongside him. He may hate her at the moment, but someday in the future he'd think back to this time and realize she called Copper to step in because she loved him. Not because she couldn't bear the thought of him killing Lefty. That was an inevitability.

It didn't take long for the lull of sleep to pull her under. When she woke, she had no clue what time it was. The first thing her brain picked up on was the throbbing in her cheek and hammering in her head. Her eyes were also gritty as though she'd been crying in her sleep. How TV movie of her. Though not entirely unexpected after the intensity of the day. With a sigh, she rolled to her back and winced at the soreness from her fight with Lefty.

Rocket

Something sounded outside her door. Chloe sat, straining her ears.

"I'm telling you this right now, bucko, you fuck this up further and I swear to God Lefty won't be the only one dying today. You catch my drift?"

"Babe, I'm pretty sure he gets your meaning. You're about as subtle as an avalanche."

Izzy harrumphed. "Just making sure we're all on the same page. And we are, right, *Logan*?"

Logan grunted and Chloe's lips quirked. Leave it to him to respond to a threat with a sound instead of words.

"Go on in," Izzy said. "I checked on her twenty minutes ago and she was passed out."

She imagined Logan nodding as he reached for the door. Footsteps indicated Jig and Izzy's retreat. As the doorknob turned, Chloe sucked in a breath and quickly smoothed her hair down. Shit, she must look like a wretched hag. She rubbed a thumb under each eye. They came away black. Great, mascara tracks were always a man-pleaser.

"Oh, you're up." Logan said as he soundlessly stepped into the room.

"Yeah, I, uh, just woke up. What time is it?"

"About four."

"Wow." She hadn't meant to sleep for two hours.

"Can I sit?" he asked, indicating the spot next to her on the bed.

"Go ahead." Chloe scooted until her back met the wall. She drew her knees up and wrapped an arm around them in a sort of metaphorical shield for her heart. After toeing off his boots, Rocket sat against the headboard and stretched out his legs.

There was a crease between his eyes. It tended to pop up when he was deep in thought. The fact he hadn't stepped right in the room and told her to fuck off had to be a good sign, right?

Who the hell knew at this point?

After at least three minutes of silence, Chloe was losing her mind. Someone had to say something before the pressure became so great, the room exploded off the side of Izzy and Jig's house. "So, uh, did you..."

"I fucked up," Logan said at the same time.

"Huh?" She blinked at him. "I mean, what did you say?"

Logan's sigh was heavy and full of pain. "I fucked up."

As her head shook side to side, Chloe said, "No. You just got caught up in the thought of finally getting Lefty. I understand why, Logan."

He huffed a soft chuckle. "Well, I fucked that up too, but it's not what I was referring to. I'm talking to how I treated you at your house. My reaction to you calling Copper."

"Oh." Not her smoothest, but she was truly stunned speechless. "No. You didn't. I—"

"Saved my fucking ass, baby."

She had nothing to say to that. It was such a one eighty from the man who'd glared at her like she'd snuffed out the sun.

"I kept seeing you. The way I found you in the motel."

She tensed and his hand landed on her thigh.

"I shouldn't bring it up."

"No." She scooted a little closer. "It's okay. Continue. Please."

"I kept seeing you that way and I didn't try to push it away. I let it come. Let it fuel the raging fire of hatred I had for the man. And then he was there. In front of me. After hurting you again," he said as he stroked a gentle finger over the two butterfly bandages on her cheek. "God, Esposito had to fuck with me one last time." Rocket's head thunked against the headboard. His eyes fell closed and he breathed in and out as though trying to get a handle on his emotions. Then he opened his eyes and those blue orbs met her gaze. "I felt so guilty I didn't check your house that I lost control when I saw that he hit you. Then this afternoon, I had my second shot at him. I did the same thing. Pictured you hurt and helpless. But this time, the image faded away. It was replaced by a new one. One of you as you are now.

Strong, resilient, so sexy my dick aches every time I so much as breathe the same air as you."

As though to demonstrate his point, his gaze drifted down between his legs. Chloe couldn't help but follow. Sure enough, there was a bulge in his jeans. She chuckled softly.

"I realized something today. We need to live for the current image of you, not the past one. Today is what's important. And today I have you. And you're whole, and healing, and strong enough to protect yourself. My guilt doesn't move us forward or show you the respect you deserve. I'll always try to protect you, Chloe, maybe even too much, but I see you for the strong, kickass woman you've become. I trust you to take care of yourself when I can't. What I'm trying to say, Chloe, is that I fucking love you."

"Logan," she breathed.

He grabbed her and hauled her into his lap. A tiny bit of wiggling later and she was straddling him with her arms tightly wound around his chest, head buried in his neck.

"Please, tell me you can forgive me for being an asshole. You saved me from losing my family, and I cast you aside. If you can't forgive me today, tell me there's a chance it can happen in the future. I'll work my fucking ass off to get back to where we were, baby." His words were interspersed with soft kisses to her cheek, the side of her head, her neck.

Though they may have been meant to comfort, Chloe's body reacted with a swift and fierce need. "There isn't anything to forgive, Logan," she whispered against his ear. One tug on her hair had their foreheads resting against one another. "I love you too. So much. You've given me my life back. Actually, you've given me an even better life than I had before you. So much better. Not only do I get you, I get your whole crazy family."

"Fuck, I love you," he said as he tightened his hold in her hair. "Kiss me, gorgeous."

Chloe's smile was so big her cheeks cramped. "You got it, *Rocket*." Their mouths met in a kiss of two people starved for each other. As though desperate to feel her skin, Logan released her hair and shoved his hands under her shirt without much finesse. She moaned as his rough fingertips scraped across the soft skin of her belly, igniting a trail of sparks. When his hands closed over her lace covered breasts, she whimpered and ground down on his rampant erection.

It was at that moment that the door flew open. "You're goddamned right you get all of us," Izzy announced as she burst into the room, completely at ease with the scene before her.

"Christ," Jig muttered behind her. He held a hand across his eyes as he blindly reached for his woman. "Sorry folks. I'll just grab her. You two go about your business."

"What?" Izzy said with a shrug. "I'm just checking to make sure he's not getting out of line in here."

"Aww, Iz, you trying to protect me?" Chloe asked with a giggle as she tried to wriggle away from Logan's greedy hands.

"Good looking out, Izzy, but Chloe can protect herself. Pretty sure she could take any one of us now," Rocket said as he winked at her.

Though it was said with the lightness of jest, Chloe's heart soared. He really did see the strength in her.

Jig's hand finally captured Izzy's arm. "We're going now, kids," he said. "Feel free to resume whatever it was we rudely interrupted. Let's go, babe." He tugged her out of the room.

"It's not rude if it's our house," Izzy said, then laughed when Jig's palm cracked across her ass.

"Lock that fucker on your way out," Rocket called. "And pay no attention to whatever noises you may hear over the next few hours."

Jig reached inside and flicked the lock before shutting the door.

"Few hours," Izzy said. "You wish!"

Chloe broke out in a fit of giggles that only increased when Logan grumbled.

"Now," he said, returning his hands to her breasts. He gave them a squeeze. "Where were we?"

Chloe leaned down. "I think you were about to tell me you love me again," she whispered against his lips.

"You're goddammed right I do." He kissed her and Chloe felt like she could fly. Nothing had ever felt so right. She'd been through hell, but then she found a man who could handle hell with his hands tied behind his back.

EPILOGUE

2 weeks later

Rocket sat in the dark, his silenced pistol laying across his lap as he stared at the man just beginning to wake up.

With a yawn, the man opened his eyes and locked on Rocket. All vestiges of sleep disappeared in a snap as the man shot up.

"Didn't think you'd be so surprised to see me, old man," Rocket said as he lifted the gun and pointed it toward Esposito. He hadn't wanted it to come to this, but Esposito left him no choice. He couldn't be allowed to run around accepting unapproved kill contracts.

"My security?"

"Needs to be fired," Rocket said with a shrug. "Though I suppose it doesn't matter since they'll all be out of a job in a few minutes anyway."

Esposito's eyes flicked to his night stand. Rocket chuckled. "Don't bother. Your gun is empty now. Been out of the field too long, old man. It's made you soft. I've been in here for a good twenty minutes while you slept like a baby."

Esposito reached into the nightstand anyway and pulled out a pack of cigarettes and a lighter. "Mind if I light up?"

"Knock yourself out," Rocket said. "Those things'll kill ya though."

A snort was the only response he got. "What do you want?"

"You broke your own rule."

Rocket

"And what rule would that be?" the old man asked as he flicked the lighter and sparked up the cigarette. Rocket had the urge to rip it from his fingers and jam it down his throat.

"Don't get greedy. You used to preach that to us. All the time. Easiest way to save our own asses. Don't get greedy. And here you are, taking on unsanctioned hits for mega cash."

"Yeah, well I found something out along the way," Esposito fired back. He sucked in a drag then blew out a cloud of smoke.

Rocket lifted an eyebrow.

"I like being fucking rich. This is about Chloe isn't it? Has nothing to do with the jobs I take. You're pissed because I let Lefty loose in her house." He shrugged. "Heard it all worked out in the end."

Rocket didn't say anything. Let the old man think what he liked. He found himself on Rocket's hit list the moment Rocket discovered one of the targets was a child. If those were the jobs Esposito was taking, the man couldn't be allowed to walk the planet.

"I've known all along." Esposito straightened, seeming to gain some confidence. Did he think he'd be getting out of this alive?

Laughable.

"I knew you didn't kill the targets. I know you got 'em stashed away somewhere. And I don't give a fuck. Cartel thinks they're dead and I got my money. All's well that ends well."

"And?" Rocket couldn't wait to hear the next words out of Esposito's mouth.

"And DarkOps is done with you. I gave you my word and you know I'll stick to it. I won't so much as glance at you, your woman, or your club again. So why not just part as past friends and be done with this shit?"

"That's an easy one." Rocket pulled the trigger twice. The muted whoosh of each bullet leaving the chamber was followed by two grunts as the slugs plunged into Esposito's jerking body. "Because you'll continue murdering innocent people as long as someone is willing to foot the bill."

Wide-eyed and slack jawed, Esposito sagged back against his pillows. He pressed a hand over the wound on his stomach as though he could somehow stem the flow of blood. Not possible. It was pouring out of two holes in the center of his body. He'd bleed out in five minutes, tops.

The other hand still held the smoldering cigarette between limp fingers. Rocket stood and strode toward the bed. He plucked the cigarette from between the old man's fingers and stood watching the man gasp and struggle to remain conscious. Just as he began to drift in and out, Rocket moved to the end of the bed.

"Told you these things would kill you," he said as he dropped the cigarette on the bed. Within seconds a small fire blazed on the blankets. Rocket shifted his gaze back to Esposito. The old man lay, eyes open, unblinking, staring at nothing.

It was done. Time to get out before the entire residence was engulfed in flames. And time to get back to his woman.

Despite having just taken a life, a sense of peace washed over Rocket. He'd finally put his past to bed. And now he was lighting the fucking thing on fire.

"YOUR MAN THROWS one hell of a party," Copper said as he took a seat next to Chloe.

She giggled. "Think he had a little bit of help." Or the ol' ladies took pity on him and did ninety-nine percent of the work.

Rubbing his chin, Copper looked around the clubhouse. "Maybe, but he put in his time."

Chloe studied him. He was looking much healthier than he did the first time she laid eyes on him. Still wearing the boot cast, but moving easier. "LJ sure seems to be enjoying himself," she said pointing toward the newly patched man with three Honeys hanging off him.

Copper huffed out a laugh. "Yeah, don't think he's hating that. Never got the chance to properly thank you."

Her forehead scrunched. "Thank me? For what?"

"For that." Copper jerked his thumb in the direction of Logan, who was walking back from the bar with a drink in each hand. Shell walked along side of him and Logan was boisterously laughing at whatever she'd said. Probably a story about her daughter's increasingly impish antics.

She cast Copper a look. "Where was he last night?"

Copper stared down at her, rubbing his chin. She didn't know why she'd bothered asking. He wasn't going to give her a straight answer, just as Logan hadn't when she asked him at least a hundred times why he was going to be gone most of the night. She had her suspicions, strong suspicions, and she was good with it, but wanted confirmation.

"Let's just say he was closing the door on his past and you'll no longer need someone from the club tailing you all hours of the day."

Just as she thought. He'd gone after Esposito. She supposed she should be more concerned with the fact that her man had murdered two people over the past few weeks, but she wasn't. Both men deserved what they got and even more. The world was two sadists lighter today. "So go back to telling me why you want to thank me. Why I'm so wonderful." She bumped Copper's shoulder, making him laugh.

But then he grew serious once again. "You're pulling him out of his shell. The man is happier than I've ever fucking seen him. No doubt that's one hundred percent due to you."

Warmth and genuine joy filled her as she watched her man close the distance between them. She was so mesmerized by the way he moved and the sexy smile he sent her, she barely noticed when Copper kissed her cheek before ambling off to meet his woman.

"Here, babe," Logan said as he handed a gin and tonic to her.

"I love you," she said in a rush, then her face grew hot. Smooth, blurting out mushy stuff in the middle of a raucous MC party.

Apparently, Logan approved. His smile grew even wider and he bent down to give her a deep, wet kiss. "Love you too, gorgeous."

"Copper is impressed with your party planning skills," she said before taking a sip of her drink to hide her smile.

Logan just snorted. "Last fucking time I'm doing that shit."

"LJ appreciates it. And he seems like such a good guy."

A grunt then a, "He is," was the only reply.

"Copper also said you're happier than he's ever seen you." Okay, maybe she was fishing a little bit, but it didn't hurt to check in and make sure he really was satisfied with what they were building.

He stared down at her, a small smile curving his lips. Seeing him without the weight of his past and her attack was an impressive sight. All their demons had been exorcised and they were free to just enjoy what they'd found in each other.

"What?" she asked.

He leaned down until he was less than an inch from her mouth. The scent of whiskey tickled her nostrils.

"Babe, I'm happier with you than I've ever been in my fucking life."

Thank you so much for reading **Rocket**. If you enjoyed it, please consider leaving a review on Goodreads or your favorite retailer.

Other books by Lilly Atlas

No Prisoners MC
Hook: A No Prisoners Novella
Striker
Jester
Acer
Lucky
Snake

Trident Ink
Escapades

Hell's Handlers MC
Zach
Maverick
Jigsaw
Copper
Rocket
❅ ❅ ❅

Join Lilly's mailing list for a **FREE** No Prisoners short story.

www.lillyatlas.com

Acknowledgments

Thank you for reading Rocket and Chloe's story. I've been dying to tell you all about how they fell in love and overcame so many obstacles both external and internal. Thank you to everyone who purchased, borrowed, reviewed, shared on social media, and read this book. I look forward to bringing you more in the Hell's Handlers series. LJ is next up!

There are quite a few people I want to thank, not only for the production of this book but for my entire writing career.

First and foremost, to my husband. Without your constant and unwavering support, I would never have published a single word. You didn't so much as blink when I announced wanting to publish my first novel. Since then you've been my most tremendous supporter every step of the way no matter how many times I freak out!

Carli, my sister-in-law – You are not only my number one fan but constant support and encouragement for me. You've read every book and not only helped me market but proofread, attended signings, brainstormed with me and listened to me complain. You're the best biscuit ever!

Leah Suttle – Thank you for your amazing and drool-worthy covers. I have no doubt they've helped get my books noticed.

Gel with Tempting Illustrations – Thank you for the

amazing, teasers, banners, and graphics that make marking so much easier. You are truly talented.

Shirley Jump – Thank you for making me think deeper about every word I write. I've learned so much from you over the past few years. When I write, I hear you in my head.

Nancy Cassidy – Thank you to and all the editors I've worked with through the Red Pen Coach. The time spent perfecting my books has been invaluable to me.

My ARC Team – Thank you all for taking the time to read and review my books. You all know just how critical reviews are to us authors and give of your time so freely to help us. Thank you!

Join my Facebook group, **Lilly's Ladies** for book previews, early cover reveals, contests and more!

About the Author

Lilly Atlas is an award-winning contemporary romance author. She's a proud Navy wife and mother of three spunky girls. Every time Lilly downloads a new eBook she expects her Kindle App to tell her it's exhausted and overworked, and to beg for some rest. Thankfully that hasn't happened yet so she can often be found absorbed in a good book.

Made in the USA
Middletown, DE
28 May 2021

40617395R00205